A new breed of
warfare calls for a
new breed of spy.

*continued . . .*

## DEBT OF HONOR

*It begins with the murder of an American woman
in the back streets of Tokyo. It ends in war . . .*

**"A SHOCKER."**                    —*Entertainment Weekly*


## THE HUNT FOR RED OCTOBER

*The smash bestseller that launched Clancy's career—
the incredible search for a Soviet defector
and the nuclear submarine he commands . . .*

**"BREATHLESSLY EXCITING."**    —*The Washington Post*


## RED STORM RISING

*The ultimate scenario for World War III—
the final battle for global control . . .*

**"THE ULTIMATE WAR GAME . . . BRILLIANT."**
                                    —*Newsweek*


## PATRIOT GAMES

*CIA analyst Jack Ryan stops an assassination—
and incurs the wrath of Irish terrorists . . .*

**"A HIGH PITCH OF EXCITEMENT."**
                                    —*The Wall Street Journal*

## THE CARDINAL OF THE KREMLIN

*The superpowers race for the ultimate Star Wars missile defense system . . .*

"*CARDINAL* EXCITES, ILLUMINATES . . . A REAL PAGE-TURNER."
—*Los Angeles Daily News*

## CLEAR AND PRESENT DANGER

*The killing of three U.S. officials in Colombia ignites the American government's explosive, and top secret, response . . .*

"A CRACKLING GOOD YARN."
—*The Washington Post*

## THE SUM OF ALL FEARS

*The disappearance of an Israeli nuclear weapon threatens the balance of power in the Middle East—and around the world . . .*

"CLANCY AT HIS BEST . . . NOT TO BE MISSED."
—*The Dallas Morning News*

## WITHOUT REMORSE

*His code name is Mr. Clark. And his work for the CIA is brilliant, cold-blooded, and efficient . . . but who is he really?*

"HIGHLY ENTERTAINING."
—*The Wall Street Journal*

*Novels by Tom Clancy*
THE HUNT FOR RED OCTOBER
RED STORM RISING
PATRIOT GAMES
THE CARDINAL OF THE KREMLIN
CLEAR AND PRESENT DANGER
THE SUM OF ALL FEARS
WITHOUT REMORSE
DEBT OF HONOR
EXECUTIVE ORDERS
RAINBOW SIX
THE BEAR AND THE DRAGON
RED RABBIT
THE TEETH OF THE TIGER

SSN: STRATEGIES OF SUBMARINE WARFARE


*Nonfiction*
SUBMARINE: A GUIDED TOUR INSIDE A NUCLEAR WARSHIP
ARMORED CAV: A GUIDED TOUR OF AN ARMORED CAVALRY REGIMENT
FIGHTER WING: A GUIDED TOUR OF AN AIR FORCE COMBAT WING
MARINE: A GUIDED TOUR OF A MARINE EXPEDITIONARY UNIT
AIRBORNE: A GUIDED TOUR OF AN AIRBORNE TASK FORCE
CARRIER: A GUIDED TOUR OF AN AIRCRAFT CARRIER
SPECIAL FORCES: A GUIDED TOUR OF U.S. ARMY SPECIAL FORCES

INTO THE STORM: A STUDY IN COMMAND
*(written with General Fred Franks, Jr., Ret., and Tony Koltz)*

EVERY MAN A TIGER
*(written with General Charles Horner, Ret., and Tony Koltz)*

SHADOW WARRIORS: INSIDE THE SPECIAL FORCES
*(written with General Carl Stiner, Ret., and Tony Koltz)*

# Tom Clancy's
# SPLINTER CELL®

# OPERATION BARRACUDA

WRITTEN BY
# DAVID MICHAELS

BERKLEY BOOKS, NEW YORK

**THE BERKLEY PUBLISHING GROUP**
**Published by the Penguin Group**
**Penguin Group (USA) Inc.**
**375 Hudson Street, New York, New York 10014, USA**
Penguin Group (Canada), 90 Eglinton Avenue East, Suite 700, Toronto, Ontario M4P 2Y3, Canada
(a division of Pearson Penguin Canada Inc.)
Penguin Books Ltd., 80 Strand, London WC2R 0RL, England
Penguin Group Ireland, 25 St. Stephen's Green, Dublin 2, Ireland (a division of Penguin Books Ltd.)
Penguin Group (Australia), 250 Camberwell Road, Camberwell, Victoria 3124, Australia
(a division of Pearson Australia Group Pty. Ltd.)
Penguin Books India Pvt. Ltd., 11 Community Centre, Panchsheel Park, New Delhi—110 017, India
Penguin Group (NZ), Cnr. Airborne and Rosedale Roads, Albany, Auckland 1310, New Zealand
(a division of Pearson New Zealand Ltd.)
Penguin Books (South Africa) (Pty.) Ltd., 24 Sturdee Avenue, Rosebank, Johannesburg 2196,
South Africa

Penguin Books Ltd., Registered Offices: 80 Strand, London WC2R 0RL, England

This is a work of fiction. Names, characters, places, and incidents either are the product of the author's imagination or are used fictitiously, and any resemblance to actual persons, living or dead, business establishments, events, or locales is entirely coincidental. The publisher does not have any control over and does not assume any responsibility for author or third-party websites or their content.

TOM CLANCY'S SPLINTER CELL®: OPERATION BARRACUDA

A Berkley Book / published by arrangement with Rubicon, Inc.

PRINTING HISTORY
Berkley edition / November 2005

Copyright © 2005 by Rubicon, Inc.
Splinter Cell, Sam Fisher, Ubisoft, and the Ubisoft logo are trademarks of Ubisoft in the U.S. and other
countries. Tom Clancy's Splinter Cell © 2004 Ubisoft Entertainment S.A.
Cover illustration by axb group / Greg Horn.
Stepback art by Greg Horn.
Handlettering by axb group.
Cover design by Rita Frangie.
Interior text design by Kristin del Rosario.

ISBN: 0-425-20422-7

BERKLEY®
Berkley Books are published by The Berkley Publishing Group,
a division of Penguin Group (USA) Inc.,
375 Hudson Street, New York, New York 10014.
BERKLEY is a registered trademark of Penguin Group (USA) Inc.
The "B" design is a trademark belonging to Penguin Group (USA) Inc.

PRINTED IN THE UNITED STATES OF AMERICA

10  9  8  7  6  5  4  3  2  1

## ACKNOWLEDGMENTS

The author and publisher wish to acknowledge the work of Raymond Benson, whose invaluable contribution to this novel is immeasurable. Many thanks go to Ubisoft Entertainment personnel Mathieu Ferland, Alexis Nolent, and Olivier Henriot for their cooperation and support, and to Vanessa Lorden for her help. Finally, a big thank-you each goes to James McMahon and Dr. Grace Stewart for their expertise.

# 1

**THE** OPSAT's mechanical alarm wakes me at eleven o'clock sharp. Since I possess the ability to sleep soundly at the drop of a hat, anywhere, at any time, the OPSAT's built-in prodder that nudges the pulse in my wrist comes in very handy. It's silent and it doesn't jolt me awake the way alarm clocks sometimes do.

I hear the wind blowing outside the small tent. The weather forecast had warned of a winter storm before midnight and it appears to be just beginning. Terrific. The subzero weather outside my bivouac would have in normal circumstances turned me into a Popsicle hours ago had it not been for Third Echelon's technological breakthrough in designing the skintight, superhero-like uniform that separates my very human body from the harsh elements. Not only does it protect me from extreme heat or cold but the threads of Kevlar woven into the fabric somewhat serve as bulletproof material. At long range, the stuff works pretty well. I don't want to have the pleasure of testing its strength at short range, thank you very much.

I crawl out of the tent, stand, and take a moment to survey the dark forest around me. Aside from the howling wind, I can't hear a thing. Lambert had warned me that I might encounter wolves this far into the woods but I must have lucked out. If I were a wolf, I'd stay in my den and keep the hell out of this kind of weather. There sure won't be any meals wandering about in minus ten degrees Fahrenheit. None except a two-legged mammal that happens to be heavily armed.

I quickly roll up the tent. The unique camouflage makes it appear to be a snow-covered rock when it's erected on the ground. One would have to examine it at close range to recognize it for what it really is. Again, a well-designed piece of equipment, courtesy of the National Security Agency. It's ironic that only a handful of the personnel within the NSA know of the classified department called Third Echelon. I'm such an elite employee of the United States government that you could count on two hands the number of people who can define "Splinter Cell." And to tell the truth, I couldn't name all those people. Aside from my immediate supervisor, Colonel Irving Lambert, and the minuscule team working in the unremarkable, unmarked building that stands separate from the main NSA headquarters in Washington, D.C., I have no clue as to what senators or Cabinet members have heard of Third Echelon. I'm pretty sure the president knows about us, but even *he* would Protocol Six me if I were caught. That means I'd be disavowed—they would wash their hands of me and pretend I never existed.

I pack the tent and lower my goggles. The night vision mode works remarkably well in a Ukrainian snowstorm. I may feel as if I'm in a scene from *Doctor Zhivago* but at least I'm not going to bump into any trees as I move forward.

Obukhiv is five miles away to the south. I'm somewhere between that small village and Kyiv to the north, which is where I began my mission. We spell it "Kyiv" now instead of "Kiev" because it's the English translation of the proper Ukrainian name for the city. Same goes for "Obukhiv," which used to be "Obukhov." The people made a concerted attempt to change all city names from Russian to Ukrainian since the nation became independent in 1991. I'm pretty sure the Russians will keep spelling them the old way.

Moving through a free Ukraine is no problem these days so I had little trouble picking up my equipment from the American Embassy in Kyiv and obtaining an SUV to drive to Obukhiv. I laughed when I saw the thing—a 1996 Ford Explorer XL with 120,000 miles on it. But it runs okay. From the village I hiked into the woods earlier today and set up camp here in the cold forest. Third Echelon intelligence confirmed that the Shop's third hangar for their stealth plane—which was destroyed a few months ago in Turkey—is located here in a clearing beyond the woods and is still in use. Satellite photos revealed that vehicles occasionally appear and men continue to go in and out of the structure. I already got rid of one of the three hangars, located in Azerbaijan near Baku. A special ops military force blew up the one that sat in Volovo, a tiny hamlet south of Moscow. Now I have the job of checking out the third one here to see what they're up to. The Shop, a notorious arms-dealing network of Russian criminals, was left in disarray after the business in Cyprus last year. We seriously damaged their organization but the leaders are still at large. Much of our intelligence indicates the Shop picked up and moved headquarters out of Russia and went to the Far East, possibly the Philippines or Hong Kong. That remains to be seen. One of Third Echelon's top priorities over the last several months has been to find the four so-called directors of the Shop and bring them to justice. Or kill them, whichever comes first.

A Georgian named Andrei Zdrok is the main man. He's number one on the "to do" list. The other directors consist of a Russian army general named Prokofiev—no relation to the composer, I don't think; a former GDR prosecutor named Oskar Herzog; and another Russian—former KGB—by the name of Anton Antipov. If I can find any information pertaining to these guys' whereabouts, I'll have accomplished the mission and can go home.

"I see you're on the move, Sam." It's Colonel Lambert, speaking to me through the implants in my ears. They allow me to talk with the team back in Washington when the reception is good. I answer him by pushing on the one in my throat.

"I'm approaching the compound now. What's the satellite show?"

"There's no activity. You're clear to infiltrate."

I move quietly through the woods, my boots inadvertently making *squish* sounds in the snow and ice. Can't be helped. I seriously doubt there are any guards this deep in the forest. I'll have to be more careful when I approach the hangar, though. And it appears to be just up ahead, where the trees begin to thin out.

Crouching, I scan the field in front of me. A building that once served as an airplane hangar sits at the end of a runway. Whoever piloted the stealth plane had to be pretty adept—there isn't much breathing space at the end before the trees become thick again. A smaller building adjoins the hangar—most likely offices and bunks for the guys working there. An electrified fence and gate surrounds the perimeter and an unpaved road—now covered by snow—runs through the forest from the facility to the highway leading out of Obukhiv. The No Trespassing and Keep Out signs have apparently done a good job keeping out the curious.

Three Taiga snowmobiles sit parked outside the compound. I see a lone guard in front of the door, smoking a cigarette. Damn. If I'm going to deactivate the fence, someone inside is going to know about it.

Wait. Someone's coming down the road. I see approaching headlights through the trees and hear the sound of vehicles.

"You've got company, Sam," Lambert says. "Looks like a motorcycle, or maybe a snowmobile, and a car. Came out of nowhere."

"Yeah, I see 'em."

I quickly move through the brush to the edge of the gate and lie flat in the snow. Most of the time my uniform is black but since it's custom-made for a Russian or Ukrainian winter, this model is completely white and thus blends in well with the natural surroundings. In a moment I'll unzip it, peel it off, and reveal the darker uniform for when I need to lose myself in the shadows.

The hum of the electrified fence suddenly ceases. They've turned it off from the inside and the gate begins to open automatically.

Another Taiga snowmobile, driven by a lone rider, sails past me and goes through the open gate. A few seconds later, a black Mercedes follows. I make sure no other vehicles are lagging behind and then I roll my body through the gate as it starts to close. I lie still and peer around to make sure I wasn't seen. So far, so good. Now's the time to play chameleon and dispose of my white outer-suit.

After stuffing the garment into my backpack, I get up and creep closer, staying to the shadows. Positioning myself behind a boarded-up water well, I watch the newcomers as they stop their vehicles in front of the small building. The guard I saw earlier goes over to the hangar and unlocks the door. He swings it open and the guy on the snowmobile guides his ride inside. After a moment, he walks out and the first guard closes the hangar door—but doesn't lock it. The Mercedes' driver keeps the motor running as four men get out of the car. One of them appears to be a Russian army general. I change the lenses in my trident goggles, focus on the men, and positively identify the officer as General Stefan Prokofiev. One of the other guys looks like Oskar Herzog, but if it's him he's grown a silly beard. The third guy I don't recognize. He's smaller than the others and has long, flowing black hair. Looks kind of like Rasputin. The fourth man is another soldier, probably just a bodyguard for the general. I quickly snap some photos with my OPSAT and beam them to Washington via satellite uplink with encrypted burst transmission.

The door to the main building opens and I see two men standing just beyond the threshold. They wave to the foursome as the men walk inside. Hands are shaken and then the door slams shut.

The driver gets out of the car and greets the snowmobile rider. They speak in Russian, probably talking about the weather. The guard offers the rider a cigarette and they walk around the building. As soon as they're out of sight, I run toward the hangar—roughly twenty meters—and peek inside the door. Where an airplane once rested, the place is now full of crates, snowmobiles, and a couple of cars. Nothing else of interest. I then reach into the backpack and grab one of the nifty homing beacons that Third Echelon created for me. It looks like a hockey puck, only smaller. It's magnetized and is activated by a twist of the top. I quickly move back outside to the Mercedes, crouch behind it, and place the device on the underside. There is a soft clink as the magnet meets metal. I push a button on my OPSAT to make sure it's receiving the signal.

Okay, let's get inside the building now. I try the knob but it's locked. So I knock and whistle loudly. My Russian isn't great but it'll do for short innocuous phrases in case I need to converse with someone.

I hear footsteps and the sound of the guard unlocking

the door. It swings open and I reach for him, pull him outside, and give him a head bonk he won't forget. The sharp
edge of my goggles slices his nose a bit but he'll live. I
drag his unconscious form around to the side of the hangar
and hide him behind a generator attached to the building. I
then hurry back to the front door, turn off the night vision,
and step inside.

The corridor is empty but I can hear angry voices in a
room down the hallway. There's a washroom next to it, so I
go in there and shut the door. I open a pouch on my leg and
remove a microphone with a suction cup attached to it. I
lick the cup and stick it on the wall, then adjust my OPSAT
to pick up the signal. Through my headset I can now hear
what they're saying. The Russian is difficult to pick up but
I can understand some of it. For good measure I start
recording it just as Carly St. John, Third Echelon's acting
technical director, speaks through the implants.

"I'll try to give you a rough translation as we go, Sam,"
she says, "then later we can do the whole thing."

Either the general or Herzog is doing most of the talking. He's giving the two men from the building a royal
chewing out.

"It's something about 'failure to do this and failure to do
that,'" Carly says. "And 'a security breach.' They're 'closing down the facility.'"

One of the men protests and sounds very frightened.
Apparently he's about to lose more than just his job.

*BLAM! BLAM!* The two gunshots startle me. They're
followed by the sound of two bodies hitting the floor. I hear
the general or Herzog mutter something and then the four
newcomers leave the room. They march down the hall, past
the washroom, and exit the building. The place is dead
silent.

I open the washroom door and look into the hallway.
Empty. I quickly move to the killing room and sure

enough, the two men who had greeted the general and his entourage are lying in pools of blood. I snap some photos and then move toward the front door. I gently crack it open and peer outside. The general is barking orders into a radio as the four men get inside the Mercedes. The driver has returned with his snowmobile rider pal.

"You've got more company, Sam," Lambert says. "Three vehicles approaching. Better get out of there now."

He's right—I see more headlights coming through the gate at the other side of the compound. Military vehicles. Two trucks and a tank! I feel my heartbeat increase as the trucks pull in front of the building as the Mercedes takes off. At least eight armed soldiers—Russian, not Ukrainian—jump out of the vehicles and rush toward the front door—exactly where I'm standing.

Well, hell. I turn and run to the back of the building, past the killing room and into a space where several cots are set up—obviously the living quarters for the men who no longer work here. There's a grille covering a ventilation shaft high on the wall. As I hear the soldiers enter the building and stomp along the corridor, I climb on one of the cots, pull off the grille, and climb inside. But I'm too late. One of the soldiers enters the room and sees my feet disappear into the shaft. He shouts loudly for others to join him. A deafening gunshot blasts part of the wall away behind me.

I snake along the shaft as fast as I can. Luckily I come to a junction just as the soldier points his pistol inside the shaft to fire at me. The shaft turns upward here so I leap above the gunfire and begin the climb to the roof. The soldier doesn't follow me. I'm sure he figures they can catch me when I emerge at the top.

The grille on the roof doesn't come off easily. I'm forced to draw my Five-seveN and shoot the corners of the damned thing. I holster my gun and then give the grille a good pounding with my gloved fist and it finally loosens. I pull myself up and out onto the snow-caked roof. The gun-fire commences immediately, the rounds zipping inches over my head. The angle isn't great for the soldiers so I'm at an advantage as long as I lie low. I reach into another trouser pocket and retrieve an emergency flare. It's not much but hopefully it will be bright enough to blind the soldiers temporarily. I aim it to the sky and set it off. The flare bursts over the compound, violently brightening the darkness. The gunfire ceases momentarily. I rise and scramble across the roof to the other side, near the hangar. It's not a big jump—I leap off the roof and land in a snow-bank. I drop, roll, and come up unharmed. But right in front of me is the snowmobile rider. He's halfway in the process of drawing a Makarov when I deliver a Krav Maga ax kick to his chest. This propels him backward and he drops the pistol. I move forward and give him another kick in the groin, which makes him completely docile. I kneel beside him, search his pockets, and find the keys to the snowmobile.

"Thanks," I say in Russian. "I'll return it. Someday."

I rise and run to the hangar, taking just a moment to look back and see what's going on. Some of the soldiers are apparently removing files, documents, maps, and com-puters from the building. Cleaning house. The Shop is def-initely closing down this facility. The Russian tank, one of the older T-72s, is moving to a position from where it can fire at the place. They're going to demolish the hangar and wipe out all traces of its existence. The rest of the soldiers, of course, are looking for me.

The Taiga snowmobile is sitting where the rider left it earlier. I mount it, insert the key, and start her up. The Taiga is a lightweight sports model, just what I need to make a quick getaway. The thing picks up on its two steer-ing skis and one track and bolts out of the hangar. Naturally, the soldiers spot me and shout in surprise. I hunker down and speed past the tank, knock over a soldier, and head for the gate.

Machine-gun fire riddles the snow around me. A round smashes into the rear fender over the track and for a moment I think the snowmobile's been crippled. The vehicle coughs and jerks but then I manage to regain control. I push the speed up to sixty as I fly out the gate.

Behind me, the tank's 125mm smoothbore gun thunders, blasting a hole in the front of the facility. The resounding boom shakes the forest around me and I can feel the heat of the building going up in flames more than a hundred yards away. This is followed by a series of smaller explosions—most likely detonations placed within the building by the soldiers.

Of course, by then several soldiers are tailing me on the other snowmobiles. I switch my goggles back to night vision and turn off my Taiga's headlights. I immediately turn off the road and head into the thick forest, zigzagging through the trees. At this speed you'd have to be crazy to try and maneuver past these natural obstacles, but I suppose I am. There's a fine line between a death wish and being a little crazy.

I notice the headlights of the tailing snowmobiles turn off the road behind me. Damn, they figured out where I went. Well, let's see if they can keep up with me. I inch up my speed to seventy-five. The trees are whipping past at a dizzying rate. I have to forget about the guys behind me in order to concentrate on steering. The last thing I need is to wind my legs around a tree trunk.

Gunfire. I feel the heat of the bullets slicing the air near my head. I duck lower on the vehicle, which hampers my steering capability. *WHAM!* The snowmobile grazes a tree and the thing wipes out. I'm aware of being in midair for a second or two and then I land hard on the ground. I thank my lucky stars I wasn't thrown into a tree or a rock.

The tracking snowmobiles come closer. I manage to pull myself up and limp to the overturned Taiga. I push it upright, get back on, and start her up again. The right front ski is bent but I think it'll still go. I accelerate and test the steering mechanism. Not bad. If I cheat to the left a bit, I can get the damned thing to go straight.

More gunfire. Great.

I increase the speed and take off into the darkness just as I hear a spectacular crash behind me. One of the enemy snowmobiles has merged with a tree in a most unpleasant manner. That's good for me but it's also set the tree aflame. If the fire spreads it could illuminate the forest and they'll be able to see me better. Gotta lose these guys and fast.

I press the implant in my throat. "Are you there? Anyone?" I ask.

"We read you, Sam," Lambert says in my ear.

"You tracking me?" I ask.

"We've got you by satellite. I'll bet you need directions."

"Please."

"I'm afraid you can't go back to the main road to Obukhiv. It's swarming with troops. Your best bet is to head for the Dnipro."

"The *river*?"

"Come on, it can't be that cold. Your suit will protect you."

"You want me to *swim* to safety?"

"Dump the snowmobile. Better yet, crash it. Your pursuers will hopefully think you're dead."

I shake my head. "Lambert, I'm beginning to feel like an underpaid stuntman. Okay, how far am I from the river?"

I hear Lambert consult with someone off mike, probably Carly or Mike Chan. He comes back and says, "You're less than a mile away. Take a thirty-degree turn to the left and you'll be heading straight for it."

"Thanks. I'm out." I make the move, dodge another tree, and try to increase my speed. Now the thing's going about fifty and it's the best I can do.

Suddenly and without warning, a snowmobile bursts out of the brush in front of me. The headlight nearly blinds me and I have to avert my eyes for a second, steer right, and perform a jump over a fallen log. My Taiga lands awkwardly and spins around. The Russian soldier slows his vehicle and fires a pistol at me. The bullet whizzes over my left shoulder as I duck and skid the Taiga in a half circle to kick up a snow spray. This gives me time to draw the Five-seveN, point it in his direction, and shoot.

Two rounds miss but the third hits the soldier in the chest, knocking him off his vehicle. I holster my gun, turn the Taiga back toward the river, and speed on.

I hear the roar of the water up ahead. I pick a nice thick tree fifty feet away and push the speed as high as it'll go. At the same time I position myself by crouching on the seat, ready to leap off at the last second. Closer . . . closer . . . and I jump, land in the snow, roll, and wait.

The Taiga slams into the tree and bursts into a fireball. The thing is obliterated.

I stand and make my way toward the roar. In three minutes I find myself at the bank of the Dnipro, a wide, snaking river that runs from western Russia through Belarus, and down into Ukraine all the way to the Black Sea. The spot I happened to pick for entry has no easy grade to climb down. I estimate it's at least a fifty-foot drop.

So I assume a stance, concentrate, take a deep breath, and jump off the bank. I hit the cold water like a knife, relax, and let my natural buoyancy lift me to the surface. Lambert was right. My suit keeps out the frigid temperature, but the ice water bites at my face. I roll so that I'm on my back—which goes a long way toward keeping my face warm—and drift to a place of safety as the strong current carries my horizontal body downstream.

All in a day's work, because I'm Sam Fisher. And I'm a Splinter Cell.

## 2

**ANDREI** Zdrok was not a morning person. If he had his way, Zdrok would sleep until noon and retire after midnight. Unfortunately, he had never been able to do that during his entire life. Coming from a family of bankers that did business in the former Soviet Union, it was always "early to bed, early to rise," etc., and he hated it. Even though he had tremendous wealth, acquired from the banks that did most of the USSR government's financial business, Zdrok found it difficult to find happiness in the world. When the Soviet Union fell and he founded the arms-dealing black market enterprise known as the Shop, he thought everything would become rosy. For a while, it seemed that it had. But things changed a year ago, after the disastrous dealings with the terrorist group known as the Shadows. The United States' law enforcement forces, namely the National Security Agency and the Central Intelligence Agency, broke through the Shadows' ranks and destroyed them. A domino effect reverberated through the pipeline back to the Shop, crippling the organization so badly that Zdrok had to pick up roots and move out of Europe. While living in Switzerland was nice, he never cared much for the places he had resided prior to the exodus— namely Russia and Azerbaijan.

He didn't much like Hong Kong either.

The Shop had set up headquarters in the Far East because the organization had friends there. A particular Triad had done business with the Shop for many years and helped establish a base of operations for Zdrok. The Shop once enjoyed a profitable territory in the Far East, especially in Macau, Indonesia, and the Philippines, until the National Security Agency—once again—caused some damage to the status quo. But there were still Shop operatives in the Far East, ready and willing to go back to work. The territory could be rebuilt. Hong Kong seemed to be the most desirable choice for a new base, despite the fact that the former British colony was now under Communist Chinese rule. Zdrok's friends had assured him that business in Hong Kong had continued "as usual," that is, in a capitalist state of mind, after the 1997 handover. This economic philosophy was *supposed* to continue as such for fifty years, while Hong Kong remained a "Special Administrative Region," along with Macau, which also was recently reannexed to China, after decades of Portuguese rule.

Zdrok walked east on Hollywood Road in the Sheung Wan district, one of the more popular areas of Hong Kong Island. The streets, occupied by antique and curio shops, Buddhist and Taoist temples, eateries, and oddly, coffin makers, always seemed to smell badly to Zdrok. In fact, the whole of Hong Kong smelled. They didn't call it "Fragrant Harbour" for nothing. At least up on the Peak, where he rented a modest but comfortable bungalow, the air was fresh. His accommodations were a far cry from what he had been used to, especially most recently in Switzerland, but they would do. What he disliked was coming to work, and that brought him down to Sheung Wan.

He turned north and then east again onto Upper Lascar Row, known locally as "Cat Street." Zdrok had no idea why it was called that. There weren't any cats that he could see. Just more antique shops. And one of them was the front for the Shop.

Zdrok unlocked the door to the "Hong Kong–Russian Curios" storefront, a place that had been there for ages but had recently undergone a name change. Jon Ming, venerable leader of the Lucky Dragons Triad, had smoothed the way for Zdrok's visa and business license and taken care of other administrative hurdles. So far everything had worked smoothly. Now if he could just get used to the smell.

He went through the legitimate shop, which was full of all manner of junk that Zdrok couldn't imagine anyone wanting to buy (but they did—the store actually showed a small profit) and stepped through the door behind the counter. It was still too early for the regular shop employees to be there. He paused at a mirror and took a look at his reflection.

At fifty-eight years old, Andrei Zdrok was still a handsome man. He enjoyed grooming himself and dressing as if he were the richest man in the world. At one time he was one of the ten wealthiest men in Russia. He had no idea if that was still true. Probably not.

The back of the store was a storeroom full of boxes, supplies, and a trick bookcase that rotated when one pulled out *The Complete Works of William Shakespeare*, replaced it, and then removed a book entitled *Bogus Bard: The Life of Christopher Marlowe*. This revealed the inner offices of the Shop, where Andrei Zdrok spent most of his daylight hours.

He closed the bookcase behind him, descended the spiral staircase to the basement, went into his personal office, shut the door, and booted up his computer. As he waited the sixty seconds, Zdrok longed for some of the Swiss coffee he had become addicted to when he lived in Zurich. There was nothing like that in Hong Kong, of course. The Chinese, and the British before them, didn't know how to make good coffee. Tea was another matter, but he despised tea.

Once the computer was up and running, Zdrok opened his e-mail and found an encrypted message from Jon Ming. Zdrok spent a moment decoding the e-mail and found that it was an order—a big one. Eight hundred thousand U.S. dollars' worth. Unfortunately, Zdrok had to hand over the arms to the Lucky Dragons at no charge. It was part of the deal he had made with Ming over two years earlier. They would provide the Shop with valuable information concerning the branch of the National Security Agency known as Third Echelon, as well as material for Operation Barracuda. In return, the Shop would supply the Lucky Dragons with all the weapons and arms they asked for. In Zdrok's opinion, he had gotten the better end of the deal. The Operation Barracuda intelligence alone was worth millions.

Zdrok had been waiting for this final order from the Lucky Dragons. It meant that the Shop's business with them was complete. The final "installment" of Operation Barracuda materials had been delivered. Of course, it would be prudent to keep relations between the Shop and the Triad pleasant. After all, Jon Ming had shown considerable "face" in helping Zdrok relocate. Zdrok owed Ming a great deal. He just didn't want to pay it.

Zdrok picked up the phone and dialed a number he knew by heart. A man on the other end answered, *"Da."*

"It's me," Zdrok said.

"Hello, Andrei."

"Good morning, Anton. How are things up in the New Territories?"

Anton Antipov, one of the Shop's directors and essentially Zdrok's right-hand man, replied, "Most likely the same as it is down on the island. Warm. Muggy. They say it might rain." Antipov was in charge of the Shop's remote warehouse, located near the residential and industrial New Town of Tai Po.

"At least we're missing the Russian winter, eh?"

"If you say so." Antipov didn't care much for the Far East either. He wasn't fond of Chinese food, and in a place such as Hong Kong that was a great disadvantage.

"I've received the final order from the Lucky Dragons," Zdrok said. He listed the desired items and quantities. "It must be shipped as soon as possible, of course."

"Of course," Antipov said.

"Do I detect sarcasm in your voice, Anton?"

"Not at all."

"Come on, talk to me."

"You know I was never happy about allowing this Triad to put our affairs in order. It's humiliating."

Zdrok sighed. "We've been over this a dozen times, Anton. What else could we do? If we had stayed in Eastern Europe or Russia we would have been found and arrested. At least here we can hide and still do business."

"How long can we hide, Andrei? How long before the United States finds us?"

"Anton. You worry too much."

"And you're unceasingly unhappy."

"Ah, well. These are our natures, yes? Let us concentrate on the matters we can control. Our customer in China will give us five million dollars U.S. as soon as we deliver the final installment of Operation Barracuda material to him."

"You have it?"

"We have it. It will go to the general tomorrow."

"Very good. We can close up that particular avenue."

"Yes," Zdrok said. "I have already asked Ming to do so. He will take care of it."

"And what happens if Ming finds out where all this Barracuda stuff is going?"

Zdrok felt himself shudder. "That would be very unfortunate. Under no circumstances are the Lucky Dragons to know our plans."

"I know that. You've said it a hundred times."

"Then that makes it a hundred and one."

"But if General Tun flaunts—"

"Quiet. By then it will be too late."

Antipov sighed. "Is that all, Andrei? I have an order to put together. In fact, most of it will have to be shipped from Russia. Tell Ming he'll have it in a week."

"That's actually good for us. Oskar can ride over with the shipment. Arrange it, please."

"Right."

Zdrok could sense that Antipov had more to say. "Is there something else, Anton?"

"Andrei, what does the Benefactor think of Operation Barracuda? He *is* aware of General Tun, is he not?"

"Of course he is. Don't be a fool. The Benefactor is on our side and always will be. It was he who initially put us in contact with the Lucky Dragons and it was he who introduced us to the general. Fifteen percent is what most authors and actors pay their agents. I think he's well worth the commission, don't you think?"

"If you say so, Andrei. You were always much wiser in these matters than me."

"Cheer up, Anton. Go have some Russian vodka for breakfast. But only after you send word to Oskar and get Ming's shipment ready."

"Have a good day, Andrei."

Zdrok hung up the phone and continued to check his e-mail. There was one from General Prokofiev. The Russian general had remained in his home country because of his position with the army. Of all the Shop directors, Prokofiev was the most protected. His cover was unshakable.

Zdrok opened the e-mail and read:

AZ—

Obukhov facility closed. General managers retired. All went smoothly except presence of Western competition. Still attempting confirmation of competition's going-out-of-business sale.

—SP

Zdrok rubbed his eyes. Good news and bad news. The good news was that the last remnants of the Shop's stealth plane activities had been destroyed. So far, the Russian government and military forces had not traced the theft of the aircraft to Prokofiev. The bad news was that an American intelligence operative witnessed the destruction of the Obukhov hangar. Prokofiev's last sentence indicated that he thought the man was dead but a body had not yet been recovered.

*Damn*, Zdrok thought. It sounded as if the operative may have been one of the men on the classified list of agents' names and descriptions that Zdrok had obtained last year. Was this man one of Third Echelon's Splinter Cells? Could he have been the nemesis that brought the Shop all of its troubles?

Could he have been the man known as Sam Fisher?

Zdrok slammed his fist on the desk and swore that the Shop would have its revenge on the man. Zdrok picked up the phone and made another call.

It would be easy to find out whether or not the Splinter Cell was still alive.

# 3

I'VE tracked General Prokofiev's Mercedes to an apartment building in Kyiv's Old Town, near the St. Sophia Cathedral. It's not far from a main thoroughfare, vulitsya Volodymyrska, and many of the historic landmarks in this cold, old city. It would probably be a bit more pleasant if it wasn't winter. Everything is gray and white and rather depressing. I've heard that spring and summer in Kyiv is really nice but I've never seen it then. It seems that the few times I've been here it's always winter.

Although I don't have much taste in the aesthetics of art and architecture, I do admit to being a history buff, and Kyiv has an abundance of antiquity. You could say it's the mother city for all Eastern Slavic peoples. After all, the Russian Orthodox Church was founded here. Outside the Upper Town—what the locals call the Old Town—is a very modern and cosmopolitan metropolis. Its urban sprawl is unequaled in Ukraine and this fact is quite amazing when you think about it. Kyiv has survived Mongol invasions, devastating fires, the rule of Communism, and the terrible destruction of World War II, and yet it manages to progress onward into the twenty-first century.

After my swim in the Dnipro, I managed to crawl out downstream and hike back to where I'd left the Ford. It took me five hours to walk to Obukhiv and I felt like the abominable snowman when I arrived. I drove to Kyiv, all the while checking the progress of Prokofiev's Mercedes on my OPSAT. The homing device was working beautifully. Prokofiev and his entourage checked in to the Hotel Dnipro, a high-end joint frequented by diplomats. I elected to stay three blocks away at the no-frills Hotel Saint Petersburg because I prefer budget places. I set my OPSAT's alarm to go off if the Mercedes left the Hotel Dnipro and then caught some badly needed sleep. The OPSAT beeped me awake earlier this afternoon. I figure I got five hours, which is pretty damned good. I left the room wearing civvies, jumped in the Explorer, and followed the blinking dot on the OPSAT's map to my current location.

The apartment building is old, as is everything else around here. There's not much parking but I get lucky after a few minutes and find a spot across the street. I stop, settle in for a spell of surveillance, and use the opportunity to contact Washington.

"Hello? Anyone at home?" I ask, pressing the implant in my throat.

"Hi, Sam." It's Carly St. John, my favorite person at Third Echelon. She's as smart as a whip and attractive as hell. I've often considered what it might be like to become romantically involved with her. I kid myself that she might be interested. The problem is that I'm not keen on becoming romantically involved with *anyone*. At least that's what I keep telling my reflection in the mirror. I made a resolution after Regan died to put women out of my mind. And

I've been pretty good at staying celibate . . . until recently. Ever since I returned from the Mediterranean last year, I've been feeling, I don't know, an *itch*. I found myself eyeing some of the women in my Krav Maga class in Towson, Maryland, where I live. And then there's Katia, the class instructor. She's absolutely gorgeous. Katia Loenstern's an Israeli woman who has made more than one pass at me and I've been a jerk and resisted each of them. Lately I've been thinking I need to change that attitude, but then the ugly realization of what I do for a living messes up everything. A Splinter Cell in a committed relationship becomes a vulnerable Splinter Cell. It also puts the partner in jeopardy. It's just too damned risky.

"Sam?" Carly asks. "You there?"

"Yeah," I say. "Sorry. I drifted off there for a second. Is the colonel around?"

"Not right now. I was about to contact you. There's a big snowstorm heading your way. What are you doing?"

"I should be eating dinner but instead I'm keeping tabs on General Prokofiev. Have you made headway on those photos I sent you? Any IDs yet?"

"As a matter of fact, I just got them back. You were right. The guy with the beard is Oskar Herzog. I guess he's trying hard to change his appearance. It's not working too well, is it?"

"No, it's not. What about the other guy? The rock star."

Carly laughs. "Your 'Rasputin' description was pretty funny. Actually, he's just as sinister as Rasputin. He's been ID'd as Yvan Putnik, a Russian Mafiya hit man. The guy has a record in Russia but he must have some powerful friends in the government because he keeps getting out of prison."

"Well, look who he's hanging with."

"Right. If you're buddies with General Prokofiev then you've got nothing to fear from the big bad law-enforcement dudes."

I rub my chin. "So what does that mean? What's this Putnik guy doing with the Shop?"

"I suppose he's working for them, wouldn't you think?"

"Well, duh. What I meant was I wonder what kind of jobs he's doing for them—wait a second." General Prokofiev just came out of the building. He's with a tall, striking blonde that must be twenty-five years younger than he is. Maybe more. I snap a couple of shots on the OPSAT. The bodyguard gets out of the passenger seat and opens the back door for the couple. After they're inside, the Mercedes drives away.

"I gotta go," I say. "I'm beaming you a couple more photos. I just saw the good general with a pretty blonde. See if you can find out who she is."

"Is it his wife?"

"No. General Prokofiev's wife is his age. This girl looks young enough to be his daughter."

We sign off and I discreetly pull into the street to follow the Mercedes, which takes the busy Naberezhna shose south along the Dnipro until the driver makes a left onto the Metro Bridge. The car moves east on prospekt Brovansky and then pulls into the small parking lot beside an old wooden mill in Hidropark. I'm puzzled for a moment until I realize that the mill is really a restaurant called Mlyn. The Hidropark, a Kyiv landmark, is an outdoor amusement park that spreads along the riverbank and encompasses some islands. The restaurant apparently offers a spectacular panoramic view of the Dnipro and its beaches.

I pull into the lot, park away from the Mercedes, and turn to watch my prey. The bodyguard opens the back door and Prokofiev and the girl step out. I'm closer now and can see that she's runway model material. Who *is* she?

More photos. After the couple is inside, the Mercedes leaves. I get out of the SUV and enter the restaurant. The maître d' greets me and asks if I want a view of the river. I tell him I'm just having a drink at the bar and he frowns as if I'm committing a grievous sin. He indicates the bar with his nose and then focuses his attention elsewhere.

I position myself on a cushioned stool where I can see Prokofiev and his date sitting on the other side of the room next to the large window. A bartender asks me what I'll have. I really don't want alcohol while I'm working but I figure *when in Rome* . . . I ask him for a recommendation and he tells me that the house special is a "KGB."

"Okay, I'll have that," I say. I'm expecting the KGB cocktail that has Bailey's Irish Cream and Kahlua in it, but instead he gives me something containing gin, apricot brandy, kümmel, and lemon juice. It's god-awful.

As I drink the wretched thing I watch the couple and discern that they're definitely having a romance. The way the good general is holding her hand on top of the table doesn't evoke a father-and-daughter relationship. She laughs at something he's saying and then—bingo, she leans across the table and kisses his forehead.

I snap the image on my OPSAT.

For the next ten minutes I sit with my drink and take a few more surreptitious photos. I even catch the general with his hand up the girl's skirt at one point. The best part comes when he presents her with a small wrapped box. She opens it excitedly and then squeals in delight when she sees the diamond necklace inside. Prokofiev stands, moves behind her, and fastens the trinket around her neck. He then leans down and she kisses him full on the mouth.

At that moment a text message comes in on the OPSAT. It reads: GIRL IN PHOTO IS NATALYA GROMINKO, FASHION MODEL, SINGLE, AGE 24, LIVES IN KYIV. NO CRIMINAL RECORD THAT WE KNOW OF. CARLY.

I force the rest of the cocktail down my throat and leave a few hryvnia notes on the bar. Just as I prepare to go outside, I see Rasputin—or rather, Yvan Putnik—enter the restaurant, scan the tables, locate the general, and rush over to him. I sit on the stool and watch them in the mirror behind the bar. Putnik whispers something to the general and a look of concern crosses the old man's face. He wipes his mouth, stands, and takes the model's hand. He says something to her—apparently he must leave immediately— and she wrinkles her brow and pouts. The general kisses her on the cheek and then leaves the restaurant with Putnik. Miss Grominko remains at the table, sulking. I wait a couple of minutes and then follow the men outside.

Great. It's snowing. In fact, it's a major blizzard.

The Mercedes is already out of the lot when I run to get in the SUV. I switch the OPSAT to tracking mode and see that the car is heading east toward Oryal. It's also the road to Moscow. They're already close to two miles ahead of me so I pull onto prospekt Brovansky and proceed to catch up. I'd never lose them while the homing device is working but I like to keep a visual on the target when I'm tailing someone. Unfortunately, the snowstorm is a hindrance and the roads are slick with ice. I'm forced to slow down when I see a policeman directing traffic through an intersection where two cars have collided. By the time I'm clear, the Mercedes has a five-mile lead on me. They're definitely traveling out of town.

Suddenly the blinking dot stops moving. The car has stopped somewhere up ahead. I'm in the outskirts of Kyiv and can't imagine what the general is up to. Surely he doesn't have another mistress living out in the burbs.

I reduce my speed when I'm within a mile of the location indicated by the blinking dot. Then, without warning, the homing signal quits on me. The blinking light disappears.

*What the hell . . . ?* I think. What happened? Those homing devices have a life of at least seventy-two hours. Did they find it and disable it?

I pull over and study the map on the OPSAT, trying to

remember exactly where the dot had been before it vanished. I pinpoint an intersection that seems to be the best possibility and then drive in that direction. I'm about a quarter of a mile away when I see, through the blinding snow, a black cloud of smoke billowing toward the night sky. I hear approaching sirens as I slowly guide the SUV down the street to a vacant lot next to a condemned building, the point where the Mercedes last sat.

In its place is a burning wreck. The car appears to have been deliberately set on fire.

I stop the SUV and watch the scene as two fire trucks and a police car appear with lights flashing. The firefighters immediately set about putting out the blaze. Once they do, I can see that the burning hulk is indeed the Mercedes.

*Shit! They must be on to me!*

The bastards dumped the car, destroyed it, and went on their way in a different vehicle.

# 4

**PROFESSOR** Gregory Jeinsen wiped the sweat off his brow as he debarked and made his way toward the Arrivals area. Hong Kong International Airport was abuzz with activity, as was usually the case, so Jeinsen felt relatively safe from being recognized. After all, who could possibly identify him? He had changed his appearance considerably since he left Washington. He had dyed his gray hair black and combed it differently, he had shaved his mustache, and he now wore glasses with fake lenses. These simple alterations made him look twenty years younger than his true age of sixty-four. If the Pentagon was searching for him, an agent would have to do a couple of double takes in order to see any resemblance to the scientist who mysteriously went missing two days earlier. His liaison in Hong Kong had paved the way for a new identity and taken care of the necessary paperwork, so Jeinsen now held a German passport and entry visa with the name Heinrich Lang. This wasn't too much of a stretch. Jeinsen had a cousin named

Heinrich and his favorite film director was Fritz Lang. The new name suited him.

The exodus had been planned for years. Jeinsen had come to the United States by way of an even earlier defection. Born and raised in Germany, Jeinsen unfortunately found himself growing up on the eastern side of the Berlin Wall at the end of World War II. As an adult he worked as a weapons development scientist for the GDR until the fateful day in 1971 when he was smuggled through Checkpoint Charlie in a laundry truck. A job with the U.S. government had already been arranged; hence for over thirty years Jeinsen lived in Washington, D.C., helping to design and develop weapons technology for the Pentagon.

After flying smoothly through Immigration and Customs with no problems, Jeinsen picked up his one piece of luggage from the baggage claim and made his way outside to catch a taxi. His instructions were clear: go directly to the hotel, check in under the new name, and await further orders.

It had been an anxious two weeks preparing to leave. He had to make sure he left nothing behind that might implicate him as a government traitor. All traces of communication with Mr. Wong in Hong Kong were to be erased. It was best if Jeinsen seemed to have simply disappeared. The D.C. police would chalk it up to a missing persons case. Because of Jeinsen's status within the Pentagon, FBI involvement in the search was of course inevitable. But if he had done everything correctly, the authorities would find no trail to follow. Jeinsen had done it once before in East Germany. He was fairly certain he had accomplished the task successfully in D.C.

The taxi dropped him off in front of the magnificent Mandarin Oriental Hotel on Connaught Road in the Central district of the island. Jeinsen knew it was possibly the most luxurious hotel in the territory, aside from perhaps the Peninsula Hotel in Kowloon. He was pleased that Mr. Wong had seen fit to treat him as a VIP and provide him with such flattering accommodations.

*Yes!* Jeinsen thought. *The decision to defect to China is already turning out to be the right one!*

The bureaucrats and military bigwigs at the Pentagon never appreciated Jeinsen's talents. Sure, he was given a top-level security position, had carte blanche in the weapons design programs, and was respected by his peers. It was the moneymen that always gave him short shrift when his colleagues received higher advances. Jeinsen had asked for better raises time and time again. He got raises but they were never what he felt he deserved. Growing up in East Germany, Jeinsen had a delusion that anyone who defected to America could become rich. It had never happened. He had made a modest income, lived comfortably, but was by no means "wealthy." Jeinsen firmly believed he was a victim of prejudice due to his former nationality. The thirty years in Washington ended up being a huge disappointment.

When Mr. Wong contacted him through a liaison in a government agency, Jeinsen was ready to consider any offers made to him. Wong promised him a fortune and secure passage to Beijing by way of Hong Kong. All Jeinsen had to do was hand over information concerning a special project he was working on and use a transmittal system that Mr. Wong specified. The process would take three years. Jeinsen didn't want to wait that long but Wong convinced him to be patient. It would be worth it in the end. Thus, when Jeinsen's role in the project ended recently and the task was complete, everything happened quickly. Wong made good on his promises, arranged Jeinsen's travel plans, and quietly got the scientist out of the country.

Jeinsen approached the front desk and checked in under his new name.

"Welcome to the Mandarin Oriental, Mr. Lang," the

registration clerk said, handing Jeinsen a key and an envelope. "Oh, someone left this for you this morning."

Jeinsen took it. It was a brown envelope addressed to him in care of the hotel. "Thank you," he said.

The physicist nearly gasped when he saw the room. It was a full suite with a terrace. He had never before stayed in such lavish surroundings. Even when he had to travel for the Pentagon, they always pinched pennies and put up their employees in midrange hotels. Mr. Wong was truly a generous man.

Before unpacking, Jeinsen opened the envelope and examined the contents. There was a small silver key with the number 139 engraved on it, a phone number written on a piece of paper, and fifty Hong Kong dollars. Jeinsen picked up the telephone and dialed the number.

Mr. Wong answered, saying, "Welcome to Hong Kong, Mr., uh, *Lang*."

Jeinsen chuckled. "Hello there. How did you know it was me?"

"No one else would be calling this number. How was your flight?" Wong spoke good English with a strong Chinese accent.

"Long. Very long."

"Yes. Do you need some time to rest?"

"No, no, I slept on the plane. I think I'm ready to . . . well, whatever you need me to do."

"Fine. Did you get the key?"

"Yes. What is it?"

"It's to a safety-deposit box in the Bank of China. Do you know where that is?"

"I can find it."

"It's very close. You could walk there if you want." Wong relayed directions. "You'll find further instructions and the rest of your payment in the box. I look forward to meeting you finally."

"Er, me too," Jeinsen said. "Thank you."

He put down the phone and rubbed his hands gleefully. Jeinsen felt like a young man again as he unpacked, freshened up, and changed clothes. In a half hour he was ready for the next great adventure in his life.

Jeinsen left the Mandarin, followed Wong's directions, and walked south across Chater Road to Statue Square. He was impressed with the collection of fountains in the square but it was too crowded with Asian migrant workers. Apparently a lot of Filipinos and Manilans congregated there, hoping to obtain employment as maids.

The impressive HSBC bank building stood towering over the square to the south. Jeinsen skirted east beyond the monumental structure and headed southeast on the footpath along Des Voeux Road, past Chater Garden, and finally to the equally impressive Bank of China Tower. The seventy-story building, designed by Chinese-born American architect I. M. Pei, was apparently the third tallest structure in Hong Kong.

Jeinsen went inside the banking lobby, approached a teller, and showed the woman his key. "I'd like access to my safety-deposit box, please," he said.

"May I have some identification?" the young Chinese woman asked. It seemed that everyone Jeinsen saw was Chinese. Most of the British minority that occupied the territory had left after 1997.

He showed her the new passport. She gave it a cursory glance, handed it back to him, and gave him a form. "Please fill this out and take it to the representative over there." She pointed. Jeinsen thanked her and moved to a counter. He wrote down his new name and indicated the Mandarin Oriental as his address. When he took it to the uniformed bank employee, the man asked to see the safety-deposit key and then led him through a vault door.

The rep used a key of his own as Jeinsen twisted his key

in the lock for box 139. The rep removed the box and handed it to Jeinsen, pointing to a private room. Jeinsen nodded and went inside. After shutting the door, he opened the box.

It contained HK $100,000 and a deposit slip indicating that two million more were in a special account with his name on it.

Jeinsen wanted to shout aloud. His hands trembled with excitement as he stuffed the cash into his pockets.

At the bottom of the box was a white envelope. He opened it and found another note from Mr. Wong. It instructed him to go immediately to the Purple Queen night-club in Kowloon. There were instructions on how to take the ferry across the harbor and the address to give to a taxi driver on the other side. He was to leave nothing in the safety-deposit box and place the key and the note in his pocket.

Jeinsen was walking on clouds when he left the bank. He didn't bother hailing a cab to take him to the Star Ferry pier. He preferred to walk, admiring the hordes of Asian people sauntering through the streets. For the first time in his life he felt superior. All these *workers*, these *common folk*! *He* was now a wealthy man. He could hire servants and *maids*. He could be the master for a change! Life was *wonderful*!

The ferry shuttled him across Victoria Harbor to Kowloon's Tsim Sha Tsui district. Jeinsen's earlier elation changed when he began to walk through Hong Kong's tourist ghetto. He found Tsim Sha Tsui crowded, energetic, and bright. It was still daylight but already the multitude of neon signs overwhelmed his senses. The streets were full of countless restaurants, pubs, clothing stores, sleazy bars, camera and electronics stores, hotels, and people. Traffic was bumper to bumper and the noise was deafening. Jeinsen suddenly felt his age.

He hailed a taxicab and gave the driver the address. The car went east past the Peninsula Hotel, recognizable by the two stone lions in front, and into what was known as Tsim Sha Tsui East, a more upscale version of its western neighbor. The buildings were more modern and there seemed to be more breathing space between them.

The taxi arrived at the Purple Queen within minutes. Jeinsen paid the driver, got out, and faced the nightclub. It was obviously an elegant establishment. The structure looked no more than ten years old and was surrounded by a series of dancing fountains. A suggestive silhouette of a nude woman was embossed on the side of the building next to the tinted glass doors. The nightclub was closed—a sign prominently read OPEN 5:00 P.M., CLOSE 5:00 A.M. Jeinsen looked at his watch and realized he hadn't reset it for local time. Counting ahead silently, he figured it to be nearly four in the afternoon. Jeinsen tried the front door but it was locked.

He knocked loudly and waited a moment. Puzzled, he started to walk around to the side when he heard the lock disengage. A very large, intimidating Chinese man in a business suit appeared and barked, "Yes?"

"I—I—I'm here to see Mr. Wong," Jeinsen muttered. He was suddenly very nervous.

The doorman glared at him for a couple of seconds and then nodded. He stepped aside and made way for Jeinsen to enter.

"Thank you," the physicist said.

"Mr. Wong back here," the big man said. "Follow me."

The doorman led Jeinsen through the nightclub's main floor. The place was lit as if it were about to open for business. Darkness prevailed but tasteful pin lights in the ceiling accentuated the tables and divans. Strategically placed planters held all manner of tropical flowers and plants. A large aquarium dominated one wall and a spacious bottom-lit dance floor occupied the middle of the room.

Jeinsen gawked at the furnishings as he trailed behind the big man. "Very nice place," he said. "Does Mr. Wong own it?" The doorman ignored him.

They went through a door marked, in English and Chinese, EMPLOYEES ONLY. It opened to a dimly lit corridor lincd with four doors.

"Last door on left, please," the man said, pointing.

"Oh. Okay, thank you." Jeinsen smiled sheepishly and went through. The door shut behind him.

Jeinsen apprehensively walked down the hall and knocked on the appropriate door.

"Come in." Jeinsen wasn't sure if the voice belonged to Mr. Wong. Perhaps it did. He opened the door and went inside. The room was obviously some kind of office, but it had been covered in the kind of plastic sheeting that painters use to protect furniture and carpets.

Without warning, someone standing behind the door shoved Jeinsen. The elderly scientist and U.S. government traitor fell forward to his hands and knees. His penultimate sensation was feeling the cold end of a gun barrel on the back of his head.

The last thing his brain recorded was the sound of the gunshot.

# 5

"**NOBODY** reads anymore, that's the goddamned problem!"

Harry Dagger drops a stack of books on the floor and surveys the overflowing shelves in his tiny English-language bookshop. He looks at me helplessly.

"Don't ask me what to do," I say.

"I stock more books than I can sell. I swear I'm going to go out of business if I don't move some of these things. Sam, you wouldn't want to buy a couple of cartons' worth and I'll gladly ship them to the States for you?"

"No, thanks, Harry. I'm afraid I have all I need," I say as I sip the glass of Russian vodka he's given me. I know you're supposed to down the thing in one chug but that's not my style. Since Harry's an American I don't feel the pressure to drink like the Russians.

Harry's Bookshop, which is tucked away a few blocks northeast of Gorky Park in Moscow, is really a safe house for American intelligence agents. Harry Dagger has been operating in Moscow for nearly forty years. He was CIA during the sixties, seventies, and most of the eighties, and retired just before the collapse of the Soviet Union. Harry set up his bookshop in 1991 and never expressed a desire to leave Russia. Possessing many friends in the government, Harry has managed to keep his nose clean and run a respectable business. The authorities may or may not know he also hosts out-of-town spies and provides them with Moscow intelligence but so far he's never had any trouble.

Now pushing seventy, Harry Dagger is exactly the kind of man you might find running an antiquarian bookshop in any American city. He's fussy, a bit unkempt, and extremely knowledgeable about the publishing business and authors in general. He also knows a hell of a lot about Russian spy networks, the Russian Mafiya, government corruption, and anything else that a lowly Splinter Cell such as myself might be interested in knowing.

He also resembles Albert Einstein, which makes him quite a character.

"But that's neither here nor there," he says, sitting in the chair across the worktable from me. He takes his vodka, neat of course, and downs it in one go. He eyes me nursing my glass and says, "Oh, come on, Fisher, that's no way to drink Russian vodka!"

"Leave me alone, Harry. I really don't *like* Russian vodka straight like this."

"Would you prefer a cognac instead?"

"How about some orange juice? Do you have that?"

"*Orange juice?* Where do you think you are? Miami?" He stands and goes into the back room, where he keeps a refrigerator, a small stove, and a food pantry. Harry lives above the shop and has a full kitchen in his flat but often "entertains" in the store. He returns with a glass of OJ and sets it in front of me.

"Here you go, tough guy," he says. "Better go slow with that stuff. It creeps up on you."

I laugh and thank him. He sits with another glass of vodka for himself and says, "Anyway, as I was saying. This Yvan Putnik is bad news. You really saw him with General Prokofiev?"

"Washington identified him in the photos I sent."

Dagger pulls on strands of his uncombed long white hair. "Very interesting. We've always suspected Prokofiev of playing footsie with the Russian mobs but I guess this clinches it. When I learned for certain he's with the Shop, I still had no concrete proof. Still don't. But all my sources tell me he's one of the four directors. I relayed all this to Lambert last year, you know."

"I know."

"If Putnik is working for the Shop now, it could put your and every other Splinter Cell's lives in danger."

"That's nothing new. Last year the Shop had all the information they needed to take us out one by one. They nearly succeeded, too. Carly's still trying to figure out how the Shop got our names."

"Well, just because the Shop has moved out of Russia and her satellites doesn't mean they're going to stop trying to track you down. I'd say with a guy like Putnik working for them, their odds for success are greatly increased. He's very good at what he does. I'd say he's responsible for some of the most difficult political assassinations that have ever been attempted in this country. He's an expert sharpshooter and probably very handy with a knife, too. He's known to use a Russian SV-98 sniper rifle with 7.62mm NATO ammunition. If you find yourself facing him, run away."

"I'd never do that, Harry. You know that."

"I know. I'm just saying . . ." Dagger downs his vodka while I take a sip of juice.

"So you have no clue where Andrei Zdrok is now?" I ask.

He shakes his head. "The Far East. That I'm sure of. It could be Thailand, it could be Singapore, it could be Taiwan, maybe Hong Kong or Macau, maybe Jakarta."

"It's interesting that Prokofiev is still here."

"He has to keep up appearances. Prokofiev's a top general." With that, Dagger opens a folder and removes a map. "Okay, since you want to go through with your cockamamie idea, here's where he lives." Dagger points to a spot on the eastern side of Moscow. "Izmaylovo. Actually between Izmaylovsky Park and Kuskovo Park. Quite a lovely mansion in a well-to-do neighborhood. Lives there with his wife, Helena. Children grown and moved out."

"And you've had your people watching the house?"

"Ever since I got your message. He hasn't returned from his 'business trip.' I'd say it's wide open for you to do what you do."

"What about the wife?"

"My watchers claim she goes to bed early and appears to be a heavy sleeper. Maybe she takes sedatives. She and her husband have separate bedrooms. She's a real battle-ax. Kind of looks like Boris Yeltsin in drag. It's no wonder Prokofiev has a mistress in Ukraine. If I were married to Helena Prokofiev, I'd never go home either. She's probably more dangerous than he is."

"Is the house guarded?"

"Only when the general's at home. All other times the place is looked after by their very well trained German shepherd."

"Oh, boy."

"Right. As I understand it, the dog is fearless and will attack anyone it doesn't know unless the general or his wife orders him down. Now. I've prepared something that will help you out in that department." Dagger stands, goes to the back room again, and returns with a small box. Inside are three oddly shaped bullets that look to be the size of ammunition that my Five-seveN takes.

"These are tranquilizers," he says. "Load your handgun with them before you go inside. They won't harm the dog—much—but one will knock him out quickly. Just make sure you shoot him before he sees or hears you!"

Dagger goes back to the folder on the table and removes a floor plan. "This is it, the ground and top levels. Prokofiev's home office is here on the ground floor. As you can see, it's on the opposite side of the house from the bedrooms, which are over here on the second floor. See?"

"Uh-huh."

"What do you think?"

"I think my best bet is to go over the fence to the back and break in through the door here." I point to an opening leading to a courtyard behind the house. "What about the security system?"

"It took some bribing to get the goods from the company that installed it. Inside the door you'll find a keypad. The code to shut off the alarm is 5-7-7-2."

"Thanks." I continue studying the floor plan. "I think once I'm safely through the door, I'll go past this living room area, into the dining room, and down this hallway. From there it's a straight shot to the office."

"Sounds like a plan. What are you driving?"

"Nothing at the moment. I had a company vehicle from the embassy in Kyiv but I returned it."

"I can't let you use my car. The Russians know it. Let me make a call and I'll rustle up something for you. It might be old and used, but it should run."

"Isn't everything old and used in Russia?" I ask.

Dagger's expression turns to mock indignation. "I resent that remark!" he says as he pours another glass of vodka.

*  *  *

**HOW** come no U.S. agency can provide a car in Russia newer than 1996? I'm driving a 1995 Ford E-350 van that Harry's friend must have driven to Siberia and back at least six times. There's 167,000 miles on it and it runs with a distinctive *clop-clop* sound in the engine. But it moves.

They call this part of town Outer East Moscow, but it's still well within the boundary of the Moskovskaya Koltsovaya Avtomobilnaya Doroga, the highway ring that designates the city limits. I've spent a lot of time in Moscow through the years and I've found I enjoy this area. Even in the winter it's scenic. Kuskovo Park was once some important count's huge country estate. It resembles a mini Versailles, with a lot of elegant buildings and formal gardens. Of course right now everything's covered in snow. The district known as Izmaylovo is definitely upper-scale for former Soviet homeowners. It's not surprising that General Prokofiev's private residence is here. Izmaylovsky Park, just south of the region, was once a royal hunting preserve next to an expansive, undeveloped woodland. It's remarkable that this exists within Moscow city limits because it feels as if you're out in the country.

While it's still daylight I do a simple reconnaissance around the general's neighborhood. His estate is set back from the road, surrounded by an iron-bar fence. Snow covers leafless shrubs and trees and I can imagine the place looking magnificent in the spring and summer. The two-story house, what I can see of it, appears to be perhaps seventy or eighty years old but it's well kept. The driveway leading from the gate to a three-car garage runs past the side of the house where Prokofiev's office is located. Unfortunately, it's impossible to tell if anyone is home. I'll just have to return after dark, find a place to park the van, and, as Harry puts it, "do what I do."

\* \* \*

**NOW** dressed in my uniform, this time a black one, I easily climb the iron fence and quietly move through the snow to the back of the mansion. Leaving footprints can't be helped so I deliberately create unreadable tracks; that is, with each step I wiggle my foot to create unshapely holes and walk unevenly. This way it's difficult to say just *what* sort of animal went through the grounds.

"Satellite reception is fuzzy, Sam," Lambert says in my ear. "Cloudy sky."

I glance up and reply, "Yeah. Once I'm inside you can watch through my trident goggles."

"As always. Good luck."

I'm now in the courtyard and can see the bedroom windows on the second floor. Perfect timing—the light in the wife's room goes out. Once again I walk like a deranged alien to create unrecognizable prints and make my way to the back door. I remove my set of lock picks from my leg pocket, examine the lock, and determine which picks might work best. The door opens in two tries.

I immediately step inside, find the keypad, and punch in the security code that Harry gave me. It works. I quietly shut the door and stand still for a moment. The house is silent. No sign of a dog anywhere. My night vision goggles are in place and I have no trouble navigating around the furniture in the living room. But as soon as I enter the dining room I hear a muffled *ruff* in another part of the house. The dog is upstairs. I quickly draw the Five-seveN, already fitted with the flash and sound suppressor, and return to the living room. I can see the staircase beyond an archway at the other end of the room, so I duck behind the sofa. Sure enough, I hear the sound of four paws padding down the stairs. I can see the animal now—he's huge and looks more like a wolf than a German shepherd. The beast halts at the foot of the stairs. He's staring into the living room but doesn't see me. He knows something's wrong, though, for he's growling quietly. The dog moves forward slowly, not sure what it is he senses. The growling grows louder. I have one chance at this, for if he sees me he'll alert the whole neighborhood.

In a smooth, fluid motion, I rise, aim, and squeeze the trigger. The dog spots me but he's so surprised that I think he forgets to bark. The bullet hits him just above the front right leg. He yelps slightly, turns, emits a low *ruff* again, and then drops to the floor. The animal is still breathing— he's just stunned. In a few seconds he's sound asleep.

Carly can see everything I can through the trident goggles. "Poor doggy," I hear her say with sarcasm. She can be a kidder when she wants.

The house remains quiet so I stand, go back to the dining room, and find the hallway leading to the office. I find the general's door locked, so I utilize the lock picks again. This one's more difficult than the house door; I guess the general is more protective of his personal things than he is of his wife. It takes me nearly three minutes to open the damned thing because there are two dead bolts on the door along with the standard lock.

I'm finally inside. I shut the door and the first thing I see is an awesome collection of antique pistols and rifles mounted on the wall. I recognize one as an Austrian Matchlock caliver from the 1600s. There's a single-shot muzzle-loading pistol from the early 1800s, probably Russian, that looks brand-new. There's even a Winchester Model 1873 lever-action repeater rifle. Amazing. They must be worth a small fortune.

I move to the desk, which is impressively neat and tidy, and boot up the computer to take a look at the contents of the general's hard drive. Since I don't want to spend too much time in here, I simply plug the OPSAT into one of the computer's serial ports and upload everything onto it. I then beam all of it to Washington; I'll let them sort through the files.

Next I open the desk drawers and filing cabinet but find nothing of interest. I then spot a small wall safe next to the desk and get down on my knees to examine it. Normally I would use one of my disposable picks—lock picks with explosive charges in them—to open a safe. They're quick and dirty, but unnecessarily noisy. When I have to keep quiet, the device I call the Safecracker is the next best thing. It's the size of a cigarette pack and is equipped with suction cups and a transmitter that sends signals to my OPSAT. It records the minute sounds the lock mechanism makes within the safe and then creates a fairly accurate estimate of the combination needed to open it. It doesn't always work. If it's a really complex mechanism, I don't have a prayer.

I attach the device to the safe and set it to work. Four minutes go by before the first number appears on my OPSAT. Damn, it's taking too much time. I'm not comfortable with this. Harry forgot to tell me how long those tranquilizers last. I sure don't want Fido coming in here after me.

Another three minutes and the second number pops up. Just one more and I can see if the Safecracker did its job correctly. But as I'm counting the seconds I could swear I hear something outside the office. I hold my breath, freeze, and listen carefully.

*Come on, make another sound. Confirm what I heard the first time.*

But there's nothing. I exhale just as the third number appears on the OPSAT. I quickly turn the knob, trying the combination the Safecracker has provided to me.

The safe opens, revealing a few file folders.

I'm able to read some of the Cyrillic and make out that one file is devoted to Russia's nuclear inventory. And *China's* too!

"My God," Lambert says. He can also see the papers

through my trident goggles. "That document lists the location of every nuclear device in Russia and China." I don't risk answering him vocally but I continue to study the file. It dates back to the eighties, when the Soviet Union was a bit friendlier with its Asian neighbors, so it could be terribly out of date. The pages go on and on . . . uh-oh. There's a page listing *missing* nuclear devices. Twenty-two of them. Holy shit. The general has scribbled coded notations beside these entries. There *is* a date on this page and it's recent.

"Snap some shots of that, Sam," Carly says. "I'll work on making sense out of those notes." I quickly do so with the OPSAT.

Another file seems to concern a Chinese general in the People's Liberation Army by the name of Tun. I've heard of him. He's a controversial figure in China, a real hawk. Tun likes to rile up the government with emotional speeches, inciting them to take action against Taiwan. I'm not sure what kind of power or influence the guy has these days but through most of the nineties he was considered a bit of a crackpot. Prokofiev's file on the man is pretty extensive. Photos, biographical info, and . . . damn, lists of arms that Tun appears to have purchased from Russia. No, wait. Not from Russia. From *the Shop*! It has to be. These are purchase orders for arms, worth millions of dollars, that Prokofiev has signed off on.

I quickly snap more photos and then carefully place them back in the safe. I close it, spin the combination knob, and stand.

"Good work, Sam. Now get the hell out of there," Lambert says.

That's when the office door opens. A woman, dressed in a nightgown and resembling Boris Yeltsin in drag, sees me and screams like a banshee.

# —6—

I jump toward Mrs. Prokofiev, grab her by her massive shoulders, pull the woman toward me, step to the side, and place my hand firmly over her mouth. This muffles her scream to an extent.

In Russian, I say, "Please be quiet. I won't hurt you!" I mean it, too.

But the woman is huge and strong. She wrestles out of my grip and swings an elbow into my stomach. The suit protects me but this woman means business.

She starts to run from the office and I tackle her. Her bulky frame falls to the carpet with a heavy thud as she screams again. I move over her and put my hand across her mouth again.

"Listen to me!" I shout in Russian. "I work for the government! I'm here to help you."

But it's like holding a 280-pound wild boar. Because I'm pulling punches and don't want to hurt her, she throws me off of her and manages to get to her feet. I hang on to one leg—it's like hugging a tree trunk—and she pulls me along the carpet back into the office. Damn, she's going for the guns.

"Wait!" I shout, but she pulls the Winchester off the wall, cocks it, and aims it at my head.

I raise my hands. "Mrs. Prokofiev," I say, "please calm down and just listen to me."

"Who are you? What do you want?" she demands. Her voice is deep and hoarse.

"I'm a private detective," I blurt out. "I work for the Russian government. I'm gathering information about your husband's extramarital activities!"

This gets her attention. "What did you say?"

"Please, may I stand?"

She keeps the rifle trained on my forehead. I don't doubt she would pull the trigger if provoked. Only now do I notice that there are curlers in her gray hair and she's got cold cream on her face. Hideous.

"All right, stand up, pig!" she shouts. I do so but I keep my hands high. I'm sure I could disarm her and send her to Dreamland if I wanted to, but I have a better idea.

"My name is Vladimir Stravinsky and I work for the Russian government," I say. "Your husband is in some trouble. I'm here to see what I can find. I honestly thought you weren't at home."

"What did you do to Ivan the Terrible?" she snarls.

"I beg your pardon?"

"Ivan! My dog!"

"Oh. He's just asleep. It was a tranquilizer. He's not harmed, I promise."

She squints at me and frowns. "What's this about Stefan?"

Stefan? Oh, her husband. "Mrs. Prokofiev, are you aware of your husband's extramarital activities?"

"His *what*?"

"May I lower my hands?" I ask as politely as possible. "I can show you some, um, pictures."

She glares at me, unsure whether or not to trust me. Finally, she nods her head but keeps the barrel in my face. "What are you talking about?" she whispers.

"Your husband has a mistress in Ukraine. In Kyiv, to be exact. A fashion model." I decide to rub it in. "She's in her twenties."

The woman's eyes flare. I swear they turn red for a moment. "I don't believe it!" she says.

"It's true. I'm afraid this affair he's having is causing some concern in the Kremlin. The general has been neglecting some of his, er, duties."

"You lie, pig!" She lifts the rifle to her eye, taking a bead on my nose.

"I can show you pictures!" I say.

Mrs. Prokofiev slowly lowers the gun again and jerks her head. "All right. Show me."

I hold out my wrist and reveal the OPSAT. "They're on here. This is like a digital camera. Look." I quickly bring up the shots I took in Kyiv and display them to her, one by one. Her facial expression exhibits incredulity at first and then her pallor changes from white to red, even through that awful cold cream. If she could breathe fire, she would.

"I'll kill him," she mutters. The woman lowers the rifle and commands me to stand. She appears a little unsteady, so she moves to the desk and sits in the general's chair. "What is going to happen to him?" she asks.

"I don't know. I'm just gathering information for now."

"You don't need to do anything," she says. "I'll kill him first."

I figure this is anger and bravado talking. "That's not necessary, Mrs. Prokofiev. I'm sure that—"

But I'm interrupted by the sound of cars moving past the office window. I remember that the driveway leading to the garage is on the side of the house directly next to the office.

"My husband!" she says, standing. "He is home!"

I curse to myself. "I'll have to hide."

She waves her finger at me. "No. Do not hide. Go out the back door. I will keep him occupied when he comes in. Hurry!"

I nod, thank her, and leave the office. Ivan the Terrible is beginning to wake up. He sees me and growls sleepily. I jump over his body and he springs to his feet. When he barks, Mrs. Prokofiev shouts, "Ivan! No!" The dog whimpers slightly and sits. He apparently knows who his master is.

I go out the back door, close it, and step into my old footprints to keep from creating new ones.

"Sam, you're not alone," Lambert says. "Man at three o'clock."

Sure enough, a uniformed guard comes around the house to the back, apparently performing a routine security sweep for the general's arrival home. He sees me and shouts for help. As he draws his pistol, I forget about the footprints and rush him. I slam into him head-on and together we fall into the snow. I punch him in the face as hard as I can but the man is well trained. He plunges his knee into my side, sending a jolt of pain into my kidney. I roll off of him and attempt to get to my feet but the guard whips his arm out and stiff-hands me in the neck. If the angle had been a little better for him, he would have broken it. As it is, I fear he's destroyed my larynx. I struggle for breath but the pain is intense.

The guard stands, draws his weapon, and points it at my head. I'm on my knees, helpless and groveling before him, but I do have the presence of mind to clutch handfuls of snow and pack them together.

The guard says, "I should go ahead and kill you but I think we'll see what the general has to say about you."

Suddenly there's a loud gunshot inside the house. The guard stiffens and looks up. I use the opportunity to throw my slush ball into his face. It's one of Krav Maga's basic tenets—use whatever you have available in order to gain an advantage. I then spring at him, pushing off with my legs like a jack-in-the-box. I ram him in the abdomen, knocking him down once again. His pistol, a Makarov, flies into the air. This time I don't give him a chance to rebound. I jump and bring the soles of my heavy boots down on his head. I twist, land with legs on either side of his temples, and then I give him a solid kick in the right cheekbone.

He stops squirming.

I pause for a second and a half to make sure I'm not leaving anything behind and then I take off toward the side of the house. As I run past the office window, I hear angry voices inside but it's impossible to identify them. And I really don't care. My throat is on fire and I just want to get the hell out of there. I got what I needed, I think.

Sticking to the shadows, I jump the iron fence and sprint down the street toward the van.

# 7

COLONEL Irving Lambert had a bad feeling about the upcoming meeting. Senator Janice Coldwater had called it,
which wasn't a good sign. In Lambert's opinion, the good
senator was trouble. As the head of a small group of Washington, D.C., officials known by its members as "the Committee," she had the power to tell him and other
high-ranking military and intelligence officers what to do.

Lambert felt the burden of his age as he walked down
the corridor toward the designated conference room in the
Pentagon. The fact that the meeting was being held in the
center of all-things-military was also foreboding. He
would be facing his counterparts in the other governmental
intelligence organizations, as well as the politicians who
made the big decisions involving Third Echelon's administrative and budgetary requirements.

Having been in the military intel business since he was
a young man, Lambert was well connected in Washington.
He could request—and receive—an audience with the

president if he wanted. He could initiate covert operations that no one else in the U.S. government knew about—or needed to know about. He often held America's security in his hands—something else that wasn't widely known or appreciated. And yet despite all this, Lambert often felt as if he were the bottom of the bureaucratic totem pole. His colleagues in the FBI and CIA received more respect. The military commanders looked down their noses at him. Only a handful of Congress members knew he existed.

It was no secret that Third Echelon was hanging on to threads. The past year, while productive in terms of crushing certain threats aimed at U.S. interests, had proved disastrous in terms of manpower and cost. The Shop had eliminated several Splinter Cells. How the Shop had obtained the agents' names was still a mystery. Lambert had been ordered to find the leak and plug it up. To date he had been unsuccessful.

Lambert entered the room and was thankful that he wasn't the last to arrive. Senator Coldwater was already in her seat at the head of the table. She gave Lambert a curt nod and went back to the notes she was studying. An easel, covered by a drape, stood at the head of the room next to the senator.

U.S. Navy admiral Thomas Colgan sat to her left. He stared into a cup of coffee, obviously concerned about something. Next to him was a man Lambert didn't know. He appeared to be a civilian—a brainy type with mechanical pencils in his shirt pocket. He was the only one who had removed his jacket and draped it over his chair. Lambert could see that the guy was nervous to be there.

Assistant FBI director Darrell Blake sat to the senator's right. He, too, ignored Lambert and continued to look at printouts that lay in front of him. The head of the National Security Agency and Lambert's boss, Howard Lewis, was the only one who smiled at Lambert. He sat away from the others, holding a seat open. The colonel squeezed Lewis's shoulder and sat beside him.

"How's it going?" Lambert whispered to his boss.

"We'll see," Lewis whispered back. Lambert rubbed the top of his graying crewcut, something he did involuntarily when he was anxious.

The other people in the room consisted of Homeland Security representatives, a member of the Joint Chiefs of Staff, the head of the DEA, and a handful of other military and political advisers.

The Committee was a top secret think tank put together by the president to tackle classified issues and to police clandestine organizations within the government. Third Echelon fell into this category. The only people in Washington who knew Third Echelon existed, other than the president and vice president, were in the conference room. No one was *really* supposed to know about Third Echelon. The NSA's function as the nation's cryptologic establishment was to coordinate, direct, and perform highly specialized activities to protect U.S. information systems and produce foreign intelligence reports. Since it was on the edge of communications and data processing, the NSA was naturally a very high-tech operation.

For decades the NSA engaged in what was called "passive" collection of moving data by intercepting communications en route. The First Echelon was a worldwide network of international intelligence agencies and interceptors that seized communications signals and routed them back to the NSA for analysis. It was a network vital to the United States' efforts during the Cold War. As the Soviet Union disintegrated and communications evolved, high technology became the name of the game. The NSA created Second Echelon, which focused entirely on this new breed of communications technology. Unfortunately, the immense volume of information combined with the accelerated pace of developing technology and encryption overwhelmed Second Echelon. NSA experienced its first systemwide crash. As communications became more digital, and sophisticated encryption more expansive, passive collection was simply no longer efficient. So the NSA launched the top secret initiative known as Third Echelon to return to more "classical" methods of espionage powered by the latest technology for the aggressive collection of stored data. As Lambert thought of it, Third Echelon went back to the nitty-gritty world of human spies out there in the field, risking their lives for the sake of taking a photograph or recording a conversation or copying a computer's hard drive. The agents—the Splinter Cells— physically infiltrated dangerous and sensitive locations to gather the required intelligence by whatever means necessary. That said, the Splinter Cell's prime directive was to do the job while remaining invisible to the public eye. They were authorized to work outside the boundaries of international treaties, but the U.S. government would neither acknowledge nor support the operations.

When CIA head Morris Cooper entered the room, Lambert groaned inwardly. He and Cooper always seemed to be at loggerheads.

"Sorry I'm late," Cooper said. "Traffic in the hallways was thicker than usual."

No one seemed to appreciate that Cooper was attempting humor. He shrugged and sat across from Lewis and Lambert.

"Now that we're all here," Senator Coldwater began, "I'd like to start with some budgetary concerns and get that out of the way before we talk about the new business at hand." Then she looked at the two NSA representatives. "Mr. Lewis and Colonel Lambert, the Committee members have been going over the budget that handles the various agencies and organizations involved in our nation's security. As you know, this includes Homeland Security, several antiterrorism task forces, and other classified groups within the FBI and CIA. I'm afraid that the NSA is high on the list for a reduction in funding because some headway must be made somewhere."

Lewis shifted in his seat and Lambert felt his stomach lurch.

"You're talking about Third Echelon?" Lambert asked.

"Yes."

Lambert cleared his throat. "With all due respect, Senator, might I remind the Committee of what Third Echelon has accomplished since its inception. In the last year alone we stopped a major conflict in the Middle East that would have brought disaster to Israel. We completely destroyed the terrorist organization known as the Shadows. We've run the illegal arms-dealing entity known as the Shop out of Eastern Europe and the Middle East. You can't say that we haven't done our jobs. Our plans for the future will make our little group even more effective. For example, we're expanding our Field Runner program. These support agents travel with Splinter Cells to sites of operations and provide much-needed back-watching."

The senator nodded. "The Committee appreciates what Third Echelon has accomplished, Colonel. But I'm concerned about Third Echelon's record of *losing* Splinter Cells. It's very high, considering there aren't very many of them. In the last year you lost how many? Three? Four?"

"That was because the Shop had the names. We've discussed this in Committee meetings before, Senator. A leak—"

"And you've had nearly a year to find that leak," Cooper said. "What is it you're doing over there in that little building of yours?"

"Well, Morris, we're not just pulling our puds," Lambert said. Cooper snorted and Lewis nudged the colonel to cool it.

The senator continued. "Colonel, the cost to recruit, train, and pay one single Splinter Cell is immense. Losing one in the field amounts to the military losing a handful of million-dollar missiles. I must also point out that the operations in the Middle East you mentioned did not occur without some public knowledge. The whole point of Third Echelon was to perform its tasks without *any* evidence of its actions. The business in the Middle East last year was very messy. People were killed. Governments knew you were there. The president was placed in a very uncomfortable position."

Lambert took a deep breath and said, "All I can say is that the results were solid. Our goals were accomplished and we prevented worldwide catastrophe. I'm sorry if the president had to tell a couple of white lies."

Lewis nudged Lambert again. The colonel continued. "As for the leak, we're doing everything we can. I'd like to remind everyone that the only people that know of Third Echelon's existence are the small group of employees working under me, the president and vice president, and the *people in this room.*"

Morris Cooper leaned forward. "Is that some kind of accusation, Lambert? You think one of *us*—?"

"Gentlemen, please," Senator Coldwater said. "No one's blaming anyone in here."

Lambert took a breath and continued. "I have a man tracking down the Shop's known directors as we speak. We have successfully identified them and we are hot on their trails."

"I'm happy to hear that, Colonel," Cooper said.

Darrell Blake came to Lambert's defense. "The FBI is looking for these men as well. What's the CIA doing?"

"Oh, we're on the lookout, don't you worry," Cooper said. He sat back in his chair and folded his arms.

Senator Coldwater nodded. "Fine. At any rate, gentlemen, nothing has been decided yet. The budget is still being broken down and analyzed. Colonel, I will take your words under advisement. Let's move on." She then nodded at Admiral Colgan.

The naval officer cleared his throat and spoke. "Senator Coldwater, gentlemen, thank you for allowing me and my colleague, Charles Kay—you all know Charlie, the director of SeaStrike Technologies?"

Some of them shook their heads. Lambert had heard of him but never met the man. SeaStrike Technologies was a subsidiary of a major defense corporation that researched and developed tools and weaponry for the U.S. Navy.

"SeaStrike Technologies has been working with the navy for several years now on our MRUUV project. You're all familiar with that."

Lambert nodded. So that was what this was about. The MRUUV program had been initiated by the Naval Sea Systems Command to research and develop the technology necessary to create a Mission-Reconfigurable Unmanned Undersea Vehicle—the MRUUV—capable of being launched from the twenty-one-inch torpedo tube that is standard on all U.S. Navy submarines. The last Lambert had heard about the project was that SeaStrike was close to realizing its completion.

"Charlie, why don't you tell everyone what you came here to say?" Colgan asked.

Kay nervously pulled on his shirt collar and then spoke with the clarity of a scientist. "At the heart of the MRUUV project is that it's the evolutionary development of the tube-launched long-range mine reconnaissance system, or the LMRS. We intend for it to be launched from a Virginia-class or Los Angeles–class attack submarine for clandestine ISR, as well as mine neutralization and tactical ocean survey."

Lambert's interest perked up. ISR stood for "intelligence collection, surveillance, and reconnaissance"—just the stuff that was Third Echelon's expertise.

Kay stood and moved to the covered easel. He removed the drape to reveal a rendering of a sleek, tubular rod with various sensors and probes sticking out of it.

"This is our MRUUV," he said. "It is mission-reconfigurable and offers advantages over single-mission UUVs because submarine torpedo spaces are too small to carry separate twenty-one-inch UUVs for each mission. By reconfiguring sensor packages and other mission payloads on the UUV either inside the submarine or at a support facility ashore, the mission payload can be optimized for the submarine's overall mission." Kay pointed to the rendering with his pencil. "The Flight 1 MRUUV has a diameter of twenty-one inches and weighs approximately twenty-eight hundred pounds. It will capitalize on the BLQ-11 long-range mine reconnaissance system to provide an initial ISR capability for current SSNs. It's operated from its mother sub and it communicates directly to the sub or indirectly via satellite communications with other nodes. The system uses its mother sub's navigation systems for mission planning and is capable of receiving mission updates from the Global Positioning System. The real beauty about it is that the MRUUV can use modular payloads that can be swapped out."

Kay turned and then smiled at everyone in the room. "And I'm happy to say that our prototype is complete and ready for testing."

There were some murmurs of congratulations but no applause.

"So let me get this straight," Cooper said. Kay turned

his attention to the CIA man. "You're telling us that thing can carry weapons? We could put a nuclear device on it and deliver it to a coastal city with utmost discretion?"

"Theoretically, yes," Kay answered.

"Then that's pretty sharp," Cooper said.

"Yes, we're all pleased with how it turned out." Kay returned to his seat. "We're hoping that the test runs can commence as soon as possible."

Admiral Colgan regained the floor. "That said, we've come here to alert the Committee that tests cannot commence due to what may be a serious security breach with regard to the MRUUV program."

The rest of the group waited for the admiral to continue. Colgan eyed Kay again and nodded.

Kay cleared his throat and swallowed. "The problem is that the lead physicist on the project, Professor Gregory Jeinsen, has been missing for a week. He didn't report for work last Monday. When an investigation was made, Professor Jeinsen was nowhere to be found."

"I've never heard of this Jeinsen," Morris Cooper said. "Who is he?"

Colgan answered. "Professor Jeinsen is an East German scientist who defected to the U.S. in the early seventies. He's worked for the Pentagon in various capacities but mostly in weapons development."

"I knew him personally," Kay said. "And worked side by side with him, of course. He's an honest and brilliant man. An American citizen."

"And what's been done to find him?" Cooper asked.

"The D.C. police searched his apartment. It looked completely normal. It appeared that Professor Jeinsen had simply got out of bed one morning, left the place, and never returned. His things are still there. Nothing is missing, as far as the police can tell. If there's a suitcase or some clothes gone, it's difficult to say. The police have a missing persons bulletin out on him but there are no clues yet."

Darrell Blake spoke up. "Our agency was alerted two days after the professor didn't show up for work. The FBI is now on the case and is looking into every possibility. We can't rule out that Professor Jeinsen met with some kind of foul play. I'm afraid it's beginning to look like that is what indeed has happened."

"You mean he's been kidnapped?" Lewis asked.

Blake shrugged. "I don't know."

Colgan continued. "What troubles us is not only the good professor's safety but also the fact that Professor Jeinsen had complete access to the MRUUV program. He was the man in charge of it. If the professor happens to find himself in enemy hands, well, the results could compromise our work on the project. It could be a very serious blow to our defense strategies."

The senator spoke next. "Thank you, gentlemen. A file has been prepared on the professor. You will all receive copies before we leave here today. I'd like all of you to look into this. The FBI is already doing what they can. I want the CIA and NSA to give this situation top priority. This is an order that comes from the president himself. Find Professor Jeinsen."

# 8

**HOME** again.

The day after my nocturnal visit to General and Mrs. Prokofiev's house in Moscow, Lambert ordered me to come back to the States. My job in Russia and Ukraine was finished.

It turned out Mrs. Prokofiev wasn't kidding when she said she'd kill her husband. She certainly tried. As soon as he walked in the front door, she shot him with the Winchester rifle. The bullet entered his body just below the Adam's apple and severed his spine on the way out. For good measure she shot him again in the head. The general was rushed to the hospital but it's looking as if we can write him off. He'll live but only as something akin to a rutabaga. Poor Mrs. Prokofiev was arrested and will no doubt go to prison or perhaps die for her crime, but her words to the police were that "the bastard deserved it." Hopefully at the very least she will gain some personal satisfaction from her deed.

Oskar Herzog, the Shop director who was with Prokofiev at the Obukhiv hangar, has disappeared. He's probably gone to wherever Andrei Zdrok and Anton Antipov are hiding. I'm sure when Lambert finds out where they are, that will be the destination of my next "business trip."

In the meantime it's good to be back in Towson, Maryland, where I live in a town house much too large for a single man in his forties. I have three floors in which to spread out and I must say it's pretty nice when one leads a solitary existence. I indulge myself in a few simple pleasures such as a supersized flat-screen television and a decent collection of DVDs. I prefer old westerns and war movies. I keep a library of reference material in the lower floor and that's also where my home office is. I don't read a lot of fiction. I mostly study the countries of the world, trying to keep abreast of everything that's happening politically and economically, especially in the so-called hot spots. Knowing who's really on your side and who's not is a primary task when you're out in the field. So every day I try to learn something new about a place. It keeps me on my toes.

I'm conveniently three blocks away from I-695 and can do most of my food shopping at a market a block away on York Road. My Krav Maga class meets in the same strip mall. My instructor, Katia Loenstern, left me an intriguing message on my answering machine.

"There's going to be a special class on Thursday and I'd really like you to be there," she had said. "Please."

Well, it's Thursday, so I change into my jumpsuit for the workout. I grab a small gym bag to carry a towel and an extra T-shirt, and I'm ready to go. It's still winter in Maryland so I wear a slick red ski jacket and set out on the five-minute walk from my subdivision. But before I shut the front door and lock it, I hear the house phone ring. I keep two phone lines—one has an unlisted number that's for personal use. Friends and family—what little of them I have—use that number. The other phone is a secure line to Third Echelon.

Since not many people have my home number, I can usually bet that a caller is not a telemarketer but instead someone I don't mind talking to. I rush back inside and grab the phone in the kitchen, which is on the ground floor next to the front door.

"Fisher," I answer.

"Dad!"

I feel my smile stretch across my face. It's worth turning around and coming back into the house to get a phone call from my daughter, Sarah.

"How are you, honey?"

"I'm fine. It's cold here. You got snow?" In my mind's eye I picture her at five or six years old, which isn't the case anymore. It's hard for me to accept the fact that she's no longer a little girl.

"No, it's melted but it's cold outside. I was just about to walk over to my gym class. How's school?"

"Good. You *know* why I'm calling, don't you?"

I think for a second. "Um, because you love your dad and just wanted to hear his voice?"

She laughs with her unique girl-giggle that tugs at my heart. "No, silly. Well, sure, that's true, too, but I called to wish you Happy Birthday!"

Damn. I nearly forgot. My friggin' birthday is tomorrow. I chuckle and shake my head. It figures that it conveniently slipped my mind.

"So why don't you call me tomorrow, too?"

"Well, I'm in school all day and then I have play rehearsal tomorrow night."

"Right."

"So, here goes!" She starts to sing the stupid song and I laugh some more. When she's done, I thank her profusely.

"You should be getting something in the mail," she says. "I gotta run. You gonna be home for a while now that you're back?"

"I hope so. At least until my next overseas sales conference."

She snorts. "Yeah, right. We wouldn't want you to miss it."

Sarah knows what I do. I was able to keep it from her for a long time until the incident last year, when the Shop got hold of her. With the loss of innocence comes the responsibility of living life as the child of a Splinter Cell.

We chat for another minute, send each other our love, and hang up. As an afterthought, I kiss my index finger and touch her photo that's held on my refrigerator door by a magnet. Then I head out the door once again.

As Splinter Cells go, I'm fortunate that I'm not assigned to a static location. Most of the other Splinter Cells are stationed in parts of the world where I certainly wouldn't want to stay all the time. I guess I have a special position within Third Echelon. Being the first Splinter Cell and an agent who can adapt easily to just about any place they send me, I'm more useful as a "contractor." In the old days, spies were often diplomats or embassy intelligence officers stationed in the country where they did the spying. With Third Echelon, though, the Splinter Cells are guys who have no affiliation with the U.S. government—at least they don't in a public sense. I've used numerous cover identities when I'm on a job and I have to sometimes learn trades and skills to make the cover more legitimate. At any rate, it's nice to be able to come home between assignments in order to see Sarah.

Third Echelon sure beats the CIA, which is where I worked before Colonel Lambert recruited me. In the CIA I had to spy in the traditional way—usually posing as a diplomat or someone in an official capacity. Later on I moved to a stateside job in weapons development. I thought I came up with some pretty good theoretical work on information warfare but the bureaucratic machine always managed to hamper my creativity. I've always been and will continue to be a man of action until my health or age prevents me from doing the job. Right now I'm pushing fifty. I don't know how much longer I'll have with Third Echelon before they forcibly retire me, but you can bet I'll stay until they do. I don't really know what I'll do with myself without the work. I truly believe it keeps me young. It's something about the danger, the thrill of the hunt, the most dangerous game. When your life is on the line, not to mention the lives of your countrymen, it tends to keep the adrenaline flowing. And I'm addicted to that rush.

I reach the strip mall and go inside the small dance studio that Katia rents for her class. She's already there, limbering up, and I'm not surprised to see that we're the only two people in the place. I'm usually the first to arrive.

"Sam!" she says as she bends her torso over her left leg and pulls on her foot. As usual, she's dressed in a leotard and tights. It's impossible not to notice her spectacular long legs. "I'm glad you're back. How was the trip?"

"Busy," I say as I place my gym bag on the floor next to the big mirror on the wall. "Where is everyone?"

She smiles flirtatiously. "I guess they're late. Go ahead and warm up and then you and I'll get started."

I start in on my stretches as I watch her. Katia, as I've mentioned before, is an Israeli-American and she's extremely attractive. She's thirty-six and keeps very fit and buff. She's got great brown eyes, a long nose, and a wonderful pouty mouth. Her long, curly dark hair flows wildly around her head unless she ties it into a ponytail. Even then the hair is so curly it just sticks out in a bunch rather than hanging like a true ponytail. I think it's cute.

While I'm warming up, Katia stands and goes over to her things to retrieve a water bottle. She takes a swig and allows the spillage to run down her chin, neck, and front of her leotard. Katia's got nice, natural breasts, and the moisture serves to accentuate them. Damn, she's never done that before and I'd swear she's doing it for my benefit. What the hell is going on here?

"So," she says, "a little bird tells me your birthday is tomorrow."

"Oh, yeah? What little bird is that?"

"Your registration form you filled out for the class."

"Really? Does it fly?" I'm on the floor now, stretching my legs. She approaches and stands over me.

"How about I bring you breakfast tomorrow?" she suggests.

"What? Katia . . ."

"No, really, Sam." She squats to my level. "You never go out and I've had enough of our friendly get-togethers to 'just have coffee.' I want to bring you a birthday present and I'm volunteering to bring you breakfast. I know where you live; it's on your registration form. How's eight-thirty sound? Or would you rather sleep in for a while? I can make it nine-thirty or ten if you prefer."

I stop stretching and look at her. The woman is serious. "Katia, we've talked about this before. I'm really not in the singles market. I really appreciate the offer but I'd rather not—"

"Bullshit, Fisher. Enough excuses. Now get up. It's time to work." She stands and moves away.

I'm beginning to understand why no other students have shown up for class. I've been set up. "The others sure are late," I say.

"Forget the others, Fisher," she says. "I wanted you all to myself today. I need you to spot me on some new moves. You game?"

I stand and shrug. "Sure, Katia."

Before I have a chance to defend myself, she charges and delivers a powerful spinning heel kick, knocking me to the mat. I fall flat on my ass.

"What's the number one rule in Krav Maga, Fisher?" she asks.

I sit up wearily. "Avoid getting hit."

She shakes her head. "Tsk, tsk, tsk . . ." Katia gestures with her hand for me to stand. I do so but now I'm on my guard. When she comes at me again I block the kick, grab her calf, and twist. She's prepared for the maneuver, though. She rotates her body in the same direction as the twist and touches her hands to the floor to support herself. At the same time she sledgehammer kicks me in the abdomen with her free leg. This forces me to let go of her calf. I step back and look at my instructor with renewed respect.

Katia's on her feet. "Throw me, Fisher," she says. "If you can."

"Katia, you know I can."

"Then shut up and do it." Before I can move, she says, "If I pin you, I'm serving breakfast at your place tomorrow. Deal?"

"Whoa, Katia. Wait a second."

*"Deal?"* This time she grins mischievously.

All right, if that's the way she wants it. "All right, Katia. Deal."

"Then throw me."

I move in to her live side, that is, the inside of an opponent using a basic stance with one foot forward. She has her left foot forward so I move ahead and to my left. Moving to this angle places me in a position where I can be struck by either her hands or feet. I want her to attack.

Katia tries another kick but I sidestep and try to grab her leg, but she moves away quickly. She circles so gracefully it's like fighting a ballerina. Before I know it, she's behind me and slap-kicks me in the kidney. I turn and let her have it on the chin with a right hook. I've never before hit my instructor with such force but she's asking for it! The blow shocks her a little. She rubs her chin, shakes her head, and then glares at me.

"You all right?" I ask. I'm actually afraid of hurting her.

"Shut up," she says. She's mad now. Katia comes at me like a wild tiger, leaps onto me, and wraps her lithe legs around my waist. She then repeatedly delivers nerve-wracking ridge-hand blows to either side of my neck. She knows where the exact pressure points are, too, so I feel sparks of pain shooting down my spinal cord like lightning. I can't help but fall to my knees with Katia still attached.

She then delivers a straight punch to my nose. I swear I see stars. But I have the presence of mind to block the next blow and then spear-chop her sternum, right between her breasts. It does the trick—she releases me from her leg lock and pushes away from me. I just hope I didn't hit her too hard.

"You all right?" I ask again.

"Shut the *fuck* up," she says. Before I have a chance to stand, she propels herself at me, slamming my lower back to the mat. I use the momentum of her own weight to throw her over my head. She lands with a hard slap. I quickly twist to a facedown position and grab her shoulders. Our heads are parallel, facing each other with my chin to her forehead and vice versa. She struggles for a moment and then brings her legs up. With amazing agility, she kicks me in the face with both feet. Needless to say, I let her up.

What's come over this woman? Does she want a date with me that badly? I admit I'd been thinking about her a lot lately and was wondering whether or not it was time to end my years of celibacy. She's being very persuasive!

We're both on our feet now. She moves in to my dead side before I can adjust my stance. This is the opposite angle of the live side. I have my right foot forward, so she steps with her left and moves so that more of her back is to me. I attempt to grab her under the arms in order to apply a full nelson, but she wiggles out of that with ease. At the same time, she back kicks my knee and stomps on my bare foot. An elbow to the lower abdomen sends me to the floor.

The next thing I know, I'm flat on my back again and she's on top of me. I push her shoulders and am fairly certain I could fling her off of me—but I just don't want to. This little "exercise" of hers has caused me to become aroused. Katia lowers herself until her face is an inch from mine. I no longer resist.

She kisses me on the mouth. It's a long, passionate, animalistic kiss, with tongues and biting and sucking. It goes on for at least a minute before we part. Her eyes are alive with excitement and she's panting with pleasure.

That's when I throw her off of me.

She topples onto the mat and looks at me as if I'd just committed a grievous sin. I do believe I've offended her.

"I'm sorry, Katia," I say. We're both out of breath. "It's just . . ."

"Forget it, Sam," she says. "You just don't want to admit you liked it."

She's right. I *did* like it. And damn it, it *has* been too long since I've had any sort of romantic involvement. Is it time? Can I forget Regan's ghost and stop ignoring the feelings in my loins and in my heart? Can I do this without someone getting hurt?

"So," she says, "I pinned you. What time is breakfast?"

And she smiles. I laugh and shake my head in resignation.

# 9

**SERGEANT** Kim Lee Wei enjoyed his early morning beat in Tsim Sha Tsui East because it allowed him the opportunity to watch the sunrise from the Promenade. This amazing waterfront walkway offered some of the best sights in Hong Kong. Specifically, one could see a postcard-worthy view of the central skyline on the island across the harbor. The scene was particularly mesmerizing at night.

The Promenade became crowded with people as the day went on, so Sergeant Wei relished the quiet and relative emptiness at dawn. Of course there were the usual early morning tai chi practitioners, joggers, and fishermen, but the number was negligible. Later the walkway would be full of musicians, photographers with tripods, strolling couples, mothers with prams, clowns and jugglers, and an overwhelming horde of tourists. During the Chinese New Year, which had recently occurred, the Promenade was *the* place to watch the harbor fireworks display. The June Dragon Boat Festival always drew a mass of humanity as well. Sergeant Wei was grateful that his beat was almost always in the morning and he didn't have to work those chaotic evening events. Like a good session of tai chi, the Promenade-at-dawn patrol was good mental therapy.

The policeman usually walked back and forth between the Star Ferry pier and the Hong Kong Coliseum. In his ten years of pounding the beat he had never encountered any serious trouble. Once he came upon a group of teenagers attempting to paint graffiti on the wall. There had been his share of drunks that had spent the night on benches. And there was the time he had found a woman's purse. She had reported it stolen the previous day and made a big stink about it. Everything was intact within the purse, including her money and credit cards. Sergeant Wei figured she had simply dropped it and not noticed until later.

On this particular morning, the sergeant strolled west from the ferry pier, past the clock tower, and on around the southern tip of Kowloon. Near the New World Renaissance Hotel, Wei always encountered "Jimmy," a fisherman who tried to catch his breakfast every morning. Wei didn't know Jimmy's full name but they always greeted each other with respect and friendliness. Wei figured the vagabond to be in his late sixties and had most likely seen it all. Jimmy never bothered anyone and was always gone by seven o'clock.

"Good morning, Jimmy," the sergeant said in Cantonese.

"Good morning, Sergeant," Jimmy replied. "It will be a very nice day, I think."

"Looks that way. Catching anything?"

"Not yet. The fish are not biting. Something else has their attention."

"And what might that be?"

Jimmy shrugged. "I don't know. If you find out, you let me know."

Wei laughed. "Will do. Have a good day."

"You, too, Sergeant."

Wei continued up toward the East Ferry pier and smiled to himself. Had he ever known Jimmy to actually *catch* a fish? He wasn't sure.

When the sergeant reached the point where the Hong Kong Bypass was directly overhead, he noticed something odd. A metal stake had been hammered into the concrete at the edge of the walkway. A rope was tied around it and connected to something in the water. The line was taut.

*What the hell?* Wei thought. He had never seen that before.

He stepped over to take a closer look and saw that there was indeed something in the harbor being kept from floating away. Wei moved to the very edge, supported himself on the rail, and began to pull the rope. It was surprisingly heavy. After four hand-over-hand tugs, a burlap bundle broke the surface. It appeared to be elongated, roughly five or six feet long and maybe one or two feet wide. Wei continued to pull it up until he was able to grab the bulky end and drag it onto the walkway.

There was no doubt about it. It was a body.

An hour later, the Promenade was swarming with policemen. Sergeant Wei had provided a statement and the homicide detectives had taken over the case. Wei couldn't believe he had run across a murder. A Caucasian man had been shot in the head, wrapped in burlap, and dropped in the water. The strange thing was that the killer or killers wanted the corpse to be found; hence, it was tied to the waterfront.

The dead man was logged as a "John Doe" at the morgue. It would take several days before the corpse was successfully identified as Professor Gregory Jeinsen.

IT was crunch time again at Third Echelon.

Carly St. John sometimes brought a bedroll with her to work when things got bad. As temporary technical director, she was more or less second in command of the team, reporting only to Colonel Lambert. Anna Grimsdottir, her superior and the regular technical director, was on the Company's mandatory annual psych leave and was due back soon. In the meantime it was Carly's responsibility to make sure Third Echelon functioned efficiently and accurately—mistakes could come back to haunt her and everyone involved in the security of the nation. That was why last year's leak of Splinter Cell names to the Shop was so demoralizing. She'd never rest until she learned how it had happened.

She had stopped working at twelve-thirty A.M. to try to get a little sleep so that she could be up and pounding on her keyboard before the colonel arrived at seven. But something was nagging at her brain and Carly knew she was close. When she realized she'd never get to sleep, Carly sat up in the bedroll—still dressed in her work clothes—and decided to go back to the computer. The clock in her office told her it was three o'clock in the morning.

As she sat in front of her monitor, the same thought kept coming back to her.

*What am I overlooking?*

After all the time she had spent hacking into every employee's computer, examining every byte of the firewall, and reprogramming the security system, Carly St. John was finally on the verge of learning how sensitive information had been leaked. But something was eluding her.

She sighed and decided a pick-me-up was needed. She left her office and went to the kitchen to make some coffee. Even though her mind was racing, her body needed some caffeine to catch up with her gray matter. When she finished the preparations, she heard noise coming from Mike Chan's office. Carly moved to his door and gave it a tap.

"Mike? You in there?"

"Huh? Yeah." Chan sounded sleepy. After a couple of seconds, the door opened. Carly was startled by his appearance. He was unshaven and appeared to be wearing three-day-old clothes.

"What do you want?" he asked. No hello. No smile.

"I didn't know you were working late," she said. "I thought I was alone, that's all."

"Nah, I'm here. I've been here since yesterday morning."

"What are you working on?"

"The usual." Mike Chan was one of Third Echelon's research analysts. He reported to Carl Bruford, the director of research. Carly had never found Chan particularly friendly. Chan was very no-nonsense with regard to fellow employees. He was a serious guy, difficult to get to know.

"Okay, well, I'll leave you alone, then," she said. Carly started to walk away but Chan stopped her.

"Wait, Carly. Sorry, I guess I fell asleep and you woke me. You know how it is."

She turned and nodded. "Yeah. You want some coffee?"

"I'd love some."

"I'm making some now. In the kitchen."

The brew was ready so she took two mugs from the drainer sitting next to the sink. "These look clean," she said. "I think."

Chan followed her into the kitchen and stretched. "So how you coming with your project? Do we still have a firewall?"

"Yeah. I don't think anyone's going to be hacking us again." She handed him a cup. They took turns putting in cream and sugar. "Actually, I think I've almost solved our problem. I'm this close." She held her fingers up to indicate an inch.

"Really? How's that?" Chan asked.

"Oh, I don't know. Thinking out loud."

"No, I'm interested. Try me." Carly was surprised. Mike Chan had never paid much attention to her before.

"Well, I discovered a back door in the old firewall that was breached. Someone from our office created the back door. Someone outside the office breached it with the insider's help. That much I know."

"Jeez," Chan said. "Who could it be?"

"That's what I'm trying to find out. There are traces of two ISP addresses that have gone through the door. Would you believe that one of them is in Washington, somewhere near the Senate building? The other one originated right here at Third Echelon."

"Holy shit," Chan said. "Does Lambert know this?"

"I'm going to tell him this morning when he comes in. I was hoping I'd be able to tell him even more by then. Hey, that reminds me. Do you know anything about Triads?"

Chan blinked. "What?"

"Triads. You know, Chinese criminal organizations."

"Yeah, I know what they are. Why do you want to know?"

"I uncovered an encrypted e-mail that mentions a Triad in Los Angeles called the Lucky Dragons. Ever hear of them?"

"Um, no, I don't think so."

"I'm trying to figure out who received that e-mail. It may be a part of the puzzle."

"You think you can?"

"Wish me luck." She gave him a little wave and walked out with her coffee. Chan watched her go and shook his head. Carly St. John was a little dynamo. She was less than five feet, five inches tall, was twenty-nine years old, and possessed a brain that could power a computer. The joke around the office was that she should wear a sticker on her head that read INTEL INSIDE.

Chan went back to his own office and looked around the mess until he found the backpack he always brought to work with him. He opened it and retrieved a Smith & Wesson SW1911 .45-caliber semiautomatic. He checked to make sure it was loaded, attached the sound suppressor that was custom-made for the weapon, racked the slide, and carried it with him toward Carly's office. Chan couldn't concern himself with the security cameras that lined the hallways. The situation had reached the breaking point and there was only one thing to do.

She had left her door ajar. He peered inside and saw her sitting at her desk. Her fingers flew over the keyboard as she stared at the monitor.

Chan knew that Carly St. John would solve the puzzle. It was only a matter of time. For months he had kept a close watch on her, trying to intercept any information she provided to Lambert. If Carly said she was close to uncovering the traitor in Third Echelon's midst, then it had to be true. And if she exposed the Lucky Dragons . . . !

Chan couldn't allow that.

He quietly pushed the door open wider and stepped inside. Chan raised the pistol, pointed it to the back of Carly's head, and squeezed the trigger. The gun recoiled with a *PFFT!* and the woman slumped over the keyboard. She might have appeared to be asleep if it weren't for the mess that was made over the desk. Chan grimaced and moved closer. He aimed at the computer tower on the side of her desk and emptied two cartridges into it. The machine sparked and went dead. Chan then kicked it over and stomped on the casing. The covering came off and he was satisfied that the hard drive had been destroyed.

He quickly went back to his own office and stuffed his personal belongings into the backpack. His heart was beating furiously and he had to sit a moment to catch his breath. Picking up his cell phone, he dialed a number and waited.

"This better be good," the voice answered in Cantonese.

"I'm sorry to wake you," Chan said in the same language. "I have to get out now."

"What's the problem?"

"I'm blown. And I've killed someone."

"Shit."

"I'm leaving for L.A. right now."

"Right. We'll be expecting you. How are you coming?"

"I . . . I don't know."

"Don't fly. They'll catch you."

"Yeah."

"Stay away from the trains and buses, too. You'll have to drive. But don't drive your own car."

Chan was now so nervous he couldn't think straight. "What else am I going to drive? Tell me that!"

"Buy a new car! Rent one! But not under your own name. Don't be foolish."

"You're going to get me out of the country, right?" Chan asked.

"Of course. Just as we agreed."

"To Hong Kong?"

"I'll begin making the necessary arrangements. But you'll have to get to L.A. on your own without being caught. You must keep calm. Do you understand?"

"Yes."

"Then I suggest you leave now." The man in California hung up.

Chan closed his phone, put it in his pocket, and grabbed the backpack. His final act was to delete everything on his own computer's hard drive. He then took one last look around his office, made sure he wasn't leaving anything important, and left. To hell with the security cameras, he thought. Third Echelon would know soon enough what he had done. The main thing was to get away as quickly as possible.

On the way out of the building, he avoided Carly St. John's office.

# —10——————

I keep a small amount of weights, a bench, and a punching bag on the lower level of my town house. The entire bottom floor serves as my library, office, and gym. I used to go to a real gym in Baltimore where a motley assortment of boxers, gang members, and toughs hang out. That was okay, but now I prefer to do my workouts at home.

I'm in the middle of bench-pressing on the lower level of my town house when the doorbell rings. The clock reads 8:30 and I wonder who the hell is at my door at this time of the morning. Then I remember—damn, it's Katia. Today's my birthday and I agreed to let her come fix breakfast for me. How the hell could I forget that?

I run up the stairs to the ground floor and open the door. There she is, looking marvelous. She's wearing tight-fitting jeans and has a winter coat on—that's all I can tell at the moment—but she's done her hair and is wearing makeup, which is something she doesn't normally do at the

Krav Maga class. And here I am wearing a T-shirt and sweat pants.

"Katia!" I say. "Is it eight-thirty already?"

Her smile becomes a frown. "Don't tell me you forgot, Sam."

"No, no, I didn't. I was working out and the time got away from me, that's all. Come in, come in." I don't think she believes me but she doesn't mention it again. I take her coat and see that she's wearing a red cami with spaghetti straps. The thing accentuates her cleavage in a most alluring way.

*Uh-oh,* I think.

She has a grocery bag full of stuff. "Where's the kitchen?" she asks.

"Right here," I reply, pointing to the archway to my left.

"Oh, so it is. Nice place, Sam. You have all this to yourself?"

"Uh-huh."

"Must be nice." She puts the bag on the counter. "Okay, you go finish your workout, take a shower, and by then breakfast will be ready."

"I'm done with the workout. Really."

"Then go get cleaned up." She bats her eyes at me. I get the hint; she doesn't want me to watch her cook.

When I come back down after showering and dressing, the table in the dining room is set with two places and lit candles. She's brought her own china and a bottle of champagne. In my spot there's one of those stupid little party hats that reads BIRTHDAY BOY on it.

"Katia, this is beautiful," I say.

"Sit down, big boy, and put on your hat."

"Katia, I'm not going to wear that hat."

She sticks out her tongue at me and goes back into the kitchen. I sit and put on the hat anyway, feeling like an idiot. When she returns carrying a tray of stuff, she sees me and laughs. "Oh, that is too precious for words."

"Can I take it off now?"

"Oh, all right. I don't want to snicker all through our meal."

The breakfast is amazing. She serves omelets made with three different cheeses, peppers, onions, mushrooms, and spinach. We have bagels and lox. A side plate holds a variety of fruit. There's fresh orange juice as well as champagne.

"Damn, Katia. I guess you'll have to marry me," I say facetiously.

"Is that a proposal?"

I don't answer. Instead I hold up my champagne glass for a toast. She clicks my glass with hers. "Happy birthday, Sam," she says.

"Thanks."

And we begin to eat. Our conversation feels awkward at first. It's like it usually is when we go out for coffee. There's that underlying sexual tension I normally like to deny is there. She knows it's there, too, but pretends that it isn't simply because I'm not acknowledging it. We talk of the class, discuss some of the talented students, and eventually the subject turns into our respective careers.

"I'm pretty happy just teaching Krav Maga," she says. "I never aspired to anything else. I'm probably too old to be a mother and too young to retire."

"Can you make ends meet just teaching those classes?" I ask. "And by the way, you're not too old to be a mother, if that's what you really want."

She shakes her head. "No, I *am* too old. I wouldn't want to go through that in my late thirties. Having babies is something twenty-somethings do. And to answer your question, no, I don't make ends meet just teaching. But I have some income in a trust that my father set up before he died. As long as I don't go crazy at the mall once a month, I'll do okay with what I make."

I decide not to push the baby issue. "Where is your mother? Do you have siblings?"

"She and my younger sister live in California. San Diego. In fact, I'm going there in a couple of days. I meant to tell you. There's no class next week. I'll let everyone else know by e-mail. I'm gonna stay for about a week, I hope. I was thinking of maybe going up to the wine country afterward but I'm not sure. Or maybe L.A."

"That sounds nice," I say. "I could use a vacation, too."

"You? Mister travel-around-the-world?"

"That's work. Believe me, I don't relax when I'm traveling."

"Just what is it you really do, Sam? And don't tell me you're in goddamned *sales*. I don't believe that for a minute."

"I *am* in sales. Sort of. International relations between the U.S. and companies that provide a lot of goods that Americans can't get anywhere else. I guess I'm what you might call an information gatherer and troubleshooter."

She laughed and shook her head. "You work for the government. That's what you do."

I shrug. "Not really."

"Come on, Fisher. I wouldn't be surprised if you're some kind of spy. You're so athletic and fit. Most guys your age let themselves go. Not you. And you're smart and seem so well traveled. You're gone for sometimes weeks at a time. And you keep your private life incredibly secret. I don't know a damned thing about you except that you have a daughter and that you're better at Krav Maga than me."

"I'm no spy, Katia. And I'm not better at Krav Maga than you."

"Yes, you are, and you know it. You could have whipped my ass yesterday. You *let* me pin you."

"Maybe I wanted you to pin me."

She looks at me sideways. The candlelight makes her brown eyes sparkle.

"Yeah?" she asks.

I take a sip of champagne and attempt to keep my face expressionless. I now know this is it. My years of ignoring the opposite sex have come to an end. It's high time I reenter the world of male-and-female relationships.

Our breakfast finished, I stand and hold out my hand. She smiles and takes it. I begin to lead her away from the table but she stops me.

"Wait!" Katia grabs the two champagne glasses and the bottle. "We might need this."

I lead her upstairs to my bedroom. The bed isn't made but she doesn't complain. Katia sets down the bottle and glasses and turns to me. I take her into my arms and we kiss more passionately than we did at the studio, if such a thing is possible.


**WHEN** we finally come up for air, the clock on my nightstand reads 1:30. We made fiercely primal love for at least an hour before falling asleep in each other's arms. The lovemaking, for me, was a revelation. It had been a long time. I guess it's one of those things you don't forget, kinda like riding a bike. Well, Katia Loenstern is one hell of a ride. She rode *me* pretty hard, too. We must have slept for a half hour, then got to it again. You'd have thought I'd been celibate for a century. After chugging down the rest of the tepid champagne, we tried another position. Katia marveled at my stamina and I welcomed her enthusiasm.

It was the best morning—and best birthday—I'd had in years.

We contemplate taking a shower together just as my beeper goes off. That means I need to make a call to Lambert on my secure line downstairs in the office. I don't want to do it. Damn it, I'm on vacation. I just returned from an assignment. It can't be that. Not now. Not as I'm just beginning *this* with the first woman I've grown to like since—

"Does that mean anything?" she asks.

"Yeah," I say. "I have to make a call. Downstairs in my office."

She smiles sweetly. "Go ahead. I'll just lie here and see if I can get my blood pressure back to normal."

I touch her face lightly and kiss her. "I'll be right back."

"Bring some water," she hollers as I bound down the stairs. Once I'm alone in the office, I make the call and reach Lambert at Third Echelon.

"Sam, thank God you're there," he says.

"What's up, Colonel?"

"Meet me at the usual place in an hour."

"An hour?"

"Why, you have something else going on?"

I want to tell him to take this job and shove it but I don't. "I, uh, I'm a little busy."

"This is priority three, Sam."

Shit. That means it's of vital importance. There's no way I can weasel out of it.

"I'll be there," I say. We hang up and I climb the stairs to the kitchen. I pour two tall glasses of water and bring them to the top floor. Katia's lying playfully under the sheet, giggling. As I enter the room, she exposes one long, shapely leg and flexes it in the air.

"You like?" she says in a phony European accent. "You *vant*?"

I sit on the bed and gently pull down the sheet. She has a cute, mischievous expression on her face.

"Here you go," I say as I hand her the water. She sits up, exposing her lovely chest.

She downs the liquid quickly, exhales, and says, "So, you ready for round six? Or is it seven? I've lost count."

"Katia, I have to leave. Business. I'm sorry."

She looks as if I've slapped her. "Really?"

"Really."

"You're not trying to get rid of me?"

"Never. If I had my way about it, we'd never leave this room."

"I bet you say that to all the girls who make you breakfast on your birthday."

I lean in to kiss her again. She lets me but the earlier passion isn't there. Her feelings are hurt.

"Does this mean you're going out of town again?" she asks.

"It might."

"Sam, *what* is so important about your job?"

"I can't tell you, Katia."

"You *do* work for the government."

I figure there's no harm in her knowing that much. If we're going to have a relationship . . .

"Yes. I do. But I can't tell you *what* I do. Please don't ask. All right?"

She considers that a moment and then says, "Okay. As long as you promise you're not going to drop the Krav Maga class now."

I laugh. "Of course not." I hold out my hand and help her out of bed. "We can still take that shower if you want."

"You bet. I don't want to go home smelling like sex. My cat will go nuts."

I precede her into the bathroom to turn on the water. I see her reflection in the mirror and notice that she's writing something on the notepad I keep on the nightstand. She joins me in the shower and we spend a luxurious five or six minutes soaping each other and getting all hot and bothered again. We do it one more time, standing up in the shower stall as the hot water rains down on us.

Afterward, when we're dressed, I notice what she wrote on the notepad. It's her cell phone number and the words, *I don't give this number to just* anybody. I smile and lead her downstairs.

"You let me know if you have to leave town, will you?" she asks.

"I promise," I say. It's the least I can do.

# —11—

IT'S begun to snow. Winter in Maryland is always unpredictable. You never know if it's going to be blizzard conditions, wet and icy, or just plain cold. The temperature isn't so low today but the snow is falling heavily. The weather boys predict six inches. Joy.

I crank up the heat in my 2002 Jeep Cherokee and drive down to D.C. on I-95. The vehicle is one of the Overland models, a rugged 4×4 with a potent 265-horsepower V8. For the city, it's way too much car, but there are times when I like to take it over more rugged territory. I happen to enjoy road trips but I don't get to take them very often. I've often fantasized of being a truck driver after I retire from the intelligence biz. I could go "searching for America," just like all the other folk heroes.

Lambert and I usually find a public place to meet. I avoid the government agency buildings in and around D.C. just in case someone's tailing me. Seeing me enter an NSA or CIA building would certainly be a tip-off that I work for the feds. Currently Third Echelon's actual headquarters is nowhere near the National Security Agency, which is housed on Savage Road in Fort Meade, Maryland, halfway between Baltimore and D.C. Third Echelon proper resides in a small, nondescript building in the nation's capital, not far from the White House. Every couple of years they move HQ to a new location for security reasons. Even though I try to steer clear of HQ, I occasionally have business there. Lambert and I decided long ago that it was best to rendezvous elsewhere. We used to vary the locations, usually meeting in shopping malls. He knows I hate shopping malls so I think he picks them on purpose just to annoy me. Lambert has a sick sense of humor. Lately we've been using the same one, located in Silver Spring, because of its convenience.

I take the exit off I-95 and follow the directions to City Place Mall on Colesville Road, park the Jeep, and go inside. The food court is easy to find and there's Lambert waiting for me at one of the tables—he's always the first to arrive—but I'm surprised because he's not alone. Frances Coen is sitting with him. I know her as one of the Field Runners that Third Echelon uses. She's in her thirties and is fairly attractive for a tomboy type. Slim with close-cropped dark hair. She's wearing professional, close-fitting rugged clothes. Lambert is dressed in a black turtleneck sweater and khaki pants. He never wears his uniform when we meet in public. It appears he's munching down on his favorite fast food, a Big Mac Combo Meal. The woman is eating a salad. I make eye contact with Lambert and then I go to the court to pick up something for myself. Breakfast was hours ago. After all that heavy lovemaking and champagne, I need something substantial. I end up buying a plate of chicken and broccoli from the faux Chinese joint.

I join Lambert and Coen at the table and see that the colonel is already finished with his meal. He has a funny habit of rubbing the top of his crewcut when he's nervous, and that's what he does when I sit down. Lambert appears to be more stressed than usual. The bags under his eyes are especially prominent today and I don't remember them being that bad. Lambert's usually a very energetic guy. He's ambitious and smart, and I'm not sure if he ever sleeps. He drinks more coffee than he sucks air. Lambert's the kind of guy who's always busy and never relaxes. From the way he looks today, I'd say his lifestyle is going to send him to an early grave.

Coen eyes me silently. For the first time I notice a large scar on the side of her neck that disappears into her collar. Possibly ex-military?

"You okay, Colonel?" I ask.

"No," he says. "Carly St. John is dead."

I feel my stomach lurch. "What?"

He nods. "Shot in the back of the head. *At our office.*"

I can't believe it. Carly is—was—my friend, the one person other than Lambert with whom I enjoyed a meaningful relationship.

"Do you know who—?"

"Not yet," the colonel says. "But Mike Chan is missing. There's every indication that he's the perpetrator. He's all over the cameras."

"Mike Chan? The analyst?"

The colonel nods. I met Chan once and only briefly. A quiet Chinese-American, he seemed to be on the ball, a real team player.

I look at Coen. Lambert notices my circumspection and says, "Sam, you know Frances Coen, one of our Field Runners."

"Yes." Field Runner. I remember discussing this program with Lambert. He wants to send not one, but *two* people into the field. A Field Runner is supposedly responsible for coordinating transportation and equipment for a Splin-

ter Cell. I made my objections to the concept known, loud
and clear. The main disadvantage, in my opinion, is that
it's dangerous enough having one agent vulnerable to cap-
ture and torture. At least a Splinter Cell is trained to with-
stand rough treatment. What happens if a Field Runner is
caught? How is this woman—Frances Coen—going to react when the bad guys try to extract information from her
with hot irons?

I save the argument for later. Right now I'm more concerned about what happened to Carly.

"Whoever killed Carly is responsible for our leak to the
Shop," I suggest.

"You're probably right," the colonel replies. "If it really
is Chan . . ."

"What's being done about it?"

"We had to bring in the FBI. This is a federal crime. We
couldn't have the D.C. police in our offices. We don't exist,
remember?"

"Yeah."

"So we have to sit on our hands while the Bureau sniffs
around." I can see that Lambert isn't happy about this.

"When did this happen?" I ask.

"Last night sometime. Carly was working late. Her
computer was destroyed as well. All the progress she'd
made on plugging the leak vanished with it."

"We do have backup tapes," Coen says. "We're starting
to go through them now. We just don't know if Carly
backed up her work in the past day or two."

"I've asked that Anna come back from psych leave immediately. Until then we're operating on thin ice," Lambert
says.

Anna Grimsdottir is just as smart as Carly, but I have—
had—a special attachment to Carly. It will be difficult to
replace her. "So I guess the reason you called me here today is to go after Mike Chan?"

"No. I'm afraid it isn't."

*Huh? What the hell?* "Sir, I *want* to go after Mike Chan."

"It's not your job. It's not Third Echelon's job. It's the FBI's job. Sorry, Sam. I want to avenge Carly's murder as much as you do. We have to let the political wheels turn the way they're supposed to."

"Then what am I doing here?"

"It's unrelated. I'm sending you to Hong Kong, Sam. You'll need to leave tonight."

"Tonight? Damn it, Colonel, I just got home from Russia! I haven't been here a week. And aren't I supposed to have mandatory psych leave?"

"I know, but you're the only available operative right now. Remember—we lost our Far East agent last year and have had to fill in with subs when we needed someone. I have the Committee breathing down my neck about budget cuts. For some reason, Third Echelon is on Washington's shit list. We have to prove our worth and soon. That's why I need *you*, Sam. I don't like to say this because I don't want you getting a big head, but you're the best we've got."

It's nice to hear but I'm too pissed off to respond appropriately. I sure as hell don't want to go to fucking Hong Kong.

"What the hell is so goddamned important in Hong Kong?" I ask.

Lambert slides a large envelope across the table. "You've heard of SeaStrike Technologies?"

"Yeah, I've heard of 'em."

"One of their top scientists went missing a week ago. We were afraid he'd been kidnapped because he was the project leader of one of our most important defense programs."

"The MRUUV," Coen says. "Do you know it?"

"No."

"All the info you need is in that envelope," Lambert says.

"So, I'm supposed to find this scientist?" I ask.

"No. He's been found. He was murdered in Hong Kong. His body turned up in Kowloon. It took the Chinese authorities twenty-four hours to identify him."

"Who was he?"

"Gregory Jeinsen. Former East German physicist, defected to the U.S. in 1971. He's worked for the Pentagon ever since."

"So what do you want me to do?"

"I want you to find out what Jeinsen was doing in Hong Kong. If Jeinsen turned or was indeed kidnapped, he may have handed over MRUUV secrets. If that's happened, let's just say that the Pentagon is not going to be very happy." Lambert rubbed his crewcut again.

"You want me to go investigate a *murder*? Colonel, with all due respect, I'm not a homicide detective. Isn't that a little out of Third Echelon's jurisdiction?" I ask.

"No, that's not what I want you to do. You're going to Hong Kong to do what you always do—extract intelligence. Gregory Jeinsen was there for a reason. I want to know why. If MRUUV secrets were sold or given away or pried out of him, then your job is to follow the trail and see where they went. If, in finding that out, you discover who killed him, then great. We'll beat the FBI and CIA at their jobs. And that'll be a feather in our cap when the Committee starts making budget cuts."

"So this is all about funding, is that it?" I'm really becoming angry now.

"Stop it, Sam. Just read the file. You'll understand why this is important once you do."

I stew for a moment and everyone at the table is quiet. Finally I take the envelope and say, "Fine."

"Thank you, Sam," Lambert says.

I wave him off. "What about the stuff I found in

Prokofiev's house? Have you had time to look into that list of missing nukes?"

"Our analysts are decoding the general's notes as we speak. I should know more in the next day or two. That was a good find, Sam."

"Thanks. So what can you tell me about that security breach Carly was working on? I think it's gotten worse. Look what happened to me in Russia. Someone *knew* I was following General Prokofiev in Kyiv. He got wise and destroyed his car because he knew it was bugged with a homing device. How did he know? And from all accounts it looks like he came home unexpectedly in Moscow because he may have known I was in his house. Colonel, you can count on one hand the number of people who knew what I was doing in Russia."

"I realize that, Sam. As soon as Anna is back in place, that will be her first priority. There's no question in my mind that an insider compromised Third Echelon. Maybe it was Mike Chan. Maybe he wasn't working alone. Maybe there's another insider that's not a Third Echelon employee. Maybe the traitor is one of the few people in Washington that know of our existence. I don't know at this point, Sam, but I'm keeping an open mind. I'd like you to as well."

I nod my head toward Coen. Lambert catches the subtext behind the move. "Sam, the Field Runner operation—"

"I work alone, Lambert. You know that."

"That may not be the case in the future, Sam. For now, yes, but we're here to tell you we've got Frances here on the fast track to become your personal Field Runner. For this assignment she'll stay in Washington and monitor you remotely. Next time, well, we'll see. The kinks in the program still have to be worked out. I understand your concerns; you've voiced them enough."

I look at the woman and say, "No offense, Frances, but I can't see how your presence in an enemy zone would make my job any easier. I have enough to worry about just looking after my own butt. I don't need another butt to watch."

"You won't have to watch my *butt*, as you put it," Coen says. "I'm thoroughly trained. I can handle myself in a threatening situation."

"How about torture?" I ask. "Can you handle that? Can you handle your fingernails being ripped out one by one, or electric prods shoved up your—"

"Sam!" Lambert almost shouts. Other people around us look up to see what's going on. He lowers his voice and says, "That's enough."

I fold my arms and sit back. "Whatever."

Coen waits a beat and then starts to talk. "You're to meet me tonight at Dulles. An army Osprey will take you to one of our bases in the Philippines and from there you'll get a commercial flight to Hong Kong. I'll have some last-minute documents for you then. Your flight information is there in the envelope. I'll see you tonight, Mr. Fisher." She holds out her hand.

I don't want to be a dick so I reach out and shake it. "Call me Sam," I say.


KATIA isn't too pleased that I have to leave the country again so soon. But she didn't make a big deal out of it. If she had, I'd think twice about becoming more involved with her. The last thing I want is a needy girlfriend. I could tell that Katia was ticked off about my leaving but she said for me not to worry about it. She understood. She explained again that she was going to California anyway so maybe we'd both be back at the same time.

I like her, damn it. Against my better judgment, I'm looking forward to us both being back at the same time.

So now I'm in Dulles Airport and I meet Frances Coen in front of the magazine shop she'd designated. We walk to an empty gate, sit, and she gives me another envelope.

"I have all your transportation arrangements in here," she says. "Instructions for picking up your equipment are in there as well. You shouldn't have any problems."

"That's what *you* think," I mutter.

"What?"

"Nothing."

"Look, Mr. Fisher, I know—"

"I said to call me Sam."

"—Sam—you're not fond of this idea of Field Runners. But I'm good at what I do. You'll have to make a leap of faith. Can you do that?"

I shrug. "I'm not a very religious person."

She frowns at me.

"Okay, I'm willing to give it a try," I finally say.

"I'm not over there with you this time around. For now you'll work just like you always have. The only difference is that you'll be dealing with me on most things. Colonel Lambert will of course be giving you instructions. Anna will be back soon. But I'm your main contact now."

"Okeydokey," I say and grin. The sarcasm is not lost on her but she holds out her hand.

"Good luck, Sam."

I shake it and nod.

At that point an army sergeant enters the gate and approaches us. "Mr. Fisher?" he asks.

"Yeah?"

"I'm to escort you to the Osprey."

"Right." I take my duffel bag and follow the soldier outside. I don't look back at Frances Coen. I don't look back at anything.

## 12

I'VE been in Hong Kong a number of times, both before and after the momentous handover in 1997. Before the Brits left the colony, there was widespread speculation that the capitalistic society that Hong Kong had enjoyed for over a century would disappear. Communist China would ruin what was up to then known as "the Pearl in the Crown." So far it hasn't happened. I can't see that much has changed except perhaps there are fewer Brits walking around. The Chinese promised to keep Hong Kong in its current state of economic enterprise for the next fifty years. Who's to say what happens after that? Are they simply going to say, "Okay, folks, no more free enterprise, that's it, you're done, now it's share and share alike"? I don't buy it. Hong Kong is a well-oiled machine and I believe it's going to continue functioning the way it always has well into the twenty-second century.

My trip to the Far East was uneventful. The Osprey flew to Hawaii first and made a stop. I had a two-hour layover at

Pearl Harbor and then we continued on to Manila. By the time we arrived in the Philippines it was too late to catch the commercial flight to Hong Kong, so I spent the night in the barracks. It wasn't bad. Since I can usually sleep on demand I didn't have any problems with jet lag. Jet lag never has bothered me much. Only after I return home does it seem to catch up with me. I guess you could say I'm the master of my internal clock.

After I land the next morning in Hong Kong, I consider renting a car but decide against it. As in London or New York, cars in Hong Kong are more of a hindrance than an advantage. I'll get around much faster taking public transportation and walking. If and when I need to get to some remote spot, I'll take a taxi. I can always rent a car later if I need one.

Frances Coen's instructions say I have to seek out Mason Hendricks, a former intelligence officer stationed in the Far East. Hendricks, an American, is ex-CIA and, like Harry Dagger in Moscow, is retired but still has his nose to the ground. I've never met him although I've had plenty of opportunities to do so. Back when I was in the CIA he was certainly around, but our paths never crossed. He's reputed to be a good man, very smart and resourceful. Coen tells me that my equipment was drop shipped from Manila to Hendricks. I'm not sure what the logistics are and how he goes about retrieving the stuff; I leave that to my so-called Field Runner.

Hendricks lives in the Mid-Levels, halfway up Victoria Peak. The Peak is *the* place to live in Hong Kong, especially when the British were here. The higher up you go, the more expensive the real estate. The Mid-Levels is the equivalent of upper-middle-class to lower-upper-class neighborhoods, if that makes any sense. It's still damned expensive.

I take a taxi to his home, a detached dwelling next to a

block of apartments off of Conduit Road. When he answers the door, I'm surprised by how young he looks. Hendricks is supposed to be sixty-one but he appears to be forty-five.

"Sam Fisher," he says. He holds out his hand. "Mason Hendricks."

I shake it, evaluating his firm grip. This is a man of strength. "Glad to meet you after all these years."

"Likewise. Please come in."

The inside of his home is tastefully decorated in a mixture of Western and Eastern styles. The British influence is definitely present but the Asian flavoring tends to dominate. For example, there's a very large Buddha in the room, something you notice when you first walk in. The smell of burning incense fills the place. Next to it is a shelf containing a collection of ships in bottles—and they're all British warships from the classic eighteenth-century period.

"Forgive the incense," Hendricks says. "I'm afraid I've grown to like it after forty-some-odd years in Hong Kong."

"Doesn't bother me," I say.

Hendricks is dressed in a simple beige tunic and loose-fitting matching trousers. He'd be at home in any beach house.

"I know what you're thinking," he says. "I look younger than I'm supposed to be."

"As a matter of fact," I reply, "you don't look fifty. But you're sixty-something, right?"

"Sixty-two next month. It's the clean living that does it. And of course, a stress-free lifestyle. I admit to having a little plastic surgery, I dye my hair, and I never eat fatty foods. My health improved immeasurably after I retired from the CIA. I also finally found time for a love life. I've had so many Chinese girlfriends in the last ten years that it puts my college years to shame. That will certainly keep you young! And that's another reason why I take care of myself. Anyway, everything I do these days for our precious government is simply for the fun of it or because it interests me. I'm happy to help out the NSA. I hope I can give you some useful information. How about a drink?"

I shrug. "Sure."

"I'm having scotch. What will you have?"

"Just fruit juice if you have it."

He goes straight to the bar on the opposite side of the room from the Buddha and fixes a couple of glasses. I take the moment to browse his bookshelf, which is full of historical military reference books and suspense novels. When he brings my glass of juice—apricot—he clicks it and says, "Cheers."

"Thank you. Cheers."

Hendricks leads the way through a sliding glass door to a terrace that overlooks the skyline. "I wish I were higher up. I bought this place twenty-five years ago for a song. I could probably make a fortune if I sold it. Or if it accidentally burned down, the insurance would make me a rich man." He laughs. "Then maybe I could buy a place farther up the Peak. The view's much better. That's where all the hoity-toity live."

"I think it's a very nice place, Mr. Hendricks."

"Oh, please, call me Mason."

"All right."

We sit on deck chairs and enjoy a slight breeze. In serious contrast to the weather in Maryland, it's quite warm on the island. I don't think I've ever been to Hong Kong when it wasn't.

"Did my equipment arrive safely?" I ask.

"It did indeed. I have it in one of the bedrooms. But please, let's relax and talk out here a while. Where are you staying?"

"I don't know."

"I'd offer you my spare bedroom but I tend to have female company at night. I hope you understand."

I smile at him. "Whatever rocks your boat. I'll find a place. I'm not picky. I may stay in Kowloon. There are inexpensive hotels I know there."

"Suit yourself."

We sit for a moment in silence. Finally I bring up the mission at hand. "Mason, what can you tell me about this Professor Jeinsen?" Hendricks relates what I already know—that Jeinsen was shot in the head, wrapped in burlap, tied to the Promenade in Kowloon, and left to float in the water until he was found. An Interpol bulletin on the missing physicist was what did the trick in helping the police to identify him. Once the corpse was ID'd, the U.S. government was notified.

"The interesting thing here is that Professor Jeinsen wasn't murdered," Hendricks says. "He was executed."

"By whom?"

"I'd say it was a Triad killing."

I nod with understanding. The Triads are the Chinese equivalent of our Mafia, the Japanese Yakuza, the Russian Mafiya, and other organized crime outfits. They've been around for centuries, originally formed to help oust the Ch'ing dynasty and reinstate the Ming. It was during the twentieth century that they became criminally oriented. As secret societies, they pride themselves on being patriotic and nationalist. Violently opposed to the Communists, the Triads primarily settled in British Hong Kong and Portuguese Macau. Eventually they spread around the globe to other Chinese communities. I know for a fact that Triads operate in the Chinatowns of big American cities. They traffic in drugs, weapons, prostitution, and slavery, as well as operate protection rackets and gambling parlors. The

Triads are fiercely anti-Western and their rites and meetings are sacred, usually never witnessed by non-Asians.

"I believe we're also dealing with a very specific Triad,"
Hendricks continues. "Most Triads use knives, hatchets,
machetes—blades—to do their killing. Jeinsen was shot in
the back of the head, gangland style. Like the Mafia does
it. There's one Triad known to use that particular method
of execution in Hong Kong. They're called the Lucky
Dragons."

"I don't know them."

"They're not the biggest Triad by any means. The Dragons are awfully small when you compare them to, say, the
14K or Bamboo Union. But they've been around as long as
I can remember. They're based in Hong Kong but I know
they have extensive branches reaching into mainland
China."

"But Triads are notoriously anti-Communist," I say.

"They are. And so are the Lucky Dragons. But I'm
fairly confident they have some pull with certain government officials. Ever since the handover, it was expected
that the Chinese government would crack down hard on
Triads because of their widespread ideology against Communism. It hasn't happened. The Triads are just as powerful now as they were under British rule. Sure, it's still
illegal to be a member of a Triad and all that, and the police make arrests all the time. It's just one of those things,
like the Yakuza in Japan. They'll always be with us."

"What's the leadership like?"

"A fellow named Jon Ming is the leader. The Cho Kun,
the Dragon Head. He's, I don't know, forty-eight or so.
About your age I think. He became Cho Kun about fifteen
years ago after a bloody coup within their organization.
Ming is a wealthy gangster that lives on a plantation-style
estate in northern Kowloon, just below the border of the

New Territories. Actually, he acts more like a Yakuza than a Triad. He flaunts his wealth and power in public the way the Japanese gangsters do. That's not the norm for Chinese Triads. Here you can be arrested for just *acting* like a Triad, yet he seems to steer clear of legal trouble. That's why I think he's got some politicians in his pocket."

"Where can I find this Jon Ming?"

"He runs a fancy nightclub in Kowloon. The Purple Queen. It's one of those hostess clubs, the kind that cost you a fortune to sit and talk with a beautiful girl. Sometimes you can get her to go home with you, which will cost you even more." Hendricks rattles the ice in his glass. "I guess you can say that's how I came to know some of my girlfriends. I do frequent the hostess clubs a lot. The Purple Queen, too. I can't take you there, though. You'll have to go alone. They know me. I wouldn't want you seen with me."

"I agree."

"Ming also owns a couple of restaurants and has his hand in some of the industries around here. He controls some of the container port so he has unbelievable access to shipping stuff in and out of the country. I left you a photo of the guy in the room with your equipment so you'll recognize him when you see him."

"So what's Jeinsen's connection to the Lucky Dragons?" I ask.

Hendricks looks at me and wiggles his eyebrows. "That's what you're here to find out, isn't it?"

"Any ideas?"

"None. If you ask me, the guy must have betrayed his second country. After all, he betrayed the first one by defecting to the U.S."

I sigh and say, "That's just what we're hoping he *didn't* do. Do you think Ming keeps anything at the nightclub I might be interested in?"

"I don't know," Hendricks says. "It's doubtful. I imagine all Triad-related business is conducted at one of their Lodges, and I'm afraid I can't help you with that. Your best bet is to get a good look at Ming and follow him. Maybe he'll lead you to the goods."

"What I'd really like to do is establish a connection between this Triad and the Shop. You think there might be one?"

Hendricks nods. "They get their arms from somewhere. I've heard rumblings that the Shop is operating again in the Far East. I'll make some inquiries this evening and see what I can find out."

We go back inside the house and Hendricks takes me to the bedroom where my equipment lies on the bed. It's the usual stuff—my uniform, headset and goggles, the Five-seveN and several twenty-round magazines of 5.7×28mm ss190 ammunition, and my pride and joy, the SC-20K modular assault weapon system. This rifle uses thirty rounds of 5.56×45mm ss109 ammunition in semi and full automatic modes. There's a flash/sound suppressor combined with a multipurpose launcher that shoots airfoil projectiles, sticky cameras, shockers, and smoke grenades. Other tools of the trade include an optic cable for looking into tight holes, a camera jammer, a couple of wall mines, frag grenades, flares, and a medical kit.

"I'm impressed, Mason," I say. "You managed to get all of it in one shipment."

"I've had a *lot* of experience, Sam."

"So where is this Triad's headquarters? Their 'Lodge,' as you say?"

Hendricks picks up the SC-20K and tests its weight. "Nice weapon." He looks through the sights and says, "The Lucky Dragons don't have a central Lodge. I imagine they have several scattered throughout the territory. Your best bet is the Purple Queen nightclub. I can assure you there will be some Lucky Dragons in the place. You might even see Jon Ming. He's known to stop in every other night or so."

"All right."

"Remember you're a *gweilo* here. I don't have to tell you that these guys are pretty dangerous, do I?" A *gweilo* is a derogatory term meaning "foreign devil."

"I'm quite familiar with Triads," I say. "They'll kill any Westerner they suspect of spying on them. They'll also die to protect their traditions."

Hendricks lowers the SC-20K, looks at me eye to eye, and says, "And don't you forget it."

# 13

"SIR, the FBI agent is here to see you."

Colonel Lambert told his secretary to send him in and then grumbled to himself. Lambert hated the idea of the FBI poking its nose into Third Echelon's affairs. He ran a tight ship and he didn't like interference. Carly St. John was part of the family and Lambert felt it was his duty to solve her murder and bring the perpetrator to justice.

But he had neither the means nor the expertise to carry out such a mission. Third Echelon was not a law enforcement agency. Colonel Lambert didn't have the authority to arrest or prosecute anyone. The matter had to be handed over to an outside party and the only one that made sense was the Bureau.

Special Agent Jeff Kehoe had been assigned to the case. Lambert had met him for the first time the previous day. He was a Texan in his early forties and was a sixteen-year FBI veteran. His specialties were homicide and arson. The initial meeting had gone well and Lambert could honestly say he liked the guy. It just rankled him that Third Echelon's hands were tied in the matter.

Preliminary investigation into the murder was swift and decisive. Kehoe quickly established that Mike Chan was their man. Everyone had to swipe a key card to enter Third Echelon. Other than Carly, Chan was the only employee logged into the building that night. The firm's security cameras showed Chan moving from his office to Carly's office and back. The fact that his computer's hard drive had been erased was another dead giveaway. Lambert now looked forward to further revelations.

Lambert called, "Come in," when he heard the knock. Kehoe entered the office and nodded at the colonel.

"Good morning, sir."

"Agent Kehoe. Would you like some coffee?"

"No, thank you."

"Then have a seat." Lambert gestured to the chair in front of his desk. Kehoe sat and removed some notes from his briefcase. "What have you got for me today?"

"Quite a bit," Kehoe replied. "First of all, what kind of background check did you perform on Mike Chan before he was hired?"

Lambert shrugged. "The usual. Complete rundown of the guy's credit history, his family, schooling . . . why?"

"Mike Chan's apartment was thoroughly searched last night. An X-ray machine revealed a hidden compartment in the floorboards of his bathroom. There were some papers there that pointed us in a new direction, mainly letters written in Chinese. They were from Chan's brother. We learned some interesting things, the most important being that his name isn't really Mike Chan."

"What?"

"It's Mike Wu. He had supplied you with a completely false identity and background."

"That's impossible. We use the same background checkers as your people do. And the CIA."

"That's the problem," Kehoe said. "Chan's background was manufactured from beginning to end and it was manipulated from the inside. In other words, he had help from someone in a government agency. Every bit of so-called factual information on 'Mike Chan' was created and put into place before the background check. It takes considerable resources to do something like that. Mike Chan, or rather, Mike Wu, is not working alone. He's part of a much larger threat. Do you have any ideas what this could be?"

Lambert exhaled loudly. He rubbed the top of his head and said, "Gee, the only thing I can think of is the Shop. If it's not them then it's a major foreign power trying to get the goods on us. As I told you, Carly was working on a security breach we experienced last year. She was close to figuring it out and maybe Mike found out she was about to finger him. Hell, now I wouldn't be surprised if it was Mike that gave the Shop all of our agents' names. The Shop. It has to be them."

"But the Shop is an arms broker, right? They are a profit-motivated organization, not political, correct?"

"Yeah."

"Then what are they doing planting a mole in your organization? Other than supplying the names of your agents, what other purpose could it serve?"

Lambert thought a moment and suggested, "They're selling information." He slammed his fist on the table. "Whatever Mike was giving to them, they're selling it to someone else. That has to be it."

Kehoe nodded. "Makes sense. If it's really the Shop he's working for."

Lambert squinted at the agent. "What do you know?"

"As we uncovered more and more about Mike Wu, we

learned that he's originally from Los Angeles. We confirmed the brother's identity, the one writing him letters. He's a guy named Eddie Wu, a known Chinatown gangster. He's suspected of being a major figure in one of the Triads that operates in southern California."

"Triads!"

"Yes, sir. A Chinese gang that operates like the Mafia."

"I know what a Triad is. Wait, you think Mike Chan, er, Mike Wu, is working for his brother? And not the Shop?"

"I don't know. According to the letters, Eddie Wu knew all about his brother's false identity. I'm just suggesting that perhaps it's not the Shop. It could be; I haven't ruled it out. But there's this other angle. The Triad Eddie Wu is hooked up with is known as the Lucky Dragons. It's a global Triad operated from Hong Kong. The Dragons have branches in Los Angeles, San Francisco, and New York. Maybe Houston, too, but we haven't established that for certain. Anyway, the Lucky Dragons are a formidable bunch of hoodlums. Eddie Wu has been in and out of jail a few times and he's on a watch list out in California. But for the last several years he's kept his nose clean."

"So could Mike be heading to California?"

"That's what I think," Kehoe said. "I imagine he changed his identity again, maybe disguised himself, and flew out there. Or maybe he's taking a safer route, like the train, or bus. Hell, he could be driving. His car is missing. It's a 2002 Honda Accord. Either he's dumped it somewhere and we haven't found it, or he's inside of it right now driving along the interstate. Which would put him in Los Angeles the day after tomorrow at the latest."

Lambert shook his head. "Unbelievable. I can't fathom how that background check didn't turn any of this up."

"Like I said, sir. He's had help from someone higher up. We'd like to find out who that might be as well."

"So what's next?"

"I'm going to Los Angeles. The FBI there will be watching Eddie Wu. If Mike Wu shows up, they'll surely be seen together. We're counting on the fact that Mike Wu doesn't know we've seen through his false identity."

Lambert nodded. "Okay. Keep me informed, will you? I know you have to report to your own people but I'd appreciate it if you kept me in the loop."

"I'll do that, Colonel."

"Is that all?"

"I think so. For now."

Lambert stood and held out his hand. "Thanks. You're doing a fine job."

Kehoe got up and shook the colonel's hand. "Thank you. I'll be in touch." He turned and left the office. Colonel Lambert sat, feeling satisfied that some progress was being made. He might not like the FBI doing the job but at least this Kehoe was actually *doing* the job. Perhaps it wasn't such a bad thing after all.

On to other things. He pressed the intercom button. "Have Ms. Grimsdottir come to my office, please."

He then turned to his in-box and picked up a memorandum from Frances Coen that confirmed Sam Fisher's safe arrival in Hong Kong. Contact had been made with Mason Hendricks, and Fisher would be following a lead that might involve Chinese Triads.

*What goes around, comes around,* Lambert thought. *Could Mike Wu be involved in the Professor Jeinsen business?*

He then opened Anna Grimsdottir's personnel file and scanned it once more before the meeting. It wasn't necessary, though. Lambert had known Anna for a long time—she was one of the original Third Echelon employees. A woman of Icelandic origin, Grimsdottir was thirty years old. She was a second-generation American and a college dropout. She had been studying computer science at St.

John's College in the nineties but decided she could program rings around her instructors. She worked as a programmer for several different communications firms contracted by the U.S. Navy. She had been recruited at the ground floor of Third Echelon and had worked as a programmer and eventually became the technical director. Grimsdottir had continuously shown a strong drive, a sharp intelligence, and a noted dedication to the work.

There was a tentative knock on his door. "Come in."

Anna Grimsdottir stepped inside. As always she wore her brown hair pulled back and resembled an attractive college professor. She was so studious looking that one's mother might say she had a "nice personality." Her colleagues knew Grimsdottir's temperament was rather staid, almost the reserve of a Brit. But they also knew she had a wry sense of humor that she rarely allowed to surface.

"You wished to see me, Colonel?" she asked.

"Sit down, Anna." She took the chair, crossed her legs, and sat with impossibly good posture. "How was your leave?"

"Nice. Hawaii, you know."

"Sorry I had to end it early."

"No, actually I'm happy that you did. I'm glad to be back."

"Good. As you know, we've lost Carly."

Grimsdottir lifted her chin and said, "She was very good. I'm sorry that she . . . well, I'm sorry about what happened, sir."

"We all are." He cleared his throat and came to the point. "Are you ready to resume your responsibilities?"

"Of course."

"You'll need to get up to speed very quickly. You've missed out on a number of developments within the organization."

"Let's do it."

Lambert looked into her eyes and saw that there was absolutely no fear. Total self-confidence.

"Let's do," he replied.


**MIKE** Wu, aka Mike Chan, passed a sign telling him that Oklahoma City was twenty miles away. He needed to find a place to stop and rest before he had an accident. Wu hadn't slept a wink since he had shot Carly St. John and left Washington, D.C. Now, two days on, he was feeling the effects of sleep deprivation and too much caffeine. He was jittery, not thinking clearly, and had a massive headache.

Before leaving the D.C. area he had parked his blue 2002 Honda Accord alongside a green one that was in front of an apartment building blocks away from his own. Armed with a screwdriver, he switched license plates on the two cars in less than a minute, and then headed west on I-70. He picked up I-81 to take him down through the Appalachian Mountains and Virginia. The highway joined I-40 in Tennessee, and he planned to stay on that road all the way to California. He knew it was probably an obvious route to take but it was also the fastest. Hopefully the police wouldn't be looking for him yet. After he had slept a little, he planned to dump his Honda and steal a car for the second half of the trip. Wu couldn't believe he had made it halfway across the United States so quickly. But then, he rarely stopped. Only to buy gas and pick up a bite to eat.

He passed a sign for a motel located off the next exit. Good. Out of the way and cheap. Just what the doctor ordered. Wu couldn't wait to get there. He'd have a shower, drop into the bed, and catch five or six hours. And then—

*Damn!* In the rearview mirror he saw a police car right behind him, lights flashing. Where did he come from? Wu looked at his speedometer and saw that he was doing ninety-three miles per hour. In his haste to reach the motel, he had become careless. Up to that point he had been so good at driving safely and staying within speed limits so as not to attract attention. Now this.

Wu pulled the car over to the shoulder and stopped. The patrol car, an Oklahoma State Police vehicle, moved up behind him. The officer sat in his car making a note and doing the routine call-in with the license plate number.

*Shit.* It's going to be reported stolen. What should he do? Think quickly!

In his sleep-deprived, anxious state, Mike Wu did what he thought was the only solution possible. He reached under the seat and grabbed the Smith & Wesson SW1911. Wu scanned his mirrors to make sure no other drivers were around to see what he was about to do.

The officer got out of the patrol car and walked toward him. Wu lowered the window and smiled at the man.

"Hello, Officer," he said. "I know, I was speeding. Sorry about that."

"Step out of the car, sir," the patrolman said.

"I have my license right here . . ."

"Please step out of the car, sir," the man repeated.

"Okay, if you say so." Wu pointed the pistol out the window and squeezed the trigger. The bullet caught the patrolman in the chest, propelling him backward to the road. Wu opened the car door, stepped out, and aimed the gun at the policeman's forehead. The patrolman, gasping for air, shook his head and attempted to cry out.

Wu squeezed the trigger a second time, got back into his car, and drove off, leaving the dead man at the side of the road in front of the police vehicle. He decided that the best thing to do next was to go ahead with his plan to stop at the motel and get some sleep. The police would be looking for him, all right, but they wouldn't expect him to be so close, set up in a fleabag motel. He'd simply make sure the car was out of sight. Later, after he was rested, Wu would steal another car and continue his journey to freedom.

# 14

I find the Purple Queen nightclub easily enough. The place is huge, more like the size of a theater. This area of Kowloon, Tsim Sha Tsui East, is a major center for nightlife in Hong Kong. All around me I see not only these ritzy hostess clubs like the Purple Queen, but also karaoke bars, disco clubs, restaurants, and even leftover British-style pubs. The neon is mesmerizing and you can feel excitement in the air. Kowloon after sundown rivals anything Las Vegas has to offer. It's difficult to believe this is now a Communist-controlled land.

Two large Sikhs stand outside the front doors ready to intimidate anyone they think might not be desirable clientele. I'm dressed in my uniform because I'd like this to be purely a reconnaissance mission. I want to get the lay of the land.

I keep out of sight in the shadows and circle behind the building. There's a small parking area with a slot marked RESERVED, probably for the big guy. All the other spots are taken. I can't imagine where the valet parks the overflow, for the streets are packed with automobiles. There's a back door, no windows, and an enclosure where they store the garbage until it's hauled away. It'd be nice to get inside that back door.

As if on cue, a guy comes out the back and throws a bag of trash into the pen. He's dressed in a suit, wears sunglasses, and obviously works as muscle for the joint. I walk over to him and say in Chinese, "That garbage stinks. How often do they pick it up around here?"

He looks at me as if I'm insane. "What?" he asks.

"I said the garbage here stinks. Oh, I'm sorry, it's not the garbage. It's you I smell."

This gets a reaction. He reaches for the inside of his jacket and I quickly chop the side of his neck with a spearhand. The gun, a Walther from the looks of it, drops to the ground. I punch the goon hard in the stomach, causing him to bend forward, then clobber him on the back of the head. Once he's in Dreamland, I drag his body into the garbage pen, stuff him unceremoniously into the only empty can, and put the lid on. That should keep him snug for at least a half hour, maybe more. I then throw his pistol into another can and cover it up.

I step inside the open back door and find myself in a corridor lined with four doors. I hear rock music and bad karaoke singing coming from the club beyond a door at the end of the hallway. The space to my immediate right is some kind of meeting room. There's a table and six chairs around it, a whiteboard on the wall, and a telephone. What's strange is that there are plastic sheets hanging on two of the walls. It's the kind of coverings painters use to protect furniture, but the room doesn't appear to be recently painted. I'm about to move on when I notice a spot of paint at the bottom of one of the sheets. I crouch to take a closer look and discover that it's not paint at all.

It's dried blood.

Looking back at the room I can picture the place entirely covered in plastic at one time. Something bad happened in here and they haven't quite cleaned it all up.

Very quickly, I tear off the section of plastic. I stuff the strip into my pocket and then move on down the corridor to try the next door. This is a messy office. Papers are strewn over the desk, filing cabinet drawers are half open, and someone's leftover takeout carton of Mu Shu Crap is smelling up the room. I glance at the papers and can barely make out the Chinese script. They're bills, orders, and employee records for the Purple Queen.

I step into the next room, expecting to bump into a couple of Triads at any moment. But it's just another office, not quite as messy as the first, containing nothing of interest.

The next room is the kitchen, where they wash the dishes and glasses. There are two guys wearing aprons, backs to me, busy at the sinks. They both have headphones on and are listening to Walkmans attached to their belts. I can see a swinging door on the other side of the kitchen that most likely leads to the club.

The door at the end of the corridor suddenly opens. I step inside the kitchen and stand on the other side of the threshold. Two men wearing suits and sunglasses walk past, ignoring the kitchen, and head down the hall. They go out the back door, slamming it shut behind them. I pause for a moment, thankful that the dishwashers are too preoccupied by their jobs to turn and notice me standing behind them.

When I feel it's safe to move, I smoothly slip out of the kitchen, swiftly dart to the back door, and crack it open. The two men are getting inside a car. I wait until they pull out of the lot and disappear before I exit the building. I figure it's time to become Joe Tourist and enter the nightclub for real.

As I find a dark corner in the alleyway to put my civilian clothes on over my uniform, I ponder what the blood on the plastic sheet might mean. Seeing that Triads run the club, I suppose it could be anyone's blood. I'll have Hendricks run it to check the blood type. If it's the same as Gregory Jeinsen's then I might be on to something.

Now appearing like an average *gweilo* looking to spend some money, I approach the front door. One of the doormen opens it and a blast of soft American rock music hits me in the face. The cover charge is five hundred Hong Kong dollars, which includes the first two drinks. Sheesh, what a bargain. After I fork out the money, four gorgeous Chinese women wearing *cheongsams* sing out in unison, "Welcome!" and pull back velvet curtains so that I may enter the main floor.

It's a dimly lit room bathed in red and there are dozens of planters holding small palm trees. An aquarium stretches along one wall. I estimate there are about fifty tables in the place, with a dance floor dominating the area. There are also several divan–coffee table combinations scattered around the perimeter. Middle-aged Chinese gentlemen accompanied by anywhere from one to four "hostesses" paying rapt attention to them occupy many of these seats. In fact, the place is surprisingly crowded. I didn't expect to find so many big spenders in post-handover Hong Kong.

Apparently the patrons of the Purple Queen can purchase "time" with a hostess. She'll sit and have a drink with you, dance with you, talk with you . . . whatever you happen to arrange. There are even private rooms you can escape to. Whatever happens in there must be arranged beforehand and probably costs you more than you can afford. I understand that naïve visitors can be taken for a ride financially; simply having a drink with a hostess can be very expensive.

I take a seat at one of the tables near the door marked EMPLOYEES ONLY, which is written in both English and Chinese. I can read Chinese fairly well and can make out some of the other signage around the place that isn't translated into English. There's an emergency exit behind the band's setup and the restrooms are near the bar.

I'm not at the seat twenty seconds before a lovely young Chinese girl wearing a *cheongsam* approaches me. "Would you like some company?" she asks in heavily accented English.

"No, thank you," I say. "Just bring me a drink, please. Fruit juice, if you have it."

The girl blinks as if I've said something completely gauche. I hand her one hundred Hong Kong dollars and this seems to appease her. She rushes off using those dainty small steps so typical of Asian women and I concentrate on the "entertainment." A Chinese—or maybe a Japanese—businessman is onstage trying to sing "We've Only Just Begun" karaoke-style. It's horrific. When he's done, the three hostesses he had been sitting with applaud enthusiastically. The man leaves the stage and a four-piece band returns to their instruments. The guitarist announces that they're ready to play another set and invites everyone to "get up and dance." The band then launches into a passable cover of "Funkytown" and maybe ten or twelve people migrate to the dance floor.

The girl brings me my juice and again offers to sit and chat. Once more I refuse and act disinterested. She glares at me unpleasantly and walks away. The girl whispers to another hostess, who decides to try her luck. Perhaps the *gweilo* prefers someone a little taller? Someone with larger breasts? Maybe the one with the blonde wig?

No, no, thank you. Just let me drink in peace so I can observe what's going on around me.

When I think they've finally got the message, I take

note of the various thugs posted around the place. I count three Chinese men—all gangster types—who are obviously keeping an eye out for trouble. Chances are I've been noticed and they're pondering why I'm not spending money on a girl. Screw 'em. I wonder if they miss their pal who's in the garbage bin out back.

The first hostess brings me the obligatory second drink before I've finished the first. Apparently since I'm not spending any more money they want to get rid of me. I thank her but she barely acknowledges me.

Before long a group of men enter the place and parade through the room as if they own it. Sure enough, one of them does. I recognize the older guy in front—it's Jon Ming. The other six must be his bodyguards or lieutenants. They're all wearing expensive suits and look as if they just waltzed out of a John Woo movie.

The group walks right by my table but none of them glance my way. They head straight for the Employees Only door and step through into the corridor where I was earlier. The door shuts before I manage a better look.

Now's my chance to slip outside and plant a homing device on Ming's car. If his bozos aren't watching it too closely I just might be able to get away with it. I quickly down my second drink and leave another hundred dollars on the table and catch the hostess's eye. I point to it and mouth the words, "Thank you." She smiles but doesn't give me much encouragement to return. I stand and begin to walk toward the front when none other than Mason Hendricks enters the joint. He looks very dapper decked out in a fancy white suit.

*What the hell?* I thought he didn't want to be seen anywhere near me. Something's up.

Instead of moving toward the door, I make a detour for the men's room. I take my time doing it, watching Hendricks out of the corner of my eye. He ignores me. Several of the hostesses greet him as a regular; he smiles, puts his arms around a couple of them, and whispers in their ears. They laugh and lead him toward a divan. I find the men's room, go inside, enter a stall, and wait.

After a minute or two, the door opens and I see the bottom cuffs of his white trousers. I open the stall and Hendricks is standing at one of the two sinks, washing his hands. I step beside him in front of the other sink and turn on the water.

"What the hell, Mason?" I whisper.

"I have some information for you. Thought you could use it immediately." He quickly lays a business card on the counter and begins to dry his hands. "One of my sources tells me the Lucky Dragons are receiving a shipment of arms tonight. I wrote the address on the back of the card. It's supposed to go down at half past midnight."

I dry my hands and slip the card into my pocket. "Thanks," I mutter. Maybe this is what I need to establish a link between the Triad and the Shop. In exchange, I give him the piece of plastic with the dried blood on it.

"Get this analyzed," I say. "It might be Jeinsen's."

Hendricks sticks the evidence in his pocket and nods. "Will do."

At that moment one of the Triad thugs enters the washroom, barely glances at us, then steps up to a urinal.

Hendricks then addresses me at normal volume with the persona of a good ol' boy who just happened to bump into a fellow countryman. "Well, friend, did you get a load of those dames out there?" he asks.

"Um, yeah, I did," I say, playing along.

He winks at me. "I think *I'm* going to get lucky tonight. Happy hunting!" Hendricks leaves the washroom and I linger for a moment to finish drying my hands. When I'm done, I go out into the nightclub and head for the front door. I notice that Hendricks is back on the divan with three of the women, having a grand old time.

Once I'm outside I circle the building to look for a limousine or something that might be Jon Ming's car. There's a Rolls-Royce parked in the special Reserved spot but two men are busy washing and polishing it. I'll have to forget planting a homer this time around. The best thing for me to do is go back to my fleabag hotel, change into my uniform, and wait until twelve-thirty to check out the arms delivery.

I have a feeling it's going to be a long night.

# — *15* —

**AT** midnight I take a taxi to a district known as Kowloon City, located near the former Kai Tak International Airport. This infamous area was once the site of the legendary Kowloon Walled City, the center of everything illegal in Hong Kong. Technically the enclave remained part of China throughout British rule and therefore became the primary stomping grounds for Triads. You name it, it was there—vice, prostitution, gambling, drugs, poverty, illegal dentists and doctors, and even black market organ trading. Even sensible Chinese were afraid to go into the Walled City, which consisted of dark, dirty, narrow streets and filthy tenement buildings. If a Westerner was foolish enough to venture inside, he took his life with him.

In 1984, though, the Hong Kong government acquired the area, rehoused the residents, and tore down the walls. Now, ironically, a beautiful park occupies the grounds. In my opinion the change certainly did away with an eyesore but it also meant the Triads had to integrate themselves throughout the rest of the territory. At least in the past they congregated in a single spot.

Today, Kowloon City is still a low-rent neighborhood and probably a place that Westerners should avoid at night. The "warehouse" I'm looking for is located very near the old airport. The building is condemned, the windows boarded over, and I'm beginning to wonder if Hendricks was given a bum steer. Nevertheless, I'm nearly a half hour early and it could be that these Triads are anally punctual.

I circle the place and consider using my lock picks to get inside the back door, a steel job that appears to have been broken into before. But there's a window with only one board tentatively fastened to it, probably a weeks-old access created by a homeless person looking for a warm shelter for the night. I'm able to leap to the bottom sill, pull my body up, and peer inside the dirty glass. With my night vision goggles I can see that the floor inside is bare save for dirty pieces of junk metal lying along the sides of the space. The slat covering the window is about to come off anyway, so with one hand I pull it out and let it fall to the ground. Sure enough, the window isn't locked—it moves inward via a rusty, squeaky hinge at the top of the pane. I wriggle inside, hold on to the sill, and then somersault into the room.

The place smells moldy. From what I can tell, it hasn't been used in ages. Even the cobwebs have cobwebs. I'm about to label the so-called tip as bullshit when I hear the sound of vehicles outside. Headlights flash across the front windows, creating eerie slats of light streaming between the boards. I quickly look around for a decent place to hide and run to a large piece of scrap metal that's leaning against the wall in a corner. I crawl behind it, crouch, and wait as another pair of headlights cross the windows.

After a minute I hear the sound of keys in the front door, which is approximately thirty feet away from where

I'm hiding. The steel door opens and three Chinese dressed in cheap suits waltz in. One of them is carrying what looks like some kind of radio transmitter the size of a boom box. Three more guys come in and shut the door. I relax a little, now that I know the odds. That's six to one, which is, of course, in my favor.

One of them hits a switch on the wall and bulbs in the ceiling flood the space with illumination. So, the building has electricity. It's not condemned at all. Perhaps the Triad always uses the place for illicit purposes and they just want to keep people out.

I switch off the night vision and watch the men through a slit in the scrap metal. The guy with the radio thingy goes over to the wall, finds an electrical outlet, and plugs in the device. He unfastens something on top of it and removes a small satellite dish. Leading thin wire out of the machine, he places the dish on the floor about five feet from the box. I find it interesting that the other men aren't watching him. Instead, they've drawn handguns and stand in a semicircle, facing out, as if they're expecting someone. I begin to worry that my cover isn't good enough and they'll be able to see me back here.

The radio guy goes back to the box and fiddles with some knobs on the side. I see a red light glow and a low hum fills the room.

*What the hell is going on?*

Then it's almost as if a bolt of lightning answers my question. My ears are suddenly bombarded by a high-pitched electronic shriek that is excruciatingly painful.

*Oh, my God! Shit, turn it off!*

I'm squinting in torment but can see that the six Triad gentlemen are still out there, standing calmly, looking for signs of movement in the room. They're not affected by the noise at all.

*Damn! Stop it! For the love of Christ!*

I realize I'm bending over, embracing the floor. My hands are clutching the sides of my head and I can't shake away the torture. This is the fucking worst thing I've *ever* felt in my life!

The implants. That's what the device is targeting! It's sending some kind of electronic signal to the implants in my inner ears. This has turned me into a dog, susceptible to pitches beyond the scope of human hearing. And, like a dog, I'm now crawling on the floor, unable to control myself. I must be drawing attention to myself, for the Triads look in my direction and walk toward me, guns pointed. One of them rips away the sheet of scrap metal, exposing me. I'm helpless at their feet, writhing in agony, pleading with gods that don't exist to somehow stop the punishment.

Two of the men grab me under the arms, take my weapon, and drag me to the center of the room.

*Do something!* I command myself. I can't be *this* vulnerable! I've been trained to withstand the worst torture imaginable and do everything I can to fight back. I can't let them win!

I'm lying on my right side in a fetal position, my legs curled to my chest. I sense that the five gunmen have surrounded me and are aiming their handguns at my quivering shape. They're going to execute me here on this cold, dirty wooden floor.

I swear I'm about to black out as my right hand instinctively moves to one of the pockets on my right calf, the side I'm lying on. I grasp one of the frag grenades I keep outside of my backpack in case I need one for an emergency. If ever there was an emergency, this is surely it.

Activating it is easy. Tossing it toward the transmitter is another thing altogether. Instead, I elect to simply roll the damned thing right between one of the goon's legs. The grenade wobbles across the floor and the five gunmen follow it with their eyes. The look of surprise on their faces is priceless, for they realize there is absolutely no time for them to do anything about the inevitable—

*KA-BOOM!*

The pain in my head abruptly ceases. I'm able to think clearly and summon all the strength I have left to leap out of the pitiful position I was in. I ram one of the men, knocking the weapon from his hand, and throw him into the fellow to his right. They collide and fall to the floor. Before they hit it I'm already swinging my right boot up and into the next closest Triad, kicking him onto his ass.

As the smoke clears, I can see that the frag grenade destroyed their little toy and killed the operator and the one goon that had been standing closest to the blast. Another man was severely wounded by it—he's crawling around in his own blood, looking for his arms. That leaves the three men I just attacked, and they're quickly rebounding from the surprise. One of them manages to retrieve his dropped weapon but I move in with a solid kick to his chin. The thug's head jerks backward so hard that everyone hears the snap of his neck. He goes down and won't be getting up again. Ever.

Two happy campers left. Their weapons are out of reach but they don't hesitate to go on the offensive. Both men rush me and use some expert kung fu moves to try to disable me. A side kick delivered to my stomach succeeds in doubling me over, allowing the second guy a clear spear-chop to the back of my neck. It's a standard maneuver and I'm trained to deflect it by propelling myself forward just a few inches so that the blow hits my back instead of the neck. It still hurts and could easily break one's spine, but the bones there are tougher than neck vertebrae.

I fall forward, roll, and lock my right boot behind one man's leg. I flex my knee and he falls to the floor. The other guy tries to kick me but I grab his foot with both hands and twist it as hard as I can. He yelps and is forced to flip in the direction of the turn to avoid having his ankle broken. He, too, is now on the floor, giving me the time I need to get to my feet. I perform a forward roll from the prone position, thrusting my upper body up and over my legs, a nice move that took a complete day of practicing to master. It's especially tough on the abdomen and thigh muscles. I quickly gain my balance and I'm standing between the two Triads.

Now that my two sparring partners are lying on either side of me and preparing to defend themselves, I figure it's best for me to take out one of them completely so I don't have to split my attention. I turn slightly and deliver a whammy kick to the guy on my right, catching him square in the sternum. Before his pal can stop me, I leap over the stunned man, get behind him, crouch, and grab him in a headlock. I twist hard and hear the sweet melody of singing vertebrae. I then drop him, a lifeless blob of dead weight.

The last guy now realizes he's in trouble. Instead of attacking me, he plays it safe and runs toward the front door. He thinks fast, too, for he knocks over an old wooden ladder that was standing by the exit. The ladder falls and blocks my way before I can retrieve my handgun and get through the threshold myself. It takes me a mere second and a half to toss the ladder aside, but by then the guy is climbing into one of the cars—a Toyota Camry—and starting it up.

I run out, draw my Five-seveN, and aim at the hoodlum through the windshield. But instead of backing away, like I expect him to do, he slams his foot on the accelerator and drives straight at me. I have to dive to the right to avoid being bisected, dropping my gun in the process. The Toyota's tires screech, spraying gravel into my face, as the driver reverses, turns around, and speeds away from the building.

I retrieve my weapon and run to the other car, a Nissan Altima, and can't believe my good fortune—the keys are in the ignition. I get in, start her up, and take off in pursuit of the Toyota.

"Sam?" I hear a woman's voice in my ear. Someone at Third Echelon.

"Sam, are you there?" she says again. "Are you all right?"

I concentrate on pulling out into the street to follow my prey before I answer. "Yeah, I'm here. Who are you?"

"It's Frances Coen."

"Oh. Right." The business with my implants temporarily threw me. I didn't recognize her voice. "What do you want?"

"What's going on? What are you doing? We lost your homing signal for a few minutes. I'm afraid your implants are malfunctioning."

"No, they're not," I answer. "The bastards had some kind of transmitter that did something to them. I don't know what it was, but I swear it almost killed me. I'm all right now."

The Toyota heads for the expressway, known as Prince Edward Road, merges onto the eastbound side, and nearly collides with a truck carrying new cars. I follow him at seventy miles per hour, barely missing the truck as it swerves to get out of the way. Even though it's after midnight, the expressway is crowded. This is going to take some concentration.

"Frances, I can't talk right now. I'll get back to you later."

"Colonel Lambert wants a report. He says—"

"Tell the colonel I'm in a *situation* here and—"

*Shit!* Some jerk in a Volkswagen doing fifty miles an hour just pulled into the lane in front of me. I have to jerk the Altima's steering wheel hard to the left to avoid hitting him, but that puts me in front of a BMW going faster than I am. The horn blares as the car slams into the back of my car. I accelerate to eighty-five and get away from him since he's probably not too happy with me.

"I heard that," Coen says. "I can see you now on the GPS. Check back when you can. For God's sake, be careful."

I play zigzag through the maze of automobiles as I attempt to catch up with the Toyota. He's ahead nearly ten car lengths and is moving dangerously fast. I push the pedal to ninety, which is about the limit I dare to speed through the thick traffic.

We go over a bridge and head east into San Po Kong, a suburb just north of the old airport. The highway forks up ahead—we can stay on this road, which bends to the southeast, or there's an alternate route directly south onto the Kwun Tong Bypass. The Toyota elects the bypass and makes a jarring exit across two lanes. I lean on my horn and turn the wheel in pursuit. A taxicab nearly hits me but the driver slams on the brakes. His tires screech, the car swerves, and he smashes into the rail.

*Sorry about that,* I say to myself.

I'm on the new highway now and it's even more crowded than the first. But the Toyota is now five car lengths ahead and I'm gaining on him. Unfortunately, we pass a police car. The cop turns on his lights and picks up speed behind me. I floor the accelerator and push the Altima to a hundred as I pass a couple of SUVs. Within seconds I'm running side by side with the Toyota. The driver looks at me, scowls, and then he points a pistol out his window. The bullets smash my passenger side, spraying broken glass over the front seat and me. Two can play at that game, so I draw the Five-seveN, aim it across the passenger seat, and squeeze the trigger. The Triad accelerates just enough so that my round smashes the driver's side rear window, missing him completely.

The cop behind us has apparently radioed for backup because another patrol car enters the expressway just past the Richland Gardens exit. I can't be bothered with the police; I focus solely on catching my prey. The gloves are off now and no prisoners will be taken.

I speed up to position my car parallel to the Toyota again and then I swerve to the left, ramming him. The Toyota screeches and scoots into the far left lane. Changing lanes to stay beside him, I take another shot at the driver. This time his back windshield shatters and I hit him in the shoulder, I think. The car skids into the rail, bounces off, and wavers perilously in front of me. The guy manages to gain control of the car and moves around a slow-moving bus. The damned thing is now between us, and the two police cars are right behind me. I attempt to pass the bus on the right but a van moves into the lane. My only option is to pass on the far left, a lane crowded with vehicles entering and exiting the expressway. I wait until I pass another taxi and then push the speedometer to the breaking point. The Altima speeds to a hundred and ten as I zoom alongside the bus and eventually overtake it. The problem is that the two police cars do the same thing. Alas, the bus driver doesn't see them because they're in his blind spot. He blasts his horn as he changes lanes behind me and the two police cars are forced against the rail. One of them smashes through it and dives off the expressway onto the streets below. The other one spins, overturns, and slides into the center of the expressway.

I hear the sounds of car horns, crashing metal, and squealing tires. The pileup behind me involves at least twenty automobiles but I can't let it bother me. My prey is making a move toward an exit and I must stay on top of him.

The Toyota takes the ramp to Kowloon Bay and I follow him off the expressway. If he thinks he's going to lose me in the crowded narrow streets of the city, he's got another think coming. Traffic essentially halts to a standstill as soon as we're at street level. There's nowhere for him to go.

What a dumb move on his part. I'm right behind him and we're sitting in a line of cars waiting for a red light to change. So what does he do? He gets out of the car and begins to run.

Hell, it ain't *my* Altima, so I get out and chase after him. More car horns blast annoyance as we maneuver through the traffic and onto a sidewalk. The Triad, who's holding his wounded right shoulder, cuts around a corner and into a dark alley. When I get to the entrance I lower my goggles, flip on the night vision, spot him, crouch, and aim the Five-seveN. I squeeze the trigger and he goes down in a tumble.

As I walk toward the wounded man I hear so many police sirens that it's difficult to tell where they are. Most of them are probably on the expressway, dealing with the pileup. But some could be after me as well, so I have to make this fast and get the hell out of here.

My Triad friend is crawling on the ground, bleeding to death. I place my right boot on the wound in his back and say in Chinese, "Talk to me."

He curses at me in English. It's funny how some words are universal.

"How did you know I would be at the warehouse tonight?" I ask.

The man curses again so I apply a little more pressure to the wound. He screams and I let up a bit. "Well?"

"It's just what we were told," he says.

"So it's true you were expecting me to be there?"

He moans but doesn't answer. I apply pressure and he cries, "Yes!"

"Good. Now tell me: Was there an arms deal going down tonight? Anywhere?"

He curses at me again so this time I practically stand on the guy's back. I don't normally go in for torturing an enemy to get information, but when time is of the essence and there's no other way around it then I'll do whatever it takes.

When he finishes screaming and I let up, he says, "It's in the morning. At Kwai Chung."

Kwai Chung is the big container port for all of Hong Kong.

"Where? What time?"

"Eight o'clock."

The sirens are really close now. I can hear policemen on foot shouting to each other on the street beyond the alley entrance. They'll be here any second.

I crouch, pull the man's head up by his hair, and ask again, "Where?"

He mutters a number.

"Is that a terminal?"

He nods and coughs. Blood spurts out of his mouth.

"You wouldn't lie to me, would you?" I ask.

His eyes flutter, he coughs again, then chokes on the blood and mucus in his throat. I know he's a goner. He won't last more than a few seconds longer and I'm not going to get much else out of him. I stand and begin to run down the alley just as two policemen appear at the entrance behind me. They shout for me to stop but I'm in the shadows now. They can't see me. When I reach the end of the alley, I dart into the street, run across traffic, and duck into another dark alley. I repeat this strategy three more times and by then I've lost the cops. The only thing to do now is go back to my hotel and wait until morning. I just hope my late Triad friend was telling me the truth.

# — 16 ——————————

"**SOMEONE** set me up, damn it!" I shout to the empty hotel room in Kowloon.

Colonel Lambert, Frances Coen, and Anna Grimsdottir are all online with me through my implants. I've given a full report on what went down at the warehouse and I'm hopping mad.

"Calm down, Sam," Lambert says. "Why do you think you were set up?"

"Because they knew I would be there. They brought along that contraption that screwed with my implants for that very purpose. The Triad I interrogated in the alley confirmed it. Someone told them to expect me. They knew I was a Splinter Cell and that I had those communication implants. I was *set up*!"

Grimsdottir speaks up. "This device, Sam, what did it look like?" She has a soft voice but one can sense intelligence behind it.

"Kinda like a boom box. There was a tiny satellite dish they pulled out of it and set on the floor."

"I think I understand how it was done," she says. "They would have had to understand the technology behind the implants and how they work. If you're right, then they must have had inside information from Third Echelon. It's the only way."

"Mike Chan again?" Lambert asks.

"Possibly. If he's the traitor."

"Of course he's the traitor," I say. "He killed Carly, didn't he? Have you caught that bastard yet?"

"No, the FBI is on his trail," Lambert replies.

"Well, it still doesn't answer how the Triad knew I'd be at the building. The only person who knew what I was doing was Mason Hen—"

That has to be it. Hendricks.

"Um, I think I need to pay a little visit to Hendricks, Colonel." I look at my watch. There are a few hours left before I have to be at the Kwai Chung container port.

"Mason Hendricks has been one of our most trusted field agents, Sam," Lambert says. "His record is impeccable."

"Then maybe he knows how there might have been a link. His source was bad or something. It's worth pursuing. Besides, I gave him a piece of evidence that needs to go to a lab. Some blood I found at the Triad's nightclub. Who knows, it might belong to Jeinsen."

"All right, Sam."

"Anything else, Colonel?"

"Yes. We've finished the analysis of General Prokofiev's materials you found in his house."

"Yeah?"

"You know that list of missing nuclear devices? The notes he scribbled next to some of them?"

"Uh-huh."

Frances Coen continues. "It's a code, all right. And it's very strange."

"Well?"

"When the code is broken, it's a recipe for Russian borscht."

"What?"

"Well, that's a guess. The words specifically decode as 'Formanova Cylindra beets, beef stock, water, vinegar, butter, cabbage, and tomato sauce.' Those are the ingredients of borscht. It leaves out a few spices and perhaps some other vegetables, but that's what it is."

"What the hell does borscht have to do with nuclear bombs?"

"We don't know. That's just what the code says when it's broken."

"I think you guys have gone loony," I say.

"We were hoping you might know what it means," Lambert says. "Was there anything in Prokofiev's house that might give us a clue as to what it's all about?"

"I can't think of anything, unless that battle-ax of a wife puts plutonium in her cooking. Which I wouldn't put past her. Look, I'm going back to Hendricks's place before the sun comes up. I'll let you know what he has to say."

"We'll talk later, Sam," Lambert says, and then we sign off.

**DRESSED** in my workout clothes and carrying my uniform in a gym bag, I take the ferry to the island, grab a taxi, and go back to the Mid-Levels just as the sun begins to rise. But the driver can't get through to Hendricks's street. A policeman tells us that only local traffic is allowed in.

"What's the problem, Officer?" I ask in Chinese.

"Fire," he replies.

I pay the cabbie and get out. Once I'm on the street I can see the thick smoke billowing up ahead. A couple of fire trucks, an ambulance, and two police cars are blocking the middle of the road. And they're in front of Hendricks's small house.

I walk up the pavement and take a look. Sure enough, his place is black, still smoldering from what was apparently an intense blaze. I move closer to the policemen who are talking with the fireman in charge. Even though they're speaking in Chinese, I'm able to catch a few words and phrases.

"Firebomb . . . through the front window . . . one in the back . . . possible Triad work . . . two bodies . . ."

I observe in fascination as firemen bring out two covered corpses on stretchers. One charred, black-and-red arm sticks out from under a sheet. I catch the words "man and woman in bedroom" before the corpses are loaded into the ambulance.

Hendricks had boasted about expecting female companionship for the night. Well, he got lucky, all right. Lucky as in Lucky Dragons. And I guess his lady friend got more than she bargained for as well. It's a shame.

Now I'm at a loss as to how I was set up at the warehouse. Apparently Hendricks was betrayed too. The Triad must have found out what he was up to, somehow intercepting the information he got from his source. Maybe it was the source who tipped them off.

And so much for the piece of evidence I took from the nightclub. It's probably long gone now.

I walk away, realizing I must disengage myself from Hendricks, finish what I came to Hong Kong to do, and get the hell out. As the new rising sun bathes the island in warmth, I make my way back to the ferry so I can get to my appointment at the container port on time.

# 17

FBI Special Agent Jeff Kehoe sat in the Empress Pavilion Restaurant enjoying somewhat authentic dim sum as he kept an eye on Eddie Wu, the brother of wanted fugitive Mike Wu, aka Mike Chan. Kehoe had arrived in Los Angeles a day earlier and, with the help of the local FBI branch, had tracked Eddie Wu to L.A.'s historic Chinatown. Kehoe had staked out Wu's apartment on Alameda and had seen the man come and go twice. The first trip Wu made was to the Phoenix Bakery on Broadway, the main drag through the district. The second outing was to the Wing Hop Fung Ginseng and China Products Center, also on Broadway, where Wu purchased tea and a few other groceries. So far the Triad had displayed innocuous activity. But it was still early in the day.

Alan Nudelman, the FBI chief in Los Angeles, had briefed Kehoe upon his arrival in the city. Nudelman confirmed that Eddie Wu was a known Triad member but had never been tied to any of the more serious crimes connected with the Chinese gangs operating in southern California. The L.A. branch of the Lucky Dragons was a small organization consisting of less than a dozen members. Wu was either the top man of the clan or one of the enforcers. He had been arrested twice for narcotics possession but he had a very good lawyer who got him off with fines and short jail time. Intention to distribute wasn't proven but the L.A. police were sure that Wu was dealing the drugs for the Triad. A more serious charge cropped up involving stolen property, including weapons, for which Wu served three years in the nineties. Since then he had stayed clean, although he was on the FBI watch list. Nudelman suspected Wu of being an accomplished thief, smuggler, and killer. Currently Wu was unemployed, yet he lived in a very nice apartment building, drove an expensive car, and always had cash to spend.

The Triads in southern California operated much like small-time Mafia families. They specialized in protection rackets, mostly among the Chinese populations in the city, ran gambling and prostitution houses, and trafficked in illegal arms and drugs. Most gangland violence that occurred was between rival Triads and rarely spilled out into the mainstream. Nevertheless, the Chinatown district's police precinct was kept very busy escorting the gang members in and out of its justice system. Most of the Caucasian officers could care less if the Chinese criminals killed each other; their main concern was for the innocent families trying to make an honest dollar in democratic America.

Kehoe finished his meal and sat with the *Los Angeles Times* in front of him, pretending to do the crossword puzzle. Eddie Wu was with two other men who had come in together to meet him. They, too, appeared to be rough types wearing black leather jackets and sunglasses. The Triads in America didn't dress as fashionably as their counterparts in Hong Kong and China did. In the United States they looked more like street punks. As for Eddie Wu, he was purportedly thirty-eight years old, which was old for a common thug.

After a while, Wu paid the bill and he and his two companions stood. Kehoe paused a moment, paid his own bill, and followed the trio onto Hill Street. The restaurant was in Bamboo Plaza, home to a variety of shops. The men turned onto Bamboo Street and headed toward Broadway. Kehoe casually tailed them, trying his best to be just another Caucasian tourist admiring the Chinese souvenirs along the way.

They passed Central Plaza, where the sounds of clicking mahjong tiles from upstairs windows and open doors mixed with authentic Chinese music being played in shops. A popular place for filming, the plaza was known for its distinctive Gate of Maternal Values, a statue of Republic of China founder Dr. Sun Yat-sen, and a wishing well dating to 1939.

Wu said goodbye to his companions at the Cathay Bank at the corner of Broadway and Alpine. The two men left, walking east on Alpine. Wu went inside the bank. Kehoe lingered outside the impressive building, which was supposedly the first Chinese-American–owned bank in southern California.

Ten minutes passed and Wu bounded out. He walked east on Alpine, past Dynasty Plaza, to his apartment building on Alameda, a block east of the array of bazaars. It was one of the more modern, upscale structures in the area, certainly not the norm for low-to-middle-income Chinese immigrants. After Wu disappeared into the lobby, Kehoe got into his rented Lexus to sit and wait.

Tracking Mike Wu westward had been easy. When a state policeman in Oklahoma had been found shot to death near Oklahoma City, evidence quickly pointed to Wu. The patrolman had stopped the Honda Accord for a traffic violation, called in the license plate, and learned that the plate was stolen. Before catching a bullet in the chest, the patrolman had informed his headquarters that he was investigating the suspect vehicle. Ballistics comparison of the round that killed the patrolman and the bullets that slew Carly St. John proved to be identical.

Nearly thirteen hours after the discovery of the patrolman's body, Wu's blue Honda Accord was found abandoned behind a convenience store in Oklahoma City. Whatever Mike Wu was driving after that was a mystery.

Kehoe was certain that Wu would come to Los Angeles to see his brother. After all, Eddie Wu knew about his brother's false identity as Mike Chan. Perhaps Eddie was going to help Mike leave the country. It was what Eddie was good at, according to Nudelman. Thus, it was only a matter of time before Mike showed up at Eddie's door. All Kehoe had to do was never take his eyes off the Triad.

At midafternoon Wu emerged from his apartment. He went to his car, a BMW 745i sedan, obviously another indication that Eddie Wu earned his money illegally. Kehoe figured the BMW to cost in the upper range of sixty thousand dollars. The BMW drove west and got on the 110 freeway, heading south. Kehoe cautiously followed him.

Traffic was surprisingly light for a weekday afternoon. The rush hour hadn't begun in earnest quite yet and Kehoe actually enjoyed driving on L.A. freeways. He considered them to be the best in the country. Unlike other big cities in the U.S., it seemed that the freeways in L.A. were planned from the beginning to hold a lot of traffic. Other places he'd been, such as Chicago and Washington, D.C., had experienced painful crowding when the population had outgrown the highways.

The BMW got on the Santa Monica Freeway and sped west. Wu opened up the car and Kehoe had to push the speedometer to stay a safe distance. No problems arose, though, and eventually the BMW reached the intersection with the 405. Wu took the northward exit and headed over the hills. It wasn't long before the BMW got off at Sunset Boulevard and turned west into Brentwood.

Following the car became tricky. The BMW took odd side streets up into the area around Crestwood Hills Park. Kehoe was worried that he would either lose his prey or Wu would make him. On many of the roads they were the only two cars moving. After nearly thirty minutes of this kind of driving, the BMW turned onto a hilly road called Norman Place. Wu eventually took a hard right onto a gravel road and disappeared into the trees. Kehoe stopped at the intersection and looked at a map. Where the hell was he?

The Getty Museum wasn't far away. It was a couple of miles to the northeast. The area was sparsely dotted with expensive homes and a few isolated businesses.

Kehoe decided to take a chance and drove onto the gravel road. After moving slowly for about a mile, he came to a gate and wire fence blocking further access. A sign read: GYROTECHNICS, INC.—PRIVATE PROPERTY—NO TRESPASSING. There was Chinese script beneath the English words; Kehoe figured they said the same thing.

The FBI agent got out of the car and looked through the steel mesh gate. Fifty yards beyond the fence was a two-story modern building that was unremarkable save for dark windows of different geometric shapes. It was similar to a 1950s sci-fi movie production designer's bad idea of what a futuristic building might look like.

He got back into the Lexus and drove back to Norman Place. He pulled over and called Al Nudelman on his cell phone.

"Nudelman."

"Hi, Al, it's Jeff Kehoe."

"Yes, Jeff."

"Ever hear of a company called GyroTechnics Inc.?"

"Uh, no. What's that?"

"I was hoping you could tell me. I followed Eddie Wu from Chinatown to this building. It's in the hills near the Getty Museum. Private property."

"I'll check it out and get back to you."

"Thanks."

Kehoe drove down the hill and parked in a more unobtrusive spot. He could see the unnamed gravel road in his rearview mirror, so if Eddie decided to leave he'd be seen. Twenty minutes later, Nudelman phoned back.

"GyroTechnics is a brand-new Chinese company. Electronics, circuit boards, that kind of thing. Says here that their specialty is guidance systems for aquatic vehicles, namely boats and ships. Been incorporated in California for three months."

Kehoe asked, "What's Eddie Wu got to do with them?"

"That's a good question," Nudelman replied. "I seriously doubt he's on the payroll."

Kehoe chuckled. "Not officially anyway. Well, I'm just going to have to camp out and wait for Eddie to leave. Or wait for his brother to show up. One way or another I'm going to find out what this company is really up to."


**ANTON** Antipov opened the antique shop door and let Andrei Zdrok in.

"This had better be good," Zdrok grumbled. "The sun isn't even up yet. Decent human beings are still asleep at this hour."

"You'll be happy when you see what we unpacked," Antipov said.

He led Zdrok through the dark Hong Kong–Russian Curios shop and into the back room. Like the Shop's director, Antipov knew how to manipulate the Shakespeare and Marlowe books on the shelf and open the secret door. Together they went down into the Shop's headquarters, past Zdrok's private office, and into a main receiving area.

In the middle of the floor sat an opened crate the size of a large television. Straw had been pulled out and now littered the floor. Antipov directed Zdrok to a worktable next to the crate, where the unpacked item lay horizontally under a bright lamp, dramatically lit as if it were on display in a museum.

It was silver in color and cylindrical in shape, much like a giant bullet in its casing. Two cushions on either side of the device kept it from rolling. On the cylinder's side facing the ceiling was a compartment that had been opened, its inner mechanisms exposed.

"Direct from Mother Russia," Antipov said, smiling. "It arrived last night after you left. Ironically, delivered by Federal Express."

Andrei Zdrok's jaw dropped and he momentarily forgot having been awakened too early. The device's beauty mesmerized him. It shone like a polished precious metal but it was worth far more than any gold or silver.

"It's too bad Prokofiev isn't conscious to hear that it arrived safely," Antipov added. "The poor guy is still in a coma."

"Screw the general," Zdrok said. "He's of no use to us now. At least he was able to have this shipped to us before he became a permanent tube sucker." He approached the device and gently placed his palm on the cone-shaped head. It was smooth and cold to the touch.

"It's magnificent," he said. "I have never seen one before, have you?"

"No. Well, yes, some of the earlier kinds. Not one like this," Antipov replied.

"Well. We have to get this to our customer in China right away," Zdrok said. "You'll take care of the arrangements?"

"It's already being done." Antipov looked at his watch.

"I have to get to Kwai Chung. Oskar is coming in with the shipment this morning."

"Good." Zdrok touched it once more, admiring the fine craftsmanship and design. "You know, I almost wish we didn't have to sell it. It's not often that a nuclear bomb passes through the Shop. You're right, Anton. The last one we sold was one of the older models from the early Cold War era. Big motherfucking thing the size of a Volkswagen. These 1980s jobs are so much more compact and . . . movable."

"That they are, Andrei," Antipov replied. "That they are."

Zdrok nodded at his partner and said, "Do you have time to get some breakfast and some coffee? I'll treat."

Antipov grinned and nodded. "Sure."

Together they walked out, past the crate lid that read in Russian, English, and Chinese: PERISHABLE—FORMANOVA CYLINDRA BEETS—KEEP AWAY FROM HEAT.

# 18

DRESSED in my uniform, I arrive at Kwai Chung container port at seven-fifteen. The place is brimming with activity so I need to be careful. I don't want to be seen wearing this getup. Someone might think I'm on my way to a costume party. To make it less noticeable, I don't wear the headset or goggles. Hopefully I'll simply look like I'm wearing some kind of protective gear for handling hazardous materials. I can't worry about it, though.

Kwai Chung is a famous shipping center, probably the busiest in all of Asia. The place also serves to export goods from the Chinese mainland because China's own transport infrastructure is so inadequate. The container port lies on the eastern shore of Rambler Channel, just north of the border that separates Kowloon from the New Territories. The area is purely industrial, so there are always trucks, construction vehicles, and moving vans going in and out of the port. The container port itself consists of six terminals, with Terminal 5 at the northern end and Terminal 6 at the southern end. Terminals 1 through 4 are in the middle. The Triad hoodlum I interrogated told me that the arms deal was going down at Terminal 6, which by my map readings appears to be somewhat set apart from the terminal buildings. That figures. The Triad wouldn't want illegal activities to be noticed.

From where I'm standing I can see hundreds of containers stacked high like colored building blocks. They all have labels and logos painted on the sides, words like EVERGREEN, HYUNDAI, WAN HAI, UNIGLORY, and many others. Tall orange cranes loom over the containers at strategic points around the port, along with equally tall blue barges. The white warehouse buildings are scattered throughout the port and are manned by security guards, terminal employees, and representatives from the various shipping companies. Security at the port has increased since the events of September 11, 2001, but probably not as much as the United Nations would like. I know that in the United States our shipping ports are still very vulnerable. It would be quite easy for terrorists or other notorious groups to place WMDs inside a container and hide them well. The containers are rarely inspected. If they are, it's done randomly.

When I arrive at Terminal 6 I see that the *Odessa*, a large Russian ship, is docked at the pier against one of the big blue barges. A crane is already at work unloading crates and containers from the ship. I make note of the ship's identification details and then attempt to creep closer to the terminal. Three workers are hovering at the back of the building smoking cigarettes next to a rung ladder that goes all the way to the roof. If I could get up there I'd have a good bird's-eye view of the proceedings taking place by the barge.

I reach into my backpack and grab one of the diversion cameras that I usually launch from my SC-20K. I didn't bring the rifle with me on this trip but I can throw the camera by hand if I need to. A diversion camera sticks to a wall or object and then makes noise on my command. There's a very creative list of sounds in its database, from effects to different types of music. It can sometimes attract the attention of nosy guards and divert them away from me. It's a camera, too, should I need photos of curious guards.

I arm the diversion camera to make noise and then toss it about twenty yards away in between a row of stacked containers. The thing begins to beep, attracting the workers' attention. One of them points in the direction of the containers and curiosity gets the better of them. When they walk over to investigate the noise, I quickly run to the ladder, climb it, and safely reach the roof.

From this position, I can see the entire barge and terminal area. In addition to five men dressed in business suits conversing in a huddle, terminal workmen are loading crates from the ship into two medium-sized moving trucks with Chinese script on the side, translated as "Ming Fish Company." I lie flat, remove my binoculars, and focus on the suits. I immediately recognize Jon Ming as one of the businessmen. He has two toughs with him—armed, from the looks of the bulges beneath their jackets. Ming's Rolls-Royce is parked near the building I'm lying on.

The Chinese are talking to two white guys who apparently came in a black Mercedes that's parked beside the Rolls. Lo and behold I recognize Oskar Herzog as one of them. He's come a great distance since I last saw him in Ukraine. But then again, so have I. The other guy appears to be Anton Antipov. Lucky me, two Shop directors in one spot. Antipov is doing all the talking.

Just from witnessing this exchange it's obvious that the Shop is doing business with the Lucky Dragons. I'd bet a Hong Kong dollar that those crates are full of weapons. The Triad has to get gear from somewhere and the Shop doesn't care who their customers are.

I aim my OPSAT's digital camera at the group and snap a few photos. Then I pull out the Five-seveN and activate the T.A.K. audio component. Quickly sticking the earplug in my right ear, I'm now able to listen to what they're saying and record the conversation as well. At first I'm surprised that they're speaking English, but then I realize the Chinese guys don't speak Russian and vice versa. Ah, yes, English, the universal language. That should tell you something about the way of the world.

ANTIPOV: —as we agreed. Your order is now complete.

MING: Thank you. Please tell Mr. Zdrok that we appreciate the opportunity to do business with you. Of course, we will need to inspect the merchandise where we can do so in privacy.

ANTIPOV: I understand. I'm sure you'll find it satisfactory. By the way, Mr. Zdrok asked me to tell you that he is sorry he couldn't be here in person this morning. He had some urgent business to attend to.

MING: Don't we all?

ANTIPOV: So, everything is good, then? This completes our end of the agreement. This is the final shipment of merchandise in exchange for the various installments of Operation Barracuda that you have graciously passed on to us.

MING: Agreed. As you know, we also eliminated the link. The American authorities should not be able to trace the professor's trail. At least he won't be able to talk about it!

ANTIPOV: (*laughs*) Why, Mr. "Wong"! The professor really believed he'd have safe passage to Beijing?

MING: (*laughs*) Apparently so.

ANTIPOV: Oh, well, he probably wouldn't have liked working in Beijing anyway.

MING: I wouldn't.

ANTIPOV: Of course not.

The men are silent for a moment as they watch the workers.

ANTIPOV: It looks as if your men are almost finished. I am obligated to bring up the issue of the final piece of the Barracuda project, which you still owe us.

MING: Don't worry. We'll be picking that up from California any day. I'm just waiting to hear from my people in Los Angeles.

ANTIPOV: Very good. Please keep us informed. Our customer is anxious to receive it.

MING: (*coughs*) Excuse me. I think I am fighting a cold. Speaking of your customer, may I ask who it might be?

ANTIPOV: Mr. Ming, you know we cannot reveal that. The Shop has built a reputation on discretion.

MING: Mr. Antipov, surely you can understand our concern. Operation Barracuda, as you call it, involves some serious technology that could very well be used against our interests if it was sold to the wrong people.

ANTIPOV: I appreciate your concern but again I must stress that we cannot reveal who the customer is.

Ming takes a step closer to Antipov and Herzog. Although Antipov is two inches taller, Ming is definitely the more threatening. I can hear the change in the man's voice. He is not someone to cross.

MING: Fine. Keep your secrets. But I should leave you with a little word of advice. I do hope you are not selling the Operation Barracuda material to anyone in mainland China.

ANTIPOV: That sounds like a warning, not advice.

MING: Take it however you wish. Some of my sources have suggested that the Shop is dealing with that devil General Tun in Fuzhou. As you know, the Lucky Dragons have a relationship with a few friends in the Communist government in China, but those relationships go only so far. Triads fundamentally hate the People's Republic and what it stands for. General Tun represents the worst of China. I shall go on the record here and now that if I find out the Shop is indeed selling this material to General Tun, the Lucky Dragons will not be happy with Mr. Zdrok. We will do everything in our power to stop it. Good day, Mr. Antipov. Mr. Herzog.

No shaking of hands, no friendly salutations. Abruptly, the three Chinese turn and walk toward the Rolls. I have to duck quickly to avoid being seen. After a moment I peer over the edge again and see that the Rolls is pulling out of the parking area and the two Russians are walking inside the building. This is my chance to get down.

Once I'm on the ground, I fish a homer from my backpack, activate it, and casually walk toward the Mercedes. I look around to make sure the Russians are out of sight and that the workers are paying no attention to me. In one fluid move, I crouch, place the homer under the car, stand, and walk away. The odds are heavily in my favor that I wasn't seen.

"Anna, are you there?" I ask, pressing the implant in my throat.

"Hi, Sam."

"I take it you received that little conversation?"

"Loud and clear. I'm analyzing it now."

"And, Frances?"

I hear Coen's voice a little clearer. "Yes, Sam?"

"I've placed a homer underneath the Russians' car. I'm counting on you to track it and let me know where they go."

"Already zoomed in on it, Sam."

Satisfied, I make my way toward Kwai Chung Road, the outer perimeter of the container port, throw my sport jacket on to cover up the more superhero aspects of my uniform, and hail a taxi.

# _19_

**MIKE** Wu drove into Los Angeles on I-40 after crossing the Mojave Desert overnight. He hit I-15 at Barstow, drove southwest into the metropolis, took I-10 west to the 405, and then headed for Los Angeles International Airport. It had been a stressful trip and he was happy it was over. Pretty soon he would see his brother Eddie and he could get the hell out of the United States and over to Hong Kong where he would start a new life with a new identity.

The plan was for him to bring the final puzzle piece of Professor Jeinsen's project directly to the Lucky Dragons. Apparently the device could be disassembled and packed in checked luggage without arousing security concerns. It was made simply of machine parts and a laptop computer. Eddie was taking care of a new passport and visa for him and soon Mike could kiss America goodbye. The most important thing was that Mike would receive his big payoff, from Jon Ming himself. For the last three years Mike had worked at Third Echelon for his regular U.S. government salary. His deal with the Lucky Dragons began with an initial advance of a reasonable amount of cash. But after final delivery of Jeinsen's materials, Mike was due to receive three million dollars. Mike never understood why he had to wait until the end to get his money but that was the way the Lucky Dragons wanted it. In the meantime, Mike had done a little side transaction with the organization known as the Shop for a comfortable sum.

Mike Wu actually liked living in the U.S. He and his brother had been born and raised in L.A.'s Chinatown. Becoming involved with the neighborhood gangs began early in their lives. Mike, being the oldest, joined a Triad at the age of thirteen. Eddie had waited until he was sixteen but by then Mike was one of the major players in the gang. The Wu brothers joined the California contingent of the Lucky Dragons when Mike turned twenty-six. He and Eddie visited Hong Kong just before the handover and met Jon Ming. He gave the Wu brothers a great deal of responsibility running the American West Coast operations, tasks they shared with members already in place. When the Lucky Dragons became associated with the Shop, a new directive sent Mike to the East Coast as "Mike Chan," and eventually he became a research analyst for Third Echelon.

He didn't know how he would enjoy living in a Communist country after the luxury of the U.S. But Mike Wu was sure that he would be free of the inherent prejudice he had experienced in America. It wasn't as bad for Asians as for other minorities, but Mike encountered it daily. Even at Third Echelon. He felt he was a much better analyst than Carl Bruford, his boss. Bruford rarely gave Mike the tough assignments and yet Mike more than once went above and beyond the call of duty to work on them. He was fairly certain that Third Echelon's director, Colonel Lambert, thought highly of him.

Well, too bad. Mike "Chan" had screwed them royally.

He drove the car he'd stolen in Oklahoma into LAX and parked it in the long-term lot, where it would stay until the authorities discovered it days later. He then took the shuttle to the nearest terminal and looked for a bank of pay phones. Wu had tossed his cell phone long ago since he knew that government authorities could trace his movements if he used the device. Instead he'd bought a prepaid phone card and used it at pay phones when he had to.

Wu dialed the number his brother had given him and waited. He smiled broadly when he recognized Eddie's voice.

"Welcome to sunny southern California, big brother!" Eddie said.

It was true. The weather was quite pleasant for winter. It was a relief leaving behind the snow and ice of the East Coast.

"I can't wait to see you," Mike said. "How do I get there?"

Mike wrote down Eddie's instructions and promised he'd see his brother within a couple of hours. He then went to the baggage claim, exited the terminal, and caught a taxi.

**EDDIE** showed his brother into his office at GyroTechnics, embraced him, and said, "It's been too long. It is good to see you."

"Likewise," Mike said. "You look well."

"And *you* look tired. Was it a difficult journey?"

"I had a few problems but I'm here. And you're right, I'm exhausted."

"We'll go to my apartment as soon as I'm finished with some things here. What did you do with your car?"

Mike said, "I dumped it in Oklahoma. Stole another one

there and I just left that one in the LAX long-term parking. If I'm tracked maybe they'll think I hopped on a plane."

"Good thinking. You took a taxi here?"

"Yeah."

"Are you hungry? Want some lunch?" Eddie asked.

"That sounds good. Then I want to sleep for a week. But I can't do that because I'm going to Hong Kong tomorrow!"

Eddie laughed. "Not tomorrow. I hope to have you leaving in two or three days. Four at the most. In the meantime you'll stay at my apartment and chill out. How does that sound?"

Mike wrinkled his brow. "What do you mean? I thought you had it all arranged."

Eddie waved him off. "There have been some complications. Don't worry about it, I've got it under control."

That wasn't what Mike wanted to hear. He was too tired to push it so instead he looked around the office and asked, "You really work here?"

"Nah. Well, yes and no. I'm not officially on the payroll. I'm a troubleshooter. I help out with immigration and work visas."

"Oh, right. Eddie Wu, the Wizard of Work Visas. Illegal ones."

Eddie laughed. "Something like that."

"So what is this place, anyway?"

"It's one of Ming's many businesses. The Lucky Dragons back GyroTechnics financially but it's a legitimate enterprise here in America. They employ top scientists from Hong Kong and China and the Lucky Dragons help to get them here. That's my job."

"You mean it's a means by which scientists defect from China?"

"I guess you can say that. So far the authorities in China haven't figured out where their physicists are going. That's why GyroTechnics keeps moving around and changing its name. We stay ahead of the Americans that way, too."

"So where's the guidance system? I've been waiting for news about the final piece of Professor Jeinsen's project for a long time."

"Right. It's done, ready to ship."

"So what's the problem? I thought I was to take it with me to Hong Kong."

Eddie frowned and looked away. "Like I said, there are some complications."

Mike didn't feel like playing games. "What is it, little brother? What are these complications?"

"Ming. He's canceled the sale of the device to the Shop."

"What the hell for? Isn't it what we've been working toward for the last three years?"

"Yes. But Ming is afraid the Shop is selling it to a general in China. General Tun. Have you heard of him?"

"Yeah. The guy that's so dead set to attack Taiwan. Is *he* the Shop's customer for all this stuff?"

"I think so. I don't know for certain. Ming seems to think so. He's ordered me not to ship it and await further instructions."

"But . . . but that means we don't get paid!" Mike said. Now he was truly alarmed, forgetting how weary he was. "This deal has to go through. I'm looking forward to my new life in Hong Kong!"

"You're still going, don't worry. You just won't be carrying the guidance system with you."

"That was my cover! I was supposed to be one of your scientists, delivering it from California. Shit, has all that changed?"

"It's still being worked out, Mike. Don't worry! We have a few days to work it out."

Mike Wu was furious. He stood and shouted, "Damn

Ming! He's screwing with a machine that was working so well. The minute you start changing things is when you get caught. I say we go ahead and sell the thing to the Shop without Ming!"

Eddie looked at his brother in shock. "What are you saying? Are you mad?"

"Screw Ming! What has he really done for me? I sat there in Washington for three years, supplying the Lucky Dragons with Jeinsen's stuff, with no payoff whatsoever. It was all on spec, to be paid in one huge lump sum when I arrive in Hong Kong with the guidance system. To hell with that! I've got my own connections with the Shop. I sold them information about Third Echelon's agents last year. I can deal with them directly. Let's you and me do that, get rich, and then go our own way. We don't need to work for a Triad, Eddie. Not anymore."

"Mike, you don't know what you're saying! Look, I'm sympathetic to how you feel. But we can't go against the Lucky Dragons. We'd be dead men. Ming would come after us and he'd find us. He has the means to do it, too. You underestimate the guy."

"Does Ming know what it's like to be wanted by the Washington, D.C., police, the Oklahoma police, the FBI, the NSA, and probably the CIA, too? I have to get out of this country before they find me! I'm *really* a dead man if they do. Espionage against the United States government is one thing they don't take too lightly. Not to mention the murder of government employees."

Mike paced the room. "Eddie, if you're not with me on this, I'm going to the Shop myself. I'll tell them Ming has stopped the sale and if they can get here then I'll sell the guidance system to them on my own. And I can ask a very high price. A few million dollars will go a long way toward protecting us from the Lucky Dragons." He pointed to his sibling and said, "And *you* will back me up!"

Eddie looked at his older brother and rubbed his chin. "Maybe," he said. "Let me think about it. I suggest we go back to my place so you can get some rest. We'll talk about it tomorrow, all right? Let me find out what Ming has planned for you. Okay? We wait a day or two?"

Mike shook his head and slapped the wall. "Damn it, Eddie." He took a deep breath and finally resigned himself to the situation. "All right. But let's go now. I'm dead tired."

**JEFF** Kehoe could have sworn he had seen Mike Wu get out of the taxi that had stopped in front of GyroTechnics' gate. The guy punched the call button and went inside before Kehoe could get a good look. The FBI agent wasn't too worried, though. What went in eventually came out. As long as Kehoe stayed put in his car and kept his eye on the one road that led out of the facility, he'd be able to make a positive ID.

One of the L.A. field agents had spelled Kehoe overnight so that the FBI agent could get some sleep. Kehoe had resumed the stakeout outside of Wu's apartment in Chinatown that morning. It wasn't long before Wu emerged from the building and got into his BMW. Kehoe tracked Wu back to GyroTechnics to sit in the Lexus parked outside the compound, waiting for a sign that Mike Wu might have come into town. When the taxi pulled up to the gate and an Asian man got out, Kehoe was almost positive the fugitive had been located.

Kehoe called in to the FBI field office and told Nudelman what he suspected. He then waited for nearly two hours until Wu's BMW finally appeared and left the premises. As the car passed, Kehoe got a good look at the two men in the car.

The driver was Eddie Wu, of course, and there was no

doubt in Kehoe's mind that the passenger was his brother Mike.

"Bingo," Kehoe said to himself as he fired up the Lexus and followed the BMW at a safe distance.

# 20

"**SAM**, the Mercedes is moving down the West Kowloon Highway."

Frances Coen's words reverberate in my ear. I type a reply to her on my OPSAT: I'M RIDING IN A TAXI AND CAN'T SPEAK. COMMUNICATE BY OPSAT PLEASE.

It was simple to grab a taxi outside of the container port. They're always hovering around the area, dropping off or picking up workers or shipping executives. I made an educated guess as to where the Russians' Mercedes would be heading, so I told the cab driver to head south toward Kowloon.

I'm now able to pull up the satellite map on the OPSAT and track the Mercedes myself. I send a quick message to Coen, telling her I've got the car on my screen. She signs off and wishes me luck, adding that Colonel Lambert is pleased with the conversation I recorded between the Shop guys and the Lucky Dragons. I've succeeded in establishing the link between Professor Jeinsen and the Triad and, indirectly, Jeinsen's connection to the Shop. Now it's up to the suits in Washington to decide what to do next. I'm wondering if I'll get to go home now, but another text message appears on the OPSAT: TRY TO FIND OUT WHAT THE SHOP IS UP TO IN HONG KONG. WHAT THE HELL IS OPERATION BARRACUDA? L.

Good question. Oh, well, I knew it was wishful thinking on my part, wanting to go home.

I wonder what Katia is doing.

The Mercedes gets off the highway at Tsim Sha Tsui, so I have the cab driver do the same. He asks me again in Chinese where I'm going—there might be a shortcut around the heavy street traffic. I tell him I know what I'm doing and to just follow my directions.

We catch up with the Russians near Harbour City. I can see the black Mercedes in front of us, pulling over near Ocean Terminal. I ask the driver to stop and wait a moment. Then Antipov and Herzog get out of the Mercedes and walk away. Their driver moves the Mercedes away from the curb and into traffic, presumably toward a parking garage. I decide to follow Abbott and Costello, since they're a part of the Shop's top brass.

I pay the cab driver and get out. I'm pretty good at tailing someone on foot. Practicing stealth when you're alone in the dark is one thing; stealth when you're on a crowded city street is completely different. You have to blend in, not look conspicuous, and be flexible with your pace of movement. It's important to keep a steady distance between the prey and yourself but not appear to be rushing. Sometimes, if the prey stops, you have to pause and pretend to be interested in something while you wait for the quarry to move again. It's pretty standard stuff. There are also antisurveillance moves you can make to ascertain that no one is following *you*. But when you're doing the tailing, that can be difficult. I'm fairly confident that no one is behind me. As for the Russians, they're pretty naïve. Any jerk could follow these guys. They seem to be paying no attention to what's behind them. They don't have a care in the world.

As I expected, they make their way to the Star Ferry, on their way to Hong Kong Island. Once they're aboard, I linger just long enough to meld into a crowd of Chinese and Caucasian businessmen swarming through the gate and onto the boat. Antipov and Herzog step into the lower-deck quarters and take seats on a bench next to the wall. They are deeply embroiled in conversation, oblivious to what's around them. I position myself across the room, picking up a discarded newspaper to hide behind. I know it sounds cliché, but that's what you do.

The ferry ride between Kowloon and Hong Kong is always pleasant. Despite the rather foul stench of the harbor, it's a short, relaxing trip that could be quite enjoyable if I weren't on the job. At one point, Antipov stands and points to something outside the window. Herzog looks and nods. Antipov resumes his seat and the two men are silent. Herzog shuts his eyes and slumps for the remaining few minutes of the journey.

Ashore, I follow the men off the ferry to the taxi stand. Damn. This is where it gets tricky. I hurry to get in line behind them, with a buffer of two parties between us, and keep my nose in the newspaper just in case one of them turns around. I note the number of the taxi they climb into and then wait as patiently as I can for my turn. When I finally get into a cab, I point to the Russians' taxi up ahead, which is luckily stuck in traffic at the end of the block. The driver understands and nods his head. He throws the car into drive and screeches away from the curb. He makes an illegal move around the stalled cars in front of him, passing them in the oncoming traffic lane. So much for not attracting attention.

But the driver is good. As soon as traffic begins to move

he slips into it, two car lengths behind the Russians. He takes it easy from then on, following the other cab with discretion.

We head west on Connaught Road until the Russians' taxi pulls off onto Morrison Street. Eventually they reach Upper Lascar Row—"Cat Street"—and stop. I pay my driver and give him a huge tip, which he appreciates by showing me his rotten, discolored teeth.

The two Russians walk up Cat Street to a small antique shop. I stand across the road and watch as they enter the building. A sign above the door says it's the Hong Kong–Russian Curios store. Interesting.

After a few minutes I cross the street and walk by the shop. I look through the window and see a Chinese man sitting at a desk in the back and polishing a small statue. The Russians are not in the store. There's an Employees Only door next to the desk, and I must presume that they went through it to another area of the building. A basement, perhaps?

I note the sticker displayed in the window that informs potential burglars that Hong Kong Security Systems, Inc., protects the shop. I press my implant and ask Coen to get Grimsdottir to hack into the company's records and come up with a security access code I can use. She acknowledges and then I go back across the street.

During the next half hour no one enters or exits the shop. I snap a couple of photos and then decide there's nothing more to do now. Best to return after dark.

That's when my job is more fun.


IT'S just after midnight when I arrive at the antique shop dressed in full uniform. The first thing I do is circle the block and pop through the alley behind the store. There's an expected employee exit but I also notice an unusual outline in the pavement on the ground next to the building. It's almost as if someone had taken a stick and drawn a ten-foot-by-five-foot rectangle in the wet cement when it was first poured. Using my thermal vision, I notice there is heat beneath the outline—I can just make out thin slivers of light. Unlike most loading lifts that carry boxes to a shop basement, someone took great care to see that this one was hidden from view. Anyone without my training would never realize it's there.

I go back around to the front of the shop and carefully peer through the display window. The place is dark except for a lamp that illuminates the desk and cash register in the back. The best bet is the alley door. I return to the back of the building and use my lock picks to unlock the door. The dead bolt gives me five minutes' worth of trouble but eventually it gives and I'm inside.

The security keypad is immediately to my left. It's blinking and beeping and I know I have fifteen or twenty seconds to punch in the code Anna Grimsdottir provided. As soon as I press the sequence of buttons, the system de-activates. Nice.

I'm in a storeroom full of boxes and dusty goods. Lots of crap that someone might call antiques. There's a full bookshelf along one wall and a small bathroom with a door. But no staircase to a basement. There has to be an-other way down there.

I look inside the shop proper and find nothing out of the ordinary. The papers on the desk are invoices and such, neatly arranged and organized. I run my hand beneath the counter, searching for trick levers or buttons, but find none. Returning to the storeroom, I begin to examine the walls for telltale signs of secret doors. Again, my thermal vision comes in handy when I get to the bookshelf. Faint traces of light leak from the edges between two sets of cases. The access to the basement is behind them.

The bookcases don't budge, though. I pull on the sides, try lifting the sides, and search for more trick levers and buttons. Nothing. I remember seeing a play on stage in which one of the characters opened a trick door by pulling out a particular book. It's a device that's been used hundreds of times but it works. I figure what the hell?—so I begin to pull out the books on each shelf, one at a time. There are about fifty but I go through them quickly. When I get to the shelf that is shoulder level, I notice two books that are slightly forward, as if they've been moved recently. A book of Shakespeare and a book about Christopher Marlowe. I figure one must go with the other, so I pull out one and then the other. I hear a latch give way and the bookcase pops ajar. I open it and, sure enough, there's a spiral staircase descending to the floor below.

The stairs squeak much too loudly as I go down so I stop and take them one at a time slowly. When I'm halfway I hear snoring. I take the rest of the stairs at a snail's pace but from the way the guy is sawing logs I don't think I have anything to worry about. When I get to the bottom, I see him sitting at a desk. He's wearing a jacket and tie and is lying on top of the game of solitaire he was playing. There's a bottle of Russian vodka on the floor beside his chair. So much for Russian efficiency.

I move to the man and ask, "Are you awake?" in Russian. He snorts, mumbles, and then turns his head the other direction. The snoring begins again in earnest. He reeks of vodka so I figure I can go about my business without disturbing him. From the looks of the guy, he's going to need several hours to sleep this one off.

There are a couple of doors along the corridor, both leading into separate offices. At the end of the hall is a larger room full of more boxes and crates. I take a look and can immediately see that this storeroom isn't for the antique shop. A wooden box the shape of a coffin is full of assault rifles. On shelves lining the walls are various hand-guns of all makes and calibers. On another shelf is a collection of timers, material that appears to be plastic explosive, and boxes of ammunition.

In the middle of the floor is an open crate, one recently unpacked. Straw lies around the crate and the lid is against the wall. I examine the interior but there's nothing inside; however, the missing contents left an impression in the straw of an object that was maybe eight inches wide by thirty-six inches long.

I examine the crate for other clues as to what it contained but it's unmarked. I then look at the lid and see the logo and words burned into the wood, along with the shipping invoice. It reads, in Russian, Chinese, and English, PERISHABLE—FORMANOVA CYLINDRA BEETS—KEEP AWAY FROM HEAT. The crate was shipped from Moscow.

Beets? No way. Then I remember what I found in General Prokofiev's house. That list of missing nuclear weapons. Frances Coen told me the general's handwritten note by one of the listings was the recipe for borscht. Beet soup. Could this be . . . ?

I leave the storeroom and make my way back to the first office. My friend the Russian guard is still building a log cabin, oblivious to the world. I close the door, sit at the desk, and boot up the computer. Much of the software is in Russian. I go to the e-mail program and try to get past the log-in screen but can't.

"Anna? Someone? Are you there?" I ask, pressing my implant.

"Here, Sam. What's up?" It's Grimsdottir.

I give her the e-mail address for the computer and its server. "I need a password, and fast."

While I wait, I putter around the hard drive, taking a look at Word files and other programs. There's a folder containing several Excel spreadsheets that are obviously inventory lists with purchase and profit designations. I run searches for "Jon Ming," "JonMing," "Ming," "Lucky Dragons," "Shop," and "Mike Chan" but come up with zilch. Then I search for "Barracuda" and come up with a folder with that name. I open it and see several saved e-mails. Some of them are from Prokofiev in Moscow. Reading them, I come to realize that once again, for the second time in a year, I'm sitting at the desk belonging to Andrei Zdrok, the Shop's leader. So he's here in Hong Kong. I might have known, seeing that his other two flunkies are in the colony as well.

Prokofiev's messages are in coded gobbledy-gook but I can make out something concerning shipments of materials to Hong Kong from Russia, and orders to make sure something from America is delivered to China.

There's a folder marked GYROTECHNICS and it contains some e-mails from someone named GoFish@GyroTechnics.com. These are written either in very poor English or it's some kind of shorthand code. I quickly scan them and then come across the word *professor*. The gist of the message is that the author's brother provided the professor's materials to "JM." Jon Ming? It's signed *E. W.*

"Sam?"

"Yeah?"

"I have something for you." She gives me a six-character letter-and-number combination. "Try that and see if you get in."

I do, and it works. "Anna, I guess you're still on my birthday card list," I say.

"What about me?" I hear Coen ask.

"You just might get a card *and* a piece of cake," I say.

"Thanks a lot."

I look through the recently received e-mails and find one from GoFish. It says that his brother is now in town and needs to get out of the country quickly. A brand-new message in the in-box is from "GoFish2." I can't believe what I see when I open it.

Andrei—

It's me, Mike Wu, formerly Mike Chan. As you know, Eddie is my brother. We have just learned that JM has canceled the purchase of the Barracuda GS. We want to sell it to you directly. Contact me ASAP. We don't have much time. I need to get out of Los Angeles immediately.

—Mike

I quickly upload these files to my OPSAT and turn off the computer. While I'm doing so I consider all the various bits of information I've gathered in Russia and in Hong Kong. The way I figure it, Mike Chan was the mole inside Third Echelon. He arranged to deliver MRUUV classified secrets from Professor Jeinsen to the Lucky Dragons. The Shop then bought this material and sold them to another party. Mike and his brother, whoever that is, are in possession of one more piece of Jeinsen's work. Jon Ming doesn't want to go through with the transaction so Mike is trying to sell the thing to the Shop without the Triad acting as middleman.

There's a noise outside in the hallway. I freeze as I realize that someone's coming down the creaky stairs. Whoever it is shouts at the sleeping guard, giving the guy a thorough dressing-down for drinking and falling asleep on the job. I hear the guard, disoriented and hoarse, try his best to apologize.

More footsteps. There are several guys out there. What the hell am I going to do? There's no way out of this office. No windows, no vents, nothing. I move to the door and stand behind it, my Five-seveN drawn and ready. If I have to shoot my way out, I'll do it.

Then I hear the newcomer ask the guard why the bookcase upstairs was open. The guard doesn't have an answer. An order is given to search the premises.

I reach into my trouser leg pocket and grab a smoke grenade. After lowering my goggles, I clutch it in my left hand and prepare to pull the pin with my teeth and throw it. Suddenly, the office door pushes inward, slamming against me and revealing my position.

# 21

I switch on my thermal vision, pull the grenade pin, reach around the open door, and drop it. The men shout in alarm and then there's a tremendous explosion in the hallway. It's just a smoke grenade but the tight confines of the quarters magnifies the intensity of the blast. Total chaos ensues outside the office as the door is bombarded with gunfire. I fall to the floor, facedown, and crawl out beneath the line of fire. With my head in the hallway I can count four warm bodies in the smoke. Three of them are shooting blindly toward the office. I calmly aim my Five-seveN and take them out—one, two, three.

"Stop!" the fourth man shouts. "Stop shooting, you fools!" The poor guy doesn't realize his men are already dead. I can see him moving toward the staircase, feeling his way along the wall. I stand, grab him in a one-arm choke hold, and place the barrel of my handgun to his head.

It's Anton Antipov.

"I should just kill you now," I say in Russian.

The guy is trembling. "Wait!" he says in English. "Please!"

"Give me a good reason why I shouldn't."

"If you kill me you'll . . . you'll never know what's going on."

"I know what's going on."

"Surely you don't know the details." The guy is desperate. The coward is ready to spill his guts. He's right, though. I *don't* know the details. I pull him back through the hallway and out of the smoke. We end up in the storeroom with the weapons. I throw him to the floor, quickly frisk him, and find that he's unarmed. Standing over him with the Five-seveN in his face, I say, "Okay, Antipov. Tell me the details. I'm listening. Don't leave anything out."

The man squints at me and asks, "Who are you?"

"The Avon Lady. Now what's the Shop doing with the MRUUV material?"

"You're Fisher! Arc you not? The Splinter Cell!"

"I asked you a question."

"I was afraid you might show up sooner rather than later. Andrei . . . Andrei wouldn't believe you'd be on our trail so quickly."

"Are you going to answer me or not? You have three seconds."

"Wait!" Antipov puts up his hands defensively. "Don't shoot!"

"Okay, I'm waiting. Now talk to me."

"We've sold the MRUUV plans to General Tun in China. He plans to attack Taiwan with his army. He's mobilizing in Fuzhou and war is imminent."

Is the general nuts? "He's crazy if he thinks he can attack Taiwan without retaliation from the United Nations, not to mention America. Surely he knows that."

Antipov nods. "The general apparently has a plan for that scenario."

"And that is . . . ?"

"I don't know!"

The guy is too scared to lie. I think back to the information I gleaned from Zdrok's computer. "What's this final piece that's coming from California?"

"You know about that?"

"Answer me."

"It's the guidance system for the MRUUV. A firm based in Los Angeles is designing it according to Tun's specifications. You know how the MRUUV works?"

Yeah, I do. It's an undersea torpedo that can be guided remotely from a submarine or ship. "Why the hell would Tun need one of those to attack Taiwan? Does he have a bomb? One of your Russian nuclear bombs? Is that what came in this crate?" I indicate the one that was marked as containing beets.

Antipov nods. "Yes, he's got it. All he needs now is the guidance system. It will be on its way here from California any day if it isn't already."

I'm confused. The plan doesn't make a bit of sense. Why would the general use a nuke on Taiwan? Isn't the whole point to annex it to China? A nuke would completely obliterate such a tiny country. And what about the Chinese government? Do they know what he's up to?

Antipov shivers. "Please. Let me go. We just . . . we're just b-b-businessmen."

Why in the world would China want to destroy Taiwan? They've been trying to get the rogue island back into their sphere of influence for decades. You'd think they'd want to inhabit the place, take it over, and exploit its resources. No, there's something missing here.

"What else do you know, Antipov?" I ask. "There's more to this than you're telling me."

I see a flicker of triumph in the man's eyes. "Let's . . . let's work out a deal. Then perhaps I can tell you more." He grins, nods, and pleads with his eyes like a hungry dog. "I can pay you! I'll give you a million dollars. American! Let's deal, Fisher!"

The guy makes me sick. The Shop doesn't care who lives or who dies after they broker a transaction. They don't think twice about selling a nuclear weapon to a madman for a bit of cash. At the moment I can't think of anything more evil. The bribe only makes me angrier.

"Sorry," I say. "No deals."

Coldly and deliberately, I squeeze the trigger. Another quarter of the Shop's leadership is eliminated.

I turn and walk through the corpse-ridden hallway back to the staircase. Once I'm upstairs I fire a couple of rounds at the store's front plate window, shattering it to pieces. This sets off an alarm. Good. Let the Hong Kong police deal with the mess downstairs. I'm sure the little cache of weapons will interest them.

Lambert's probably not going to approve of what I've done. But I have no regrets. Just like General Prokofiev in Moscow, Antipov needed to be taken out of the picture. When I run into the other two, Herzog and Zdrok, I plan on doing the same thing to them. If Lambert wants to remove me from the assignment, then so be it. The way I see it is this: A job that began over a year ago was never finished. The damage the Shop has done to Third Echelon is immeasurable. They killed several of our agents. Mike Chan and the Triad may have been responsible for Carly St. John's murder, but if it hadn't been for the Shop pulling the strings it wouldn't have happened. So I say *enough is enough.*

I quickly leave through the back door, stick to the shadows, and make my way back to the ferry.

# 22

**JEFF** Kehoe looked at his watch and whispered into the microphone of his headset. "Thirty seconds. On my signal."

"Roger that."

The FBI field office had provided Kehoe with six men to stage the raid on Eddie Wu's apartment. As long as no other Triad members were present, the operation was expected to go smoothly.

Kehoe had waited until the two Wu brothers were safely inside the eight-story apartment building and then set up a stakeout until nightfall. At just after one in the morning, the team arrived in full riot gear, ready to storm the residence. The Bureau had previously taken care of contacting the building's management to warn them of what was about to take place. Warrants and legal formalities were executed by the book. An ambulance and fire truck were waiting a block away in case they were needed.

The apartment was on the top floor, one of three penthouses in the building. There was only one way in—and out. Since the brothers must be asleep, the element of surprise was in the team's favor.

Kehoe gave the signal and three men moved down the hall with the battering ram. Assault rifles ready, the trio looked at Kehoe for confirmation. The special agent nodded. The first man knocked loudly on the door.

"Open up! FBI!"

By rote, the team didn't wait for the door to open. They slammed the battering ram against the door, knocking it off its hinges. The two other agents stormed into the living room, followed by Kehoe and the four remaining officers.

Mike Wu was in a deep sleep when the crash of the door jolted him to reality. The feds surrounded him before he could sit up in bed. With three rifles pointed at his head, Wu had no choice but to raise his hands.

As the Third Echelon traitor was taken into custody, the other men searched the rest of the apartment for Eddie Wu. He was nowhere to be found.

"Where's your brother?" Kehoe asked Mike as the handcuffs were snapped onto the man's wrists.

"I don't know!" Mike said. "He was here when I went to bed."

Kehoe had not seen the guy leave the building. He couldn't believe Eddie wasn't there. He angrily turned to two team members and told them to tear the place apart. Kehoe then jerked his head at the men holding Mike and said, "Let's go."

Unbeknownst to the FBI or to his brother, Eddie Wu had built an escape hatch in the closet floor of his bedroom. The idea to do so had come from Jon Ming himself back when Eddie set himself up in Los Angeles. The FBI would eventually find the trapdoor, but not until after Wu was safely away. The door led to a passageway much like an air vent through which Eddie could crawl to the stairwell on the eighth floor. When Eddie heard the crash at the front door, he immediately went for the closet. He knew he couldn't save his brother; the important thing was to get away quickly. It took him forty-two seconds to move from his bed to the closet, open the trapdoor, and snake to the stairwell. It was then a simple matter to run down the stairs and leave the building without the FBI ever seeing him.

It worked like a charm.


"I want a lawyer."

It had been twelve hours since his arrest.

Mike Wu sat in the bare interrogation room under intense bright lights with nothing but a cup of coffee on the table in front of him. Other than the mirror on the wall, which Wu obviously knew was for observation, nothing else adorned the cold, concrete space.

He was exhausted and uncomfortable. His hands were still cuffed behind him and he was barefoot. Wu had been forced to discard the T-shirt and boxer shorts he had been wearing in bed and now wore standard prisoner's trousers and a tunic.

Kehoe and L.A. FBI chief Al Nudelman sat at the table with the captive and were getting nowhere.

"Mike, you're being held under the Homeland Security Act," Kehoe said. "You don't have the same rights normal, ordinary, everyday criminals have. If I had my way, I'd organize a little lynch party right here and now for what you've done. You've betrayed your *country* by passing classified defense secrets to enemy organizations and you're responsible for the murder of a federal employee and the murder of an Oklahoma state employee. You're up shit creek, mister."

"I still want a lawyer. And something to eat, man. You can't treat me like this. I'm an American citizen."

"You sure don't act like one."

There was a knock on the steel door. Nudelman stood, opened it, and conversed with another agent. The chief nodded and closed the door. He stepped over to Kehoe and delivered the message.

"Oh, good news, Mike," Kehoe said. "An old friend is here to see you and he'd like to ask you some questions. He flew all the way from Washington, D.C., today just to do so."

The door opened and Colonel Lambert walked in. Mike Wu shut his eyes and shuddered. He had honestly respected his boss at Third Echelon and dreaded the moment when he would have to face the colonel.

"Hello, Mike," Lambert said with no indication of warmth.

Mike looked up and nodded. "Colonel."

Lambert sat across from the prisoner and acknowledged Kehoe. "Good afternoon."

"Is it afternoon already?" Kehoe asked. "Feels like next year already."

"Thanks for letting me know about this. I got here as soon as I could."

"I think you made it in record time, Colonel. Did they beam you here?"

Lambert looked at Mike and said, "So has this lowlife said anything yet?"

"Not a thing. Keeps asking for a lawyer."

Lambert grunted. He stared at his former employee and then leaned forward. "Mike, listen to me. It's in your best interest to make a statement. Sign a confession. You know what you've done and we've got the proof you did it. Now we could go through a lengthy trial and cost the taxpayers a lot of money and draw this out to painful proportions . . . or you can simply confess and we'll try to go easy on you."

"Easy? How easy can a death sentence be?" Mike asked.

"Well, for one thing, maybe you'll get life. I'll recommend it. No guarantees, though."

Mike didn't say a word. He looked at Lambert for a full minute as if they were in a stare-down contest. Finally, the prisoner leaned forward and said as slowly as he could, "I. Want. A. Lawyer."

Lambert and Kehoe looked at each other and sighed.

"Hey, Mike, you remember Sam Fisher?" Lambert asked.

"I met him once."

"But you know who he is. You know what he's capable of."

Mike shrugged.

"Well, guess what. He's on his way here. He finished his assignment in Hong Kong and I told him to head on back to the States. When he heard you were in custody, he couldn't wait to have a word with you. He was very fond of Carly, you see. I have a good mind to let Sam in here and, well, Agent Kehoe and I will leave you two alone for a while. I can't vouch for how Sam will react when he lays eyes on you. And seeing as how you're in Maximum Security Unit Six, which no one the *fuck* knows exists, you might as well wish you'd died in a hail of bullets."

Mike knew exactly what the colonel was talking about. Everyone at Third Echelon held the Splinter Cells in awe—especially Sam Fisher. It was almost as if the guy wasn't human. He was a very dangerous machine.

Lambert stood and said, "You think about that for a while, Mike. It'll take another half day or so before he gets here. Plenty of time to write and sign a confession. Come on, Agent Kehoe. Let's leave this scum alone with his demons."

The two men left the room and locked the door. Mike Wu nervously cracked his knuckles but stared defiantly at the mirror. He knew they were behind it, watching him. After a moment, he picked up the half-empty coffee cup and threw it against the dark glass. The brown liquid ran down the wall and made an ugly puddle in the otherwise stark and sterile room.

"I want a lawyer!" he shouted again.

ANDREI Zdrok was the only man in the Shop administration who knew the Benefactor's identity. The man who acted as an agent for the Shop in the Far East had been a longtime associate of the group and had stepped up to the plate to help when the organization lost its foothold in Eastern Europe. To the others on the board, the man was known simply as "the Benefactor" because that was the way he wanted it. Zdrok was happy to comply with the man's every wish. After all, Zdrok had to grudgingly admit that the Shop would be defunct had it not been for the Lucky Dragons on one hand and the Benefactor on the other. Now it appeared that the relationship between the Shop and the Triad was going sour. Zdrok knew the partnership with Ming would completely dissolve once General Tun had the guidance system in his possession.

The disaster at the antique shop would further deteriorate the Shop's standing in the area. Antipov was dead. Their offices were destroyed and were now being picked apart by the Hong Kong police. No doubt several international intelligence agencies would be hovering like vultures over the remains. It now looked as if Zdrok might have to pick up roots and leave *again*.

He picked up the phone on his desk and dialed one of the few numbers he knew by heart. The Benefactor picked it up and said in English, "Yes, Andrei?"

Zdrok attempted English as well since the Benefactor's Russian wasn't great. "Good day, sir. How are things in your new—"

"They're fine, Andrei. What can I do for you?"

"One of our men in California was arrested. He was to be the one bringing the guidance system to the Lucky Dragons. And as you know—"

"Jon Ming canceled the sale. But I understand the men in California have offered to sell it to you directly. How much do they want?"

"That's still being negotiated. Oskar will handle the transaction. But there's one other thing."

"What's that?"

"This National Security Agency man. Sam Fisher. The Splinter Cell. He's responsible for what happened at the antique shop. It's time we do something about it. Once and for all."

"I couldn't agree with you more. Go ahead. Make the call. I'll front the down payment. Offer him more than usual."

"Thank you, sir."

"You're welcome."

The Benefactor hung up and Zdrok dialed another number he knew without looking it up. The phone rang five times before the man answered. *"Da?"*

Andrei Zdrok said, "Thank goodness you're there." He told the man what had happened at the antique shop. "It's the last straw. Sam Fisher must die. And you're just the one to do it. You're the *only* one who can do it."

Zdrok waited twenty seconds before the other party replied. "I want double the usual fee. You can understand why."

"Of course. Let's say two and a half times the usual fee. How's that?"

"Very generous of you. Where do I find him?"

"He has just left Hong Kong and is now on his way to Los Angeles. You can pick up his scent there."

"I'll leave on the first flight I can get."

"Thank you."

"I'll be in touch."

The two men hung up and Zdrok felt the first glimmer of hope after an anxious twenty-four hours since he discovered what had happened to Anton Antipov and the Shop's headquarters on Cat Street.

All would be well now. The Shop's most trusted killer, Yvan Putnik, was on his way to America to set things right.

## 23

THE ride across the Pacific in the Osprey was uneventful and I slept most of the way. However, when we landed in California I still felt weary. I suppose I could attribute it to getting older but I'm not going to. Maybe I just need another vacation. Two overseas missions back to back are enough to exhaust anyone, even guys twenty years younger than me.

Frances Coen picks me up at the base. I'm surprised to see her on the West Coast but she explains that she flew over from Washington with Colonel Lambert. She and Anna Grimsdottir think they've solved the problem of how to protect my implants from the electronic transmitter the Triad used on me. I'll need to submit to a minor operation for an hour while the adjustments are made. This will involve cutting into my skin to get to the little buggers. At the moment it's not a prospect I look forward to but I guess it has to be done.

She takes me to Maximum Security Unit 6, a classified

holding pen for prisoners who represent a great threat to national security. It's the kind of place where they hold terrorists and traitors without access to legal counsel, at least for a while. This policy is part of the Homeland Security Act and the so-called War on Terrorism that's been in effect since September 11, 2001. The unit is located east of L.A., near San Bernardino. From the street it appears to be a public parking garage, which it is. But by keying in an access code in the elevator, you can descend to the lower levels some fifty feet underground. That's where they keep America's Most Wanted.

After I'm cleared to enter the place, Coen leads me to Lambert. He's temporarily taken over a small office that has a cot. He looks as if he just woke up.

"Sam, good to see you," he says.

"It's good to be back." We shake hands and he offers me a seat on the cot. He takes the chair behind the desk upon which he's set up his laptop computer. Coen leaves us alone, saying she'll be back to get me for the surgery later that afternoon.

"Forgive me if I seem disheveled," Lambert says. "I was up most of the night talking with Mike."

"I'm tired, too," I reply. "Am I on vacation yet?"

Lambert grins; he knows I'm being facetious. "Not yet, Sam. You can have a day or two to rest up but we need you here. I'll explain later. Want some coffee?"

"Sure. I want to call my daughter. Is there a line I can use or should I use my cell?"

"Here, you can use this one," he says, pointing to the phone on the desk. "It's a secure line. I'll be right back." He leaves the room and I make the call.

Sarah's answering machine picks up. *"Hi, this is Sarah, leave a message."* I look at my watch and figure there's no reason why she should be at home midmorning. She's probably at school.

"Hi, honey, I'm back in the States," I say. "Just letting you know. You can reach me on the number you have when you get a chance. If I don't pick up right away, I'll call you back. I love you."

I hang up and lie on the cot. I'm just about to fall asleep when Lambert returns with the much-needed coffee.

"Thanks," I say. I sit up and take it.

Lambert returns to his chair and then announces, "I read your latest report."

Uh-oh, here it comes. I was brutally honest with what happened at the antique shop in Hong Kong. He's going to tear me a new asshole for killing Antipov in cold blood. At least I know he's not going to fire me, because he's already said I'm still on the job.

"I'm glad you wrapped up that end of the Shop's operation," is what he says. "That's two down, two to go."

I certainly didn't expect that. "Thanks," I say. Somehow I feel the need to explain myself. "Listen, Colonel, about Antipov—"

He waves his hand at me. "Forget it, Sam. The guy was a major enemy. All those Shop guys are supreme shits. As far as our laws go, you were in a combative situation. We'll say no more about it."

I nod and sip my coffee. After a moment of silence, I ask, "So how's our prisoner doing?"

"I believe he's about ready to talk. I think he was waiting for you."

**MIKE** Chan, er, Mike *Wu* rather, looks pretty haggard. They've kept him awake and under intense interrogation for the last forty-eight hours. I met the guy once at Third Echelon and barely remember him. He was supposed to have been very good at his job as a research analyst. Why does greed turn so many good people into villains? I'll never understand it. We all want to make money and live comfortably, but selling out one's country or friends or family to do so is beyond the scope of my comprehension.

As soon as I walk into the interrogation room, Mike sits up and widens his eyes. They must have really built up my visit. The guy looks scared.

"Relax, Mike," I say. "I'm not going to hurt you. Not right away."

"Why are you here?" he asks. "This isn't your job. Since when do Splinter Cells get recruited to interrogate prisoners?"

"They don't. I'm here of my own free will. I'm here because Carly St. John was a friend of mine. I'm here because your friends the Lucky Dragons tried to kill me. I'm here because I'm patriotic and love my country and you're a son of a bitch that isn't worth his weight in excrement."

The prisoner sighs and nods. He's resigned to his fate. "I still want a lawyer."

"You might get one after you confess. I'm not really sure how it works with you special combative types. All I know is that I'm not going to leave this room until you make an official statement and sign it."

"So, what, are you going to lean on me? You're going to show how tough you are and beat me up a little bit?"

"I'm hoping you'll come to your senses and realize that you've got no way out of this. You're caught. Lambert and the FBI have all the evidence they need to convict you. You don't *have* to sign anything. You'll still get the death penalty. We'd like to prevent that. Life is a lot better than death."

"Depends on what you're doing with your life, doesn't it?"

"Perhaps. It's too bad Carly can't do anything with hers now."

Mike looks down. I sense he's not altogether happy about what he did. Bastard.

"Why, Mike? Why did you have to kill her? You know, Carly once told me what a great worker you were. She said you were the best analyst in the firm and that you'd probably advance quickly."

"Screw you, Fisher."

Well, something in me snaps. Maybe I was overtired. Maybe I was trying to grieve for Carly. Or maybe I was fed up with all the *shit*.

I stand, walk over to Mike, grab him by the lightweight shirt he's wearing, and I punch him in the nose. He flies backward and falls to the floor. I expect Lambert or someone to come in and bitch at me but nothing happens. After a moment, Mike stands and faces me. His nose is bleeding.

"Hit me again, Fisher."

"What?"

"I want you to hit me. I want you to rough me up a little. I deserve it."

"Come on, Mike. Sit down."

He shouts, "You bastard! Hit me! It's what you came to do!"

"Sit down, Mike!"

"Screw you, Fisher! Hey, guess what! I blew Carly's brains out and I enjoyed it. I deliberately walked into her office, pointed a gun at the back of her head, and pulled the trigger. You should have seen it, Fisher. Her brains went all over her goddamned computer!"

That does it. I give the guy what he wants, and hell, it's what I want, too. To the devil with proper procedure. Besides, the little shit has made me mad. I grab him by the collar and pull him up and over the table. The guy is lightweight, so throwing him across the room and into the wall is nothing. For the next few seconds I totally lose it. I don't remember whaling on him but I must have hit him two or three times. I think that maybe I kicked him once, too.

When I come to my senses, he's lying on the floor in a mess of blood.

"Thanks," he says. "You won't believe this, but I needed that."

"Like hell," I mutter. I reach into my pocket, find a handkerchief, and throw it to him. He wipes his face and then slowly crawls back to his chair. Once he's sitting, he lays his head on his arms on top of the table. After taking a couple of deep breaths he looks up at me. I can almost see the gears working in his head as he tries to come to grips with spilling the beans. After a long pause, he speaks.

"She was about to find out I was the leak out of Third Echelon."

Finally, he understands the situation. "But killing her didn't prevent us from finding out," I say. "It was a stupid, foolish thing to do. Kill her, then run. Real smart, Mike. Of *course* we'd figure it out when you do something like that."

"I thought I'd be out of the country before the FBI caught up with me. I was supposed to be in Hong Kong. Things got all fucked up. I guess most of all she was about to uncover the link with the Lucky Dragons. I couldn't allow that to happen. I panicked. Killing her was a knee-jerk reaction."

"Keep talking. Everything we say is being recorded. Just let it spill. Then all you'll have to do is sign your name once we have it typed up."

Mike continues, "All right. Here it is. Everything you guys know is true. My brother and I are members of the Lucky Dragons. We were recruited in Los Angeles six years ago. The Triad was already in league with the Shop and has been for some time. They arranged for me to change my identity and apply for work in the NSA."

"How did the Triad manage that?"

"They didn't. It was the Shop. But they had some help in Washington."

"What do you mean?"

"Someone high up on the food chain. I don't know who it is, I swear. The person's identity is very well protected."

I rub my chin and ask, "Someone in Congress?"

"I really don't know, Sam. I swear. Whoever it is has a lot of connections. They were able to whitewash my background, create a new existence for me as Mike Chan, whatever it took. And they initiated the contact with Professor Jeinsen."

"So you're saying there's a traitor high in our government that's been orchestrating this whole thing with the Triad and the Shop?"

"Yes."

"How did the relationship between you and Jeinsen work?"

"I never met him. He would deliver electronic files to a drop box in the city. I would pick them up and send them to Jon Ming in Hong Kong. Ming then sold them to the Shop. Or maybe there was a different kind of deal between them. The Lucky Dragons got weapons for the information, or something like that."

"And there's one more piece of Jeinsen's work to be delivered?"

Mike hesitates and then probably figures he's gone this far so why not spill it all. "Yeah. It's the guidance system for the MRUUV. Comes in a laptop computer. GyroTechnics designed it to Jeinsen's specifications with some input from the Shop's customer. I was supposed to deliver it to Hong Kong along with my defection but Ming suddenly decided not to buy it. He's had a falling out with the Shop because of some political reason."

"So is the deal completely dead?"

"No. Earlier on the day I was arrested I made contact with the Shop and offered to sell the thing to them directly. Eddie and I went around the Lucky Dragons."

I whistle. "Gee, Mike, you'd better be glad you were arrested. The Dragons would have killed you in a most unpleasant way for doing that. Where's your brother?"

"I don't know. Hiding, I imagine. The Shop is in contact with him, though. I made sure that if I wasn't available then they could deal with him. He's going to sell the guidance system and it's going to happen any day. It may have already occurred."

"He's dealing with Zdrok?"

Mike nods.

I stare at the traitor for a full minute and then stand. "Thanks, Mike. Everything you've said will be typed up and you can sign it. You've helped yourself today. For the record, though, I still think you're scum. Sorry about the mess."

After my little speech, which doesn't really make me feel any better about the guy, I turn and leave the room.


"I'M going to have to break into GyroTechnics," I tell Lambert back in his office.

"We're way ahead of you," he replies. "Anna Grimsdottir has been busy hacking into their server, collecting e-mails and downloading other secure files. Our analysts are already at work picking them apart. We're sharing everything we have with the FBI and they're cooperating with us. The Bureau already knows that GyroTechnics is up to no good. An official investigation is under way for a number of crimes, including providing sensitive and classified military information to foreign powers. We know they've been working with the MRUUV material and they shouldn't have any access at all to that project. Special Agent Jeff Kehoe is now in charge of the investigation into the firm. I've told him you would do what you do best and get inside GyroTechnics and see what you can find. In the meantime, he's searching for Eddie Wu and trying to pinpoint when the guy might be making contact with the Shop."

"Do you have a photo of Eddie Wu?"

Lambert digs through the pile of stuff on his desk and comes up with one. I memorize the guy's features. He looks a lot like his brother.

"We have to prevent the exchange of that guidance system," Lambert continues. "There's no telling what General Tun is using the MRUUV for. We have to assume he's built one from Jeinsen's plans."

"What does our government have to say about this General Tun?"

"The Secretary of State has been in contact with the Chinese government. We've issued a stern warning that Taiwan is not to be harassed. Of course, China's playing dumb. They say General Tun is simply performing military exercises and war games in and around Fuzhou. He supposedly has no intention to attack Taiwan, nor has the government given him the authorization to do so. So, to make a long story short, our government has assumed a 'wait and see' position."

I stretch and can't quite stifle a yawn.

"Am I boring you?" Lambert asks.

"I'm exhausted, Colonel. It's been a tough week. Hell, it's been a tough couple of months."

"Fine. You have twenty-four hours' leave, Sam. Get some rest. Go get laid. Do what you need to do to get recharged. We have a car in the garage upstairs for you to use."

"Thanks, Colonel."

Right on cue, Frances Coen enters the office. She looks at me expectantly.

"Oh, I almost forgot," I mumble. "I have an appointment before I go, right?"

She nods. "The doctor is here. You want to come into

the prep room, Sam? I promise we'll get this over with quickly. It'll be painless. I think."

Lambert gives me a grin. "It won't be any worse than it was when you first had them put in."

"That's comforting," I say. The original surgery was horrific.

I stand and follow Coen into a sterile room where I meet a Dr. Frank and his pretty nurse Betsy.

At least I'll get a good drug out of the ordeal.


**AFTER** all that, there was nothing to it. I feel a little discomfort in my ears, kind of like when there's water in them and you can't get it out. The doc told me it would clear up in a few hours and I'd be as good as new. The car they've given me is a 2005 Nissan Murano, a roomy vehicle with a V6 engine and "continuously variable transmission." I'm impressed. It's the best company car Third Echelon has ever given me.

I have no idea where I'm going to spend the night in Los Angeles. While I'm cruising into the city on I-210, I phone my house in Maryland to pick up any messages that might be on my personal answering machine. Much to my surprise, there's one from Katia Loenstern.

*"Hi, Sam, it's Katia. I know you're probably out of town but I just, I don't know, I just wanted to call and say I miss you. I had a nice time with my mom and sister in San Diego and now I'm in Los Angeles. I felt like coming up here to spend some money. What can I say?—I like to shop, and L.A.'s a good place to do that. I just checked in to the Sofitel Hotel across from Beverly Center and I plan on hitting the mall in a minute. I'm probably gonna stay here a few days and then go back to Baltimore. Hopefully by then you'll be back, too. Anyway, I hope you're safe and I'll talk to you soon. Bye."*

Well. What did Colonel Lambert say about me needing to get laid?

I'm suddenly faced with some decisions to make. On one hand I should probably stay clear of her, get some rest, and focus on the job. On the other hand, I'm dying to see her. But am I ready to dive headfirst into a relationship? Because that's exactly what it would be if I return her call—a relationship. Damn, just the thought makes me nervous.

Screw it. I need this. It's been too long. Call it Mental Health Therapy. Hell, call it Gonad Therapy. I may be a Splinter Cell but I'm also a man.

At least now I know where I'm going. After the 210 becomes the 134, I take the 2 down to the 101 and head west. It isn't long before I get off at Santa Monica Boulevard and make my way to Beverly Boulevard and La Cienega. Right to the Sofitel, across from Beverly Center.

# 24

I check in to the hotel, go to my room on the third floor, dial the front desk, and ask to be connected to Katia's room. I expect her to be out so I'm pleasantly surprised when she picks up.

"Hello?" There's a slight puzzlement in her voice. Who could be calling her in Los Angeles?

"Hi, Katia," I say. "It's Sam."

"Oh, my God, Sam! What a surprise!"

"How are you?"

"I'm . . . I'm fine! My gosh, I'm flustered. What are you doing? Are you back in the States?"

"Yes, I am."

"What's it like in Baltimore? Still cold?"

"I don't know, I'm not there."

"Where are you?"

"Two floors below you."

She's not sure if she heard me right. "What?"

"I'm in the hotel. Two floors below you. In Los Angeles."

"*What* are you doing here?" Now she's laughing. "Oh, my *God*!"

"I got the message you left me at home. I was in L.A., so . . . here I am."

"This is amazing. I was just thinking about you."

"Yeah? Well, me, too, you."

"Do you . . . do you want to get together?"

"Well, *duh*."

"Are you hungry? I haven't had lunch yet."

"Neither have I. Let's do it."

We meet in the lobby twenty minutes later. Katia looks better than I remember. She is dressed in tight-fitting black capri pants that accentuate the shape of her long legs, a red cami, and a short black jacket. I ask her if garlic is okay for lunch and she tells me that as long as I'm having it, too, it would be great. I know a terrific place within walking distance of the hotel, just down La Cienega a couple of blocks, so we decide to hoof it. The weather in Los Angeles is slightly cool but certainly nothing like the winter temperatures back east. Neither of us needs a coat.

"How's your family?" I ask as we stroll. She takes my hand and I welcome it.

"They're good. It was a nice visit. My mom hasn't been well. She had some kind of weird infection in her toenail and the doctor was afraid she might have to lose it. The toe, that is. But the nail was removed and . . . well, you don't want to hear about that, do you?"

"I don't mind. I think I can take the image of a missing toenail."

"Anyway, I think she's gonna be fine now. And my sister is fine, too. Nutty as ever. She's getting her second divorce. I have a feeling she'll never be happy being married. She's too much of a free spirit."

"Like you?"

"Well, I'm a free spirit, too, but not like her. If she'd been around in the sixties she'd have been a hippie. What about you? Where have you been?"

"Oh, overseas. Nothing to write home about. Just the usual business."

"Yeah, right. International sales. Information gathering and troubleshooting. I remember, Mr. Mysterious."

"It's true!"

"Sure. So what are you doing in L.A.?"

"Had to make a stop. A business stop. But I've got twenty-four hours of free time."

"Aww, and you chose to spend it with me?"

"If you'd like."

"Of course I'd like."

"I *do* have to get some rest, though. I'm pretty exhausted."

She punches me on the upper arm. "Don't give me *that*, buster. We might spend the next twenty-four hours in bed but we ain't gonna be *sleeping*!"

We reach the restaurant, one of my favorites in L.A.— and San Francisco, too. It's called the Stinking Rose and it specializes in garlic dishes. Katia's never been there, so she's in for a treat.

The place is nearly full, as usual, but we're a little on the late side of the lunch hour. There's no problem getting a table. The hostess must sense the romantic tension between Katia and me so she sits us in a dimly lit corner and lights a candle. Katia scans the menu and proclaims that it all sounds good. I assure her it is and suggest the appetizer of bagna calda. We order a bottle of the house red wine and settle in for an enjoyable hour or two.

"So where in the world were you, Mr. Salesman?" Katia asks. Her brown eyes sparkle in the candlelight and I'm tempted to open my soul to her. For once, the specter of Regan is nowhere around. Perhaps my late wife is looking down from the heavens and wishes me well. Regan would have wanted me to get on with my life, find someone to love. After all, Regan and I had separated and weren't living together when she succumbed to her illness. We remained cordial mostly because of Sarah but I know Regan and I continued to have enormous affection for each other. I also believe Regan would have liked Katia.

"I was in the Far East," I say. I really don't want to give away too much about my job. Obviously, Katia has guessed quite a bit. It's an ongoing debate with myself whether or not to tell her the complete truth. I suppose that if our relationship truly becomes something serious then I'll have to.

"Let's see, the Far East," she says. "That must mean . . . Japan? Korea?"

"Nope."

"The Philippines? China?"

"Nope."

"Hong Kong? Indonesia?"

"Closer."

"Look, Sam, one thing I ask is that you be honest with me." She takes a sip of wine and then looks at me intently. "I realize you have a rather hardened heart when it comes to relationships and I don't want to scare you off. I'm independent, too, and I assure you I'm not a needy person. But I've been thinking about our short time together and, well, I just think we'll have a pretty good time if we keep at it. I'm not asking for a *commitment* or anything like that, but I am asking that you tell me the truth about yourself."

Before I can say anything, the appetizer arrives. Bagna calda is an awesome concoction of soft garlic cloves ovenroasted in extra virgin olive oil and butter with a hint of anchovy. Served in a little hot tub, it's spreadable on the freshly baked bread it comes with.

"My God, this is fabulous," Katia says when she tries it. "I could just fill up on *this*."

"It's good, isn't it? You can buy a book of recipes from the restaurant at the front desk if you're inclined to try it at home."

We order entrees and talk of other things, the question of my *honesty* temporarily placed on the back burner. Krav Maga is a big topic of conversation, along with our personal habits for keeping fit. She tells me a little about her life in Israel before coming to the United States. Her father was Israeli but her mother is American, hence the dual citizenship. After her parents' divorce, her mother brought Katia and her sister to California. Her father died of heart failure six years later.

The food arrives and it's overwhelming. She has the lemon-baked Atlantic salmon with garlic caper sauce served with *acini di pepe* pasta. I go for the garlic-roasted medium-cut prime rib, which comes with, naturally, garlic mashed potatoes. As I tell Katia, the Stinking Rose is a great place to take a date because you know you'll both have bad breath afterward.

Halfway through the meal the conversation returns to what I do for a living. She mentions that she loves to travel but doesn't get to do it very much. "You're lucky. It must be nice being able to go places in your job," she says.

"Sometimes it is. Depends."

"On what?"

"On what I have to do there."

"Sam, you *do* work for the government, don't you? Come on, your secret is safe with me."

I don't commit to an answer, but I do shrug my shoulders to indicate she's on the right track. It's the best I can do.

"I knew it. Look, I've known other men that work for government agencies. I dated a CIA guy once. We went the longest time before I found out what he did for a living and it really pissed me off."

"Why?"

"Because he'd been lying to me. He told me he was a lobbyist. He exhibited all the same signs as you—he was secretive about his job, he was gone for long periods of time, he was unbelievably fit for his age, and he was a devotee of martial arts. Believe me, Sam, I know the type."

"And that's my type?"

"Isn't it?"

I let that one ride. The meal continues pleasantly and the conversation moves along to safer subjects. At one point during dessert—we share the Irish coffee chocolate brownie mousse—I feel her bare foot brushing against my calf. She's removed her shoe and has begun to rub my leg, inching higher and higher until her foot is in my lap. She presses her toes into my crotch, all the while looking at me with a glint in her eye that means business. I'm suddenly immensely aroused, a reaction I know has to do with coming back from a life-or-death assignment. The NSA psych doctors who examine me every year always express surprise when they learn of my years of celibacy. Most guys who perform dangerous missions for the government have a libido that won't quit. Maybe that's now finally coming to the fore.

"What say you we pay the bill and get the hell out of here?" I ask.

"I was wondering when you were gonna suggest that," she says, a mischievous grin playing on her wet lips.

WE spend the rest of the afternoon and evening in my room at the hotel. The sex is as intense as it was on my birthday back home in Towson. Katia is insatiable, it seems, and I no longer feel the fatigue that was plaguing me when I arrived in California. Maybe it's the pheromones surging through my body or something like that, if you believe in that kind of stuff. Whatever it is, the chemical reactions in my loins don't fail to do the job.

By nine o'clock that night we're hungry again. I order room service and we have a couple of sandwiches and sodas. We sit on the bed, naked, eat our dinner, and laugh at the absurdity of how we must look. After the meal Katia offers to give me a massage and I readily accept. As she works me over with her strong hands I begin to feel tired again. I'm wonderfully relaxed and seem to be floating on water. The next thing I know, the room is pitch-dark and Katia is in bed next to me. I must have fallen asleep during the rubdown. The digital clock on the nightstand reads 2:35. I slept for a good six hours.

I quietly slip out from under the sheets and sit for a moment just watching Katia. She's sleeping soundly. In the dim light her dark curly hair, spread over the pillow, looks like splashed paint.

*Yes,* I think. This could be it. The years of celibacy are over. My daughter, Sarah, just might have to get used to me being with a new partner. I'm not thinking about marriage or anything that drastic. I'm not even sure I'd want to live with Katia. But I do know I want to continue seeing her. If what she said about both of us remaining independent is true, then the relationship might be ideal. I suppose I'll just have to cross each bridge as I come to it. For now, though, I feel . . . happy.

As if on cue, though, my OPSAT beeps quietly. I grab it, shut off the noise, and see the text message from Coen. All the details I need to find GyroTechnics have been beamed to me. Agent Kehoe has reported that the building was mysteriously evacuated and as of midnight no one is there. Lambert suspects that Mike Wu's arrest has prompted the firm's management to take some drastic measures. Lambert wants me to get over there as soon as possible.

Katia stirs and opens her eyes. "What time is it?" she mumbles.

"It's the middle of the night," I say. "Go back to sleep. I'll be back in the morning."

She sits up and asks, "Where are you going?"

"I have a job to do. I'll be back. I promise."

"Are you in danger?"

"No. Katia, go back to sleep. I'll be back when it's time to get up."

Her brow wrinkles and there's a moment when I fear there might be a conflict of interests. But instead she smiles, reaches out, pulls my head toward hers, and kisses me.

"Just be careful," she whispers. She then lays her head back onto the pillow and closes her eyes. She adjusts her body beneath the sheets and snuggles over onto the warm spot I left on my side of the bed.

I get dressed in my uniform and leave the hotel in the Murano.

# 25

I find GyroTechnics easily enough. It's an odd place to stick a technology development company—isolated in the hills, surrounded by trees, standing at the end of an unmarked gravel road—but then again it's a firm doing illegal shit. If what the FBI discovered is true, and I don't doubt it for a minute, the place is financed and run by a Triad. It just goes to show that these criminal organizations like Triads, Yakuzas, and Mafias are branching out beyond their normal expected enterprises like drugs, arms, prostitution, and gambling. Now they're in the global crime market and that means sponsoring and developing technology to use in committing offenses.

I park the Murano on Norman Place and walk to the gravel road. I stay off of it, though, electing to make my way through the dense growth of trees. With my night vision activated, it's not a problem. I come to the wire fence and can now see the futuristically designed building that is

GyroTechnics. A couple of floodlights illuminate the empty parking lot but otherwise the place appears deserted. I draw my Five-seveN, attach the noise and flash suppressor, and aim at the floodlights.

*Bing, bing.*

Now the grounds are pitch-black, dimly lit only by the hazy night sky. I climb the fence, dart to the employee entrance, and find a code access keypad next to the door.

Pressing my implant, I say, "Hey, Anna, are you there? I need an access code for GyroTechnics."

"Hold on, Sam," she answers. "I thought I'd have it for you by morning and didn't know you'd be ordered to infiltrate the place at this hour."

"Well, I'm standing out here in the dark. Hurry."

I suppose I could blast the damned thing but it would probably set off all sorts of alarms and the police would show up before I could say "Oops." Instead I circle the building and look for another entrance. The really odd thing about this place is that there's no front door for Joe Public. The only people that go in and out of GyroTechnics are employees. UPS must bring deliveries to the back door and the postman shoots the mail through a slot. I guess the management doesn't do much in the way of entertaining clients.

Before Grimsdottir comes back with the access code, a pair of headlights swings toward the building. Uh-oh. I make a run for the fence but have no time to climb it. I hit the dirt and lie facedown as the car pulls into the parking lot and stops. It's a Corvette. The driver extinguishes the lights and gets out. He's alone. It's too dark to discern who it is, even with my night vision. He's Asian, I can tell that much.

The guy goes to the employee entrance and punches in the code. The door opens and he's inside. I quickly get up and run to the door, switch my goggles to thermal vision, and note the keys that are still warm from his touch—9, 7, 2, 0, and *. I have no idea in what order they're supposed to be. I snap a shot of the keypad with my OPSAT camera and adjust the controls so the thermal readings are indicated on the screen. Usually I can make an educated guess as to which keys were pressed first and last—the first one will be the dimmest and the last one will be the brightest. The difficulty is if a key is pressed more than once.

I take the chance and press the combination I think might be the one. It's like playing roulette in Vegas—the odds are outrageously against me. Of course, nothing happens. I try a slightly different combination and again come up with zilch. Sometimes these keypads are rigged to set off an alarm if someone tries incorrect codes more than three times. Should I risk it? As far I know, there's only one guy in the joint. I imagine I can take him, but it's possible the alarm could bring others.

Before I take the risk, another pair of headlights swings toward the building from the gravel road. Damn! Once again I move around the corner of the structure, where I figure it's safe to wait. The new car, a Porsche, parks next to the Corvette. Again, the driver is alone. He extinguishes the lights, gets out, and goes to the door. I watch as he punches in the access code but the door doesn't open. He knocks. After a moment, a voice on the intercom answers.

The new guy can't remember the code. I quickly draw the Five-seveN and activate the T.A.K. Aiming it at the door, I hear the following conversation in Chinese:

INSIDE GUY: What do you mean, you don't remember the code?
OUTSIDE GUY: So sue me. What is it?
INSIDE GUY: Nine-nine-seven-two-two-zero and star.
OUTSIDE GUY: Thanks.

He punches the correct numbers and the door opens. Once he's inside, I hear Grimsdottir in my ear. "Sam? We have that code for you now."

"Never mind. I have it," I say.

"It's 9-9-7-2-2-0 star."

"I *said* I have it. Thanks."

"Oh. You're welcome."

*Brother.*

I wait a minute and then go to the door. I punch in the code and hear the lock disengage. I peer inside and see an empty corridor illuminated by overhead fluorescent lighting. Slipping inside, I'm aware of voices at the end of the hall. The two men are speaking in Chinese and it's difficult for me to understand them at this distance. I move farther down the corridor and slide into what appears to be a break room. There are vending machines, a couple of tables and chairs, a microwave and kitchen fixtures, and an employee bulletin board. Tacked onto the board are a couple of dozen color snapshots depicting a company picnic. A hand-printed banner reads, in English, HOLIDAY PICNIC, MARINA DEL REY HARBOR. I take a moment to scan the photos. They're the usual silly poses you see at company-sponsored events—people making goofy faces with beers in hand, a guy grilling burgers and hot dogs, a group playing volleyball. Someone has labeled each photo with a small piece of paper written in Chinese: *Ken making dinner*, *Joe and Tom getting drunk*, *Kim and Chang score a point*. All the subjects in the photos are Chinese and are of varying ages, mostly men. I'm about to turn my attention back to the two guys in the building when I notice a shot of Eddie Wu staring at me. I'm sure it's him. He's standing on the deck of a motor yacht docked at one of the marinas. The boat is named *Lady Lotus* and from the proud expression on Eddie's face it appears as if he's the skipper. Sure enough, the label proclaims, *Captain Eddie and his boat.*

I take the snapshot off the board and stuff it in one of my pockets, then turn back to the hallway.

The two men move deeper into the building. I creep along the corridor, moving from corner to corner, until the duo go inside a couple of swinging doors marked, in Chinese and English, DEVELOPMENT. Each door has a square window and through one I can see one of the men, his back to me, fiddling with something on a worktable. It's not a leap in logic to assume that the room they're in is the lab—the place where the GyroTechnics employees build all their crap.

I remove the optic cable from my backpack, switch it on, and slowly feed it along the floor and underneath the swinging doors. The headpiece just fits so I slide it through about an inch. I then open up the lens to a fish-eye and adjust the focus on my OPSAT. I now have a fairly clear picture of what's going on in there. A flick of a switch turns on the audio, which is transmitted to my implants.

The two men are busy creating explosives. One of them has a block of nitro from which he squeezes a little at a time, like toothpaste. The stuff goes into a metal cylinder that the other guy places in hockey-puck-shaped containers wired with detonators and timers. They're very similar to my own wall mines.

The conversation, being in Chinese, goes by fast but I'm able to pick up words here and there. I'll be able to have the team in Washington translate the whole thing later.

FIRST GUY: . . . Eddie . . . in big trouble . . .

SECOND GUY: I wouldn't want to be in his shoes.

FIRST GUY: And he has the . . .

SECOND GUY: Ming will find him.

FIRST GUY: . . . can't hide forever.

SECOND GUY: I still don't understand why . . . to destroy . . . the place.

FIRST GUY: Orders from Hong Kong.

SECOND GUY: . . . get rid of the trail?

FIRST GUY: Exactly.

SECOND GUY: Where did everyone . . . ?

FIRST GUY: They've been moved out. Some will go back to Hong Kong. The scientists that defected will be placed in new positions somewhere else.

SECOND GUY: . . . some dumb town in Arkansas . . . (*laughs*)

FIRST GUY: (*laughs*)

SECOND GUY: Are you almost done?

FIRST GUY: Yeah. Here. You need to set the timers.

SECOND GUY: What do you think? Ten minutes?

FIRST GUY: Five. No, make it eight. Just in case our cars don't start. (*laughs*)

SECOND GUY: (*laughs*)

FIRST GUY: So do you know where Eddie . . . hiding?

SECOND GUY: No. At least I think I know where he'll be . . . LAX tomorrow.

FIRST GUY: How do you know that?

SECOND GUY: I helped arrange it before Ming told me to shut down the firm.

FIRST GUY: You talked to . . . ?

SECOND GUY: No, Eddie did. I arranged the flight. It's not easy dealing with Russians.

FIRST GUY: He's coming from Russia?

SECOND GUY: No, he's coming from Hong Kong. Eddie will . . . meet . . . at LAX . . . American Airlines . . . or send someone . . .

FIRST GUY: . . . reward, you know? Ming said so.

SECOND GUY: I know, I know. Let's finish this job first. Then maybe we can meet the plane tomorrow, too. We follow the Russian, we'll find Eddie.

The two men begin to gather their materials. They've made, I think, eight explosives. I retrieve the optic cable, coil it, and place it in my backpack. One of the men leaves the room and takes a nearby staircase to the second floor while the other one places two or three of the devices within the lab.

Damn, they're about to blow up the place. Jon Ming must have heard of Eddie and Mike Wu's betrayal and ordered GyroTechnics to be closed down. The hard way.

Maybe I better get the hell out now. While the two arsonists are busy planting their devices of destruction around the building, I leave the way I came in. It takes me three minutes to jump the fence, run through the trees, and find the Murano.

In exactly six minutes and twenty seconds, I see the Corvette and the Porsche emerge from the gravel road, turn onto Norman Place, and drive past me down the hill. I start the engine, make a U, and follow them.

Right on time, I hear a tremendous sonic boom behind me. The ground shakes as if an earthquake has struck. In the rearview mirror I see that the night sky is orange and yellow. The blast sets off dozens of car alarms in the area and now the hills are alive with the sound of honking.

When I get to the bottom of the hill, the two arsonists are gone. I'm not concerned about them. They're just soldiers. What interests me is what they said about meeting a plane at LAX tomorrow. I'll have to get the complete translation but from what I could gather, Eddie Wu is meeting someone from the Shop at the airport tomorrow. The Russian is flying in to close the guidance system deal. Could he possibly be Oskar Herzog or Andrei Zdrok? Zdrok surely wouldn't dare set foot in the United States. I'll let Lambert deal with the logistics of what *we* can do to meet that plane.

Sirens fill the air now. As I turn onto Sunset Boulevard, two police cars zip around me, lights flashing. A fire truck, its horn blasting, is not far behind.

I press my implant. "Frances? Are you there?"

"I'm here, Sam."

"Is Lambert around?"

"No, he's asleep."

"Do you ever sleep?"

"Never. Field Runners load up on coffee twenty-four hours a day."

I pull out the photo I took off the bulletin board and look at it as I drive. "Listen, do we have any information about Eddie Wu owning a boat? A yacht, maybe?"

"Hold on."

While she's looking, I get on the 405 and head south toward Marina Del Rey. If my hunch is right, I think I might know where Eddie is hiding.

"Sam?"

"Yeah?"

"There's nothing in the files. But FBI agent Kehoe's last report stated that he was investigating a lead at Marina Del Rey Harbor. He's been on Eddie Wu's trail."

"The FBI is sharing that with us?"

"Yeah, apparently we really *are* cooperating on this one."

"Where's Kehoe now? Can we get in touch with him?"

"I don't know. Why?"

"I think I have a lead in Marina Del Rey, too. I'm going there now."

"Hold on, I'll check with my counterpart at the Bureau."

I exit onto 90 and am heading for the coastline when she comes back on the line. "Sam, Kehoe's last report was transmitted two hours ago. He was observing a boat at Pier 44 at Marina Del Rey Harbor. He's supposed to check in soon."

"Doesn't he have a partner with him?"

"No."

That isn't right. Don't FBI agents always take backup with them when going into a situation like this?

"Mr. Nudelman tells me Kehoe went off on his own because the L.A. Bureau couldn't spare another man tonight," Coen adds, answering my unasked question.

"Kehoe sounds like some kind of cowboy. He could get himself killed," I say.

"Can you tell me what you're thinking?" she asks.

"It's just a hunch I have. Let me check out something and I'll get back to you."

It's four-thirty in the morning. I can find the *Lucky Lotus*, see if anyone is there, and still might make it back to the hotel before Katia wakes up.

# 26

PIER 44 is on a section of the marina called Mindanao Way. The harbor itself is part of Santa Monica Bay and is supposedly the largest artificial small-craft harbor in the world. (My OPSAT automatically comes up with these facts when I'm mapping out a location.) It also tells me that the harbor consists of over eight hundred acres. The breakwater is 2,340 feet long and there are two miles of main channel. It's an ultimate example of joint planning and implementation of a major metropolitan recreation site. It's too damn bad I'm not a yachtsman!

I get off of Highway 90 at Lincoln Boulevard and then turn right onto Mindanao Way. I park the Murano on the street and walk toward the pier. Nightlights illuminate the marina but there are plenty of dark spots to use for cover. Moving from shadow to shadow exposes me for a second or two but I'm not going to worry about it. Eventually I arrive at Pier 44, a private outfit that rents slips to those with the dough to pay for these kinds of things.

Eddie's *Lady Lotus* is a ninety-four-foot Eagle/Westport Cockpit motor yacht. The lights are on in the salon and galley so I know there are people aboard. I see no sign of Agent Kehoe.

"Frances, you still there?"

"I'm here, Sam."

"Send me the blueprints for an Eagle/Westport motor yacht. Ninety-four-footer."

After a moment she asks, "You know what year?"

"I'm guessing latter half of the nineties."

"I have three to send you."

I go through the plans one by one and settle on the 1996 twin diesel engine model. It's a match for the *Lady Lotus*.

If anyone needed proof that being a member of a Triad is lucrative, then this is it. I have no clue what a yacht like this might cost but I'm sure it's in the millions. It's a beauty, all right. And very private, too. There's a walk-around deck but most of the floor space is inside. From the blueprints, I see there are three staterooms, three heads, a very large main salon, a sizable galley, and a comfortable pilothouse.

Now if I can climb onto the boat without rocking it and alerting everyone inside that they've got company . . . The only way on is by traversing the ramp from the dock to the deck. I'm about to do that as gently as I can when someone comes out from below. It's a goon, someone whose job it is to keep an eye on the harbor. The guy's most likely armed. I duck into the shadows as he scans the pier until he's satisfied they're alone. Then he lights a cigarette and strolls along the walk-around deck at a snail's pace. I wait until he's on the opposite side of the boat, masked by the pilothouse, and then I swiftly move up the ramp and onto the deck. With the lookout walking around the outside of the boat, I figure that any extra noise I make will be mistaken for him.

I move aft and crouch, ready to spring at the guard as he comes around the yacht's stern. I hear him approaching, closer . . . closer . . . and then I rise and deliver a solid punch to his nose. Before he can utter a sound I lunge forward, slap my hand over his mouth, move around him, and then lock his neck inside my free arm. The choke hold takes roughly thirty seconds to render him unconscious. When he's limp in my arms, I silently lay him on the deck.

Since the lights are on in the salon, they can't see out the windows. The glass is tinted so I don't have a very good view of what they're doing in there. To compensate for this disadvantage, I pull out the optic cable again and thread it into the gangway leading below. It doesn't have to go very far before I'm able to see the entire salon.

It's roomy, with a sofa, dining table, stabilized chairs, a television, stereo system, and even a dartboard on the wall. But a plastic sheet covers the floor and in the middle of the sheet is a man with his hands tied behind his back. He's lying on his side with his knees to his chest. His face is covered in blood.

I'm guessing it's Agent Kehoe and he's not moving at all.

Eddie Wu sits in a chair, looking at his victim. Wu wears leather gloves and an apron that is splashed with Kehoe's blood. Two more Chinese hoods stand on either side of the helpless man.

"Now we know what happened to Kehoe." It's Lambert in my ear, obviously awake now. Coen must have got him up. They can, of course, see everything I see through my headset.

"Try to take 'em out, Sam," he says, "but we need Eddie Wu alive."

I quickly retract the optic cable and stuff it in the backpack, and then remove a CS gas grenade from my trouser pocket. The CS gas is good for knocking out the enemy if it's used in a confined space such as the yacht. In larger areas the CS is more of a deterrent, like tear gas. Third Echelon also supplies a CS grade that is lethal but I rarely carry it unless I know I'm going to need it.

Grasping the grenade in my right hand, I pull the pin just as a bullet sears past my head. I feel the heat of the thing on the bridge of my nose—too goddamned close! The round smashes through the tinted glass, alerting the men inside of my presence. I hit the deck as another round streaks above me. Someone is on the marina taking potshots at me!

"Damn, where the hell did he come from?" Lambert says. "He was well hidden from our satellite. Sam, the SAT images reveal the sniper to be one man," Lambert says. "Repeat, it's one guy."

Before I can adequately plan a defense strategy, the two Chinese gunmen appear on deck. They're armed with semiautomatics, which they're all too eager to point at the guy in the strange uniform that they see lying at their feet. The only thing I can do is to toss the live CS grenade into the air, right in front of their faces. I roll myself into a ball, covering my head as the damned thing explodes. The two men scream in pain and surprise. One of them falls off the boat, hitting his head on the edge of the dock as he plummets into the water. The other guy tumbles back through the gangway into the salon. The gas is affecting me and I find it difficult to crawl along the deck to the other side of the boat. At least the sniper can't get at me there. I take a moment to breathe the fresh air, clear my head, and attempt to ignore the ringing in my ears. Finally I stand, lower my goggles, and switch on the thermal vision. Using extreme caution, I peer around the foredeck and focus on the marina. Sure enough, I see the heat-outlined shoulders of a man crouching behind a collection of barrels on the pier. He's got a rifle, probably a tactical sniper model, and he's ready to fire again. I draw the Five-seveN and aim but he shoots at me, forcing me back behind cover.

At that point I hear steps on the gangplank as someone

runs out of the yacht and onto the dock. In a few seconds I see him running toward Mindanao Way. It's Eddie Wu, abandoning ship. I'm just able to aim the Five-seveN from my prone position and get off a shot in his direction. The round chips the wood beneath his feet but doesn't do any damage to him. Wu disappears around a corner and there's no way that I can pursue him. Why didn't the sniper shoot *him*? Unless the killer is on Wu's side . . .

Moving around to the dockside of the yacht is impossible with the sniper over there. He doesn't seem to have any intention of moving. I have no choice but to reach into my backpack and grab a frag grenade. It's my last one—I should have stocked up when I was with Lambert and Coen yesterday. That's one of the problems with taking detours when you're on the way home from an assignment. You don't always follow the normal routine of debriefing and restocking.

Okay, this one has to count. I pull the pin, stand, and throw the grenade over the top of the yacht toward the barrels. The sniper fires again while I'm visible and he catches the top of my backpack. Luckily I'm in the act of dropping to a crouch position—if I'd lingered at full height for a split second longer I'd be a dead man.

The grenade explodes, momentarily brightening the pier with a blinding flash of lightning. I wait a good ten seconds before I carefully peer around the foredeck again. Nothing happens. With the night vision on, I see that the barrels are smashed to bits and there's a hole in the boardwalk. No sniper.

"Do you see the shooter on the SAT image?" I ask, pressing my throat implant.

"Negative," Coen answers. "Either you got him or he slipped away under cover."

"What about Wu? Don't tell me you lost him."

"I'm afraid he's merged into traffic patterns."

"Great."

I stand and cautiously move around the deck to the gangway and go inside the boat. The Chinese guard that caught the CS grenade in the face is lying dead on the plastic sheet next to Kehoe. I kneel and examine the FBI agent and see that they really worked him over. He apparently suffered some serious damage to the inside of his mouth. What did they do? Then I notice the pair of bloody pliers on the floor next to the chair in which Wu was sitting. I can't help but grimace when I see at least three of Kehoe's teeth lying next to the pliers, the roots torn and mangled. And . . . oh, no, it's the agent's tongue lying on the plastic sheet beside his head. The poor guy bled to death.

There's an open bottle of bourbon sitting on the dining table. I can't help grabbing it and taking a swig. I've seen some terrible things in my time and this has to be in the top ten.

Pressing on my implant, I say, "Frances?"

"Sam?"

"Shit, Frances, tell the FBI that Kehoe has been tortured and killed."

"What's the pier number?"

"Pier Forty-four, Marina Del Rey. I'm on the yacht *Lady Lotus*. It's pretty bad."

"Are you all right?"

"Yeah, I'm fine." I'm a little shaken from the sniper attack and seeing Kehoe in such a condition but I don't mention that.

"I'll get on to Kehoe's people right away."

She says the FBI will pick up their boy and clean up the mess. I need to disappear, and fast. As I return to the deck I carefully scan the pier with my thermal vision turned on and see no trace of the sniper. The cops will probably be here any minute, thanks to the noise of the grenades.

I scuttle down the ramp and run to the smashed barrels.

As I search the boardwalk for any clues indicating the identity of the sniper, I find three spent shells. I take one of them and recognize it as a 7.62mm NATO—a common round used in sniper rifles. This rings a bell somewhere in the back of my head but at the moment I don't know what it is. I pocket the shell and head for the marina exit before the cavalry arrives, all the while slightly paranoid that a damned competent assassin most likely has his eye on me.

# —27—

ANDREI Zdrok had experienced many setbacks and successes in his long career as an international criminal. While he maintained his status as an extremely wealthy man, the ups and downs of his business constantly drove him into states of unbearable anxiety and worry. He was often surprised that he had never developed ulcers.

To his comrades, Zdrok was very good at exhibiting a self-confident persona regardless of what turmoil the Shop might be suffering. This character trait was essential for leadership. His fellow board members—Prokofiev, Antipov, and Herzog—were aware of the hardships the Shop had faced over the past year and in many instances displayed despair and fatalism in the face of an uncertain future. Not Zdrok. He continued to push his team into new frontiers and new partnerships in order to put the Shop on the map again. Zdrok knew his fellow workers perceived him as a crotchety and humorless slave driver, but that pressure was what kept the Shop alive.

Just when it seemed that the organization was back on its feet in the Far East and making progress toward becoming a powerful force in the arms black market, the Shop had suffered another setback. It was clear that the Lucky Dragons were no longer their allies. America's National Security Agency, Central Intelligence Agency, and Federal Bureau of Investigation were sniffing around in the Shop's Asian headquarters, not to mention interference from Interpol, the Hong Kong police, the Red Chinese, the GRU, MI6, and countless other intelligence and law enforcement agencies around the world.

In short, the Shop was on the run again.

Zdrok had packed up his flat on the Peak and disappeared before the authorities came looking for him. The antique shop on Cat Street was now a crime scene and completely inaccessible. The Triad that protected him had turned their backs on him.

The Benefactor was his only friend and it was to him that Zdrok fled.

**ZDROK** took the glass of bourbon from the Benefactor and thanked him for the hospitality.

"Don't worry, Andrei," the Benefactor said. "You've been in worse scrapes. It won't be long and we'll be out of Hong Kong."

"Going to China seems more like jumping from the frying pan and into the fire."

"That's a very good English expression, Andrei. Your English is getting better."

"But my Chinese is shit. I don't even know how to curse in Chinese."

"That you'll learn quickly, my friend."

Zdrok looked at his ally and studied him. It was such an unlikely relationship. Who would have thought the Shop would benefit from a man so well connected with the organization's enemies?

"Have you heard anything from the police?" he asked.

The Benefactor shook his head. "No more than what I told you last night. They know the antique store was a front for the Shop. They're probably tearing apart your computers and looking into the facility up in the New Territories. They're searching for you but they won't find you. And since Mr. Herzog got away safely there are less of you for them to chase. When does he arrive in America?"

"Tomorrow."

"Let's hope for our sake he gets the guidance system from that Triad fellow and gets to China with it in one piece."

"That's putting it lightly," Zdrok said. "If Herzog fails to do that, then the Shop is forever dead. I might as well go to Siberia, find a nice iceberg to sit on, and freeze to death." He took a sip of bourbon and then asked, "What does your friend in Washington have to say about all this?"

The Benefactor gave Zdrok a sharp look. "Leave my Washington friend out of this. Suffice it to say our ally there is fully aware of the situation and is monitoring it closely. If help is needed, then our friend will supply it."

Zdrok often wondered who the Benefactor's contact in the American government really was. The person had powerful connections. It was because of this "friend" that Mike Wu had been able to become Mike Chan and secure a job within the NSA.

"Have you heard from Putnik yet?" the Benefactor asked.

"No. I have to assume he's located Fisher and is putting together a plan to wipe the man off the face of the earth."

"Putnik is the best at what he does. He'll succeed."

Zdrok stood with his drink in hand and looked out the Benefactor's hotel room window and tried to admire the

Hong Kong skyline. "You realize what General Tun will do if he doesn't get the guidance system?"

"Yes."

Zdrok turned to his friend and said, "He will crush us. He will alert the Chinese authorities to our presence and we'll be doomed. Not just me. You, too, you know."

"I'm aware of that. A lot rides on this deal, Andrei."

"The general is already unhappy that the system is late. It should have been in his hands days ago. The MRUUVs have been built and are ready for use." Zdrok turned back to the window. "I can't wait to see them work. They are formidable weapons. Operation Barracuda, if it ever gets off the ground, will take the world by surprise. When it's discovered that the Shop brokered the deal to create them, we will be back at the top of the game. Yes, a lot rides on the deal. That's putting it mildly."

IN another part of Hong Kong, Jon Ming awoke in his spacious master bedroom also feeling anxious. He wasn't afraid of the law, though. His home, a fortified mansion just south of the border between Kowloon and the New Territories, was perhaps the most secure private residence in the colony. Surrounded by an electrified security fence and watched by four armed guards around the clock, safety was not a cause for the Cho Kun's concern. He was easily one of the most powerful men in Hong Kong. He was beyond the reach of the law. He had the respect of the politicians and judges. In fact, he could give *them* orders.

What worried Jon Ming was something more personal, more political, and more *nationalistic*. Taiwan was under the threat of Red China. Ming, as a dedicated Triad leader, was violently opposed to China's government and sociological philosophy. The Communist ideology was anathema to him and to every other Triad on the face of the earth. The Triads had a long-standing tradition of nationalism and the expression of freedom. In the ancient times, the Triads were secret societies formed to bring about a regime change in the Chinese government. Today the Triads still believed in a China ruled by an emperor, for only in a capitalistic state could a criminal enterprise such as a Triad exist.

Jon Ming knew of General Tun. General Lan Tun was the equivalent of the warmongering right-wing hawks that were so prevalent in the United States military these days. Tun was also a bigot. He looked down his nose at the Taiwanese and considered them to be inferior to the Communist Chinese on the mainland, even though they were of the same race. The fact that Taiwan had managed to stay independent of China for so many years irked him and he was very vocal about what should be done about it. General Tun was about to make good on his threats.

The Cho Kun had another personal reason for opposing General Tun. Jon Ming's mother was Taiwanese and lived in a nursing home in Taipei. Although physically frail, she had full use of her mental faculties. Ming often spoke with her and had promised that one day he would move his "business" to Taiwan before she was gone. He knew that was unlikely but he dreamed of at least creating that illusion for her so she would believe he was near. He wanted to be able to visit his mother frequently before she slipped away.

Thus, it was imperative that General Tun not be allowed to attack Taiwan. Operation Barracuda, as Tun and the Shop called it, would be a foolproof and deadly means by which China could conquer Taiwan without interference from the West. Ming felt terrible that he had been instrumental in helping to bring about the situation. When he learned that the Shop was selling the Operation Barracuda designs and specifications to General Tun, he'd nearly had a heart attack. How could the Shop betray them after Ming had done so much to help the organization reestablish itself in Hong Kong? Ming cursed Andrei Zdrok and vowed to bring about the Shop's destruction.

Ming was forced to close down GyroTechnics, the Triad's technological development firm in the United States. This was a preemptive strike performed to stop the sale of the final piece of Professor Jeinsen's creation to General Tun. The MRUUV guidance system was the most important component, and the Lucky Dragons had nearly unwittingly delivered it into the hands of the Triad's mortal enemy!

The two Triad brothers in Los Angeles were now the targets of his wrath. One of them was in custody and would probably never be heard from again. No doubt he was singing to the authorities and revealing everything about his relationship with the Lucky Dragons. The other brother was hiding somewhere in L.A. and had the guidance system in hand. Ming had issued orders to the remaining Lucky Dragons in southern California to find Eddie Wu and recover the device before the traitor could sell it to the Shop directly. Surely by now Zdrok had sent a minion to California to pick it up. If Ming's people failed to stop the exchange, then Ming would have no choice but to consider assembling a small army of loyal Triads to take on General Tun before the attack on Taiwan commenced.

Ironically, it was thanks to the Shop and their arms deals with the Triad that it was entirely possible for the Lucky Dragons to take on a Chinese army. Ming knew his men were fierce and loyal fighters. They would do anything he asked. He was the Cho Kun. Just last night there had been an initiation ceremony in one of the Triad's many Lodges scattered throughout the colony. The three new recruits swore blood oaths to defend the principles of the Lucky Dragons. They were not like their American counterparts in California's Chinatowns. American society had corrupted the Wu brothers, who were too easily swayed into betraying the Triad. The native Chinese Lucky Dragons would never do that.

Whatever the Cho Kun asked them to do, they would perform to the best of their ability. If it meant fighting to the death, then so be it.

# 28

**AS** I'm driving back to the hotel, Lambert speaks to me through the implants.

"Sam?"

"Yeah?"

"We have information on upcoming American Airline flights from Hong Kong to LAX. The first one arrives around three o'clock today. There's another at five. We have the passenger lists but nothing is raising a red flag."

"Anyone can use an alias," I reply. "What about security cameras at the points of origin?"

"Haven't got 'em yet. There's a lot of red tape involved in getting hold of those things quickly. We should have them in hand by the time the flights arrive. I want you to be at LAX and meet the first flight. If there's no luck with that one, stick around for the other one."

"Will do, Colonel."

He gives me the airline and flight information. "Now you can go get some rest."

"I want to get this empty shell to you. I'm dying to find out who the bastard is that shot at me."

"Put it in an envelope, write 'Frances Coen' on it, and leave it at the front desk at your hotel. She'll come by this morning and pick it up before we head back to D.C."

"You're leaving today?"

"Yeah, we have to get back. Mike Wu is under wraps and we don't need to babysit you here."

"I hope not."

The sun is just beginning to rise when I arrive at the Sofitel. I leave the Murano with the parking valet, enter the lobby, and ask the concierge for some hotel stationery. I drop the shell into the envelope, write Coen's name on it, seal it, and give it to the nice lady at the front desk.

I then go up to the room and quietly let myself in. The bed is empty and unmade but I hear a feminine voice humming in the bathroom.

"Katia?"

The door flies open and there she is, naked as the day she was born and more beautiful than I can describe.

"Damn, it's Aphrodite herself!" I manage to say.

"Don't tell me . . . Apollo?" she says, pointing at me with feigned surprise. "Mars? Zeus?"

"Pick one and that's who I'll be."

She saunters over to me and helps me take off the uniform. She notices the bullet hole in the top of the backpack and wrinkles her brow. "Sam?"

"Don't worry about it," I whisper, taking her by the back of the neck and pulling her close. "Everything is fine." And I kiss her.


**WE** fall asleep again after a couple hours of fiery lovemaking. When I wake up the digital clock tells me it's nearly eleven. Having skipped breakfast, I'm famished. Katia stirs beside me and must be thinking the same thing, for the first words out of her mouth are, "Where are the eggs and toast?"

I suggest exploring the outside world for a while, perhaps find a nice place to have brunch, and maybe go shopping for an hour. I express the desire to buy her something.

"You don't have to buy me anything."

"I know I don't have to. What I want to do and have to do are always two different things. But in this case, I want to *and* I have to. Besides, I have to be at LAX at three o'clock."

Her eyes widen and she asks, "Are you leaving?"

"No. I have to meet a plane. Business."

"Oh. So you'll be back."

"Definitely."

"All right then. In that case we don't have much time."

We take a shower together, soap each other up, and resist the temptation to heat things up again. She spends ten minutes in the bathroom primping. I kick her out to shave and she goes upstairs to her own room to find a new change of clothes. Fifteen minutes later we meet in the lobby. To save time we elect to go to the hotel's restaurant, Gigi's Brasserie. It's French cuisine with a good selection of breakfast and lunch items. We order eggs and share a plate of fruit, cheese, and bread. The coffee and juice are tasty and we agree that it was a good choice.

"We'll go over to Beverly Center," I say. "Let's find you something you like, something women enjoy buying. Shoes? Jewelry? Lingerie?"

She kicks me under the table. "Lingerie is something men enjoy buying."

"Okay, let's buy that, then."

While we're eating I can't help but be constantly aware of our surroundings. Am I being too paranoid? With that sniper loose in the city, there's no telling where he'll show up next. If I was indeed his primary target then how did he know I would be at the pier? There's no way. I have to believe he was after Eddie Wu. Maybe he was sent by the Triad to eliminate the guy for turning coat. I just happened to be in the way. That seems to be a very logical explanation of what happened and the more I repeat it to myself, the more I believe it. I'm trained to detect when I'm in danger and right now the internal radar simply isn't beeping. This makes me feel more secure in going out in public with Katia but I can't be too careful. I'll just make sure that we stick to indoor places, avoid walking on the street, and spend our time in shops. We should be fine.

When we're done, I pay the bill and take a look outside while she uses the ladies' room. Traffic is typically busy for a midweek midday. Katia comes out in a moment, gives me a big smile, and we head outside. I take her hand as we walk to the corner, wait for the light, and cross the boulevard. I've said it before—I hate malls. I can't stand them. But for some strange reason, entering one with Katia is a different experience. I'm suddenly one of the normal Americans who don't have to think about national security, counterintelligence, and terrorism on a daily basis. I could be another average Joe, out at the shopping mall with his wife, the kids at home with a sitter or at school, with nothing on my mind but car payments and taxes.

Yikes.

I put those thoughts right out of my head and concentrate on pleasing Katia. We go into Adrienne Vittadini and she spends some time looking at clothes. Next we visit Banana Republic and she spends some time looking at . . . clothes. She then decides to go into Macy's to look at *more* clothes, so I pop over to Niessing to look at the jewelry. I feel like being extravagant for the first time in years so I buy her a unique pearl necklace. The pearls are framed in black, white, gray, and yellow gold. It sets me back a tidy sum but I don't give it a second thought. She's worth it. I have it gift wrapped and I suddenly feel that funny warmth in the center of my chest. It's been so long since I've experienced that particular sensation I've almost forgotten what it is. Am I falling in love? Is it just infatuation? A little of both?

Screw it. Stop analyzing and let it flow. Whatever happens is what happens. I've lived too many years to know not to try to predict things. One thing is certain—I feel great and it makes me happy to buy the gift for her.

I find her looking at shoes in Macy's and present the package to her. She nearly cries when she opens it and sees what's inside. I help her put it on and she gives me a big hug and kiss right there in the middle of the store. An elderly shopper mutters, "Aw, isn't that sweet?" and I think I'm supposed to be embarrassed but I'm not.

Katia is beaming when we leave Macy's. The gift has overwhelmed her and she can't concentrate on shopping anymore, so we wander around the mall looking in windows. I still have a little over an hour before I have to leave for LAX so I suggest we go back to the hotel. She thinks that's a marvelous idea.

We go down the big escalator that empties onto the street and prepare to cross Beverly, but I hold her back for a second while I take a look.

"What is it?"

"Just being cautious," I say. "It's in my nature."

"You really do dangerous stuff for the government, don't you." It's a statement, not a question.

"Let's not talk about it, Katia."

We start to cross the boulevard and I scan the buildings in front of us. The hotel swimming pool is on the roof of the building next to the Sofitel and I can see something glittering at the edge. The sun reflects off a metal object and for a split second I think it's the sniper. I grab Katia and pull her back.

"Sam!" she shrieks as I push her, perhaps a little too roughly, back under cover next to the escalator. "What the hell?"

"I thought . . . I thought I saw something," I say. My heart is pounding as I look up to the roof again. Then I realize it's just some kid with sunglasses playing with a squirt gun. I silently curse and apologize.

"You scared me," she says.

"It won't happen again," I reply but of course that's not true. It will always happen again. Suddenly, all the doubts and fears of being in a relationship come rushing back to me. I've put Katia in danger simply for being near me. It's no good. Everything I'd been feeling for the past several hours vanishes in the blink of an eye. My heart hardens once again and I dread having to tell her that whatever it is we're doing must stop. But perhaps I can put it off until we're back home in Maryland. Yeah, that's it. No need to spoil her vacation. No need to wreck my last hour with her. We'll say, "See you soon," and then I'll wait until a better time to break it off. That way we can both retreat to our private lives in Towson and do whatever grieving needs to be done.

"Come on, let's try that street-cross again, shall we?" I smile and take her arm.

She laughs and says, "They say practice makes perfect."

As we stand at the corner of Beverly and La Cienega to wait for the light, I'm suddenly aware of everything around me moving in slow motion. Katia turns to me and begins to close in for a kiss. At the same instant the traffic on La Cienega moves forward and out of the corner of my eye I notice a white van crossing the intersection much too slowly. Two men are inside—one driving, of course, and the passenger, who is holding what appears to be a rifle out the window.

Oh, my God, it *is* a rifle!

Katia's face is suddenly obstructing my view. I can't stop her as her lips meet mine. I instinctively push her away as the harsh crack of gunfire rings through the air. Katia's body jerks as I throw her to the street. I leap on top of her to shield her from the sniper, then roll my head back to look at the van. I can just see the face of the gunman as the vehicle zips through the intersection and disappears, blocked by Beverly Center.

It all makes perfect sense now. The gunman is Yvan Putnik, the Shop assassin. No wonder those 7.62mm shells rang a bell.

Turning back to Katia, I shout, "Are you all right? Did I hurt you?"

I roll her over to face me and I see that her eyes are open but staring blankly. She must have been stunned by the fall so I lightly pat her cheek. "Katia, it's all right. They've gone."

But she doesn't move. I panic, roll her to her side, and then I see it. The bullet meant for me struck her between the shoulder blades.

**FROM** this point on, everything is a blur. I seem to remember crying out in anguish. A couple of pedestrians leaving the mall ask if they can help. I remember telling them to call an ambulance.

In a case like this, Third Echelon protocol calls for me to leave the scene as quickly as possible. I'm not supposed to get involved with local law enforcement, whether it's in a foreign country or here at home. I'm trained to simply get up, walk away, and let others clean up after me. This time, however, I'm unable to do so. I continue to kneel beside

Katia and cradle her in my arms. I gently close her eyes and then hold her head against my chest. I feel the new pearl necklace against my sternum so I press her even harder into me, perhaps so the necklace will make a permanent indentation in my skin.

"Sam?"

It's Coen's voice but I ignore it.

"Sam, you have to get out of there."

I can't leave Katia. She's not dead. She's going to make it. Where's the fucking ambulance?

This time Lambert gets on the horn. "Sam! Get out of there! That's an order!"

This gives me the presence of mind to grasp Katia's wrist and feel for a pulse. There isn't one.

"Sam, you're to stand up, cross the street, and go inside the hotel," Lambert says. "Go straight to your room and gather your things. Frances and I will be there in five minutes. Do it now, man!"

I brush the curly hair off of Katia's face and kiss her lightly. I'm unable to say anything to her so I gently lay her body back on the street and stand. Paying no attention to whether or not the traffic light is against me, I walk across the boulevard. A small crowd has gathered around Katia and some of the people shout at me. I enter the hotel and go straight to the elevator. As soon as I'm in my room, I put my head in my hands and begin to curse. I damn them all to hell—the Shop, the Lucky Dragons, the NSA, Third Echelon, Colonel Lambert . . .

But I save the worst of the obscenities for myself.

# 29

I sit numbly in the passenger seat of Frances Coen's Lexus. We're on our way to LAX. Colonel Lambert is in the backseat.

The last couple of hours slipped by seemingly without my participating in them. I remember Coen and Lambert showing up at the hotel and picking me up. Lambert insisted I wear a bulletproof vest beneath my civilian clothes just in case the sniper was still around, so I took a moment to put it on. I also held on to my backpack. There was no way I was letting them have it. We left the Murano in the hotel's garage for some other NSA flunky to take care of. Other government bureaucrats are dealing with the police and clearing me of any involvement with Katia's murder. It's the kind of cover-up the U.S. government is good at. All the alphabet organizations—the CIA, the FBI, the NSA, you name it—have damage control teams in place that immediately jump into sensitive situations like this one. From this point onward, as far as the Los Angeles Police Department is concerned, I was never at the Sofitel and didn't know Katia Loenstern. The poor woman was the apparent victim of a random shooting.

After handing Coen my duffel bag and equipment, I was quickly ushered into her car and now here we are.

Coen and Lambert are unaware of how I felt about Katia but they suspect something. We drive in silence for a long while—traffic is typically heavy on the 405 heading south—until finally Lambert speaks up.

"Sam, this woman, was she your girlfriend?"

At first I don't answer. I continue to stare out the window and play mindless games such as counting all the red cars.

"Sam?"

"Colonel?"

"This woman. Was she your girlfriend?"

"Not really," I answer. "She was my Krav Maga instructor in Towson."

"Why were you with her in L.A.?"

I shrug. "She happened to be at the same hotel as me."

Lambert sighs and waits a moment before he continues. "Sam, we know you were seeing her. We know she was in your hotel room last night. It's our job to know these things."

"I know."

"So you don't have to hide anything from us."

"Why would I want to hide anything?" I ask. "If you know everything already then there's nothing to hide."

"Sam, I'm sorry about Ms. Loenstern. Really. If she meant something to you then it's all the more reason why we need to continue the job at hand. We're close to ending it, Sam. We can put these people out of business for good."

My heart is currently somewhere else and I just don't feel like chasing Shop personnel. That said, I *would* like to find Yvan Putnik and shove his head down a toilet, flush it, and let him drown in his own filth.

"Sam, we'll be at LAX in ten minutes. You're the only man that can do this job at the moment. No other Splinter Cells are in the vicinity; they're all overseas. You're familiar with the case, you know the people involved. I understand how you feel but the best thing for you to do is to leap right back into the action. It'll help get your mind off of—"

"What the hell do you know what the best thing for me is, Colonel?" I snap. "You don't know a damn thing about how I feel!"

Lambert is used to occasional spats between us. He ignores what I realize is an overreaction and says, "That may be true but you have to snap out of it, Sam. Perhaps you need to go on psych leave as soon as we're done, and then you can go on a long vacation. You'll feel differently then."

We begin to approach the LAX exits. Of course Lambert's right. I just don't feel like walking away from Katia and pretending that nothing happened. I'm going to blame myself, dammit, and I *want* to blame myself. I *need* to blame myself. I want the time to do that.

On the other hand, if avenging her death is a priority then I do have to keep going. I do want to catch Putnik and the other Shop vermin he works for. Meeting the plane from Hong Kong is the first step toward accomplishing that goal.

"All right, Colonel," I say. "I'm sorry."

"Forget it, Sam."

"Just don't say, 'Forget it, Sam, it's Chinatown.' "

Lambert doesn't get it but Coen chuckles.

**LAMBERT** gets off his cell phone as we're about to separate in front of Bradley International Terminal. There will be some undercover FBI agents working backup for us. I guess the Bureau figures I can't do this alone. Coen and Lambert postpone their trip back to Washington for another day so they can keep an eye on me and make sure I don't have a nervous breakdown or something.

I must admit I feel a little better now that I'm "working." In the car I was ready to murder anyone that so much as smelled like a government official, and that includes Lambert and Coen. It's typical that I would beat myself up over Katia's death. I certainly did the same thing over Regan, and she died of fucking *cancer*. The CIA shrinks at the time kept telling me it wasn't my fault but for some reason I felt better if I could blame myself. I know it doesn't make a bit of sense.

Anyway, now that I'm here at the airport and am in the thick of things, so to speak, my mind is clearing. I'm pretty sure I can focus on the task at hand and I told Lambert that when we got out of the car. He put a hand on my shoulder and squeezed it. That gesture alone was worth more than any stupid words of sympathy he might have said.

The security photos from the Hong Kong airport are transmitted to my OPSAT right on time as we walk inside. We take a moment to go through them and I'm damned if I recognize anyone.

"Maybe seeing the passengers in the flesh when they come off the plane will help," Lambert suggests.

My NSA credentials get me past airport security at the terminal. The flight is on time and will arrive in minutes. I wander into the gate area and take a look at the people waiting there. Because of security rules these days, only ticketed passengers are allowed to access the gates and it's even stricter in the international terminal. So it's a pretty good bet that the people I see here are waiting to board the next flight out, not waiting for incoming passengers. At any rate, there are no Asians in the mix. In fact, the folks here appear to be no one of interest.

"Sam?"

"Yeah?" I whisper. It's Coen. I have to be subtle pressing the implant in my throat. It's one thing to talk on those in-ear cell phones in public, it's another to simply push on your Adam's apple to speak to someone.

"I'm patching in FBI agent Firuta. He's in charge of the three-man team here."

"Okay."

In a moment, I hear his voice. "Agent Fisher?"

"That's me."

"Special Agent Gary Firuta. There are three of us here. I've got two men in the baggage claim area. I'm stationed just outside of Customs at the escalator connecting Immigration with the baggage claim. If you spot anyone coming off that plane we should be pay attention to, let us know."

"Right."

I stand at the back of the hallway to have a full view of the gate area. Finally, the plane is here and passengers begin to disembark. Since it came from Hong Kong it's only natural that most of them are Asian. I scan the faces as they come through the door and don't recognize a soul. Then, when it seems that no one is left aboard, a lone elderly Caucasian appears. He's using a walking cane and carries a briefcase. His hair is white and he has a neatly trimmed white mustache and beard. But there's something about him that's very familiar. *I've seen him before.*

I quickly snap a shot of him with my OPSAT. Even when I'm dressed in civilian clothes, my OPSAT never leaves my wrist.

The old man walks slowly into the waiting area, looks at the signs, figures out which way to go for Immigration, and moves in that direction. I follow him at a safe distance and inform Agent Firuta of what's happening. In the meantime I rack my brain trying to recall where I've seen the old man before.

The lines at Immigration are long. I move on through to wait on the other side. The old man stands meekly in line and doesn't appear to be threatening at all. While there's time to kill I pull up his image on the OPSAT screen and study it. Zooming in, I focus on the guy's eyes, his nose, his . . . beard. It's the beard. Oskar Herzog. The last time I saw him he had the same beard. He's changed the color to white, applied some aging makeup, and is doing a good job hobbling with the cane.

"Alert," I whisper, pressing the implant. "Old man now approaching the Immigration desk for passport clearance, using a walking cane. It's Oskar Herzog."

"Hold on, Sam."

I see the Immigration official pick up his phone as Herzog hands over his passport and visa. The agent listens a moment, nods his head, and hangs up. He then stamps Herzog's passport and clears the man through.

"We're letting him in," Firuta says. "His passport says he's Gregor Vladistock, a Russian national living in Hong Kong."

"The guy's really German," I say.

"He spoke convincing Russian to the agent. My two men will pick up the tail downstairs at baggage claim."

"Don't lose sight of him. He's here to meet someone."

I take the escalator down with everyone else and find the baggage claim to be very crowded. Several flights have come in during the last half hour, which isn't unusual for LAX. But the place is more chaotic because a couple of carousels are down and the only three working have been relegated to all incoming flights. On top of that the ground crew is running behind unloading the planes.

As I follow Herzog toward the carousels I notice two Asian men in business suits standing near the rental car counters. They're obviously poised to catch anyone heading toward the baggage claim. Every now and then they whisper something to each other. Now that I think about it, the two guys look too punkish to be wearing business suits. I'd bet the farm they're Triad hoods attempting to look mature.

I press the implant and whisper, "There are a couple of suspicious Asian guys by the rental car counters."

But Dopey and Goofy pay no attention to Herzog as he passes them. In fact, after the man is several yards away, they shake their heads in disappointment. Whoever they were sent to meet didn't show. The pair turns and begins to walk closer to the carousels.

Standing near the exit doors, close to the carousel designated for the Hong Kong flight, are three limousine drivers carrying signs with their clients' names on them. I notice that Herzog nods at one of them and the driver—who happens to be Asian—smiles. His sign reads MR. VLADISTOCK. Bingo.

Just as I'm about to call attention to the limo driver, Dopey and Goofy surprise everyone by causing a well-orchestrated disturbance. They both jump onto the moving carousel and shout in English, "We have a bomb! Nobody move!"

Of course, the entire crowd panics. People scream and make a mad rush to the exits, dropping and leaving behind their baggage. Security personnel blow whistles and yell for everyone to calm down but it's no use.

"Damn!" Firuta says. "What just happened?"

I keep my eye on Herzog. I don't give a damn about the two Asians. The limo driver sneakily takes Herzog by the arm and hustles him out the door. I try my best to push my way through the chaos in order to keep up with them but the crowd is too thick. Police arrive on the scene and immediately take Dopey and Goofy into custody but people are still not cooperating.

"Firuta! Where are your two men?" I ask.

Apparently the FBI agents responded to the two Asians—exactly what the fake Triads wanted. I now realize that the two Asians were working for Eddie Wu, not Jon Ming. They were sent to cause a diversion so Herzog could get away unnoticed.

Screw that. Like a raging bull I shove my way through the crowd, throwing people aside with no concern for politeness, and burst through the exit doors. I spot Herzog getting into the backseat of a limo that's illegally parked at the curb. The driver gets in and the car takes off.

I rush madly into the roadway and stop the first taxi I see. With no concern for protocol, I open the door, reach inside, unsnap the driver's seat belt, and pull him out.

"Hey!" he shouts. He starts to hit me but realizes I'm a lot bigger than he is.

"You'll get it back in one piece," I say. "I hope." With that, I'm already in the driver's seat and slamming the door. Leaving the speechless driver on the street, I take off in pursuit.

# — *30* —

TRAFFIC is heavy on the 405 going north, so there isn't much I can do but stop and start. The limo is four car lengths ahead of me. The situation is compounded by the onset of a rainstorm. Thunder cracks in the sky and the clouds overhead look villainous.

The limo eventually turns off the freeway and gets on I-10 heading east. I smoothly change lanes and exit also. Traffic is lighter but it won't be long before rush hour congestion slows the main arteries. Along the way I give Lambert a report. Apparently the FBI back at LAX are pissed off at me for taking off after Herzog without them. Tough shit, I say. They were in the wrong place at the wrong time. Lambert tells me that the two Chinese guys were arrested, even though they claimed to be "pulling a joke." Lambert agrees with me that they were most likely placed there to create a diversion. Agent Firuta is berating himself for not being on top of the situation. I sign off after Lambert reminds me to keep him informed and mentions that Coen will be following me in her car.

"What's with the weather?" I ask. The rain has become torrential, making it difficult to see out the windshield.

"Severe thunderstorm alert," Lambert says. "It's already flooding the roads west of you. Be careful."

Great. I thought it was supposed to never rain in L.A. but today I have the pleasure of chasing a limo through the middle of a freak downpour. I guess that's showbiz, folks.

Eventually the limo gets on the 110 and heads downtown but then it makes a left onto the Hollywood Freeway. By now the 101 is packed with vehicles. It isn't long, though, before the limo gets off the highway at Sunset Boulevard and turns east toward Silver Lake. I manage to stay on their tail and keep a reasonable distance behind them.

It isn't long before the limo turns in to a shabby motel parking lot. The place looks like it's from the thirties or forties. I pull the cab over to the other side of Sunset, where I'm lucky to find a parking space at the curb. From here I have a good view of the motel and watch as the limo parks awkwardly across three regular spaces. After a moment, the Chinese driver gets out and opens the back door for his passenger. Herzog steps out, shakes the driver's hand, and goes to one of the motel doors. The driver gets back into the limo and waits.

I quickly pull out the scope I use on my Five-seveN and focus on Herzog. He knocks on the door, briefly turns to look around and make sure no one is watching, and then faces the door again. When it opens, I see a Chinese man standing on the threshold. He smiles and shakes Herzog's hand. It's Eddie Wu. I'm sure of it, even through this downpour. Great, no more passive surveillance. It's time to kick some butt.

I get out of the taxi, dart across Sunset, and approach the driver's side of the limo. It's raining so hard I feel like I'm taking a shower. I rap on the window and the driver lowers it just in time to receive a powerhouse punch in the nose. Before he can react, I reach inside and apply a choke hold. Thirty seconds later he's in Dreamland. I open the door, search the guy for a weapon, and find a Browning 9mm inside his jacket. I take it, push him over, and shut the door. As I walk toward the motel room door, I drop the handgun into a trash bin.

Quietly, I approach and put my ear to the door. I expect to hear conversation but there's nothing but silence. Are they in there?

To hell with knocking. I kick the door in and go inside, my Five-seveN drawn and ready. It's a bungalow-style place with a bedroom, living room, and kitchenette. And the place is completely empty. The back door, leading to a parking area behind the motel, is wide open.

*Damn!*

I look out the door and see *another* stretch limo pulling out of the parking lot. The bastards pulled a switch! These guys certainly aren't stupid. I run out of the room and back to the limo in the front parking lot. To hell with darting back across Sunset to the taxi—it's raining too damned hard. After opening the limo, I grab the still unconscious driver and pull him out onto the pavement. I jump inside, shut the door, and start the ignition. I'm not used to driving a stretch limo—I back right into a Volkswagen hiding behind me. I throw the limo into drive, turn the wheel, and screech onto Sunset Boulevard. Hmm, maybe I *should* have taken the time to get into the taxi again.

The other stretch limo is already ahead of me, driving west. I change lanes, speed around the traffic, and pull up next to it. The windows are tinted, naturally, so I can't see the passengers. But I can see the driver, and he's an ugly

Chinese guy with an eyepatch. Just as he turns his head to glare at me, I rotate the wheel and ram my car into his. Horns blare behind us as Enemy Limo slams into three parked cars on the north side of Sunset. The driver quickly recovers and gets back into the lane. He takes a risk by increasing his speed to move in front of me, momentarily merging into the oncoming traffic lane to go around a truck, and then continues in the westbound lane at around seventy.

Fine. Look out, people.

I accelerate and tear around the truck as well, forcing a splash of water the size of a small tsunami onto it. But I accidentally swing the long tail end of my limo too widely, hitting a BMW Z3. Yikes, sorry about that, fella. I hear him cursing at me and I don't blame him. They say people in L.A. don't know how to drive in the rain and I'm sure he's thinking the same thing about me.

"Sam, what is going on?" Coen's voice surprises me. I forgot she's in the vicinity somewhere.

"I'm after Eddie Wu," I announce. "He and Herzog are in a limo heading west on Sunset. I'm behind them . . . in another limo."

"My God, Sam, it's rush hour."

"Tell me about it. It looks like they're getting on the freeway up ahead. I'm on their tail. I'll talk to you later. I need to concentrate here."

"I've got your position by satellite—barely. This rain is really hurting us. I'll follow the best I can. Good luck!"

Sure enough, Enemy Limo gets onto the 101 and heads northwest. Traffic is a bitch. I lean on my horn, indicating to the bozos in front of me that I'm going around them whether they like it or not. I pull out of the line of cars waiting on the entrance ramp, pass them by driving on the curb and splashing them with Niagara Falls, and shoot onto the freeway in front of a ten-wheeler doing sixty. The driver's horn screams at me with the subtext of a million obscenities as I swing out of his lane.

Enemy Limo is speeding ahead, maybe six car lengths in front. The driver has no regard for the traffic around him. He zigzags through the stream of vehicles, knocking cars out of the way as if he's playing a video game. I fear this chase might end up being deadlier than I anticipated. I'm not sure if it's a blessing or a hindrance when I hear police sirens in the background.

I press my implant. "Coen?"

"Yes?"

"Get on to the police. Let them know what's going on. Maybe they can divert traffic or something. It's gonna get messy up here the way that guy is driving."

"Aerial traffic control is grounded because of the storm," she says, "but I'll see what I can do."

We pass Universal City on the right as we approach the fork separating the Hollywood and Ventura Freeways. Enemy Limo changes lanes and makes like he's going to stay on the Hollywood, but at the last possible second he slides over and exits onto the Ventura. Two cars are plowed aside in his wake—and I do mean wake. One of them does a flip over the side of the damned freeway and sails to the ground below. Christ.

It's tricky but I make the exit. Like a good boy I put on a signal, honk my horn lightly, and get over to one of the correct lanes. I see Enemy Limo a quarter mile in front of me, so I step on the gas, scoot around a U-Haul truck, and gain on my prey. I'm now directly behind them, so I speed up a little more and ram their back fender. This is the catalyst for a man to lean out of a lowering passenger window. He points a handgun at me and fires. I duck as the windshield shatters with tremendous force. I'm covered in broken glass and feel the sting of what seems like a hundred needles pricking my face. My limo invariably swerves across the freeway and I barely get it under control before I crash into the rail.

Pulling the car back into the lane, I take a moment to brush myself off. The rain batters me through the gaping hole, now making it nearly impossible to see. I reach into my backpack with one hand, grab my goggles, and slip them on. Now I could drive through a dust storm and it wouldn't bother me. I then glance in the rearview mirror and see that my mug is lightly dotted with streaks of blood. Sons of bitches. I draw my own handgun and speed up. Most of the other drivers on the freeway are now aware of us and try to give us a wide berth. It's as if they're all communicating with each other—"Stay away from those mad men in the limos!" Only in Hollywood.

I'm now neck and neck with Enemy Limo, riding alongside his left. I lower the passenger window, point the Five-seveN, and squeeze the trigger. The round sears the driver's nose, destroying his window in the process. I hear the guy yell as he grabs his face. Enemy Limo skids into mine and we both careen across the lanes, out of control. I'm forced to apply the brakes to avoid spinning into another goddamned limousine. They're all over this town! Enemy Limo has a few seconds to recover and the driver picks up speed. I straighten the wheel and take off again in pursuit. With the gun in my left hand, I reach out the window and fire at the limo's back tires. The road is too bumpy and my aim isn't great with my left. I succeed in knocking out a taillight but that does little good except prompting the bozo with the weapon to lean out his window again. This time, however, he's got a rifle.

The guy is Yvan Putnik! Katia's killer! He was in Enemy Limo all along.

He fires but I'm already jerking the wheel to the left and guiding the limo into the next lane with the force of a tank. I broadside a taxicab but bounce back into the lane as I hear police sirens growing louder. I can see them now, three patrol cars with lights blazing, making their way through the scattered traffic behind us. We're getting closer to the 405 again as we cross over Sherman Oaks on the left and Van Nuys on the right. I can see another block of congestion ahead and I dread there's going to be some real carnage if I don't put a stop to this real soon.

Enemy Limo finds itself trapped between a ten-wheeler in front and a bus in back. This gives me the chance to floor the pedal and shoot up the lane beside it. I raise the handgun, aim out the passenger window, and squeeze the trigger as I pass the driver. This time I don't miss. The guy's head explodes in a mass of red and black goo.

Whatever causes the ten-wheeler's driver to suddenly change lanes, I don't know, but that's what he does—right in front of me. With no one at the wheel, Enemy Limo wavers, finally moving on a collision course with the right rail. I desperately try to steer around the stupid ten-wheeler when the asshole slams on his brakes. I remember two things. The first is that I see someone in Enemy Limo climbing over the partition to grab the steering wheel. The second thing is the back end of the ten-wheeler in my face.

**"SAM?** Sam? Sam? Sam? *Sam? Sam . . . ? . . . Sam . . . ? . . . Sam . . . ?"*

I think I hear Coen's voice. I'm not sure if it's a dream or what the hell it is. I feel pain in my shoulders and back. I'm aware of a puffy balloonlike *thing* in my face and then realize it's an air bag. I'm wedged in the front seat of the limo. I see my arms and hands flailing on the outside of the bag and there's blood on them. I then notice the odd angle of the horizon outside the bent and misshapen dashboard.

The road is perpendicular to the limo's hood. Damn, the car is on its side and I'm stuck inside. And there's water everywhere.

And then everything goes dark.

I open my eyes inside an ambulance. Coen is sitting beside me with an expression of concern on her face. The vehicle shakes and bounces over the road and I hear the piercing siren above the rumble of the engine. I take stock of my body and am happy to find no oxygen mask attached to my face. I feel pain in my side but for some reason I'm not dead.

"Hey," Coen says. "Look who's still with us."

"What's going on?" I manage to ask. My voice comes out hoarse.

"You're on the way to the hospital, pal. Doesn't look too serious, so you can relax."

Then I remember. "I wiped out."

"Yeah, but your bulletproof vest saved your life. And the air bag."

Damn, I forgot about that, too. Lambert and Coen made me put it on under my civvies before I left the Sofitel.

"They have to X-ray you," she continues. "You're gonna

be pretty bruised up. And your face looks like a pizza. But other than that you're probably gonna be fine."

I'm suddenly overwhelmed by fatigue. "Then if you don't mind, I'm going to take a nap until we get there," I say.

"Go right ahead."

And I do.


**I'M** released from the hospital around dinnertime. Coen was right, it wasn't too bad. I have two cracked ribs that should heal on their own *if I take it easy.* There's a bad gash on my left leg from when the limo crashed into the truck. That required eight stitches. My shoulders hurt like hell from the impact but thankfully nothing was broken or sprained there. I suppose my neck might have been broken, but as they say, I was lucky. Finally, my face looks like I've been through a perforator. Again, it appears worse than it is. The nicks and scratches should heal within days and leave me with no permanent scars.

However, for the wound on my heart—Katia's death— they couldn't do anything.

In the morning I'll be flying to China via Osprey. Lambert and I had a long talk at the hospital and we agreed it was the best thing for me to do. If I went home to Maryland now I'd simply go nuts. I'd be so consumed with the thirst for revenge that I'd probably go berserk in a shopping mall. Cracked ribs aside, I'm in good enough shape to go after the bastards. Mentally, I'm focused and determined. I have to see this mission through to the end.

The three characters in Enemy Limo got away, of course. By the time the police arrived at the scene, the dead driver had been thrown onto the road and someone else had taken the wheel. Because of the rainstorm there were no police helicopters in the air to follow the car. However, the limo was found abandoned off of one of the freeway's exits. We figure the passengers were Oskar Herzog, Eddie Wu, and Yvan Putnik. Where the trio is now is anyone's guess but Lambert believes they're already out of the country. A chartered plane registered to GyroTechnics and carrying three passengers left Burbank Airport a couple of hours after the freeway incident. An hour ago, when the FBI figured out that GyroTechnics was now a defunct company, it was too late to stop them. The plane had already landed in Hawaii and was left on a private runway. The three fugitives must have caught another means of transportation back to Hong Kong or wherever they're headed. My guess is that they're going straight to China to meet up with the controversial General Tun in Fuzhou. And they're most likely carrying the MRUUV guidance system device.

As for the outspoken general, Tun has stepped up his television appearances in China. For the past two days he's been delivering barbed speeches against his own government, accusing them of not having the guts to take what naturally belongs to them—that is, Taiwan. He pointedly states that China is afraid of the United Nations and the United States. The main thrust of his rhetoric is that it's time for him to take the matter into his own hands, with or without the support of the Chinese government. Of particular concern is that Tun's army, which has mobilized in Fuzhou across the bay from Taiwan, appears to be readying for an offensive strike.

The vice president has flown to Beijing to speak with China's president. So far the word is that General Tun has been sternly warned to temper his statements but we all know that means nothing. General Tun apparently has the support of most of the CCP Politburo. The highest authority in China rests with the Standing Committee of the Politburo, which comprises twenty-five members, and, below that, a 210-member Central Committee made up of younger party members and provincial party leaders. The

CCP also controls the State Council, which supervises the day-to-day running of the country.

Another wild card in all this is the power of the military branch in China. The nearly three million members of the People's Liberation Army are divided into seven military regions, each with its own leadership and strong territorial affiliations. The Chinese army, navy, and air force function under one banner and stand as a very strong voice in the actions of the government. General Tun is considered something of a folk hero in his region and has been successful in recruiting the common men and women from the rural areas around Fuzhou to join his cause. To discipline Tun would be embarrassing to the Chinese government. As we all know, the culture there is about saving face. I suppose if General Tun makes a stupid blunder, attacks Taiwan and fails miserably, then the government can then discipline him and say, "I told you so." On the other hand, if he attacks and is successful, the government could rally to his defense and challenge the rest of the world. It could be an extremely serious situation.

Lambert provided me with satellite photos of General Tun's camp on China's southeastern coast. His army is nearly 200,000 strong, consisting of land, naval, and air forces. There are three suspicious structures built right on the coast that appear to be airplane hangars. I have a feeling they're submarine pens. It's difficult to determine what kind of firepower Tun's got up his sleeve but we know about the MRUUVs, of course. And we know he probably has the missing nuke that was shipped to Hong Kong from Russia. The problem is that our intelligence has no idea what the general plans to do with the MRUUVs. Attacking Taiwan with a nuke doesn't make sense. But the presence of the submarine pens tends to refute that line of thinking, doesn't it?

My job is to find out what the hell the guy plans to do with his nuke.

When we get to Edwards Air Force Base, Coen and I spend several hours going over my equipment. She helps me restock my supplies and ammo, fixes the bullet hole in my backpack, and provides me with maps, papers, and passports. It's tricky going into a Communist country on a Third Echelon assignment. I'll have to enter illegally and for all intents and purposes I do not exist. Coen will not be going with me; it's just too dangerous. The political ramifications of being caught in China would be a public relations disaster for the NSA. I'll pick up my equipment and be in direct communication with an official at the U.S. Consulate General in Guangzhou, but even the consul will Protocol Six me if I'm arrested. I don't relish the thought of being accused of spying in the People's Republic of China. The unfortunate souls who have had that experience most often do not live to talk about it.

Before I retire for the night, I arrange for five hundred dollars' worth of flowers to be delivered to Katia's mother. Coen tells me that Katia's body was shipped to San Diego, where she'll be buried after a quick Jewish funeral. The official explanation for her death is that she was a victim of gang violence and caught a stray bullet. I suppose her mother is not going to question why gang violence erupted at Beverly Center, one of the more fashionable parts of Los Angeles.

In my note to Katia's mom, I say that I was one of her daughter's students and was very fond of her. I also provide my personal contact information in case there's anything I can do to help settle Katia's estate in Maryland. There will be the Krav Maga class to deal with and all . . . hell, perhaps I should offer to take it over. I'll have to think about that. It would be a good way for me to honor her memory.

As I settle in for the night, I think of Regan. I haven't thought about my former wife in depth in a while and I try to define my feelings for her at this point in time. I'll always love Regan even though she's a distant figure in my past. Katia would never have replaced her. No one could. After a stormy and intense relationship, Regan and I ultimately couldn't continue living together. She's been gone a long time but our hearts were always linked. At least I still have the result of our union, my dear Sarah. I'll have to call my daughter in the morning before I leave.

As sleep overtakes me, I wonder who will occupy my dreams tonight. Will it be Regan or Katia? One or the other would be nice. I just hope it's not both of them. I couldn't face being in the same dream with two lost loves.

I don't think I could handle the guilt.

# *32*

I make an unscheduled stop before slipping into China. Lambert knows I'm doing it but no one else does.

I'm in Kowloon again, keeping watch over the Purple Queen nightclub. It's the middle of the afternoon and I'm waiting for Jon Ming to arrive. The entrance to the back parking lot is visible from my seat in Chen Wing's coffee bar, located across the street from the club in Tsim Sha Tsui East.

A slightly altered passport and visa got me into the colony. We changed it just in case the authorities might have linked me to some of the violence that occurred here a few days ago. It will also be much easier for me to enter mainland China from Hong Kong instead of trying to get in through Shanghai or another major city. From Kowloon it's a straight overland journey to Fuzhou. I can stop in Guangzhou and visit the consul, pick up my stuff, and make my way to the east coast. It's a good plan.

The only problem now is that I'm unarmed and without my uniform. With Mason Hendricks gone, there's no one in Hong Kong I can rely on to provide me with a weapon. My chat with Jon Ming will have to depend on the old Sam Fisher charm, what little of it there is.

Contacting Ming proved to be much easier than I expected. When I arrived and checked in to a fleabag hotel in Kowloon, I phoned the Purple Queen and in my best Cantonese asked to speak with Ming. The exchange went something like this:

"There is no Jon Ming here. Wrong number."

"Excuse me, but I know this is Ming's nightclub. I'd like to speak to him."

"You have the wrong number."

"Tell Ming I will call back in five minutes. Tell him I have information about the Shop, Andrei Zdrok, and General Tun."

I hung up, waited the allotted time, and called back.

"Who is this?"

"Did you give Mr. Ming my message?"

"Yes. Just a minute." There was murmuring in the background before the guy got back on the phone. "Mr. Ming wishes to talk to you. Come to the Purple Queen at three o'clock today."

At exactly five minutes of three, Ming's Roll-Royce slides into the parking lot and disappears behind the building. I finish my tea, pay the bill, and walk across the street. The big Sikh standing guard glares at me, ready to pull his weight.

"Don't sweat it, big guy, I'm here to see Ming," I say.

The Sikh goes inside and I wait nearly three minutes before I become impatient and step into the club. Two Chinese thugs in suits are waiting for me. With no questions being asked first, thick strong arms grab me from behind and hold me with a viselike bear hug. It's the Sikh and he's a walking lump of muscle. Once I'm sufficiently immobile, "Joe" and "Shmoe" move forward and take turns delivering spear-hand chops to the sides of my neck. On top of the injuries I suffered in the L.A. limo crash, the pain is immense.

"Hey! What's this about?" I gasp.

"Who are you? Why are you here?" Joe asks in English.

"I was *invited*. My name is Fisher."

He says, "You were the man at the warehouse. You are an enemy of the Lucky Dragons." The thug gives me another spear-chop that sends shock waves down my spine.

At first I don't know what he's talking about—there have been so many warehouses in my life. Then it comes to me. The time they had the device that wreaked havoc on my implants. I ended up killing a handful of their men.

"That's before I was on your side." I cough.

"We don't believe you," Shmoe says. He moves in to hit me again but I use the Sikh's arms as leverage, raise my legs, and kick the man in the face. Before Joe or the Sikh can retaliate, I swing my legs back, bend my knees, and ram the soles of my boots into the Sikh's knees. He bellows in pain and releases me. That gives Joe time to perform a jump kick, hitting me squarely on the sternum and knocking me backward into the Sikh. The two of us tumble to the ground. The Sikh is pretty much out of the game—I may have broken his kneecaps—so I concentrate on the two Chinese hoods. As Shmoe moves in to kick me in the ribs, I roll toward him like a log and manage to trip him up. He falls into his partner, allowing me the opportunity to jump to my feet. I immediately spin, thrust out my right foot, and connect the heel to Joe's chin. I follow through, place my right foot on the floor, bend the right knee, and spring forward with my left foot pointed at Shmoe. Bull's-eye, right in the solar plexus. I drop back, assume a defensive stance, and wait.

"Stop!" Jon Ming stands a few feet away. He looks at me and says, "I've seen you before."

"I've been in your club," I say.

Ming turns to Shmoe and orders, "Frisk him. Then

bring him to the conference room. There is no need to play rough." He focuses on the Sikh, who is rolling on the floor in agony. "And see to his needs." Ming shakes his head as if the guard hadn't studied for a school quiz and had failed it miserably.

I hold up my arms and Shmoe does a thorough job of patting me down. When he's satisfied I'm not there to assassinate his leader, he gives me the dirtiest look he can muster, jerks his head, and says, "Follow me."

We walk through the empty club. I notice the pretty hostess who served me the night I was here. She's busy wiping the tables, preparing the place to open. She looks at me and wrinkles her brow, trying to remember where she's seen me before. Of course, all *gweilo* look alike to Asians.

They lead me through the Employees Only door and into the hallway where not too long ago I performed a clandestine search. I'm not surprised when I'm ushered into the very room that was once covered in plastic, the room where I took a specimen of dried blood. Now, however, the place is tidy and devoid of plastic. Jon Ming sits at the small conference table and gestures to one of the other empty chairs. Joe and Shmoe remain standing behind me. One of them shuts the door.

"Mr. Sam Fisher," Ming says in English. "You are a Splinter Cell from the branch of the National Security Agency known as Third Echelon."

Dripping with sarcasm, I say, "I can't imagine how you'd know that."

Ming smiles. "You have a sense of humor, I see. That is good."

"Oh, it's a million laughs that one of your people penetrated our organization and then sold information to the Shop. Yeah, we find that extremely funny, Mr. Ming, but that's not why I'm here. By all accounts I should be at your throat. Not only were the Lucky Dragons in league with the most dangerous arms-dealing outfit in the world, but you also tried to have me killed not too long ago."

"We thought you were a threat to us," he answers. "I apologize. Since you did away with six of my men at the time, I assume you will agree that the score is settled. And you did just break one of my employees' kneecaps just now. Are we even?"

"Perhaps," I say. "That depends on how our conversation goes today."

Ming is silent for a moment as he lights a cigarette. He offers one to me but I refuse it. "May I offer you a drink?" he asks instead.

"No, thanks."

"Very well. What is it you wanted to speak to me about, Mr. Fisher?"

"Let's go back to the beginning of all this. Once upon a time there was a physicist working in weapons development in my country. His name was Gregory Jeinsen. He died here in this room."

Ming registers no reaction when I say this but he also offers no refutation.

I continue. "Through Mike Wu, your mole at Third Echelon, you obtained information from Professor Jeinsen over a period of time. This consisted of the specifications, plans, and everything else that's needed to create an MRUUV. Am I right so far?"

"Operation Barracuda," Ming says. "Yes, you are correct."

"Of course I am. You then—wait, why do you call it 'Operation Barracuda'?"

"Because an MRUUV is long and cylindrical, like a barracuda fish."

"I see. Anyway, you then sold all of Jeinsen's material to the Shop."

"We *traded* it for goods, but that's neither here nor there."

"Whatever. There was one piece of the pie you didn't

give them, though—the guidance system that your illegal research outfit in Los Angeles created. By then you had called off your business relationship with the Shop and closed down GyroTechnics."

"You are exceptionally well informed, Mr. Fisher. I wouldn't expect anything less from someone with your aptitude and abilities."

"Are you aware that Eddie Wu managed to sell the device to the Shop anyway? And that he and the Shop have delivered it to General Lan Tun in Fuzhou?"

For the first time since we began, Ming registers concern on his face by blinking several times. He adjusts himself in the seat and says, "Go on."

"The United States has reason to believe that General Tun is about to attack Taiwan with a nuclear device. I'm not sure why he wants to *blow up* Taiwan, but all the intelligence we've gathered points to that scenario."

"And why do you tell me this, Mr. Fisher?" Ming asks after a pause.

"Because I know you hate General Tun and Communist China. It's a basic, fundamental tenet of the Lucky Dragons, as it is with all Triads."

"That may be true," Ming says. "But are you asking me for something?"

"I'm asking for your help." There. I've said it. Lambert and I debated for over an hour whether or not we should seek an alliance with a criminal organization that has in the past done damage to the United States. In the end I convinced him there might be some wisdom to it.

I elaborate. "Mr. Ming, you have the means to lead men to Fuzhou and do something to General Tun before he attacks. You have a small army at your disposal. You have people that believe in your cause. Do you understand what will happen if General Tun—if *Red China*—attacks Taiwan? It would lead us all into World War Three. You and your little empire here in Hong Kong would not go unaffected."

Ming takes a drag from his cigarette and asks, "Are you absolutely certain the MRUUV guidance system is in General Tun's hands?"

"No, but I know Eddie Wu was in possession of it and he was last seen in the company of Shop personnel. We have evidence that they fled the United States and were headed for Asia. They have the ability to get into China and deliver it right into the general's hands. You know they do."

Ming crushes the cigarette into an ashtray. "Is there anything else, Mr. Fisher?"

I consider my words for a moment and then say, "Yes. When I encountered your men at that warehouse near the old airport, they had a device, some kind of transmitter."

"Yes."

"How did you know the thing would be useful against me?"

"That machine was loaned to us by the Shop. It was created by and belongs to them. We gave it back to them. You should direct that question to someone in their organization."

"Interesting." So the knowledge of my implants and how they work most likely came from the Shop's source within our government. Possibly the mysterious informant Mike Wu mentioned? The one who sits "high on the food chain" somewhere in Washington?

"And how did you know I would be at that warehouse?" I ask. "Only two people were aware of my movements that night and one of them is dead."

"Again, Mr. Fisher. The Shop. Our source in the Shop knew where you would be at all times."

"Did you know a man named Mason Hendricks?"

"Yes. He was one of our best customers here in the club. I was very sorry to hear of his unfortunate accident. I believe he perished with a woman who worked for me. Very tragic."

"That fire at his home was deliberately set. Any idea who was responsible?"

Ming shakes his head. "None whatsoever. Although I suspect—"

"I know: *the Shop*. Regular scapegoats, aren't they, Mr. Ming?"

Ming's eyes flare and then he asks, "Is there anything else, Mr. Fisher?"

I sit back in the chair and say, "No. That's it."

"Very well. It was a pleasure talking with you." Joe and Shmoe move forward and stand on either side of me, ready to escort me out.

"That's it?" I ask. "You have nothing to say?"

"The conversation is over, Mr. Fisher. Let us say that I shall take your words under advisement. You are still an enemy of the Lucky Dragons. I cannot and will not divulge my thoughts to you. Good day and good luck, Mr. Fisher. My men will see you out."

Fine. I've tried my best. I stand and leave the way I came. Little Miss Hostess is still cleaning the tabletops when I go by. This time she smiles at me—if I was important enough to gain an audience with Jon Ming then I must be a VIP of some kind. I ignore her and head for the door. Before I get there, Joe puts his hand on my shoulder as if to give me a word of advice. With the speed of a snake I grab his wrist and twist it, sending him to his knees. Shmoe moves in to defend him but I hold my hand out in front of him, warning him not to get any closer.

"It was a pleasure meeting you guys," I say with a smile, then I let go of Joe's hand. If looks could kill . . . but I pay them no mind as I turn and walk out the door.

# 33

THE trip to the coastal region of Fujian was uneventful. I made my way to Guangzhou by train on a falsified work visa and passport that indicated I'd be consulting with high schools on creating a "foreign government policies" curriculum. The U.S. consul received my equipment via the diplomatic bag and provided me with an imported Cadillac to drive to Fuzhou. My passport and visa were changed and the consul sent through the paperwork indicating that my first identity had left the country. Now I'm a U.S. environmentalist studying global temperatures. I just hope I don't have to actually talk about my "work" because I'd fall flat on my face.

Most Taiwanese people consider the Fujian province to be their ancestral home, which is ironic seeing that the country is about to be attacked from there. The language spoken in the region is essentially the same as Taiwanese, although officially it's supposed to be Mandarin, like everywhere else in China. Prior to the fifteenth century, the region was a major port for travelers moving from China to Taiwan, Singapore, the Philippines, Malaysia, Indonesia, and back. Today it's still a heavily used shipping harbor. The capital, Fuzhou, is a city dating back to around the third century and was reportedly one of Marco Polo's favorite stops when he was running around Asia at the end of the thirteenth century. I won't be spending much time in the city, though. I'm heading closer to the coast, where General Tun's encampment lies. I find the area beautiful, to an extent, in that it is fertile and green and typifies the images one might think China is supposed to look like. The land is flat nearer the coast and is covered by rice fields and other farmland, so everywhere you turn there's a bare-legged guy wearing one of those broad Chinese straw hats and leading a team of oxen over his field.

China's situation with Taiwan is akin to that of a strict parent and an estranged child. After being ruled by the Japanese for something like sixty years, the Taiwanese rebelled when Chinese Kuomintang officials occupied the island and imposed their rule on the people. This led to unrest and rioting and the KMT ended up massacring tens of thousands of Taiwanese civilians. This event is still commemorated in Taiwan. Chiang Kai-shek's son and successor eventually executed the KMT military governor responsible for the atrocity. By the time the Korean War erupted in 1950, the United States sided with the KMT and Taiwan against the Communist Chinese forces supporting North Korea. It was a case in which Taiwan became a democracy almost by default.

China's government is under the mistaken belief that Taiwan still belongs to her. The island has governed itself since the Chinese Nationalist forces fled to Taiwan in 1949. Most inhabitants of the island view Taiwan as already sovereign even without a formal declaration. The Chinese government has offered the island autonomy if it will come under China's direct rule. Thus, Taiwan is a major thorn in China's side because the small island country has shown itself to be economically successful on the world stage. The end of military rule and the beginning of full democracy challenged notions that China was better off as a communist country. Now that the capitalist colony Hong Kong is in the fold, there is some thinking this will have an influence on the way China does things in the future. The jury's still out. In the meantime, there are hard-liners like General Tun who insist on reunifying China and throwing a net over Taiwan.

Tun's army encampment is set up along the coast just north of Fuzhou. After nightfall I do a reconnaissance around the place to get an idea of what I'm up against. Satellite photos provided to me by Third Echelon come in very handy. The technology has become so advanced that they can zero in on a chessboard on the ground and determine what the next move should be. From these pictures I can tell how many men are gathered in a particular spot, what kinds of vehicles are present, and how much firepower is sitting around. Sometimes we can get X-ray pictures and see inside certain structures, such as tents and temporary buildings. Thermal vision shots allow us to see where living beings are grouped. This intelligence shows that the army is housed in six barracks lining the perimeter of the base. A command post is set up next to the three large hangar-type buildings on the shore. The analysts at Third Echelon are now certain these buildings are submarine pens. The water happens to be deep enough where they've set up camp as opposed to the beachfront just east of Fuzhou. It makes sense.

Just before I arrived in Fujian province, several Chinese landing craft were mobilized at the shore. Two Luda-class destroyers, one Luhu-class destroyer, and two Chengdu frigates are busy doing maneuvers in the strait. Chinese air support will come from a base in neighboring Quanzhou. If these guys aren't preparing for an invasion then someone's playing a very unfunny elaborate joke. Our own naval forces have gathered nearer to Taiwan and outside of the strait, standing guard like floating sentinels just waiting for something to happen. It's a tense situation.

"We have you by satellite, Sam," Lambert says in my ear. "Just watch the patrolling guards. Otherwise you're good to go."

Temporary wire fences surround the base. Two gates allow entrance, one on the north side and the larger main access on the south. It appears that only two guards stand duty at the main gate at all times, but only one mans the north one. I elect not to use either. Instead I crawl through what foliage there is on the north side of the encampment, about sixty feet east of the gate, and use my wire cutters. There's no moon tonight and it's cloudy so the darkness provides me with a fair amount of cover. I'll still have to be careful, though. There are no trees or other thick vegetation to hide behind if I need to. The base itself is illuminated by a number of floodlights set up at strategic locations.

One of the barracks is right in front of me. I quietly move behind it and can hear snoring through the walls. Everyone's asleep, or at least they should be. From observing the site before I crawled in, I determined that four single-man patrols cover quadrants, moving back and forth within each man's specific section. I imagine they'll be spelled after three or four hours.

I make my way around the barracks, darting from shadow to shadow. I'd like to shoot out the damned floodlights but that certainly would be an attention grabber. When I crouch behind what appears to be the mess hall I see a lengthy stretch of brightly lit turf to the submarine pens. Unfortunately that's where I need to go to learn what I can about Operation Barracuda. How the hell am I going to get from here to there?

"Guard approaching from the east," Lambert says.

There's my answer—walking toward me in the form of one of the soldiers patrolling his quadrant. He's lost in his thoughts, not paying much attention to his surroundings, and probably figures there's no way in hell he's going to encounter any trouble in the middle of an army base. I wait until he's nearly upon me and then I spring forward, clasp my hand around his mouth, and butt him on the back of the head with my Five-seveN. The soldier falls limp in my arms. I drag him into the shadow behind the mess, remove his jacket and helmet, and try them on for size. A little tight but they'll do. I take his assault rifle—a QBZ-95—then I stand, get into character, and slowly walk into the light. I'm now a patrolling Chinese soldier.

As inconspicuously as possible, I slowly and surely make my way to the command post and submarine pens. It's out of my guy's quadrant but I don't think anyone's going to notice. I just don't want to run into the guy who *is* supposed to be patrolling this quadrant or there might be some fireworks.

The entrance to the first pen is open. I stand to the side and carefully peer in. Sure enough, there's a submarine sitting in the water. Work lights illuminate the pen and I see a couple of soldiers on the platform at the side of the sub, sitting at a table and playing cards. They, too, probably figure no one's going to bother them this late at night.

As I study the submarine I realize it's not a class I recognize. I remember reading a Pentagon report that was distributed to Third Echelon operatives regarding a new class of sub the U.S. military believed China was building.

Known at the Pentagon as a Yuan-class sub, it is speculated to be a new type of attack boat that's diesel-powered and built from indigenous Chinese hardware and Russian weapons. I quickly snap some shots of it with my OPSAT and move on to the next pen. There's a little more activity inside this one so I'm unable to get a good look. I do, however, note that a sub is indeed in the pen and might be a nuclear-powered Xia-class.

The third pen is empty. No submarine at all. Yet there are several soldiers moving things around on the platforms on the sides of the slip, cleaning up after a launch operation or preparing for the arrival of a boat.

Then I recognize a guy in civilian clothes standing over a control board some forty feet away. It's Oskar Herzog, now without the white in his hair and beard that made him look older. He's talking with a man in a sharp-looking uniform whose back is to me. From this angle it's difficult to discern his rank.

I carefully slide inside the pen and crouch behind three oil drums so I can get a better look. Finally, the man turns away from the control board and I'm able to snap a shot. It's General Tun himself.

He and Herzog walk away from the control board and head in my direction. I hug the floor as they move past the drums and step outside. I quickly make sure no one is following them or watching, and then I slip out the door and tail them. They head straight for the command post, a small temporary building not far away from the pen.

After they go inside, I move around to the back of the small structure, where there's a window at shoulder height. I reach into my backpack and find what I call my "corner periscope," a device that's really a lot like a dentist's tool—it's a thin piece of metal with a small round mirror at the end. The metal is bendable so I can adapt it to just about any kind of space. It's best for looking around corners when you don't want to be noticed but in this case I use it to look inside the window.

Well, well. A bunch of late-nighters. I've got all of them in one tidy package. General Tun, Oskar Herzog, and Andrei Zdrok stand over a worktable studying maps. Eddie Wu sits on a stool in the corner looking as if he's about to nod off. And lying on a couch, barely awake, is Yvan Putnik.

I'm extremely tempted to lock and load and end it here and now. I press my implant and ask for Lambert.

"I'm here, Sam. What is it?"

I type in a text message: I HAVE ZDROK, HERZOG, PUT-NIK, TUN, AND E WU TOGETHER IN CONVENIENT TARGET LOCATION. SHOULD I?

After a moment, Lambert says, "Do you know what they're planning to do with the nuke and the MRUUV?"

I respond: NOT YET.

Lambert says, "Then you'd better wait. Please proceed with the primary directive. Then get the hell out. We'll leave that other thing for the U.S. military. It's not your job, Sam."

Oh, man. Putnik is the one I really want. It's my deepest desire to make the guy suffer for what he did to Katia. As I curse Lambert's orders, I put the corner periscope in my trouser pocket and activate the T.A.K. on my Five-seveN. I aim it at the window and listen in on the conversation. Since the general can't speak Russian and the Shop guys can't speak Mandarin, they've opted for very bad English.

TUN: . . . they tell me submarine *Mao* do reach American west coast seven day.

HERZOG: Are you sure about that, General? Only seven days?

TUN: *Mao* is fast submarine we have. Xia-class.

ZDROK: I was impressed with how it looked today when it left the pen.

TUN: It beautiful boat. New diesel-powered sub very nice, too. United Nations not know about.

*They do now,* I think.

ZDROK: So, General, I believe this finishes our business together. You have the warhead my comrade General Prokofiev supplied to you, you have all the pieces of Operation Barracuda and they appear to be working, and now Mr. Herzog and I would like to leave you with your plans. That final payment . . . ?

TUN: It is done. Here receipt for wire transfer into Swiss bank account.

ZDROK: Oskar, take a look, is this in order?

HERZOG: Appears to be. The figures are correct.

TUN: You not see Barracuda work, Mr. Zdrok?

ZDROK: Uh, no, General, I got here after your sub left.

TUN: Please. Allow me show. Come see before you go.

ZDROK: (*big sigh*) All right. Yvan, wake up. The general wants to demonstrate his new toy. Eddie, you coming?

WU: (*grumbles, unintelligible*)

I hear them shuffling about and finally all five men leave the structure and walk toward sub pen number two. I wait until they're inside and then move around the back of the building. By doing so I discover metal rungs attached to the side of the structure, obviously there so soldiers can climb to the roof if they need to. I ascend to the top and come face-to-face with an infantryman who is very surprised to see me.

"Hello," I say as I swing the butt of the QBZ-95 around and into his face. The guy plummets to the metal roof, making a bit more noise than I'd like. I quickly roll him against a ventilation pipe to conceal him a little and dump the Chinese rifle in the shadows. I don't need it as long as I have my SC-20K.

There's an open trap in the roof near the ventilation pipe. I look inside and see rafters along the underside of the ceiling. Perfect. I slip inside like a snake, grab hold and straddle a rafter beam, and scoot away from the opening. I'm now in the darkness and can see everything happening below me. General Tun has led his spectators to the front of the Xia-class sub and is directing soldiers to bring out equipment. A long coffinlike trunk is placed on the platform that runs alongside the boat. Inside is one MRUUV and it looks just like the one Professor Gregory Jeinsen drew up in the Pentagon. It's long and cylindrical, about six feet long and maybe three feet in diameter—kind of like a cigar holder with flat ends instead of rounded ones. I aim the Five-seveN, adjust the T.A.K. frequency, and listen in.

ZDROK: So that's it, huh. This is what all the fuss was about?

HERZOG: It's a marvelous invention, Andrei. It's beautiful.

ZDROK: How many of these things can your subs carry?

TUN: Launch from torpedo tubes. *Mao* has three Barracuda. Like this one.

ZDROK: Okay, so one of the MRUUVs has the warhead. What do the other two have?

TUN: Nothing! They decoy.

HERZOG: When do you plan to make your announcement to the United States, General?

TUN: When *Mao* reach target area. Seven day.

HERZOG: And you really plan to use it if they don't let you take Taiwan?

TUN: (*nods enthusiastically*) No more Disneyland! Boom!

ZDROK: What will you do if the United States comes down on you before then?

TUN: "Comes down . . ."?

ZDROK: Attacks you. What if they attack you first?

TUN: (*laughs*) You funny man, Mr. Zdrok. Joke, right?

Whoa. I get it now. The general isn't planning to use his nuke on Taiwan at all. He's using the MRUUVs to deliver the weapon as close as possible to a major American city on the west coast. Los Angeles, from the sound of it. And that's his insurance policy for attacking Taiwan. He'll let us know that the weapon is in place and will be detonated if we try to stop him from invading the little island. Since they're using a submarine to launch the MRUUV, it's going to be difficult as hell to track it. From what I understand of the MRUUV technology, it can be shot from the sub's torpedo tube and then be guided remotely to its final destination. The sub doesn't even have to be in American coastal waters; it can sit right on the edge of the international boundary and do its thing. Ingenious.

It's time to get out. I begin to scoot backward along the rafter beam toward the opening when I hear a rumble down below. An entire platoon of armed men barges into the place. The sergeant runs to another uniformed officer, who in turn whispers something to the general. Then everyone looks up at the ceiling as the general is escorted out of sight.

*Shit.*

Did they find the guard I knocked out earlier? Or the guy on the roof? They're sure acting like they know someone's up here.

A soldier brings out a searchlight, sets it on the platform beside the sample MRUUV, switches it on, and shines it at the ceiling. He slowly moves it along each beam as every man in the place studies what it reveals. I stay perfectly still and pray that not too much of my body extends beyond the outline of the beam I'm on.

Another couple soldiers bring in a device that looks familiar. In fact, it's the boom box sonic transmitter I saw in Hong Kong. They plug it in to an outlet, point the little dish at the ceiling, and turn it on. I can hear the familiar hum as before, but this time my implants are not affected. Thanks to Grimsdottir's work and the operation Coen had me undergo in L.A., their sonic torture device is no longer effective.

The men look at each other questioningly. One man checks the machine to see if it's working properly. He shrugs his shoulders. One guy shouts some orders. Men hustle back and forth. They're not sure if I'm really up here or not. Meanwhile, Zdrok, Herzog, Putnik, and Wu huddle near the door, watching and waiting to see if their intelligence proves to be correct.

So far they haven't seen me. Hell, I'll stay here all day if I have to. As long as I don't move I just might be safe. My biggest worry is how did they learn I'm here?

A man wearing civilian clothes walks into the pen from the front door. Before I have a chance to get a good look at him, he turns to Zdrok and his crew, has a word with them, and then moves onto the ramp by the sub. When he looks up at the ceiling, I feel my heart skip a beat. I now have the answers to a lot of questions. I now know how the enemy has been able to track my movements in Hong Kong, in L.A., and here. I now know how the Shop knew where I'd be and when.

Mason Hendricks, alive and well, shouts, "Fisher, you had better come down like a good boy. Otherwise they're going to shoot you down."

# 34

A soldier brings in another searchlight and aims it on the trap in the ceiling, so I won't be going out that way. To put it bluntly, I'm trapped. Sooner or later one of those light beams is going to catch a part of my leg or shoulder and it'll be all over. The only thing I can do is to make it more difficult for them to see me.

But I have to risk moving to reach into my trouser pocket and retrieve three smoke grenades. The eye is most attracted by motion, so I inch my hand along my side as slowly as possible. I finally reach the pocket and unsnap the flap but I forgot that I placed my corner periscope in there, loose. The damned thing slides out and gravity does the rest. I watch in horror as the device falls to the platform, hitting it with a *ding*.

"There!" Hendricks shouts, pointing at me.

The soldiers aim their assault rifles as I reach into the pocket and grasp a grenade. I pull the pin and let it drop. The *boom* is louder than it is damaging, but the dark cloud of smoke it produces is what I really want. I quickly grab another one, pull the pin, and let it fall. Then the gunfire begins. The bullets spray the ceiling around me but I'm now able to scoot along the rafter beam out of harm's way. I don't move toward the trap door because they'll be expecting that. Instead I go the opposite way with no clue as to how I'm going to get out of there. The gunfire continues to spread in all directions—they're leaving no room for doubt.

There's one other option. I reach into my backpack and grab my only wall mine. It takes me five seconds to activate it and another five to attach it to the ceiling. I set it to explode in ten seconds, which better be enough time for me to scoot along the beam far enough out of the way!

The men below are still blinded by the smoke and are wildly shooting their guns. The wall mine is a gamble I have to take. I'm counting on it to blow a hole big enough for me to get through and at the same time provide even more smoke to cover my escape.

I move to the far end of the beam I'm on and cover my head as bullets rattle the ceiling around me.

*KA-BOOM!*

The building shakes with unexpected roughness, causing the beam I'm sitting on to jerk precariously and come loose! I hug the girder, feeling it sway with my body weight. I can't see a damned thing—smoke has filled the place and I have no idea if I'm falling or hanging by a couple of steel bolts. After a moment my equilibrium calms down and I perceive the beam isn't dropping, it's just dangerously close to doing so. I flip down my goggles and turn on the night vision, which sometimes helps to see through smoke screens. It outlines some objects and I can now plainly see the big hole in the ceiling that's at least six feet in diameter. The smoke will ventilate quickly so I'd better get moving.

The girder I'm hugging is still attached to the ceiling behind me by a few bolts. The end in front of me is hanging out into space above the slip. I have to inch my butt in reverse, move up the beam to the ceiling, and then grab hold of another girder to do a hand-over-hand in order to reach the hole. If I move too quickly, the girder I'm on will surely come loose. And of course the soldiers below are still firing their weapons into the air, creating a random hazard no matter what direction I go.

Ain't this the life?

When I'm about five feet from the ceiling, I hear the bolts begin to give way. There's a horrible wrenching sound behind me as I feel the beam jerk and drop a few inches. I can't risk sitting on it any longer, so I focus on the stationary beam above my head and try to propel myself those five feet from a sitting position. This is where that Krav Maga training comes in handy. By using the muscles in my thighs and performing a painful stretch between my waist and arms, I'm able to *elongate*—that's the best way I can put it—and give a little push-off at the same time. As soon as I do, the girder breaks loose and falls. For a split second I'm weightless in the air and then I feel my hands around the ceiling beam. I clutch it tightly, catch my breath, and then begin the hand-over-hand trip, twenty feet to the hole.

I don't look down but I can hear the men shouting to each other. The girder must have fallen on a few of them. It seems like an eternity before I reach the hole and the smoke clears quickly while I'm in transit. Sure enough, just as I reach the hole I hear Hendricks shout, "There he is! Shoot him!" The bullets fly but I'm already climbing through the opening and crawling onto the roof. I roll my body toward the edge of the building as the rounds perforate the steel, inches behind my trail.

As soon as I figure it's safe to do so, I stand and run to

the rung ladder on the side of the building. Three guys are in the process of ascending it. I draw the Five-seveN and shoot the first man. He falls, knocking off the two behind him. The ground is crawling with soldiers and they're surrounding the building. For the second time in the last ten minutes I'm trapped, so I reach into the backpack to check my stock of smoke grenades. Damn, only two left. I do have a couple of chemical flares, though. And something else that might be useful.

I swing the SC-20K from off my back and load it with a diversion camera. Timing is crucial. In situations like this I wish I had four more hands. First I run to an edge of the building where there are fewer soldiers below. It happens to be the north side, in between submarine pens one and two. If I can get to the ground, at least I'll have a *chance* to shoot my way out of the base. I lay the two chemical flares and the smoke grenades in front of me, then prepare two diversion cameras—one loaded on the SC-20K and the other at hand, ready to load.

Next, I take a chemical flare, break the seal, point it laterally from the pen's roof, and shoot it over the soldiers' heads. It bursts beautifully, spreading flame and sparks over the area. It won't hurt them but hopefully it will cause confusion. A smoke grenade is next—I pull the pin and toss it below me. It explodes and covers the ground with thick darkness. Flare number two is next and this time I aim it laterally in the opposite direction from the first one. It, too, explodes neatly and serves to disorient the men. I then drop my last smoke grenade, allowing it to detonate in the space between pens.

Finally, I launch a diversion camera, aiming the SC-20K at the side of sub pen one that's nearest to the coast. As soon as the camera sticks it begins to broadcast the sounds of single-shot gunfire. I then quickly load the second diversion camera and fire it over the soldiers' heads, sticking it onto the side of a military jeep about thirty yards west of sub pen two. For a gag I set it to play—very loudly—a marching band's rendition of "Stars and Stripes Forever."

Total chaos on the ground. The Chinese soldiers don't know what the fuck is going on. They think someone's shooting at them from the beach side of the pens and a fifty-piece band has suddenly appeared on the other side. The flares continue to burn brightly over their heads, illuminating the smoke as if it were part of a psychedelic concert stage show.

I take the opportunity to leap off the roof. Because of the smoke, it's difficult to determine exactly where the ground is. I've made jumps like this before and know how to fall and roll to avoid hurting myself—but that's usually when I can see where I'm going to end up. My night vision goggles don't help much in this particular instance, either.

Hell, there's no use fretting about it. I take a stance and jump.

I hit the ground sooner than I expect and feel a tremendous pain in my right ankle. I try to compensate and roll but the damage is already done. I plummet to the earth like a lead weight. Just when I expect a dozen soldiers to attack me, nothing happens. The soldiers are still running around blindly, wondering where the heck I am. I manage to stand, wince in pain, and limp away. Damned ankle. I'm sure I didn't break it but I know it's sprained. As I move along, the pain diminishes. It can't be too bad. Down on the ground the night vision works a bit better and I'm able to navigate around the buildings. I pass the first sub pen and head for the north side of the camp. Behind me I still hear shouts and gunfire but by now the smoke is clearing.

The noise wakes up the rest of the men. I can see soldiers stick their heads out the barracks doors and windows. With my limp it probably looks as if I'm a crazy man skipping across the base. One guy sees me but he's too sleepy to figure out I'm the enemy.

It's a miracle that I make it to the fence. I hit the ground, crawl to the section that I cut earlier, and then slide through. By golly, I'm nearly home free. If I can just get clear of the base, hide somewhere in the dark, and avoid being found, I just might get out of this alive. I cross the road and move beyond the illumination of the base lights. The main highway to Fuzhou is up ahead. I'll probably have to avoid that for now and find a ditch or something and hole up inside it.

But now I can hear their vehicles revving up as they broaden the search. Changing direction and favoring my bad ankle, I jog parallel to the highway but stay in the shadows. It isn't long before they pull onto the road and begin to patrol at slow speeds. Obviously, they know I'm not too far away. When one of the jeeps suddenly stops and turns its searchlights in my direction, I drop to the ground. The beams cross over my prone body and then remain stationary. I hear the vehicle doors open and close. Uh-oh.

"Sam!" Lambert says. "You're surrounded! Get out of there!"

Movement headed my way. Soldiers.

I grab my SC-20K, make sure it's set for spray fire, and get ready to blast my way out of there. I remain still, wait for the right moment, and then release a volley of fire in the direction of the noises. I hit a group of men just as a searchlight finds and totally illuminates me. The soldiers fire at me as if there's no tomorrow, forcing me to hit the ground again. By then, I'm completely covered. It's no use. A dozen rifle barrels are aimed at my head.

I have no choice but to drop my weapon and raise my arms.

# 35

THEY take me in a jeep back inside the compound. My backpack, SC-20K, Five-seveN, headset, and OPSAT are confiscated. They also empty all the pockets on my uniform and remove my boots. Two guns held to my head keep me compliant. During the short ride back to the base I hear Lambert's voice in my ears: "Sam? What's happened? Are you all right? Out satellite tracker's lost you."

In order to answer him, I feign a cough. In doing so I bring my right hand to my throat, press my implant, and say, "Throat hurts." The Chinese guards nudge me with the gun barrels—*Put down your hand.* I nod, smile, and do as they ask. Back in Washington, Lambert will know I've been taken prisoner. When the implants were first integrated into a Splinter Cell's standard equipment, a series of code words were created that could mean a variety of things. Hypothetical scenarios were constructed to which we matched these codes. As long as we're able to press the throat implant and speak, we can communicate with Third

Echelon. The best way to do that in the company of the enemy is with something natural, such as a sneeze or cough—thus, my message to him told Lambert everything he needs to know.

As soon as we're back at the submarine pens, though, a soldier ties my hands behind my back with a strong nylon cord. Hopefully Lambert will begin to take steps to try to get me out—unless I've been Protocol Sixed. There's always that possibility. The rules of this dangerous game state that if the enemy captures us, then we don't exist. I've never been in such a situation before so I don't know how serious Lambert will be about it. I know of one Splinter Cell who was Protocol Sixed after being arrested for spying in North Korea. If there are other cases, I'm not privy to them. I suppose I'll just have to assume I'm on my own from here on out. To hope for something as rash as a rescue would be foolish.

I'm marched into a temporary building not far from the command post. Made of steel, aluminum, and some concrete and wood, it appears to be an all-purpose facility with offices and supply rooms. I'm taken into an approximately ten-foot-by-ten-foot cell containing a bunk built into the wall, and thrown to the floor. The soldiers leave, slam the door shut and lock it, and I'm alone.

I pick myself up and attempt to stand. My ankle still throbs with pain but I can live with it. Then I sit on the bunk and attempt to empty my mind of anything that could hamper my resistance to torture. Who knows what they'll do to me? Most likely they'll just execute me and get it over with but one never knows. Perhaps they'll use some exquisite Chinese "persuasion" to get me to reveal NSA secrets, not that there's anything for me to tell. I really don't know much classified stuff that might be damaging to our government. Third Echelon keeps it that way. At best I could give them details on how Third Echelon is structured and I doubt they'll even get that from me. I plan on saying absolutely nothing, no matter what they do to me.

Roughly twenty minutes go by before the door opens again. Mason Hendricks and Andrei Zdrok enter the room and shut the door behind them.

"I see you've made yourself at home," Hendricks says. "Sorry. We didn't mean to keep you waiting."

"Screw you, Mason," I say.

Hendricks chuckles and looks at Zdrok. "Fisher's a man with a big vocabulary." Zdrok smiles but looks at me coldly. "Oh, do you know Andrei? Andrei Zdrok, Sam Fisher."

"We bumped shoulders once but we've never been formally introduced," I answer. "Forgive me for not shaking hands."

"I think we should kill him now," Zdrok says. "He's too dangerous."

"Wait, my friend, wait. Don't you want to see him suffer? After all the harm he's caused our organization?" Hendricks asks. Zdrok doesn't answer but I can see he's chomping at the bit to get at me.

Hendricks leans against the wall and says, "Fisher, I suppose you want some answers."

"I don't give a shit, Mason," I say. "You're a traitor and a scumbag. That's all the answers I need."

Hendricks frowns and continues, "Come on, Fisher. You know as well as I do that the United States is heading in unfathomable directions. America's foreign policy has gone berserk. I simply shifted my allegiance. I don't live in the United States, Fisher. I've lived in the Far East for half my life. It's time I stop kidding myself and do what's in my heart."

"And that's to join a black market arms-dealing operation that supplies terrorists?"

"Fisher, I've been a Shop supporter for years. Long before you'd even heard of them. In fact, Andrei here refers to me as 'the Benefactor.' It's because over the years I've provided the Shop with a great deal of intelligence with regard to recruiting customers."

"You mean you've given away government secrets. You've compromised our own intelligence agencies."

"Perhaps," Hendricks says.

"So, Mason, now I know how the Lucky Dragons and the Shop have always managed to stay a step ahead of me, no matter where I went," I say. "You had access to Third Echelon's movements. Lambert told me as much. He trusted you. So you knew where I was at all times. Even in Los Angeles. Your hit man Putnik knew exactly where I'd be."

"That's right, Fisher. Of course, we don't talk to the Lucky Dragons anymore. We've had something of a falling out."

"So I hear."

"Now Andrei and I are going into business together. I'm leaving Hong Kong. Since he's lost two of his partners—*thanks to you*—I'll be joining him in the Shop. With my connections worldwide, it will be a wise investment. If I could trust you, I'd offer you a job within the organization. We could use a man like you."

"Go to hell, Mason."

"I figured that's how you'd answer so I didn't bother to ask."

"So what happened at your place in Hong Kong? Who did you burn up in your place?"

Hendricks shakes his head and says, "Tsk, tsk, tsk. It's shame that Yoshiko had to die. I was rather fond of her but she was conveniently in the right place at the right time. She worked at the Purple Queen, you know. As for the male corpse, he was someone the Shop provided to me. Some Caucasian they'd kidnapped from the street, cleaned up, and dressed in my pajamas. I had to make the Lucky

Dragons, as well as Third Echelon, think I was dead, you see. You understand."

"Oh, of course. Very well done."

"Thank you. Now the problem is that I'll have to change my name and appearance and settle my old estate through a third party, which is such a bore. Oh, well, it had to be."

"And now you're free to help a mad Chinese general attack a defenseless country and extort the United States into not interfering. You're an enterprising guy, Mason."

"Oh, you've figured out our scheme, have you? Do you know what we're extorting the United States with, as you so delicately put it?"

"You've got a Russian warhead and you're putting it in one of the MRUUVs that the submarine headed for America is carrying."

"I'm impressed, Fisher. Two hours ago you didn't know that."

"And I've already transmitted the plan to Third Echelon. You'll never get away with it."

Hendricks's eyes flared. "You're lying, Fisher. You haven't told Third Echelon squat. The last communication you had with them was around the time you were caught and you didn't say anything about it. I think you just figured it out and haven't had the time to make a report. I monitor all of Third Echelon's communications, Fisher. How else would I have been on top of you every step of the way?"

He's right. I believe him. He had full access to our satellite feeds and could plug into my implant conversations.

Hendricks removes something from his coat pocket. He discreetly hands it to Zdrok, who grins for the first time since he entered the room.

"Andrei here has something for you. He wants you to know how much he appreciates everything you've done for him and the Shop."

Zdrok holds a pair of brass knuckles. He makes a big show out of slipping them on his right hand, over black leather gloves. While he does this, Hendricks motions for me to stand. I have no choice so I do so. He then moves behind me and tightly wraps his arms around my chest, preventing me from going anywhere.

"Don't try any of your Krav Maga moves, Fisher," Hendricks says. "I'm quite proficient in self-defense myself." I know he speaks the truth.

"Mr. Fisher," Zdrok says as he approaches me, "you have seriously damaged my company over the last year. It gives me great pleasure to hurt you in this way."

With that, he carefully lifts his fist, aims at my stomach, and lets me have it with as much force as he can muster. When the brass knuckles connect to my solar plexus it feels as if my entire abdomen has exploded. The pain is worse than anything I've ever known and I'm overcome by a wave of nausea and blackness. I vaguely remember falling to the steel floor like a sack of rice.


**DAYS** go by. I know that because the guards bring me a plate of soggy lukewarm rice every twelve hours or so. Mealtime is an extremely pleasant experience, seeing as how my hands are still tied behind me. I get to lap the rice off a plate on the floor as if I'm a dog. And twice a day they come and escort me to the head. If I don't have to go when it's time, then tough luck. If I have to go when they're not around to take me, then tough luck. But I'm happy to say I haven't made a mess of myself yet. For the most part, though, they've kept me in this stupid cell for nearly a week. I'm very much alone.

And my stomach hurts like hell. A horrendously ugly bruise covers my solar plexus and I fear there may be internal damage. For the first day or so there was blood in my urine and stool but that seems to have subsided. Nevertheless, the area of my body between my rib cage and hip bones is in constant pain and is incredibly tender to the touch. Those cracked ribs I sustained in Los Angeles don't help either. Zdrok's brass knuckles really did a number on me. I hope I don't have a ruptured spleen or something like that, but then again I'd probably be much sicker than I am if that were the case. I'm no doctor. If any of those internal organs were indeed busted up, wouldn't I be dying? I suppose I should be thankful I'm not worse off than I am.

What the hell are they keeping me alive for? Every time one of the goons comes in with food or to take me to the head, I ask for Hendricks or somebody. The Chinese guards ignore me and just do their jobs. What's the point of keeping me here for days? I don't get it. They don't provide any medical attention for my stomach, they keep me in isolation, and yet they feed me.

I haven't heard a peep from Third Echelon. Perhaps they really have Protocol Sixed me. I would have thought that Lambert or Coen or *someone* would have spoken through my implants and told me *something*. Instead it's been completely dead. The radio station is completely off the air.

There have been times when I've heard activity outside—shouts from soldiers, vehicles moving, even airplanes flying overhead. Yesterday it sounded as if the entire company was moving out of the base. It's been deadly quiet since then.

Then, out of the blue, the door opens and in walks Mason Hendricks, accompanied by Yvan Putnik, who is carrying a gym bag. I'm sitting on my bunk and don't make any effort to move. Hendricks greets me and doesn't bother to introduce his pal.

"How are you feeling, Fisher?" he asks.

I just glare at him.

He snorts. "That good? You look awful, too." He jabs me in the stomach and I wince. "That's a nasty bruise you've got there."

"What do you want?" I ask.

"Oh, nothing, really. Thought you might like some company after all this time. Perhaps you'd like some news of the outside world?"

I wait for him to go on but I try not to appear eager.

"A skeleton crew is here on the base. General Tun and the rest of his men are on a frigate off the coast of Taiwan. The attack is imminent." He looks at his watch. "I'd say it's going to begin in about an hour. They'll start with an air bombardment and then a sea assault."

I sigh but it comes out as a groan.

"Yes, I know, Fisher. Sounds pretty bad. And you know what? Our country is not going to do anything to stop them. Oh, we talked tough for the last several days, and I believe our president is in seclusion with the Chinese president right this minute. You see, General Tun told the United Nations this morning that the United States would be the target of his 'secret weapon' if we lift a finger to help Taiwan. China is claiming no responsibility but they're not raising any hands to stop him."

Hendricks begins to pace back and forth as he speaks. Putnik stands there solemnly, his spooky gaze fixed on me. He really does look like Rasputin.

"The Chinese submarine *Mao* reached the coastal waters of Los Angeles earlier today. Three MRUUVs were launched from the torpedo tubes. Two decoys and one armed with the warhead. Before the U.S. Navy could pinpoint the sub's location, the *Mao* had moved back into international waters. The bomb can be detonated manually from a control panel located on the submarine or here in the command post. Andrei Zdrok, Oskar Herzog, and I will have the pleasure of watching the drama unfold. We were going to leave last week but General Tun made us an inviting offer. You see, we had no place to go, so the good general offered us safe haven here on the base at least until after all this has blown over. He's going to help us relocate the Shop headquarters and he'll probably take over the position once held by General Prokofiev in Moscow."

"What about me?" I ask.

"Oh, what about *you*? You're wondering why we've kept you alive all this time. You can thank General Tun for that. As soon as he saw that a National Security Agency Splinter Cell had been arrested and was in his custody, the general left strict orders to keep you alive—for a while. I think he wanted to figure out what he wanted to do with you. Perhaps you could be some kind of bargaining chip in the talks with the U.S. I'm not really sure. I said it was a dumb move but he wouldn't listen to me. At any rate, all that doesn't matter now. We got word just a little while ago that the general no longer has any interest in you. With talks deteriorating between China and the U.S., with the attack on Taiwan imminent and Los Angeles about to be destroyed if the Americans defend the Taiwanese—he finally figured you're just useless to him. So Yvan here has volunteered to make you go away. Permanently."

Putnik grins at me. So this is it. They've kept me here like an animal and now it's time for the slaughter. Fine. Get it over with.

"Oh, Yvan doesn't speak English. But he wanted me to tell you he's going to take his time. He's interested in seeing how much pain a tough Splinter Cell like you can take. It's for his personal research, you see. I told him you'd be happy to contribute statistics to his work. I'll leave you two alone now. Goodbye, Fisher."

Hendricks raps on the door and a guard unlocks it. It slams shut behind him and I'm left alone with my executioner. Damn, I wish I had the use of my hands. I could take this guy, I know I could. Just give me a fair fight. *Please*.

Putnik slowly removes his jacket. Underneath he's wearing a T-shirt. He opens his gym bag and removes a roll of tape, the kind boxers wrap around their fists before stuffing them inside their gloves. I watch as he methodically covers his hands and every now and then punches the palm of one hand with the fist of the other. He then takes out a couple of knives. One is long and slender, like a stiletto. The other is clearly a Rambo knife the size of an American bowie. He places these on the floor next to the bag. Then he looks at me, smiles, and nods his head. He's ready.

I waste no time. I leap from the bunk and ram my head into his stomach, throwing him against the wall with a loud *clang*. Not stopping there, I kick him repeatedly until he manages to grab my bare foot and twist it sharply. It happens to be the ankle I sprained a week ago and the pain surges back. I can't help yelling as I fall to the floor.

Putnik stands and is no longer smiling. He moves forward and delivers a fast kick to my weakened, sore stomach. The pain is immense and it effectively paralyzes me for several seconds. Putnik walks around me, obviously intending to draw out the punishment as promised. But just as he's standing directly behind me, I recover enough to roll over onto my back and jab my feet into his crotch. The man cries out and twists away, holding onto his groin as if I'd set it on fire. I grin in satisfaction as I pull myself up and face him, ready to attempt a side kick to his chest. But he's ready for me; Putnik lashes out, growling like a wild animal. His eyes widen with madness, drawing further comparisons to old photos of Rasputin. The assassin leaps at me with the speed of a tiger and we both fall to the floor. His hands are around my neck as I try to buck him off. With my own hands tied, all I can do is jerk my upper body like a fish out of water and hope for the best.

Then, as if storm clouds suddenly decided to open and release a torrential rain, the high-pitched whine of an incoming missile fills the air. This is followed by an explosion that rocks the building so hard that Putnik falls over.

For a moment the two of us remain frozen. Then we hear gunfire outside. Shouts and screams. Then more gunfire. Putnik stands and raps on the door. No one comes to open it and he looks worried.

Another incoming shriek is even louder than the first. This time the temporary building we're in is hit dead-on. It's like being in the center of a vacuum—it feels as if the very air around you is imploding and your physical surroundings have ceased to be solid. I experience the sensation of falling but there's nowhere to descend. All I know is the world around me no longer exists and smoke and flames have replaced it.

# — *36* ————————————

**DAZED,** I kick rubble off of me and attempt to assess the damage. The smells of gunpowder and burning metal are the first things I'm aware of. Then I see the blue sky and white clouds above me and realize the building I was in has been blown to bits. I'm covered in ash, pieces of steel and aluminum, and chips of concrete, but my body appears to be unharmed, I think. But my hands are still tied, damn it.

There's more gunfire all around me. I see Chinese men running, shooting at soldiers. These men are not dressed in uniforms but rather in clothing you'd expect guerilla fighters to wear. Their heads are wrapped with red scarves.

Civilians! Civilians have attacked the base!

I roll over and brush against a jagged edge of metal that cuts into my arm. After cursing for a moment, I get an idea. I position myself in front of the sharp edge so that it rests against my wrists. As carefully as I can, I rub my wrists up and down against the serrated metal and allow it to dig into the cords that have bound my hands for a week. I manage to slice my skin a bit while doing so but I'm willing to with-stand a few seconds of discomfort to be free. A minute later and the cord snaps loose. My arms groan with pain when I move them in front of me for the first time in days. It hurts so good—the relief is unbearably sweet. The cuts and nicks are bleeding all over the place but I don't give a damn.

I push the rest of the rubble off and sit up. That's when I see Yvan Putnik lying under a piece of concrete support. He doesn't look too good.

The gunfire draws closer and I see a squad of soldiers retreating and firing at a group of the civilian warriors. The army seems to be no match for the newcomers. The civil-ians appear to be well armed and relentless. One of them carries a pennant on a stick and then I understand what's going on. I recognize the Chinese characters on the pen-nant as the sign of the Lucky Dragons. Jon Ming listened to me after all. The Triad finally came to try to stop Gen-eral Tun. I just hope they're not too late.

Putnik groans and moves. Being the compassionate son of a bitch that I am, I lift the pylon off of him and slap his face a little.

"Hey!" I shout. "You all right?" Then I remember to speak Russian, so I do. Putnik opens his eyes and looks past me. He's having trouble focusing. Finally, recognition sets in and he actually *snarls* at me.

With an unexpected burst of energy, Putnik brutally jabs his knee into my side. I gasp in pain and fall back onto burning wood and metal. I scorch my back and roll off in alarm. Putnik pulls himself to his feet, brushes off the soot, and comes at me. Krav Maga teaches you to fight as if your life depended on winning. If that means you have to fight dirty, then so be it. There are no rules in Krav Maga.

Therefore I grab a piece of the burning timber beside me and hurl it into Putnik's face. It shatters and he recoils, clutching his eyes. Ignoring the ache in my side, I manage to stand and deliver a ferocious kick to his abdomen. The Russian doubles over, still blinded by the fiery splinters in his eyes. His position allows me to grab him from behind and apply a choke hold to his neck. Putnik struggles against me as I lift him off the ground by his head. I tighten the grip around his throat and whisper in Russian, "This is for Katia, you bastard."

The man jerks and kicks like a wild beast but I don't loosen the vise. After all the pain I've suffered in the last week, his clumsy attempts at self-defense are trivial. Finally, after thirty or forty seconds, the killer weakens. His struggles become slower and less effective until eventually he collapses in my arms. Then, for good measure, I twist his head sharply. The sound of bones cracking is music to my ears. I let him go and the corpse crumples to the ground like a rag doll.

The base is in shambles. I'm not sure what the Triad hit it with but they've got some heavy-duty firepower. It's ironic that most of it came from the Shop. I make my way out of the rubble and realize I must be an incongruous sight. I'm barefoot, wearing Chinese pajamas, and I'm bloody and bruised.

Two armed Triads appear in front of me and shout a command. I'm too dazed to understand. I try to tell him in the best Chinese I can speak that I'm an American captive. They don't understand. Then I mention the words, "Cho Kun, Jon Ming," and their eyes light up. They nod enthusiastically and motion for me to follow. I can barely walk so one of them lets me lean on him a little. We move toward the beach, where the submarine pens are in flames. A group of Triads are standing outside the unharmed command post and waving automatic rifles in the air. They shout something that resembles a victory cry. The mass of men parts and I see Jon Ming standing in the middle and pointing a handgun at the head of another man who is on his knees. The prisoner is Andrei Zdrok.

Ming sees me and grins. The Triads all turn and look at me as I approach. Zdrok eyes me with fear and hate. His expensive suit is covered in soot and grime, and one of the sleeves is nearly torn off his arm. There's a gash above his eyebrow but otherwise he looks none the worse for wear.

"You look terrible, Mr. Fisher," Ming says.

"I feel terrible," I answer. "Thank you for coming."

"It is our pleasure. Look what we have here. What shall I do with him, Mr. Fisher?" Ming asks.

"Was he armed?"

"Only with this." Ming shows me the pair of brass knuckles that Zdrok used to make mincemeat of my stomach. I take them and slip them on my right hand. Zdrok's eyes widen and he shakes his head.

"No! No!" he cries.

I slug Zdrok as hard as I can, crushing his nose and possibly fracturing the bone beneath it. The man screams and falls to the ground. The Triads cheer.

"He's all yours," I tell Ming as I let the brass knuckles fall to the ground.

Exhausted and weak, I push my way into the command post to see what's left of it. The place is littered with bodies and the equipment has been destroyed. The body of Mason Hendricks lies awkwardly on the floor, his torso riddled with bullet holes. Close to him is Oskar Herzog, also perforated in a dozen places. His body is draped over the smashed control panel that might have disabled the MRUUV.

I press the implant in my throat and say, "Colonel, if you're there, I really need to talk to you." But all I receive is silence. "Colonel Lambert? Coen? Anyone?"

I collapse into a chair as a wave of nausea and dizziness overwhelms me. I'm about to lose consciousness when Ming comes in and squats beside me.

"Mr. Fisher," he says. "Americans are here. They're looking for you."

•

ONCE again I sleep through a series of transitions. My dreams are troubled and feverish. Part of the time I believe I'm back in Towson, Maryland, working out in the gym or practicing Krav Maga with Katia. Then I'm teaching a very young Sarah how to swim in the military base's pool in Germany. Images of Andrei Zdrok and Yvan Putnik interrupt the serenity and suddenly I'm dodging bullets. The final part of it is terrifying. I dream that Third Echelon has Protocol Sixed me and left me to rot in a Chinese prison. I see myself growing old and thin, wasting away until finally there's no reason for me to keep living.

And then I wake up. The first thing my eyes focus upon is the face of Colonel Irving Lambert. He has a goofy grin on his face and he says, "There you are. Welcome aboard, Sam."

My tongue feels heavy and my mouth is dry. "Hi," I say. What did he mean by *aboard*? Then I'm vaguely aware of a gentle rocking motion. "Where the hell am I?"

"You're aboard the USNS *Fisher*," he answers. The *Fisher*? How appropriate. I recall it's one of Military Sealift Command's LMSRs, a large, medium-speed, roll-on, roll-off navy ship, mostly used for transporting armies, equipment, and vehicles. "How long have I been here?" I ask.

"About eight hours. We flew you to Hawaii yesterday afternoon and gave you a sedative to help you sleep. We then dropped you onto the *Fisher* a few hours later and here we are."

"Where are we going?"

"California. We're three hours away. How are you feeling?"

I take stock of my body. There are aches and pains everywhere. My stomach is the worst but it doesn't seem as bad as it was.

"Okay, I guess." I try to sit up and realize I've got an IV in my hand and there's a tight bandage wrapped around my middle. "What's going on?"

"We're building up your strength, Sam. You were dehydrated and had gone without substantial nourishment for what, a week?"

"Something like that."

"You'll be happy to know that your insides are all right. Nothing badly damaged. You had a ruptured peritoneum but by some miracle you didn't develop peritonitis. The doc says you should have received a very bad case of it and perhaps even died, but someone upstairs is looking after you, Sam. The tear in the peritoneum began to heal on its own and you're well on the way to recovery. Doc says it's most likely due to your healthy lifestyle, the fact that your abdominal muscles are in tip-top shape and you do a million sit-ups a day, or whatever it is you do. You're living proof that exercise and diet can save your life. What happened to you, anyway?"

"Andrei Zdrok punched me in the stomach with brass knuckles."

Lambert almost laughed. "I understand you paid him back with interest."

"Yeah? What's happened to him?"

"The Chinese have him in custody. He's in a hospital in Fuzhou and probably not a very good one. You messed him up pretty bad, Sam. The front of his facial bone plate is broken and the orbit of his right eye dropped. If he doesn't die then he'll stand trial for terrorism and espionage in China. He and Eddie Wu, too. They caught him trying to run away from General Tun's base."

"Wait. What happened at the base? The Triad—"

"Your little talk with the head of the Lucky Dragons apparently did some good. The Triad brought an army of three hundred men up from Hong Kong and bombed the place with some Stinger missiles and mortars before rushing in and taking it over. Of course by then most of Tun's men had already moved out. The Lucky Dragons didn't know it, but the Chinese army was three miles away, standing ready for orders from Beijing to do something about General Tun. Those orders never came. When our spy satellites picked up on what was going on, the CIA got together a crew posing as a Red Cross team. They asked for and received permission from China to do a reconnaissance flight over the base for the sole purpose of locating you. We knew you were still alive. Those implants told us that."

"Why didn't you get a message to me? Colonel, I thought I had been . . . I thought you had abandoned me."

"Sam, I won't lie to you," Lambert says. "We almost activated Protocol Six. If Tun had attacked Taiwan and forced us into a skirmish with China, then that's what would have happened all right. We would never have been able to get you out. We couldn't communicate with you because Mason Hendricks was monitoring our transmissions. We had to stay silent. I'm sorry, Sam."

I nod and shrug. "And the Triad?"

"Most of them got away. When they attacked the encampment, Beijing gave the orders for the Chinese forces to storm the base. That happened shortly after the CIA got you out. The Triad dispersed because technically they're traitors. It's a very strange situation. We think China wants General Tun to fail in a big way before he attacks Taiwan so they don't have to lose face in stopping him. If he doesn't mess up, then they'll have to appear as if they're supporting their general. The hard-liners in Beijing agree with Tun's motives. Anyway, some of the Triads were caught and will most likely be tried for treason."

"What about Jon Ming?"

"As far as we know he got away."

"And nothing has happened in Taiwan?"

"Not yet. It's been a standstill for twenty-four hours. Tun has threatened us with his nuke off the coast of California—he won't say where exactly. I'm hoping you have some things to tell us."

"That I do." I proceed to relate everything I learned. That Tun's submarine launched three MRUUVs off the coast of Los Angeles. One of them is armed with the nuke. Since the control panel at the base in Fuzhou is destroyed, the MRUUVs are operated solely from the sub. Lambert confirms that the U.S. was aware of the Chinese sub when it approached American waters but now it's moved out to international waters where it can't be touched. However, Naval Sea Systems Command provided Anna Grimsdottir with all of Professor Jeinsen's MRUUV specifications. She's currently working on how the guidance system can be altered if the correct "barracuda" can be found. Certain satellite technology will be instrumental in locating them in the water.

"And what are we going to do with those fuckers when we find them?" I ask.

Lambert winks at me. "Let me ask the doc if you can get out of bed. I have something to show you."


THE LMSR is Military Sealift Command's newest class of ship and provides afloat prepositioning of a heavy brigade's equipment and a corps' combat support, as well as surge capability for lift of a heavy division's equipment from the United States. LMSRs can carry an entire U.S. Army Task Force, including fifty-eight tanks, forty-eight other track vehicles, plus more than nine hundred trucks and other wheeled vehicles. The ship carries vehicles and equipment to support humanitarian missions as well as combat missions. The new construction vessels have a cargo carrying capacity of more than 380,000 square feet, equivalent to almost eight football fields. In addition, LMSRs have a slewing stern ramp and a removable ramp that services two side ports, making it easy to drive vehicles on and off the ship. Interior ramps between decks ease traffic flow once cargo is loaded aboard ship. Two 110-ton single-pedestal twin cranes make it possible to load and unload cargo where shoreside infrastructure is limited or nonexistent. A commercial helicopter deck is used for emergency daytime landing, which was how I was brought aboard. The *Fisher* is a prime specimen of an LMSR.

After the doc removes my IV and clears me to leave sick bay, Lambert leads me through a dozen passageways and hatches to one of the storage decks. Aside from an assorted allotment of military vehicles, I see three strange-looking contraptions that look like wet bikes from the future. Lambert speaks to a crewman, who turns on some lights so we can examine one of the devices up close.

"This is what the U.S. Navy calls a CHARC," Lambert

says, pronouncing the word as "Shark." "Or, to be more specific, a Covert High-speed Attack and Reconnaissance Craft. Have you heard about it?"

"I vaguely remember reading about it being developed," I say. "Tell me more."

"Lockheed-Martin designed and developed it to protect the navy's surface vessels from high-speed armed boats and submarines. Ideally the CHARC will help provide a lethal response for some of the emerging littoral threats that face naval forces today, including small-boat swarm attacks and diesel-electric submarines. Remember what happened to the USS *Cole*? The creation of the CHARC is a direct response to that incident."

"It looks awesome," I say. And it does. The CHARC is about twelve meters long and consists of two levels of hydroplanes topped by the actual boat in which one or two men can ride. "I imagine it's portable?"

"That it is. The entire thing can be collapsed to fit into a 3.6-by-3.6-by-12-meter box and transported on deck or in a cargo hold. Think of it like an attack helicopter, only it's in the water on a high-speed platform that uses SWATH, or Small Waterplane Area Twin Hull, technology. It's small and stealthy and is plated with bulletproof material. It can attack on a moment's notice using an array of Hellfire missiles, twenty-millimeter guns, forty-millimeter grenade launchers, and torpedoes. We added drop-mines that will sink to the bottom of the sea and knock out anything in their paths. The navy will use it to loiter, patrol, and attack in shallow littoral waters. What's really nice is that it sits low in the water for long periods and can then pop up and dash to suspected threats when speed is needed. And it's fast, too."

I run my hand along the side of it. "Very nice," I say.

"Now here's where it gets interesting," Lambert says. "The designers installed several intelligence-gathering tools that are helpful to us. For one thing it has mine-hunting capability—it'll sniff out and destroy mines as it encounters them in shallow water. By the same token it can detect other objects and zero in on radiation. The Geiger counter and sonar equipment will let the rider know when he's on top of dangerous material or even vehicles."

"So it'll find the MRUUVs."

"Precisely. Another cool feature is the homing beacon. The pilot wears it in his belt, so if he leaves the CHARC for any reason, such as a dive, the CHARC will follow him along the surface on automatic."

"Damn, it's like a loyal dog. Great, let me at 'em," I say. "You have the owner's manual handy?"

"Whoa, hold on, Sam. You're not well enough to do this. I was just showing you—"

"What do you mean I'm not well enough? Are you out of your mind?" He can't keep me out of the fight. Not now. Not after what I've been through.

"Sam, we have some Navy SEALS aboard. They're going to pilot the CHARCs."

"I'm a Navy SEAL, too, Colonel. You know damn well that I have to do this. I *need* to do this."

"It's been more than twenty years since you were a Navy SEAL, Sam. And you just got up from a hospital bed. Be realistic! We're going to have to launch these things at sunrise. That's only four hours from now."

"Oh, come on, Colonel! You know I can do this. I'm *fine*. I feel great. You know me." I didn't feel great but I wasn't about to let someone else do this job.

"Sam, if we find the MRUUVs, it's going to take someone to dive down there and disarm the bomb. That means scuba gear and the works. You're just not up for it. You're not healed. The mission is too important. I'm sorry, Sam."

I don't know what to say. I'm so angry I could slug the

guy but of course I'm not going to do that. Deep down I know he's right. If I were in his shoes I'd make the same call. With a sigh I simply nod my head and walk away.

"Sam . . ."

"It's okay, Colonel. Just have someone show me to my quarters, if I have any."


A loud knock on my compartment door disturbs my sleep. At first I think the bulkhead is collapsing but then my senses spin me back to reality. I turn on the overhead light above my bunk and say, "Come." The digital clock tells me I've been asleep for two hours.

Colonel Lambert takes a step into the small quarters and says, "Sorry to disturb you, Sam. May I come in?"

"Sure." I sit up and rub my eyes. "What's up?"

Lambert sits on the end of the bunk and replies, "I've come to eat crow. And apologize."

I wait for him to go on.

"One of our Navy SEALS . . . he . . . well, hell, he's got goddamned *food poisoning*. Or something. He's throwing up every half hour and is running a temperature. Doc says it's either food poisoning or a stomach virus. That, uh, leaves a vacant seat on one of the CHARCs."

I'm suddenly wide awake. "Are you telling me . . . ?"

"The job's yours if you still want it, Sam."

"Of course I still want it!"

"Get dressed and meet me on the same deck where we were earlier. You'll suit up in diving gear and we'll run you through the basics on how to operate the CHARC. We're an hour outside of Los Angeles so we'll be launching as soon as we can." He stands and goes for the door. "I just hope I don't regret this."

"Don't worry, Colonel," I say. "And thanks."

\* \* \*

**THE** two Navy SEALS are young guys—well, young compared to me—named Lieutenant Junior Grade Max Carlson and Ensign Ben Stanley. When I walk onto the deck I can feel the skepticism oozing from them. They look at me as if to say, "Who the hell is this old guy?" I introduce myself and shake hands with both of them and they reply politely, but I can tell they are not happy about me joining the team.

Colonel Lambert stands on the sidelines trying to be as unobtrusive as possible while the commanding officer, Lieutenant Don Van Fleet, welcomes me and then addresses the three of us.

"Men, we don't have much time. I just received word that Taiwan has been attacked. Our forces are holding back until we find that nuke and neutralize it. So for every minute that goes by, more Taiwanese are dying. I understand that General Tun's forces bombed Taipei with a warning volley to get the Taiwan government to surrender. Of course they refused. A sea assault followed and now Tun's armies are storming the island's beaches. It's not pretty, especially with our navy sitting there with thumbs up their asses. Lieutenant Carlson, I'm giving you five minutes to teach Mr. Fisher everything he needs to know about the CHARC. We launch two minutes after that. Before I turn over the floor to Colonel Lambert, are there any questions?"

We shake our heads. Lambert steps forward and says, "You've been supplied with schematics of the MRUUVs. The CHARCs' reconnaissance capabilities have been set for picking up metal that measures the approximate size of what we believe the MRUUVs to be. In addition, the Geiger range depth has been set to fifty feet below the surface. Hopefully the damned things aren't swimming deeper than that because we lose effectiveness beyond fifty feet. Your best tool will be the sonar, which will give a return of any object of that size. Unfortunately you'll probably also pick up sea life—sharks, maybe some dolphins, but hopefully no whales. The NSA is monitoring three suspect areas of the coast. According to some initial readings from some of our intelligence buoys we've narrowed the logical points of interest to Santa Monica and Venice, Marina Del Rey, and Playa Del Rey. From a tactical standpoint, we believe these three areas make the most sense for targets. Lieutenant Carlson, you'll patrol Playa Del Rey. Ensign Stanley, you'll cover Marina Del Rey. Fisher, you've got Santa Monica and Venice.

"Once you've located a possible MRUUV, you'll have to put the CHARC on automatic standby and take a dive to confirm. Make sure your homing beacons are working. Once you've confirmed you have an MRUUV, you report in and we'll give you further instructions. Any questions?"

Carlson speaks up. "Sir, is it possible this bomb will go off while we're there?"

Lambert replies, "General Tun has said that he'll detonate the nuke only if his forces are attacked by anyone outside of Taiwan. But you never know. There's always that risk."

Stanley asks, "Will we have to disarm the bomb?"

"My team in Washington is working on that. What we do when we find the bomb will depend on a number of factors. Just report in when you've found it."

There aren't any more questions, so we go to it. Carlson reluctantly takes me through the CHARC's controls and it seems pretty straightforward. Anyone who has operated a wet bike should be able to handle it. I'm also issued standard SEAL diving equipment. Along with a military wet suit, I have an upgraded LAR-V (Mod 2) rebreather with a large oxygen gas cylinder, a military diver broad that integrates with a compact depth gauge, a G-shock watch, an underwater compass, and a built-in adjustable chem-light holder. I try on a new Aqua Sphere SEAL diving mask that is supposedly leak-free and surprisingly comfortable; AMPHIB boots, which are all-terrain multifunctional boots that work well in and out of water; Rocket II fins that are designed to be worn over the boots; and HellStorm NaviGunner water ops gloves. We each have a single tank of air and a tool belt containing various items we might need when we encounter an MRUUV.

The CHARCs are lowered into the water with each of us sitting in our respective vehicle. Like the MRUUVs, a CHARC uses SWATH technology to propel it. SWATH gives a craft the ability to deliver big-ship platform steadiness and ride quality in a smaller vessel and the capability to sustain a high proportion of its normal cruising speed in rough head seas. The waterplane is the horizontal-plane cross-section of a ship's hull at the water surface. Thus, the CHARC has two submarinelike lower hulls completely submerged below the surface; above the surface the CHARC resembles a catamaran with a wet bike on top of it. Ship motions are caused by the waves on the ocean surface, which produce forces on the hull that decrease rapidly as the hull is moved farther below the surface, as with a submarine. Wave-exciting forces can also be made smaller if the amount of waterplane area at the design waterline is decreased. However, the objective of SWATH is not to minimize ship motions at the expense of speed/power or payload capabilities. Instead, the relative proportions for the strut waterplane area and submerged hulls are selected to reduce motions and accelerations well below accepted criteria for seasickness or onset of degraded performance of personnel or equipment. All SWATH crafts will have less than 50 percent as much waterplane area as a monohull of equal displacement.

We never had cool toys like these when I was a SEAL!

The weather is typical southern California—breezy, sunny, scattered clouds. The sun hasn't been up too long and it's still winter, so riding at a fast speed would be quite chilly if I wasn't protected from the elements. The driver's seat is inside a bulletproofed canopy so there's a bit of a jet cockpit feel to it. It's soundproofed, too, so all you hear is a pleasant *whir* that could easily lull you to sleep if you were so inclined. The controls are brightly lit and intuitive; a monkey could pilot the thing. And best of all it smells like the interior of a new car. I love it!

The CHARC handles so smoothly that it's hard to believe I'm on the surface of the Pacific. The water is choppy but the CHARC seems to glide right over it. Before long I'm within a mile of the Santa Monica Pier and I can see the Ferris wheel and other amusements glistening in the early dawn. I reduce speed and concentrate on what the instruments are telling me. There are schools of fish moving underneath me. A large stationary metal object lies at the bottom, most likely a sunken speedboat.

"I'm in position," I say into the intercom. The two SEALS and I are hooked up to a ComLink originating at the *Fisher*. Lambert and the Third Echelon team in Washington are also monitoring the mission through my implants. I guess I'd better watch my language.

"Roger that," Carlson says. "I'll be in my position in about twenty seconds."

"Same here," echoes Stanley.

And so it begins. The search is tedious and painstaking. After thirty minutes all three of us comment on how the job is like trying to find a needle in a haystack. Each of our sections encompasses thirty or forty square miles of ocean.

"Colonel, is there any chance of getting more men and CHARCs to help with the search?" I ask.

"We've already tried, Sam," he says. "More are on the way but by the time they get here it will be noon."

"I'm afraid it's going to take us longer than that just to locate something worth diving for."

"Just keep looking."

Anna Grimsdottir comes on the line and says, "Our intel buoys have picked up a total of sixteen objects that might be MRUUVs in the three sectors. I'll give each of you the coordinates for your respective sector. At this point it's difficult for us to tell if they're moving or not. You'll have to determine that."

She gives the three of us separate coordinates to check out. It takes me three minutes to guide the CHARC to my first one only to find that the object is stationary. Another sunken wreck. Grimsdottir calls out the next location, which turns out to be a mile closer to shore. I reach it in forty seconds and once again am disappointed by the discovery.

This process continues for the next hour until finally Stanley calls out, "Hey! I think I have one." Grimsdottir quizzes him on some of the instrument readings and he answers promisingly. The object is moving with the speed of a barracuda and is the correct size and shape. "I'm going for a dive," he says. Carlson and I continue our search as we wait with anticipation for good news. Six minutes pass and finally Stanley's voice rings in our ears.

"Affirmative," he says. "It's an MRUUV." Grimsdottir asks him about Geiger readings, but this time his answers are negative. There's no indication that this is the one with the bomb.

"Blow it out of the water," Lieutenant Van Fleet commands. Stanley confirms the order and tells us that he's activating the drop-mines. They're powerful explosives but nothing so serious that he'd be in danger by being on top of them.

"Mines released," he says, and we wait for the sound of fireworks.

But the tremendous noise we hear in our headsets is shocking, overamplified, and distorted. After a few seconds we hear nothing but static. Then everyone talks at once.

"Stanley? Ensign Stanley?"

"Oh, my God!"

"What happened?"

"Did you see that?"

"That geyser was sixty feet high!"

Lieutenant Van Fleet quiets everyone down and says, "I'm afraid the MRUUV was booby-trapped with a powerful explosive. When Stanley's mines hit it, the MRUUV blew the CHARC to pieces."

Well. I guess that's going to change our strategy.

# 38

"I just received word from the White House," Colonel Lambert announces to me through the implants. The other SEAL can't hear him. "The president is going to issue the go command in thirty minutes whether or not we find the nuke. People in Taiwan are dying and General Tun's forces are on the outskirts of Taipei. The president is going to call Tun's bluff."

"Won't China protect their general?" I ask.

"That we don't know. The vice president is in seclusion with China's president in Beijing. We're not privy to what communications are going back and forth between Beijing and Washington. The bottom line is we have thirty minutes."

"Then get Anna to give me and Carlson something to work with."

"I'm working on it, Sam," Grimsdottir cuts in. "I'm tracking two possibilities in your sector and one in Lieutenant Carlson's sector. Give me five minutes to narrow them down to the best choice." She sounds calm and collected in a stressful situation that would have anyone else at the breaking point.

The CHARC purrs closer to Santa Monica Pier as I study the sonar screen for anything unusual. Fish set off minor readings every few seconds. There's a lot of junk down there that causes the metal detector to jump continuously. I'm beginning to understand the various meter levels and what they might mean so I don't spend too much time looking at something that turns out to be nothing.

"Sam, I have coordinates for you." Grimsdottir reads them out and says, "Something's in motion there and it's bigger than what you've seen so far."

"I'm on my way."

I guide the CHARC about four hundred yards to the south and watch the screens for any blips. Sure enough, there's something down there. It's metal, it's moving at a slow speed, it's about six feet long and approximately three feet wide. More promising is the fact that the Geiger counter is going nuts. I snap some sonar pictures of it and transmit them to Third Echelon, all the while staying above the thing. I reckon the speed to be about fifteen knots and at that rate it'll be very near the shore in less than a half hour.

"Take a dive, Sam," Lambert says. "Anna thinks that's it."

"Roger that."

I put the CHARC on idle, lower the face mask, and insert the rebreather into my mouth. The backward dive off the vehicle pulls on my abdomen, which delivers a jolt of pain through the sore spots, but I ignore it and allow myself to descend. It's been a while since I've been diving. It's a lot like riding a bike, though—you never forget how.

The water here is murky and not very clean. L.A. must have one of the most polluted shorelines in the world, yet people swim in it all the time. This far out I would have expected it to be a little clearer but no such luck.

I switch on my lamp and shine the beam across the
ocean floor until it finds the object. Sure enough, it's an
MRUUV, just like the one I saw in the submarine pen in
China. It's an odd thing to see down here. The device is
shiny silver with several indicator lights burning brightly
along the side. My earlier thought that it looks similar to a
giant cigar tube is even more apropos down here.

I quickly surface, climb aboard the CHARC, and transmit my message. "You're right, Anna. I've got one. And the
Geiger is about to jump out of its skin."

"Excellent," Lambert says. "Stay on top of it, Sam.
Stand by until we figure out what we want to do about the
damned thing."

"Well, hurry up. I'm not very fond of nuclear enemas."

A few minutes go by and Anna says, "Sam, can you
hear me when you're underwater?"

"Yes."

"Then go on back down."

Another backflip off the CHARC and I'm below the
surface. I break open a chem-light and place it in the holder
so I can see what's in front of me.

She continues. "Sam, I want you to swim alongside the
MRUUV and look for something. Tap your OPSAT to let
me know you're there."

I keep up the pace, swimming four feet above and parallel to the device, then push a button on the OPSAT.

"Okay, good. Now, do you see the rectangular panel on
the top? It should be directly behind the antenna in the
front." I see it. The lid is roughly two feet by one foot.

AFFIRMATIVE, I type.

"Right. Now get on top of the thing like you're riding
a motorcycle. You're going to have to unscrew that
panel."

*Ride it?* Is she kidding? The other one blew up beneath

poor Ensign Stanley. How do I know just touching the damned thing isn't going to set it off? I tap out the question on the OPSAT.

"Sam, it won't blow up just by touching it. It's got to be protected against minor bumps and scrapes down there. The thing's probably collided into a rock or two since being launched from the sub. Not to mention fish or other plant life. Go ahead, you'll be okay."

Fine. I swim a little faster so that I'm gliding evenly with the thing, then I reach down and grab the front end. I try not to flinch when I do so and thankfully "the Barracuda" just keeps purring along. I let it pull me through the water for a few seconds and then I lower myself onto its back. I'm now riding it as if it was a dolphin.

AFFIRMATIVE.

"Good. Now get that panel off. It's the only way to get to the booby trap and, if I'm not mistaken, also to the guidance system controls and the bomb."

I take a screwdriver from my utility belt and begin to work. The panel is lined with twelve screws; so it takes a few minutes to get them all off. I put them in a pouch on the belt in case I need them again later. The panel comes off and I hold it in one hand. In order to work with both hands I have to grip the MRUUV with my thighs.

"You can let go of the panel. You're not going to need it again." Okay, so I let it float away. I indicate that it's off and she says, "Good. Now look carefully inside the compartment. I assume you have a chem-light? You should see plastic explosive attached to the inner surface, probably encased in waterproof material. It's probably brick shaped and has wires coming out of it."

I would have found it without her description. Recognizing explosives is part of my job. In fact, I'm pretty sure I can dismantle the thing without her instructions. It's pretty straightforward. "What you need to do is determine which is the positive lead and which is the negative lead. The wires go to a—"

AFFIRMATIVE.

"Oh, okay, you know what you're doing. Sorry."

It's a simple matter of disconnecting the explosive from the igniter. There's probably a sensor located somewhere in the device that tells the igniter to do its business but I don't have to worry about that. With a pair of wire cutters, I snip the appropriate leads and that should do the trick.

AFFIRMATIVE.

"Good. Now you should be able to get to the guidance system controls. Do you see what looks like a closed laptop inside the compartment?"

AFFIRMATIVE.

"See if you can open it."

I do. It's exactly like a laptop computer, complete with keyboard and monitor. A screen saver displaying Chinese characters and a GyroTechnics logo flashes on.

"All right, now you need to get into the main menu. Press any key to do so."

AFFIRMATIVE.

It asks for a password. She tells me the password is "Taiwan000" and I type it in. I'm amazed that she knows that. It appears that Anna Grimsdottir is back in action.

"Sorry to interrupt, folks, but I have some news." It's Colonel Lambert. "The thirty-minute time limit has elapsed and the order's been given."

Damn, the time flew by.

"Our forces are attacking General Tun's army at this moment. The navy, the air force, the marines—you name it. They're unleashing hell on Tun's little army."

*Shit!* What does that mean? Is Tun going to set off the bomb?

"Keep working, Sam," Grimsdottir says calmly. "Tun

will have to get a message to the submarine and give the order to blow the nuke. They're not going to do it without his say-so."

I hope you're right, sister. Okay, let's keep going. She instructs me how to get into the programmer's main menu. Everything is in Chinese so it's a little more difficult for me. Grimsdottir's Chinese is "fair" and mine is "okay" so together that makes a "pretty good," right? Accurately translating these commands is essential.

Once I'm inside she relays a series of coded commands. It's tough typing on the keyboard while riding the MRUUV in cloudy water. The chem-light is sufficient but with the gloves and everything else, it's easy to make errors. I have to use the backspace key several times during the course of typing. Finally I've got it all in and press Enter. The screen changes and there are several options available, all in Chinese.

"You'll need to select the option that says 'Course' or 'Direction,' something like that."

AFFIRMATIVE. I find the one that translates to 'Heading,' and select that. This takes me to a screen displaying the current course in common submariner terminology.

Then something odd happens. A red light illuminates within the compartment and starts to flash slowly and repeatedly. I tell Grimsdottir this and she says, "Oh, no. If it's what I think it means, then they've activated the nuke. Sam, do you see any kind of digital readout inside there? Something that looks like a clock counting down?"

*I hate clocks that count DOWN!* Yes, I see it. It must have started at 10:00, for now it's at 9:52 and decreasing a second at a time.

"Okay, Sam, you've got a little time but you have to work fast. The MRUUV is equipped with an automatic diagnostics program that checks the entire system to make sure the bomb goes off properly. It takes roughly ten minutes to go through all the tests and as soon as it's done, the bomb will explode. Try to ignore the countdown and go back to the laptop. I want you to type in these new course headings." She gives them to me and I try to enter the data, but I keep punching the wrong keys. Damned gloves. I finally pull them off so my fingers can be a little more accurate. The water is cold but not unbearable. I'm sure, though, that if I'm in the water for too long my hands will stiffen from the low temperature.

I finally get the new course heading entered but it suddenly changes back to the original!

*What the hell?*

I tell Grimsdottir this and she says, "Damn, it's the control on the submarine. They see what you see on their monitor and realize someone's tampering with the guidance system. I have to figure out a way to cut them out. Stand by."

*Stand by?* The fucking nuclear bomb is ticking and the clock now reads 8:43! The Barracuda is on a steady course right for Santa Monica Pier and I'm sitting on the goddamned thing.

I type into my OPSAT: IS THERE A WAY TO DEFUSE THE BOMB?

Grimsdottir replies, "Not in this amount of time, Sam. Hush, let me think."

All right, now I'm considering what kind of damage a nuclear bomb will do if it explodes out here in Santa Monica Bay. I'm just guessing, but I would say half of Los Angeles would be gone in an instant. Hollywood, Beverly Hills, Santa Monica, Venice—*poof!* Millions dead. The nation's economy in chaos, which of course dominoes into the world's economy being in turmoil. World War III with China.

I can't let this happen.

"Sam! I want you to type in exactly what I tell you to," Grimsdottir says. "Make sure it's correct before you press

Enter." It's long and it's complicated but I do it. It seems like it takes forever. I indicate that I'm done and she reads it again slowly so I can proof what I've typed. I hit Enter and a bunch of code appears on the monitor at a high rate of speed. After ten seconds of this, the screen goes blank.

No! Is it dead? What happened?

I begin to type on the OPSAT and tell her what's going on but Grimsdottir beats me to it and says, "You should have a blank screen when it's done processing."

Fuck, I wish she'd told me that before.

AFFIRMATIVE.

"Good. Now let's go back to the course settings menu and retype the new coordinates." I follow her instructions and repeat what I did earlier. This time the new settings stay on the screen. We've successfully shut out the Chinese sub's control.

The MRUUV suddenly begins to turn in a wide arc. I ride along with it as the device makes a U-turn and heads away from shore. But it's going too damn slow and I tell Grimsdottir this.

"Then we'll have to increase its speed. Go back to the main menu, can you do that?"

The clock reads 4:35. Now I'm getting nervous. I bungle the first try and end up back at the course settings menu. A second attempt gets me to the main menu and I'm ready. This time I'm way ahead of Grimsdottir. I see the option for "Speed" and begin to raise the scroll bar.

"Find the option for speed. When you do that . . . oh, I see you're already there. Good work, Sam."

The MRUUV accelerates and becomes much more difficult to hold on to. I glance upward and see the dark shapes of my CHARC's pontoons following along on the surface. The homer beacon is working beautifully.

"See if you can get it up to at least sixty knots. That's what it's going to take to get the thing out of range of the city. You can also direct the nose downward at a twenty-degree angle. That way it'll go deeper, which is what we want."

I use the touch-pad cursor and manage to steer the Barracuda into a dive but the damned thing is moving too slowly. Something's hanging up the computer.

The clock reads 3:20.

"You've got it to forty knots, Sam. You're almost there."

The speed is doing a number on me now. My legs are beginning to ache from holding on so tightly and I have to use one hand to secure myself while the other one works the computer.

"Fifty knots, Sam."

The clock is at 2:48.

Damn, I'm going fast. I'm not sure I can hold on much longer. And what the hell am I going to do when it's at sixty knots? Just jump off? Where am I gonna go?

The clock is at 2:29.

"Sixty! Get off, Sam! Surface and get in your CHARC! Go! Go! Go!"

I release the MRUUV and it cuts through the water ahead of me. Floating stationary for a few seconds, I watch it until it disappears into the murky blue-green darkness.

"Go, Sam, go!"

Her words jolt me out of the temporary haze. I immediately turn and start ascending as hard and fast as I can. Shit, how far am I from the goddamned coastline? I want to ask Grimsdottir if she has a fix on me but I can't afford to stop and type the question. If ever I needed to rely on my Navy SEAL training to save my life, this could be the prize event.

I move closer to the surface where the CHARC's pontoons are resting. As soon as my head is above water I look to see if the coastline is even *visible*. It appears to be a couple of miles away. But I know distances are deceiving when you're in the water. I grab hold of the CHARC's struts, climb aboard, buckle myself in, and close the canopy. It takes five seconds to turn the thing around and open her up to a high speed. Lambert was right, this baby is *fast*! Before long it's going eighty miles an hour.

The shoreline is closer . . . closer . . . I grip the controls and concentrate solely on putting as much distance between that damned bomb and me as possible. The CHARC reaches its limit, practically flying along the surface at eighty-five. The Santa Monica Pier's Ferris wheel looms larger in front of me. I'm almost there . . .

Then it's as if the world collapses around me. A deafening sonic boom literally *pushes* the CHARC forward at what feels like an impossible rate of speed. I'm spinning in total darkness, completely weightless and vulnerable. A painful ringing in my ears won't let up and I'm not sure where I am . . . it's dark . . . and I can't stop spinning . . . and . . .

# 39

THE so-called Battle for Taiwan lasted just under four hours. The first two hours belonged to General Lan Tun and his small but superbly equipped army and navy. While he had sufficient firepower from his destroyers and frigates, the air support he had counted on from the Chinese base in Quanzhou never came. The effects of his ships' bombardment of Taipei were greatly exaggerated in the world media. At first the reports indicated that tens of thousands of people had been killed and the city had been destroyed. In fact, the loss of life numbered in the low hundreds and only 20 percent of the metropolis was hit. By the time all the general's landing craft had brought his army to Taiwan's shores, the island's own forces had gathered en masse to repel the invasion. Tun, aboard one of the Luda-class destroyers in the strait, watched with horror as his plans to conquer the island and become a national hero in the People's Republic diminished with each passing minute.

Then, despite his warnings to the U.S. government that

he had a powerful weapon at his disposal, the American military joined the melee. The navy's ships had been stationed around the island all along, watching and waiting for the moment when those in charge in Washington gave the command to strike. Tun had warned the U.S. that any attempt to stop his invasion would result in the loss of a major American city. For the first two hours of the assault, the Americans did nothing. As soon as it was evident that Tun's army had failed to establish a beachhead, the U.S. destroyers moved in and began to fire at Tun's ships. In actuality, the orders were given to go ahead and strike before the armed MRUUV was found in Santa Monica Bay and just happened to coincide with the first inklings of Tun's defeat.

In a panic, General Tun had issued the orders to the submarine *Mao* to activate the nuclear bomb. The device was programmed to explode after the ten minutes of diagnostic testing was complete. The *Mao*, safely hidden in the deep waters of the Pacific Ocean, had no reason to fear retaliation. All they had to do was make sure the bomb went off.

Thus it was a heart-wrenching blow to General Tun when he learned that the bomb did indeed explode—miles away from the California coast and very deep below the surface. He couldn't understand why the MRUUV hadn't been closer to shore. What had gone wrong? The plan was foolproof. Even though sketchy reports were coming in that as a result of the explosion Los Angeles had suffered an earthquake and considerable damage, nothing along the magnitude Tun had envisioned had taken place.

In a last-ditch appeal, Tun contacted Beijing and asked for support from the rest of the PLA. The Politburo refused to acquiesce. In short, General Tun was on his own. China wasn't going to lift a hand to help or protect him. Several powerful officials in the military protested the Politburo's decision but there was nothing that could be done unless other independent branches of the army joined the battle on

Tun's side. To have done so would have meant political disaster for the generals involved. It became a case of China at first believing her arrogant son was making a risky but necessary challenge to Taiwan, but in the end the child had become an embarrassment and needed to be disowned.

Tun also didn't know that China's president gave the U.S. permission to stop the general. The Politburo had to do so to save face with the rest of the world. Nuclear bombs exploding off the coasts of countries were not acceptable forms of diplomacy. China conveniently blamed General Tun for the "unfortunate incident" and thus sacrificed him to world justice. During the fourth hour of the conflict, the U.S. Navy sank General Tun's Ludo destroyer with torpedoes. The general and his entire command support team went down with the ship. Shortly afterward, his men on the beach were forced into surrendering. American forces joined the Taiwanese in rounding up the surviving army and eventually turned them over to Chinese authorities. Most of them would undergo trials for treason.

While all this was going on, Andrei Zdrok lay in a hospital bed in Fuzhou. He had slipped into a coma shortly after his skull was fractured by Sam Fisher and had remained in critical condition ever since. The medical facilities in Fuzhou were far from adequate even though the doctors did everything in their power to save Zdrok's life. The Chinese government had expressed a fervent desire that the man would answer for his crimes against the country. But it was not to be.

Ironically, Andrei Zdrok died peacefully in bed at the exact moment when the nuclear bomb he had supplied to General Tun exploded off the coast of California. His last great arms deal was, to that extent, a success.

The Shop, however, would no longer be a threat to world peace.

# —40—

ONCE again I wake up in a hospital bed. I have no clue as to how I got here or how much time has elapsed since I was swept away in the aftermath of the explosion. Frankly, now that I think about what happened, it's difficult to believe I'm alive. I note that my arm is in a cast and my hands are covered in gauze. There's an IV stand and the usual clap-trap of machines around the bed. But oddly enough, I feel no pain or discomfort. In fact I feel more rested than I have in weeks. The only minor problem is I feel hungry and my mouth is as dry as cotton.

A young nurse's pretty face comes into view and she smiles. "Hello!" she says. "You're awake! How do you feel?"

My voice comes out sounding like nails on sandpaper. "Okay."

"Let me get the doctor. I'll be right back."

A few minutes go by and a U.S. Air Force doctor enters the room. "Good morning, Mr. Fisher," he says. "I'm Dr. Jenkins. How are you feeling?"

"Okay," I say again. "Thirsty."

"I'll bet you are. Nurse, give Mr. Fisher some water."

She puts a straw to my mouth and I suck the cool, lovely liquid into my throat. It's like heaven. When I'm done, I ask, "Where am I?"

"Edwards Air Force Base," the doctor answers.

"How . . . long have I been here?"

"Three days."

"I've been out for three days?"

"Mostly out. Occasionally you'd wake up for a few minutes at a time in a feverish state. Perfectly natural for someone who went through the kind of trauma you did."

"What happened? I remember the explosion—"

"The protective shell of the CHARC and your scuba equipment saved your life. You rode a tsunami wave as if you were a piece of driftwood and ended up on the beach near Santa Monica Pier. It's a miracle you weren't killed but the CHARC is one tough piece of machinery. All you have to show for it are a broken arm and a lot of bruises and cuts."

"What about . . . what about radiation?"

"Well, that's what we're not sure about but we think it's going to be all right," the doctor says. "The bomb went off deep underwater. Most of the radiation was contained below the surface. A lot of fish have died. Our beaches are littered with thousands of dead sea life—whales, fish, sharks, dolphins—it's tragic. We think the wave you rode in on was well ahead of the spread of radioactivity. The air, ironically enough, is no worse now than it was prior to the explosion."

I shake my head. "Amazing."

"The military picked you up and whisked you away before any news teams got to the beach. No one saw you. Now get some rest, Mr. Fisher. You're going to be fine. I'll have the nurse fix a small meal for you and we'll see how you take it. We've been feeding you intravenously since you were brought in. I'll let Colonel Lambert know you're back in the real world." He pats my shoulder and says, "It's good to have you back. It's no secret around here that you're a hero."

**AFTER** a yummy meal of Jell-O and ginger ale, with promises of a more protein-based lunch of eggs a little later, Colonel Lambert walks into the room. He's all smiles and I'm really glad to see him.

"How are you, Sam?"

"Good, Colonel. I'm almost ready to get out of here."

"Well, you probably need to stay put another day or two. We have to check you out through and through. You were awfully close to a nuclear explosion, you know."

"Yeah. I don't remember much of it, though."

"I bet you have a lot of questions."

"Colonel, I bet you already know what they are, so why don't you fill me in on what's been happening while I've been in never-never land."

Lambert pulls up a chair and sits beside the bed. "To put it bluntly, Sam, you saved Los Angeles. And you've saved Third Echelon."

"What do you mean?"

"We were in danger of losing funding. The Committee in Washington had intimated as such but now they're all conciliatory. Senator Coldwater and the other alphabet agency directors have sent congratulations to us for saving the day. I think the FBI and the CIA are kicking themselves that they didn't get the chance to go after those MRUUVs, which technically is probably the way it should have played out. It just so happened we were there first and we had the intelligence. So, bottom line is you put a feather in our cap, Sam. Thanks."

"Does this mean we can skip my performance evaluation for this year?"

He smiles and continues. "The nuke did some damage, though. Los Angeles experienced an earthquake that was five point three on the Richter. Most of the damage was on the beachfront communities and around LAX. The federal government will be putting together a relief package for those that qualify."

"It could have been worse."

"Definitely. Farther north, a tsunami hit Topanga, Santa Monica, Venice, and Marina Del Rey and that caused a lot of damage as well. We believe that's how you ended up onshore—you must have been in it or on one of the smaller waves that preceded it."

"Where'd they find me? *Who* found me?"

"The coast guard found your CHARC very near Santa Monica Pier right there on the beach. It was pretty banged up but you were snug as a bug inside. Surprisingly, the tsunami receded and didn't leave much flooding except farther north in Topanga State Park. Most of the residential areas between the park and Santa Monica are now wading pools. All in all, the estimated death toll is around five hundred and fifty. There are roughly a hundred missing small craft that were at sea when the bomb went off. I imagine we'll have to write those poor people off, too. They're still taking radiation level readings but it doesn't look as bad as you might think. I imagine the beaches will be closed for a year or so. The economy will be hit and it won't be pretty. But, like you say, it could have been worse. It wasn't as bad as the tsunamis that hit the Indian Ocean a year or so ago. If you hadn't changed the course on that MRUUV, it would have been a completely different story."

It's sobering news and very difficult for me to comprehend that such a fate was in my hands. "How do things stand internationally?"

Lambert tells me how the military conflict in Taiwan turned out and that things are basically back to the status quo between the island and China. As for relations between China and the U.S., it's too early to say.

"China assumes no responsibility for the bomb. They're blaming that entirely on General Tun and the Shop. Of course, Tun is dead and the Shop is no more. So they're convenient scapegoats. I imagine our government will issue some kind of declaration condemning Tun's attack on Taiwan and subtly insinuate that China could have done more to stop him. Anyway, that's not our problem right now. We'll let the elected officials handle that stuff."

"So the Shop is really gone. Hard to believe."

"Yes, but don't go thinking your job is finished, Sam. There are plenty of other enemies in the world."

"Well, I hope you don't mind, but I'd like to take at least six months off."

"Sam, I'm giving you a *year* off. You've earned it."

"You're kidding."

"No, I'm not. However, there's a catch."

"If there's an emergency . . ."

"Right."

"Figures. There's always an emergency."

Lambert laughs a little and I manage a smile. "How did you like working with Frances? And Anna again?" he asks.

I have to admit the truth. "They're great, Colonel. Give 'em raises."

"I already have. You'll be receiving a nice bonus as well. Oh, that reminds me. I have a surprise for you."

"I hate surprises," I say.

"You'll like this one." He stands and walks toward the door. "Don't go away, I'll be right back."

"Where the hell am I gonna go, Colonel?"

He leaves and I have a moment to look out the window. The sun is bright in a very clear sky. Spring is around the corner and I'd swear there are birds chirping outside. You'd never know that an atomic bomb exploded in the region just three days ago.

Lambert sticks his head in the room and says, "I'll leave you alone with your visitor for now. We'll talk again later. Take care, Sam."

"Okay, Colonel. Wait, what visitor?"

He opens the door wider and my heart sings when I see who it is.

"Hey, Dad!" she says.

Sarah runs to the side of the bed and plants a big kiss on the side of my face. I wrap my free arm around her and hold her close as Lambert winks at me and closes the door.